JOURNEY TO THE MIDNIGHT SUN

LOVE CONQUERS ALL
Book I of III

James Sheldon

Sheldon Publishing
Winchester, KS
USA

Acknowledgments

With heartfelt gratitude, I thank Mr. D.B. Bennett for his artwork on this book's title page and his artwork on map one's upper left quadrant. Doug is a lifelong artist whom I have known since early childhood. I would also like to thank Mr. Mark Lysaught, a retired cartographer who advised me on my maps. Mark is a dear friend from boyhood, the best man at my wedding, and worthy of mention; he made the maps in my non-fiction book, *American Errand, Rivers of the North.*

With regard to editing: Although my creative work, including the structuring of text, is not AI-assisted, I would like to thank Grammarly and their AI for helping me check for typos and make minor grammatical corrections in the final edit.

I would like to thank Google, their search engine, and their Gemini AI for helping me tremendously with my research. I'm old enough to remember going to the library and checking out armloads of books.

I would like to thank HP, Flux.1 AI, Canva Draw, and MS Paint for their help in creating the artwork on this book's jacket. By running Flux.1 AI on my somewhat standard HP VSD9VLCR laptop, I was able to get a rudimentary foundation to work from, which I extensively altered using Canva Draw and MS Paint. I am not an artist, but fortunately, using the tools above, I was able to create a book jacket that I could accept.

I would like to thank Canva Pro for the human images on the back cover. I input snippets from this book into their 'Dream Lab' AI image generator, and on its first try, the AI produced the images as shown. I would also like to thank Cava Pro and MS Paint for helping me create the compass roses on maps one and two.

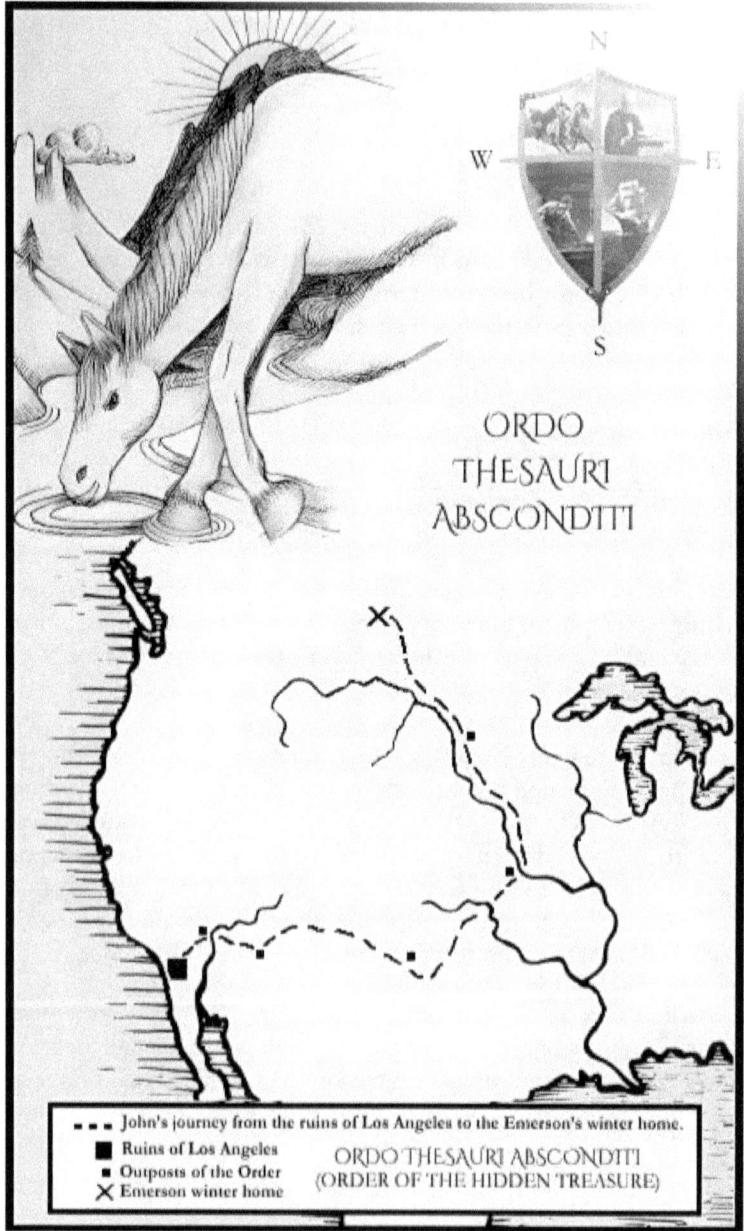

ORDO
THESAURI
ABSCONDITI

- - - John's journey from the ruins of Los Angeles to the Emerson's winter home.
■ Ruins of Los Angeles
■ Outposts of the Order
✕ Emerson winter home

ORDO THESAURI ABSCONDITI
(ORDER OF THE HIDDEN TREASURE)

N
W — E
S

Lake of the Swans

Montreal River

Old River Crossing

Rendezvous Campgrounds

Montreal Lake

Emerson Clan Summer Home

Ruin of Prince Albert

THE BIG RIVER, N. FORK

THE BIG RIVER, S. FORK

Ruin of Saskatoon

Emerson Family Winter Home

The Little River

Total distance traveled: 341 miles

"THE TRAGIC RAMIFICATIONS OF
BEING HUMAN ARE LEFT BEHIND IN
THE SOUL'S UNFATHOMABLE DESIRE
TO FIND ITS WAY HOME."

Old Kasskatchen saying

Journey to the Midnight Sun

LOVE CONQUERS ALL
Book I of III / Chapter 1

WITH THE EYE OF AN EAGLE, you may have spotted John Summerfield on the vast Dakota plain, a solitary man walking in sailing veils of snow. With the vision of an eagle, you may have seen him, bound as he was, head to toe in the fur of the wolverine. In any case, you couldn't miss his companion close behind, his trusty draft horse, Ellie. She bore her packsaddle with one eye bright as a sapphire in the sun, the other dark as a moonlit pool. A few steps behind John, she followed of her own accord, towed by an unseen bond formed from mutual reliance in the wild, unfretted by the snow devils that rose and fell.

Under the snow-filled whip of the wind, one could not know the storm had passed until looking across the horizon, clouds began to break first over here, then over there. Subsequently, dim patches of light appeared as though from lighthouses along fog-shrouded shores. The wind relented, the snow it bore diminished, and the indistinguishable grayish-white of earth and sky divided to reveal the shelter John sought. The great hardwood forest of the north stood a mere mile ahead. Still only a shadow to the naked eye, it appeared as a continuous wall, dark and mysterious, grown up gradually through earth's ever-changing climate. Stretching east to west along what had once been the border of the USA and Canada, it divided the bygone states and provinces of Montana, Alberta, North Dakota, Saskatchewan, and Manitoba. A two-hundred-mile-deep sash of oak, ash, and maple, itself the facade of a much larger boreal forest, it marked the end of the known world if one could be generous enough to call it that.

Civilization in John Summerfield's day existed in precious few pockets along the east and west coasts of the continent previously known as North America. Few souls strayed into the sparsely populated interior, a vastly unknown realm save for tales of no return. Dark forests prowled by ravenous beasts. Haunted mountains. Windswept plains roamed by savage horse clans. A faraway inner wilderness. Magnet to curious misfits drawn to fatal attractions, or so told the storytellers.

It was the dawn of the 31st century and although primitive in comparison to 21st century technology, the handcraft with which John had been outfitted had no superior in any century. His boots, tent, and cookware, his knife, bow, and spear, the best wood and steel, leather and fur, wool and linen—all painstakingly crafted to fit his own person.

The same went for his four-legged companion. Ellie's packsaddle had been made especially for her. The enigmatic insignia branded on her left shoulder marked her as the cream of a lineage that, having outlasted the age of mechanization, reigned once again as the most advanced system of transportation available to man. The special brand she bore belonged to John's Order and could be found on most everything he possessed. Add to this a lifetime of intense training and John Summerfield represented an investment amounting to no small fortune in any millennium. And being only twenty-one years of age, one might assume him the son of a powerful chieftain or king but that was not the case.

To understand how and why John came to be where he came to be, we need only a brief overview. Before John's time, in the 'Realm of the Golden Coast' (once known as California), impassioned men had lived and died to find a treasure trove of lost scientific knowledge—its existence known only through oral storytelling that had been put down in writing. It was a story so fantastic as to be unbelievable, and yet, as undeniable as the ruins that stood along the ocean. It was a story for a present with no past, its tales of old lost like ships that sink to watery depths, all but beyond reach, casualties of a catastrophic storm. And so it was, the story of the 'Data Block' was the legend of lost legends—the greatest of all legends. And great legends can lead powerful kingdoms and their men to tremendously expensive undertakings (as history shows us in the Fountain of Youth and Golden City of El Dorado).

In the search for the Data Block, the leaders of the expeditions had not been called Knights or Conquistadors but Seekers. Seekers believed the Data Block contained lost knowledge with which men had once risen like gods to fly above the clouds and even walk on the moon! Utterly unbelievable stuff if not for the stumps of fallen skyscrapers and bridges standing amid the rubble of ghost cities strewn here and there across the continent. And yet, despite so much jumbled proof of former glory, the expeditions had ended in a string of failures culminating in bankruptcies and not-so-glorious revolts. Seekers were put on trial and executed, their great quest banned under penalty of death. Fortunately, the ban would not last more than a few generations thanks to the resilience of the renaissance that had fostered the search in the first place.

Thus the great quest began anew, albeit with ramifications. Reorganized after a revolt, those in charge did not outright abandon the search but largely sought economy and longevity by replacing risky expeditions with celebration and ritual to maintain the status quo. So things weren't quite like the old days. Still, the great ruins of the Golden Coast stood as a source of awe and inspiration to the people. In the cool of their shadows, believers preached the fulfillment of the ancient promise. The Data Block would be found. Men would once again rise to be as gods. And who would not want to fly? None more so than our hero! In the meantime, however, daily life had gone on up and down the Golden Coast. Agriculture, textiles, metallurgy, stone masonry, architecture, and trade, to name a few, kept the people occupied. And while the legend of the Data Block placed it very far away, there were those who, being fortunate enough to secure a license from those who held power in the name of the promise, made a living exploring the local ruins of Los Angeles, San Diego, and San Francisco.

It was no easy job mining massive ruins with nothing but picks, shovels, mules, and carts. Cave-ins and casualties were commonplace. And still, it was an elite industry, for the clues salvaged from the mines brought heightened knowledge, and knowledge was power, and given that human nature remained unchanged, the new power brokers were perfectly willing to go along with a legend if it helped keep their subjects manageable. Thus, to foster and maintain the promise of a beautiful future, they established a special order somewhat like a knight's order of old and charged it with finding the Data Block, perhaps not so much to find the Data Block but to perpetuate its legend through pomp and ritual, which culminated once every five years with the celebration of a new champion. On the other side of this coin, however, the men of the special order saw themselves as true believers. Life in the order began at age six when a boy was selected and placed in the care of dedicated instructors who would rigorously train him to adulthood—a badge of honor for the boy's family, even though they would scarcely ever see him again.

At age eighteen, John Summerfield graduated at the top of his class. A fledged member of the 'Seekers of the Trove,' he could henceforth wear the order's enigmatic insignia. Three years later, and our radicalized hero grabbed the brass ring, so to speak, when the order awarded him the appointment of 'Seeker.' The post of Seeker, being specifically for young men, lasted five years, a time frame in which the appointee was to sacrifice every aspect of his life to find the Data Block. Hidden far away for safekeeping in a mythical realm known only to the ancients, the Data Block waited in a place of such beauty and purity that no man could make it his home. Or so the legend told. By law, only the Seeker could go in search of the legend

4

because, he was the one put forth by the Order, itself an arm of those who held power in the name of the promise. This guaranteed legal custody to the right people if, by chance, the Data Block actually existed and was found.

Also of great importance, John's role as Seeker was to serve as an example for the people to follow. He, was the new renaissance man. He was young, strong, courageous, intelligent, and if only for the sale of a myth, extraordinarily handsome. This was our hero, an instrument of misdirection, and a prelude to hope. A would-be astronaut of the 31st century, the believers had cheered him like a rockstar. Coming together upon his naming, they had paraded him through the ruins of old LA. Pressed together, dressed in costumes depicting the old expeditions and the hope they stirred in the hearts of men, they had carried the Seeker for all to see, a symbolic sacrifice to be witnessed only once every five years. A picture of piety and madness, it ended with a glorious send-off that saw the Seeker riding off into the desert alone. And that was the last of most Seekers, save that their names were glorified in memorials that lined the dusty parade route. Not all died, though. Facing deadly desert heat, high-country blizzards, wolf packs, grizzly bears, and, worst of all, savage clans of various origins, some Seekers survived thanks in part to support from a handful of tiny outposts established by the Order.

Traveling what we call the Old Spanish and Santa Fe Trails, few Seekers made it as far as the Missouri River where a remote outpost had been established in the stone skeleton of what had once been Leavenworth Penitentiary. From there, any surviving Seeker was to continue by way of the old Lewis and Clark Trail until he reached the confluence of two great rivers, the Missouri and the Yellowstone. There he was to turn north where, as legend told, the great hardwood forest would appear like a wall in the distance—a realm completely unknown to civilization, same as vast areas of land had been for most of recorded history. Presumably, the Seeker would continue north through the hardwoods and directly into a second forest, an ancient boreal forest said to be without end. And yet as legend told, somewhere beyond the endless forest lay the Land of the Midnight Sun. There, in plain view, stood a monolith of black onyx, the Data Block. That was the legend. In reality, if the Data Block did exist somewhere under the northern lights in a million square miles of tundra, it may as well have been a needle in a haystack. Also worthy of note, ocean-crossing journeys had yet to be made in John's time but the ability to sail along the west coast of the continent provided knowledge of the inland mountains, being that they continued unbroken into the far north like an impenetrable wall. And so it was, the hope and belief that a glorious promise waited at the top of the world lived via the overland route. And in the year 3010, our Seeker, young John Summerfield, had earned his shot at it.

And now we are almost up to speed. John had made the confluence of the great rivers and turned north. He had walked north for three days when the forest came into view only to vanish in a whiteout caused by a freak polar vortex. And as we already know, John had fought his way through the storm to stand before the forest. Now, one final important detail to cover is that winter had come early to the Dakotas. Even before summer was officially over, three weeks back at the ruin of Bismarck, the weather had turned. And it was there, in a tiny fortified dwelling at the end of the known world, itself the last in a series of remote outposts with great distances between that John had received the last help he would get from his Order. It came from a handful of believers as ardent as warrior monks. They had given John a hero's welcome, fed him as well as they could, and fostered his convictions with powerful evidence. For although the city of Bismarck had sunk into the earth, the remains of a great monolith still stood. Heavily made from white limestone and green granite, the old State Capitol building stood alone on the windswept plain. An art deco monument to glory and untold mystery. Thus fueled in body and spirit, and resupplied as best as could be afforded, our hero had departed to meet his destiny in the north.

We now join John and Ellie at the end of the known world. A mere mile ahead, a new world with new possibilities, beheld by only a handful of Seekers, none of whom had ever returned. And looking upon it, the Seeker spoke just a handful of words: "We've made it, Ellie." And while his four-legged companion may not have understood her master's words, she most certainly knew his conviction. Side by side, they paused to take it in. Bedecked in the first snow of the season, the forest glistened in a coat of white. The wind had calmed to a brisk breeze, and the sun, now dominant in the western sky, made all the difference.

Pushing back his hood, Summerfield removed goggles of lead glass and leather. He looked forward to a reprieve from the wind. There would be wood for fire. There would be water for drinking and cooking. And as so often the case in sun-touched openings along forest streams, he expected to find patches of grass for his horse to eat. He expected this because, although it had been unseasonably cold, a slightly warmer climate worldwide had brought more rainfall, making the region unrecognizable to our 21st century eyes. Behind John, the grasses of the Great Plains still reigned. Further back in his home along the Golden Coast, the ocean had risen several feet over the past millennia. Not a huge difference there. Along the old US/Canada border, however, the changing climate had tipped the scales to make a significant difference. The trees had taken over, blocking the sun and wind, allowing the soil to hold moisture that would otherwise evaporate. Slowly but steadily, the increased moisture and longer growing seasons com-pounded by centuries of undisturbed growth and natural soil enrichment had given rise to deciduous giants. Ash, maple, walnut, and white oaks nearly four hundred years old towered to heights above two hundred feet! Only prairie fires, both natural and manmade, had checked the forest's southward advance, resulting in a meeting of prairie and forest with no transition zone, creating a tree wall at once abrupt, impressive, and starkly beautiful in young Summerfield's eyes. Indeed he marveled, for the hardwoods overhung the snow-covered prairie in a continuous eave that extended to both horizons, east and west.

With all its beauty, the forest nevertheless appeared as a mighty shadow realm risen up to tower over man and beast. Therefore feeling a healthy dose of instinct, John reached for the rifle on his packsaddle. A technological wonder of its day, the rifle had been designed and developed based on the rusty remains of a 20th century BB gun mined from the ruins of San Diego. A child's toy reimagined as a deadly weapon with craftsmanship inseparable from art, the rifle's forward pistol grip operated in dual function. It could be pumped like a shotgun to load marble-sized slugs, and it could be ratcheted down and away from the rifle's stock through which a force multiplier made of levers and cams pumped air into a steel high-pressure storage tube.

As awesome as his weapon was, it should be noted that John still relied on traditional weapons: both spear and bow. As for his super-weapon, it was one of only three in existence. The other two remained under lock and key in the Order's armory. Countless man-hours of metal smithing had gone into each, as the renaissance of the Golden Coast had only begun its advance into the sciences and was still very far from mass production. Nonetheless, by putting bits and pieces of ancient knowledge together on a clean slate, craftsmen had made three remarkable weapons. A man of average strength could quickly pump one up to 2,500 psi, good for approximately 10 rounds of .50 caliber ammunition, each round capable of killing man or beast. Presently, John ratcheted the pump once to get a feel for the pressure in the storage tube, and the pressure was good. Thus he hung the rifle over his shoulder and took his mare's lead rope in hand.

Due to weeks of unseasonable cold and wind, the trees stood bare. Only the oaks retained their leaves, brownish-green and dried out in the breeze, they rattled like talismans high in the eaves. Below them, John could see deep into the wood, an impenetrable wall at distance now up close revealed its own kind of spaciousness. Mighty tree trunks stood as columns in an ancient temple. The floor lay mostly free of undergrowth, and with several inches of snow reflecting the daylight, the forest appeared void of the darkness associated with long-standing woods.

Proceeding in, John found and followed a subtle downward incline several miles to the edge of a ravine. Rugged in places, the ravine's steep slope appeared manageable. A tiny stream wound like a ribbon at the bottom, its vertical cutbanks of black earth woven with tangled tree roots. Opposite the cutbanks, inside the stream's many bends, miniature beaches of sand and pebbles lie beneath several inches of snow. Here and there along the stream, flats built from centuries of silt lie covered with grass and kissed by sunlight thanks to the opening that the waterway created in the canopy above. But of course, there was no direct sunlight in the ravine at that late hour, and John understood that cold air accumulated in low spots. Still, he needed fuel for his horse and water for them both. And so it was, he picked his way down into the ravine, leading his mare carefully, that she not slip and trample him on the snowy incline. Then, on a flat a few feet above the stream, he wasted no time making camp in the precious daylight.

As always, the horseman's horse came first. Both warhorse and packhorse, John began by removing the packs from Ellie's packsaddle, then her packsaddle, and finally her buffalo cloak. He brushed her thick fur coat quickly but thoroughly so that it could best insulate her. Ellie, being naturally suited to cold climates, hadn't needed her cloak due to cold but as a shield against unrelenting wind. A Clydesdale of the famous black and white variety, her particular bloodline could be traced to a large ranch for Clydesdale horses that once existed in the Flint Hills of Kansas. It was there, at the abrupt end of the Industrial Age, that a small herd of Ellie's forerunners found themselves free on the very plains where horses had first evolved. And by the laws of nature, being that the well-suited not only survive but thrive, the Clydesdales roamed the vast plains where having already been set on a genetic growth path by man, they grew larger still from one generation to the next. The result being that, whereas a 21st century Clydesdale could weigh as much as 2,800 pounds and stand 7 feet tall, Ellie weighed 3,200 pounds and stood 8 feet tall. Of course, there were other breeds of smaller horses, and they were the ones that dominated the plains. And there were humans on the plains, advanced stone age tribes that had become expert riders. Humanity had come a long way from the late 21st century when the very survival of the species lie in question. But coming back to Ellie's bloodline, the giants had remained largely separate from the smaller breeds for the same reasons that wolves and coyotes remain separate: the bigger kill the smaller when given the opportunity. They were not the 'gentle giants' of the 21st century. They were wild and could be as mean as nature demanded. They were the black-and-white giants of the plains, given special spiritual status by the savages on account of their majestic nature. And most recently, they had been discovered by a graduate from John's Order. And so it was that a number of the Clydes had been captured and taken back to the Golden Coast where they were selectively bred. And Ellie, being the cream of that crop, had been selected for the quinquennial sacrifice. Her massive body, although very dark brown, appeared black. Her mane and tail also appeared black. Her belly showed a patchwork of black and white that continued to her knees. From her knees down, she was snow white with long feathery hair that shrouded bell-shaped hooves the size of dinner plates. Large black splotches like paint thrown on Ellie's otherwise white face encompassed both her eyes and made for a natural work of art in which random chaos gives rise to stunning symmetry. Horse eyes, the largest eyes of any land animal—one lit like a sapphire, the other a moonlit pool. A magnetic gaze in a big white face, looking down from an animal three times the size of a bull moose. A loyal warhorse in possession of a battle switch that, if flipped, sent the beast into fight mode with shocking speed and agility. Ellie was wonderful as a friend, and dreadful as an enemy.

"Give me that paw!" John ordered with a fake growl, tugging the long hair around Ellie's massive hoof. Only with the giant's help did he inspect the underside of her hoof which the snow had cleaned to perfection.

After rewarding Ellie with a few handfuls of grain, John fenced off a grassy area by running a cord from tree to tree along with a few fence poles cut with a hatchet and driven into the gravelly stream bottom. He had often let her graze free on the plains providing there were no wild horses to draw her off. He penned her up in the forest because it was not her natural habitat. Too hungry to care, Ellie grazed the grass that lay under the snow, pausing now and then to sample the tips of shrubs that grew along the creek.

Moving with minimal waste, John cleared a sleeping spot, then dug through accumulations of leaves, taking the driest ones to use as padding and insulation under his ground tarp. Atop this, he pitched a small tent in which he laid a bed of wool and animal furs. Finally, John built a cookfire and celebrated his success by cooking something out of the ordinary: chicken, a gift from his fellow believers in Bismarck. He had kept it for weeks in a tiny cage on the packsaddle, fed it grain from Ellie's stores, let it stretch its legs on a tether and peck about until travel time. It had managed the cold surprisingly well but with the combined stress of cold and travel, it hadn't laid a single egg. John apologized, explaining how he had given it all the time he could. He then killed and cleaned it beside the stream, after which he cooked it in a cast iron skillet with oil and potatoes.

In the waning light, Summerfield ate with a mixture of gratification and encouragement. He had gained the protection of the forest with twelve weeks remaining before the winter solstice. Chewing his last bite, he wiped out his skillet and put food-related items in a rodent-proof box. He urinated along the borders of his camp as a fair warning to any hungry animal that might follow its nose there and end up the victim of a .50 caliber slug.

Finally, John crawled into his tent under a beautifully bleak forest canopy backlit with stars. Ellie, being too tuckered to sleep standing, slowly lowered her front knees to the ground and rolled onto her side with a mighty exhale. Then, stretching out over the snow like a beached whale, she went straight to sleep. Likewise, John had only laid down his head when he fell fast asleep.

Traveling north, John and Ellie made excellent progress due to the forest floor presenting no serious impediment, being largely flat and devoid of dense undergrowth. In good order they covered two hundred miles and entered the transition zone where deciduous forest gave way to ancient boreal forest. Adding to John's good fortune, the weather had moderated. Easy to understand then how John might wonder if the stories about a forest of no return were overblown. Then again, he could not know how the tragedy of that day, in which he would play a part, would change his life forever.

Dawn had just broken. It was day sixteen in the woods where, once again, he had camped beside a small stream in a ravine. Having bundled his bedding up tight, the horseman performed a series of tasks for which he needed little or no light. He then exited his tent where Ellie, quietly grazing in the dim, lifted her head and let out a nicker to greet him. Her great size and the angle of her stance there in the darkness of the woods with clouds of steam flowing from her nostrils might, at first glance, be mistaken for a dragon.

"How's my little girl?"

With a coincidental nod of her head, Ellie returned to grazing.

High above them, the dawn filtered down through the forest canopy. From the shadows below, the sound of water trickled around roots and stones. Countless branches, bare of leaves, formed an intricate lattice that appeared as an all-encompassing web. And in this dim textile of black and white, the form of a man moved busily about, smoothly, as a spider might go about its web. For thousands of miles, mile after mile, day after day, the wild had drawn John further and further from spectator and closer and closer to participant.

John took down Ellie's portable pen so she could have fresh grass for breakfast. He then fueled up on a bowl of hot farina, nuts, honey, and an apple from his dwindling stores. Later, he would eat chunks of venison while walking through the day. He needed lots of fuel to make the kind of progress he had. And for the same reason, at any stop, no matter how brief, Ellie was allowed to eat whatever grass or foliage lay at her feet. And because it took considerable work and time to break down and set up camp, Ellie had plenty of time to eat in the mornings and evenings. Presently, while John packed their gear, she munched one mouthful after another, a four-legged colossus with a baby-soft nose.

Using his powerful six-foot-three build, John lifted the awkward frame of Ellie's pack saddle above his head and eased it as gently as possible onto her back. She would not need her buffalo cloak that morning. The pack saddle, a hinged contraption of wood, iron, and leather, constituted a custom-made frame into which six custom-made packs fit three on either side. The six packs, each of wood and leather, were the size of small chests and could be taken from the saddle and carried by a man as a backpack. John moved the saddle's frame a smidgen this way and that to settle it just right on Ellie's back. He knew her comfort and well-being went hand in hand with his survival. On a side note, the way he baby-talked her like she was his wee little daughter may have gotten him thrown out of a rough and tumble 19th century cowboy camp. Then again, it was his only soft side.

"That's my girl! Oh—that is just right!"

13

And tightening her cinch strap, he went on talking as though to a child about the goodness of it all, "That'll keep ya comfy!"

Ellie, having heard it all before, seemed to ignore him.

Placing the first few packs into the saddle frame but still yet to strap them in, John pulled on Ellie's halter to bring her head up out of the grass. She wanted to eat. It was her nature. She was an eating machine but for the sake of proper adjustment, John needed her upright.

"Up, girl," John ordered, "up."

Giving way, Ellie rose to her full 8ft height, and John installed another pack. Then pausing for no apparent reason, he placed his left hand on the bridge of her nose to steady and lower her head, whereby using the outside edge of his right palm, he gently wiped a gooey from the corner of her eye.

"You're too pretty for gooeys."

No more had John turned to fetch another pack then Ellie went back to grazing. She had only begun to chew when quick as a bear trap, she snapped to attention, her ears perked stiff as pikes. Her eyes grown large, she blew out a mighty snort, then stood on point, wound up like spring steel.

In one smooth motion, John set down the pack and brought his air rifle from his back to his front. Following Ellie's line of sight, he scanned for something more than just another squirrel or raccoon, something more than a deer or other harmless creature of which there had been hundreds (to which his horse had grown accustomed).

Ellie bobbed her head and blew out another snort, sending a pair of steam clouds into the crisp morning air.

"Easy girl," training his eyes and ears.

The forest seemed unnaturally quiet. Nothing stirred, not even a bird. Only the sound of the stream as it ran through the splotchy shadows of leafless trees.

Stepping back, Ellie tried to turn and run but John jumped in her face, "No you don't!" aggressively.

Restrained by her master, the giant set to bobbing and fussing. A small dance made big by 3,200 pounds of wound-up flesh and blood.

"Ellie!" through grit teeth, pulling her lead rope, "Calm down!"

Wide-eyed with fright, Ellie breathed heavily while John turned his attention to the wood, his brain in high gear. Ellie was no spooky horse. Something was there, something significant. Grizzlies were known to sneak up before charging in, contrary to popular belief. Wolves would charge in a coordinated bluff to panic their prey so they could bring it down from behind after exhausting it in a chase. A mountain lion would sneak up and remain unseen until its moment to pounce. But easier prey filled the wood, and John suspected a more sinister creature.

Unknowable though it be, that thing called the 'sixth sense' reached out to tap on John's shoulder. Invisible fingers from the ether, cold as death, raised the hair on the back of his neck. Calm and quick, John looped Ellie's lead rope over her neck and secured it to a halter ring under her chin (to serve as a makeshift pair of reins). He undid the cinch straps that held her packsaddle, and as the saddle fell to earth, he stepped on it like a stool and leaped onto her back.

"Yah!" shouted the horseman, digging his heels into the giant's flanks. "Yah!"

Ellie launched into the creek and, with a single bound more, landed on the opposite bank. As if possessed by a demon, the war horse plowed through the undergrowth that grew along the opposite shore. Her rider encouraged her on, and while he could not be sure in the chaos, he thought he heard an arrow or two fly past.

"Yah, yah!" up the slope John went, his giant warhorse kicking and thrusting with branches busting.

Reaching the top of the ravine, John spun Ellie around hard so that he could take aim from the high ground and dispatch those who had attempted to ambush him. But there was nothing there—nothing visible, anyway.

John moved Ellie this way and that to get different angles of sight through the trees. Meanwhile, shafts of morning sunlight flowed through the wood to lay down a quilt of brightly illuminated patches in sharp contrast with dark impenetrable shadows. It was beautiful and, when taken together with a cloudless sky and a south breeze, held the promise of a good day.

"I don't know, girl," stroking Ellie's neck, "maybe we just freaked one another out."

Be it truth or wishful thinking, man and beast remained in battle mode. Instinctively, Ellie remained particularly on edge. A spirited herd boss, her agility and speed in the hands of an experienced horseman came as an abrupt surprise to all who misjudged her by size alone. Like John, she had cleared a high bar to be there.

Reining his horse to the left, John rode along the ridge looking for tracks.

With every step, Ellie bobbed on the verge of explosion. She hadn't gone fifty yards when John suddenly stopped her. Directly before them in fallen leaves lie the tracks of four or five men.

The thought of flying arrows nearly sent John jumping to the ground. He did not jump, as doing so would cripple his sight advantage. Instead, he wheeled Ellie around and trotted her, weaving between trees, keeping to the high ground above his camp, and scanning the terrain below. And sure enough, his sharp eye caught the silhouette of a human shifting in the shadows.

"SHOW YOURSELF!" Summerfield shouted.

Down in the ravine, a tall lanky man stepped out of a shadow and, with a few steps more, stood boldly at the center of John's camp. Then another man and another came out of the shadows to join him. Four men in all and a boy of about 13. The boy, being the silhouette John had first seen, crouched

16

on the far side, just a stone's toss beyond the others. They were clansmen. Blond-headed forest dwellers of the north. Blue-eyed warriors with bush bows and spears, out on a hunt.

"GAU-AH-WAY," shouted the first clansman, gesturing with his arm and hand for John to move on.

"GAU-AH-WAY," he repeated loudly, making animated gestures for John to leave while his companions held their bows and spears at the ready.

The clansmen had meant to capture John but the giant had worried them greatly. None had ever seen a horse giant but had heard stories about the extra powers such creatures gave to men. As a result, they had approached John's camp with extreme caution.

Knowing he was out of their range, John swung his leg over Ellie's neck and slid down her side in one smooth motion. Then, kneeling in the leaves, he leveled his air rifle, aimed, steadied, and fired. The shouting savage fell straight back and hit the ground with a thud.

Initially shocked, the others were momentarily at a loss, unable to understand how John had killed their leader.

Quick as shooting skeet, John pumped the pistol grip to load another round into the chamber, aimed, and dropped a second man like a sack of potatoes.

The surviving men jumped for cover along the creek bank. The boy crouched further down and vanished in the shadows.

John leaped onto Ellie and charged. He didn't need to ponder to know he could not allow the savages to vanish into his surroundings from which they could then ambush him as they had nearly done only minutes before. Nor would he be taken alive, to be hauled away and tortured while the clan whooped and howled like theatergoers at a wildly entertaining comedy.

As John came down the slope, the bowman rose, his arrow drawn to fire. John reined Ellie to the right and vanished into the thicket above the stream. Ellie plowed like a locomotive. John hunkered down, gripping her mane as branches whipped and raked his body. In the next instant, the giant exploded from the thicket and flew airborne over the stream in a cloud of sticks, twigs, dirt, and leaves before landing on a pebbly beach opposite the cut bank.

Reining Ellie left, John charged the two men.

The bowman, unable to get a shot at the rider hunkered behind the giant's neck, lowered his aim and shot the beast in the chest. Ellie flinched and stumbled but bore down hard and trampled the bowman, crushing his ribs into his lungs. Simultaneously, the spearman came on with a wild shout to launch his weapon into the rider's left side but missed as John twisted and jumped like a cat. Then, as the horse ran out from between the two men, they remained facing one another on the beach, not six feet apart.

John stood with weapon aimed point blank.

The spearman had taken his hatchet from his belt. His arm cocked, he hesitated in the knowledge of John's magic terror weapon.

John also hesitated. He had the man beat and they both knew it.

The two were roughly the same age, the one dark-eyed, the other blue-eyed. Outside of that, they could have been brothers. Their exchange lasted but a second. It was all over in a second. John fired and the man fell into the stream with a bullet between his eyes. He and his companions were not the first savages the Seeker had dispatched on the trail but this particular event would alter John's life in ways he could not possibly foresee.

Scanning the woods with heart pounding, crouching, breathing hard, pointing his weapon this way and that, John glanced at the man Ellie had very intentionally trampled, and seeing he was dead, he turned to where he had last seen the boy. But no sooner had he focused in that direction than a warning came via his peripheral vision, and yanking his head back, an arrow flew past his face so close it nearly grazed his nose. He spun and aimed. He had the boy dead in his gunsight. He hesitated on the trigger, and the boy took off like a rabbit.

Dropping his aim, John watched as the boy disappeared over the crest of the ravine.

Glancing about for his horse, John spotted Ellie about thirty yards off with an arrow protruding from her chest. Ellie was the last of the original animals John had when he departed old Los Angeles two years earlier. The horseman had begun his journey with two horses: Ellie, his heavy battle and pack horse, and a lighter riding horse aptly named Bolt, as in a bolt fired from a crossbow. John also had a dog. Unfortunately, Rex had been mortally wounded in a run-in with wolves on the high plains of New Mexico and John had to put him down. Bolt then went lame and John had to leave him behind. The Seeker got another riding horse at the ruins of Fort Leavenworth but it caught and broke its leg between submerged roots on a muddy bank and John had to put it down.

Presently, John approached Ellie slowly, his air rifle in hand, "How ya doing, girl?"

Ellie stepped away before John could get hold of her lead rope. Her large eyes told of her dread. Meanwhile, crimson droplets fell steadily from the end of the arrow's shaft.

"It's okay, girl," John reassured, taking the rope in hand. "You did good," holding eye contact, gently stroking her neck, "you did real good."

Ellie relaxed a bit, munching her lips like horses do when recovering from trauma.

With a light touch, John ran his hand down to the wound, and as he felt the blood-soaked area, he exhaled with audible relief, "This is your lucky day, Ellie."

Although the arrow looked awful when viewed from Ellie's left side, in reality, it had traveled just under the hide of Ellie's right shoulder. John could feel the shaft, and at its end, the arrowhead felt like a hard knot under her skin. She bled not from arterial or organ damage but simply from elevated blood pressure due to the pounding of her huge heart.

19

John moved Ellie only a few steps to cross-tie her, then got to work with a first-aid kit. Ellie flinched and fussed but mostly she just watched John intensely with an animated eye that seemed almost human.

Having made a small incision, John removed the arrowhead and then withdrew the shaft. He sewed Ellie up tight in the knowledge that they couldn't remain there. Ellie would have to work but hopefully only enough to secure a hideout for a few days while her shoulder muscle healed. That was the plan. John knew it unwise to remain in the area while hostiles were aware of his presence, but he had no choice.

Finishing up, John quickly examined several cuts that Ellie had received in the thicket. As he did, a black-capped chickadee landed nearby and lent its voice to the quiet of the wood. Well known for its habit of freezing in the presence of danger, the songbird had come out to sing its equally famous 'all-clear' song so that all may know the danger had passed, "See-Saw. See-Saw."

With packsaddle loaded, John and Ellie set out northward.

All that afternoon and evening, wails and cries echoed through the woods as the women buried their fallen men. The clanswomen had lost all their men. They wailed violently because the 'law of the jungle' allotted them little time to grieve, and in a culture that would be alien to us, they had no choice but to put their grief behind them and move on as their situation demanded. Not that their hearts were any less broken, not to deny them their pain, not to deny them their humanity but rather for the sake of understanding; it is perhaps helpful to look at scientific observations from the 21st century in which wolves in the wild mourn their dead for a week whereas wolves that were cared for in sanctuaries away from nature's hard side mourned their dead for six months or more. The women were of a capacity far superior to wolves, and still, nature did not care any more about their feelings than those of wolves. Winter loomed just around the corner. Time was of the essence. It took many years to master a vast palette of survival skills and they had lost half in one fell swoop. Without the lost half, they would lose what the whole had supported: their home, their way of life, their freedom, prosperity, and happiness. This, however, is not to paint them as entirely innocent, for had their men captured John and brought him back to camp, odds were strong that the death he'd feared would come—slowly and painfully.

Having come down from their summer home in the north, the forest people had only recently settled into their winter home. Nestled in the bosom of the wood, primitive yet suitable for a postcard, their dwelling sat beside a low cliff inside the bend of a small river.

The following day, with but a trace of twilight remaining, the dogs of the clan suddenly sprang to their feet barking and snarling. The creature that had slain half the family stood just there where the firelight flickered and danced on the cusp of the wood.

Scarcely more than a shadow, he appeared to stand on two legs but with hulking shoulders like those of a bison from which extended multiple limbs. Some of the limbs ended in hands, others ended in hooves. Gazing upon this form with horror, a little girl named Sophie let out a bone-chilling scream.

Summerfield heaved a whitetail deer from his shoulders. It landed on the ground before him with a thud. It had been gutted and bled, and lacked only its heart and one backstrap.

Taking several steps back, John vanished into the forest.

Chapter 2

If Ellie had not needed time to heal, John would have hightailed it out of the area directly after the battle. But he had held up, and as a result, his plans changed as we shall now see.

It was mid-October and for the past two weeks, John had appeared regularly on the edge of the hunter-gatherer camp. Always he hung up a deer, or a few grouse, or a pair of squirrels. More than once he hung stringers of bass or trout (the forest transition zone supported both species). He befriended the dogs and, of late, they wagged their tails and danced around him. He never stayed but disappeared into the woods without a word. He should not be given too much credit, though. Like the conquistador Coronado, John was searching for his lost city of gold. As for the women, they shouted, screamed, threw rocks, and shot arrows at John even as their world demanded they make use of everything he brought. In their world, John's presence was a reflection of the wild that surrounded them. One buck defeats another and adopts a harem. One wolf defeats another and assumes leadership of a pack. Even among the forest tribes, such things, while rare, had precedent.

During this time, while out collecting nuts which were plentiful, two of the women discovered John's camp tucked into the edge of a glade. They were country neighbors not a mile apart even though no cordial contact took place between them. That changed one particularly beautiful October day after conditions had calmed enough for John to play his hand. The four women were sitting in their camp, bathed in sunlight, talking as they worked. They sat round a large firepit, itself positioned like a fountain some distance out from the steps of a modest structure called a longhouse around which several huts were neatly ordered. Below the structures, a stairway cut into a limestone cliff angled down to a pebbly beach on the river fifteen feet below where a pair of birch bark canoes were tied. The small river, known as the Qu'Appelle River in the 21st

century, had returned to its original northwesterly course after the failure of Diefenbaker Dam a thousand years before and not twenty miles to the northwest.

"Good afternoon, ladies," said John, speaking clearly from the cusp of the wood.

Startled, the women turned to look.

Straight-faced, Summerfield tipped his wolverine cap, and as the women looked on in silence, he walked in and took a seat among them—

"My name is John," pointing to himself in a businesslike manner while moving his eyes from woman to woman until his gaze came to rest on the eldest. A tall woman of sixty and some years, Emma had become the clan's Matriarch at an early age when her mother and father drowned. Along with her parents, several of her children, her siblings, aunts, uncles, and cousins had also perished. It had happened while camped at a river crossing during a rainy season many years before. A tumbling wave of logs and debris had decimated the unsuspecting clan in a flash flood resulting in part from an earlier forest fire. Emma's once golden hair, now mostly gray, was kept in a large braid that came over her shoulder before disappearing in a cloak of woodland caribou trimmed in red fox. She was fine-figured for her age and must have been a rare beauty in her day. Her large green eyes were not naturally menacing but sharpened by the responsibilities that had fallen on her early in life.

"Ma'am," John continued, addressing the Matriarch with a nod of respect, "may I ask your name?"

Holding her work in her lap, the Matriarch looked on soberly. At her knee, a little girl named Sophie had been learning to tease tread from strips of sinew. The child, being less restrained than the adults, stared at John with a mixture of fear and curiosity.

John smiled at the child. She smiled back and the Seeker, somewhat swedged, lifted his eyes to the Matriarch, "I mean you no harm."

23

The Matriarch looked on with suspicion.

"Can you understand me?" John asked. "I have not come here to harm anyone."

Speaking cautiously, the Matriarch replied, "Ya say no haam us?"

"Yes," said John, nodding, "I mean no harm." And looking around the fire, he added, "I regret what has happened, but…it is what it is."

In the silence that followed, the chickadee sang its song, "See-saw, see-saw." Perched on a twig beside the river, it pruned its feathers and soaked up sunlight. The little river meanwhile, gently sparkled and rolled along.

Both Seeker and clanswomen could not in their wildest dreams imagine where the coming alliance would take them but as it is said; 'the past is prologue.' The women, though they knew it not, were the long-lost legacy of farmers and ranchers, shopkeepers and tradesfolk. Eleven hundred years before in that very neck of the woods and throughout the region, there had come a people from the north of Europe. Tracing their lineage to Viking, Goth, Saxon, and Celtic ancestors, they were migrants in search of new and better lives. Few had survived the cataclysm of the 21st century. Those who did, sifted through the shattered remains and salvaged what they could to survive. The need for survival forced them together. Organically and surprisingly fast, they formed into clans and tribes. They congealed around likeness of being as well as the absorption of anyone who, by some outstanding ability, could add to the group's chance of survival. Time rolled on, the centuries accumulated and a rich forest culture developed with villages along the many rivers and lakes. Some of the villages grew large. A few grew into super-villages not so different from the Stone Age super-villages that rose in the Neolithic and Chalcolithic periods of civilization seven thousand years before. These people, descendants of 21st century Canadians, called themselves Kasskatchens. The central hub of their Nation, a super-village named Grandal, stood on the shore of what we call Lake Winnipeg. From Grandal, Kasskatchen chieftains ruled over what had once been Saskatchewan, Manitoba, northernmost Minnesota, and southwestern Ontario. Presently, the clanswomen lived in the western reaches of the realm and were known as people of the frontier. Beyond the frontiers, across vast areas of unknown territory, there existed other realms. For example, the descendants of the Cree plied the waterways to the south and east of old Hudson Bay. In the far north, descendants of the Inuit made their livings along the Arctic coasts. They, like everyone else on earth, lived in the aftermath of a civilizational collapse. Not a new thing but the same rise and fall that has occurred throughout history. And perhaps it is at least plausible then that the collapse of civilization in the 21st century dramatically dwarfed all its predecessors because technology, the very thing that dramatically decreased distances around the world, also increased the distance for the world to fall. From the skyscraper heights of the Digital Age to the ground level of the Stone Age was a very long drop. A drop perhaps not so different from the fall of the Assyrian and other great empires, where people living only a few centuries later had no idea who built the massive ruins that stood along the rivers. And still the English language survived in derivatives which should not be too surprising as history shows that language survives even as reading and writing are forgotten. Moreover, English had dominated the entire continent, a first in human history. Of course, distinct dialects had developed among surviving groups. And yet, for those that spoke the old tongue, enough similarity remained to make communication possible much like Latin and Italian remained similar a thousand years after the fall of Rome. And so different groups could trade without having to learn a language entirely foreign to them. Of course, English was not the only language but outside a smidgen of Spanish, the writer of this story is limited to it. I am also limited by my training in Western literature and 20th/21st century culture, with which I can only do my best to convey the richness and unique complexities of 31st century Kasskatchen culture. On a similar note, their lexicon contains words and terms of pre-existing origins. For example, the original agricultural meaning of the term "the seeds we sow" has morphed over time to become a popular reference to human behavior. And being flawed as I am, and owning the awful way in which this story begins, I nevertheless will do my best to recount all following events in a manner that clears the bar of common decency without undue austerity, like this current meeting for example, to which we will now return without further interruption.

"Ma'am," John inquired, addressing the Matriarch while gesturing to the woman beside her, "if I may ask, is this your daughter?" The similarity being obvious.

"Yes."

Receiving no further reply, John shifted his attention to the daughter, "Ma'am, may I ask your name?"

"My name is Jessie," apprehensively.

"And may I ask your mother's name?"

"Emma."

John lifted his wolverine cap and gave nods of respect to Emma and Jessie, "Ma'am...ma'am."

Jessie, tall and well-made like her mother, appeared young for thirty-eight. Somewhat more outgoing, she gestured to the woman sitting to the other side of her, "This is my cousin, Mia."

"Ma'am," gesturing again with a lift of his cap.

Initially an outsider from the southeast corner of the realm, Mia had married into the clan and was mother to twins named Noah and Sophie. At age twenty-five, Mia rivaled her blond-headed kin with dark Aegean eyes, large and widely spaced above high cheekbones framed by dark brown hair. Her expression spoke of apprehension mixed with curiosity.

Jessie next introduced her daughter, Laureal, who bore her mother such strong resemblance as to be the image in the tale of the reflecting pool at the heart of the enchanted forest, of which we are all familiar. More than a few times, John had gone out hunting only to end up spying the young woman walking the forest paths, gathering herbs in sunlit glades, or digging nuts from squirrel caches. More than a few times, she had yelled and screamed at him.

At present, suffering the terrible consequences of John's arrival, Laureal spoke no words even as she sized him up beginning with a search of his eyes before unconsciously looking him up and down once.

Years of rigorous training aimed at keeping our hero faithful to his mission could not protect him from the overwhelming gravity of nature but, as we already know, there's more to it than all that—

"Ladies, I have come here to propose a trade. I offer you my continued assistance, and in return, I ask for your assistance."

The twins, who usually helped the adults and by such means learned skills critical to their survival, were released from their training to play with the dogs in the safety of the compound. And regarding the boy who had shot an arrow at John, the Seeker already knew him to be hunting squirrels deep in the wood. Thus having their full attention, Summerfield began, "This is my offer. I will aid you in securing your survival. For example, perhaps I can escort you to another dwelling or village where you have kin?"

Gaining no response, John continued, "In return, I ask only for information regarding the territory to the north. In particular," scooting out on his seat, "the realm beyond the forest. I am looking for an object there; a monolith said to be the size of a great boulder, rectangular in form, standing upright and...shining like polished onyx."

With every word, the Seeker grew more and more acute, "According to the ancient account, it stands in plain view on a barren expanse of such beauty and purity that no man can make his home there. And yet, it is there that it awaits our return."

Finishing, John appeared kindled with the passion of a zealot.

Visibly apprehensive, Laureal opened her mouth to speak only to fall silent on a look from her grandmother.

"What?" asked John, his dark eyes suddenly fixed on her. "Please, tell me what you know!"

Laureal's mother jumped in, "We know nothing of the realm beyond the trees!"

Turning to Jessie, the Seeker's glare was hard and long, "But then, you do know that a realm beyond the trees exists."

"Yes, but that is all."

"Sir," Mia began, hoping to placate the stranger, "if I may ask, when you look to the north, do you see the hovering lights?" referring to the Aurora Borealis.

Staring at the woman, John nodded slowly, "Lately, I have glimpsed some strange things there. In the night sky, faint traces of red and green."

Mia nodded like one who knows, "What you have seen will grow stronger as you travel north, and according to some, it is the reflection of the world beyond the forest." Then, with an air of wonderment, "Sir, could it be that by following those lights, you may find what you seek?"

"Perhaps there is something to that," the Matriarch broke in at last, "but seeing as how the further north one travels, the larger the lights grow, where would one turn to search when having traveled far, the lights cover the breadth of the sky?"

"The forest is what we know," Jessie reiterated with a raised brow. "There are things here that cannot be explained, one such thing not five days north of here."

On John's entreaty, Jessie described an aberration deep in the wood which, in reality, was only the ruins of a city once known as Saskatoon. Mia further expanded and, being keen on the oral mythology of the Kasskatchen people, recited the closing verses in the epic saga of the Niths:

28

"…their cloaks fallen
from their shoulders,
their memories, their spirits,
their futures, all lost,
all fallen into darkness.
Alone, only the Nith remains,
biding its time, until the
new host cometh within
the fallen walls of
its own making."

Jessie and Mia's accounts, well-meaning though they be, were in reality little more than a mix of superstition and vague oral reference to an epic cataclysm ten centuries before. Long since swallowed up by the forest, the ruins of Saskatoon, Winnipeg, Prince Albert, and Regina, to name a few, were known as 'Niths' to the forest people and were considered taboo. Nevertheless, the ruin of Saskatoon, as we shall see, would prove pivotal to the Seeker's mission.

Presently out on the edge of his seat, John had only opened his mouth to speak when the Matriarch cut him off, "Sir, I pray you have not come here in search of evil."

"No ma'am!" incredulously. "My mission is to recover lost knowledge!"

"Well, whatever it is you are after, we will not give you any more information…not today."

In great surprise, John stared at Emma. And she, glaring back at him, continued, "You said you would help us in return for what we know. All right then, but do not think that because we have lost our men you can strut in here expecting us to trade our world away."

"I would remind you, ma'am," growing heated, "that your men could have approached me peacefully but instead chose to ambush me, to capture me, or kill me! And when that failed, they tried to take my equipment, without which I might die. But it did not turn out that way. And now I have come here, not seeking revenge but offering my assistance, and asking for nothing in return but information!"

"Our men were protecting us!" Jessie stated, her intensity boosted by her impressive beauty and keen emerald eyes. "They died protecting the land on which our lives depend. They died doing what their fathers' fathers before them did. And we miss them terribly!"

In the silence that followed, only the voices of the children could be heard, playing in their own little world.

John dropped his eyes to the ground. Withdrawn in thought, uncertain of himself and of whom he was dealing with, he lifted his eyes only to come eye-to-eye with Laureal. They had never been so near, and still, even without their awful circumstance, a great gulf lay between them, one raised in a renaissance, the other brought up in the wild. And yet, something more powerful than hate and mistrust had brought their paths together, out in the allure of the forest, in hallways of trees illuminated by shafts of sunlight where, stopped in their tracks and fallen into silence, each had beheld the other.

Summerfield was first to look away, into the surrounding wood. And Emma, gaining Laureal's eye, shot a look of her own, to silently tell her granddaughter, *"Don't you look at that animal…or so help me God, I will thrash you with a switch!"*

John returned his eyes to Emma, "Ma'am, what would you have me do?"

"Precisely as you said, sir. You have offered your assistance in exchange for what we know. Well, I can assure you our knowledge of the north is extensive and should be of immeasurable value to you. But first, you must cut log poles and build us a wall to keep out the ill-intended, be they four-legged or two. I'm sure that beast of yours will come in handy. And since, as I well know, you like to prowl these woods, and I give you your due, for you are a good hunter, but on that account you can also help us stock our stores for winter. That way, if we can get through the winter, then come spring, our kin can help us find honorable replacements for the men we have lost. And by such means, we can keep our home, our land, and our way of life."

With his mouth partly agape, Summerfield stared at the Matriarch. What she asked would be a monumental undertaking. To his mind, it seemed she was thinking of a well-stocked motte-and-bailey.

"Do you not have family you can go and live with now?" he asked.

"Our clan is not as numerous as we once were. Our kin would accept us, but we would come as a burden just when they were preparing for winter. And since the territory of our particular family lies on the fringe of the realm, it would be a journey of many days. Who knows how long our home would sit abandoned? Mia and her late husband stayed here last winter…one of our couples always does, but now, in our absence, the wild animals would do their worst. And the destruction might be many times greater if word of our demise spread to certain animals of the two-legged variety."

Turning the possibilities over in his mind, John gazed into the fire pit where tiny flames danced atop a bed of coals. Perhaps the Matriarch was not asking too much. Given that the compound already sat perched on a small cliff above the river, perhaps he could fortify it with a partial wall. That, and a few extra deer or caribou to supply them with meat for the winter months. It was certainly a lot, but perhaps not impossible.

"Think it over," said the Matriarch, "then we will talk."

Over a barrel, young Summerfield's expression told of his disappointment even while he did his best to retain the courtesy in which he'd been rigorously trained, "Well…alright then, ma'am." And somewhat aimlessly, he added, "I suppose I should be on my way."

"Stay," Emma softly ordered, putting her hand out, that he remain seated. Then turning to her daughter, "This man has been feeding us. Now it is our turn to feed him."

Laureal rose from her seat, "I'll get him a bowl."

"No," Emma ordered, "you will sit down and remain there."

Jessie brought a set of clay-fired bowls and, from the blackened pot, drew ladles of steaming porridge made from bread root and rabbit. From a second pot, Mia produced bowls of wild rice spiced with forest herbs. And Laureal, who had gained permission, brought roasted acorns on a wooden dish. For dessert, there would be pears, harvested from rugged little trees that grew in forest glades. Fruit not native to the region but imported and selectively bred by 21st century researchers at the University of Saskatchewan, presently a ruin and all that remained of Saskatoon a hundred miles to the north. The pear trees, a custom-made subspecies, had established their niche with a thousand years of help from birds and other animals that spread their seeds. Also, the forest people periodically burned off the forest glades and clearings along the rivers to allow for more fruit-bearing trees and plants. The pears, being specifically bred for it, had weathered the cold snap of early autumn and, as a result, provided fruit for the fall harvest.

Himself being raised in a renaissance and therefore no stranger to civilized food, John was visibly surprised and, having complimented the women, continued to savor the unexpected goodness of his meal. While they supped, the conversation turned to that of edible plants and herbs, forest medicines, animal pelts, and storms to remember. They spoke of iron, wool, and cotton, relatively new commodities from trading routes that had connected the forest realm to lands beyond the Five Seas in the east (the Great Lakes). In the course of such conversation, Summerfield gained valuable information and wondered if perhaps it was the women's way of showing goodwill. Indirectly, John also learned some history about the family and the men he had killed. They had been Emma's husband, Emma's son-in-law who had been Jessie's husband, Emma's nephew who had been Mia's husband, and Emma's oldest grandson who had been Jessie's son and Laureal's big brother. The family had only recently returned from their summer home and hunting grounds except for Mia, her late husband, and the twins. They had stayed over the summer to keep and maintain the family's winter home.

John lowered his eyes to his plate, the weight of their loss growing on his shoulders. He was too young to figure it out. Perhaps it was not something that could be figured out. From childhood he had been trained to find the Data Block, to fight his way there, to do whatever was necessary. Not only had the clansmen threatened his existence, they had threatened his reason for existence. Still, he was the one with the giant and the overwhelmingly superior firepower. And at that moment, sitting in silence, if he could go back and do it over again, he would have fired a shot across the bow.

The women had also fallen silent.

The day was getting on. Trees cast their shadows across the river. Wispy signs of dusk gathered on the horizon. Snow geese were honking somewhere just out of sight, slowly descending to earth, looking to overnight on their long journey south. Then, like thunder in John's ear, there came the snap of a twig.

Summerfield spun in his seat while slinging his rifle from his back to his front. All in the same instant, Laureal nearly collided with him as she leapt past like a cat.

"NO!" cried the Matriarch, rising, shaking her head and extending her hands with palms facing the boy on the edge of the wood, "NO!"

The boy, standing with an arrow drawn to fire, shouted at his sister, "Get out of the way!"

Laureal stood with arms extended, blocking both the boy's shot at Summerfield and Summerfield's shot at the boy.

"Get out of the way!" shrieked the boy.

Acting on the quick, Laureal strode to her little brother and slapped the shaft of the arrow, setting it free to fly astray.

In the next instant, John lifted the boy into the air and slammed him to the ground, knocking the wind out of him.

"Don't hurt him!" cried Laureal, following close behind as John drug the boy roughly into camp, pushed him down hard to sit on a bench, and while he gasped to breathe, got in his face and warned, "Try that again, and I will kill you!"

In silent rage, Summerfield dropped into a seat opposite the boy where he sat glaring across the fire while contemplating his next move. Only a week before and undisclosed to the women, the boy had crept to the edge of the Seeker's camp and shot John with an arrow. Fortunately for the horseman, he had risen from his seat at the very instant the boy released his arrow. Thus the shot only grazed John. The incident had remained a secret in part because John had chased the boy down, put a knife to his throat, and swore he would kill the boy's entire family if he ever tried such a thing again.

Presently, Jessie and Laureal stood in near shock, fearful, not knowing what to do.

John glanced up at Laureal, "Thank you for what you did. I won't harm him…this time."

Laureal nodded numbly. Then, obeying her grandmother, she went to help Mia quiet the crying children.

Emma approached John and gestured with a solemn look, "Walk with me."

A short distance into the woods, the Matriarch stopped and said, "Night will fall soon. You should return to your camp."

"I am very sorry about this, ma'am, but you must tell the boy if he tries that again, I will have no choice but to kill him."

"Please do not do that, sir. He is all we have left."

"Then you must see to it that he understands."

"I do not believe you intended to break our family," said Emma, "but we have suddenly found ourselves very broken and…struggling to salvage what is left."

At a loss for words, Summerfield tipped his cap, "Good night, ma'am," and he went away toward his camp.

That night, John lay in his tent pondering his options. Firstly, he decided he must—he absolutely must—get Laureal out of his thoughts. But no matter how he tried, he could not.

He and Ellie had had time to rest and heal. He had carefully repaired and prepared his gear as needed. All that remained was to shoe Ellie. She currently walked barefoot and that was good but she would need her shoes soon. Size 10s with cleats for ice travel on frozen rivers. Other than that, everything was ready for whatever lay ahead. From his arrival in the forest, John had hoped to find a frozen river that he and Ellie could follow north like a highway. And he had found the perfect starting point at the camp of the forest women. But after the cold snap of late September, an "Indian Summer" seemed to have set in. So it might be necessary to continue traveling through the forest at least until the rivers froze. Certainly the women knew of trails he could take. Just knowing the trails existed meant he could find them. They would run along the rivers for sure, but what about elsewhere? It would be a priceless advantage to know what the savages knew. He wished the old woman didn't have him over a barrel. If only he could kidnap the little children and then trade them back for information, but he had taken an oath, something like a knight's oath of old that forbade such behavior.

Pushing back against anxiety, unable to sleep, Summerfield crawled from his tent. Nearby, his horse stood sleeping, breathing so gently with her giant lungs as to be indiscernible. She lifted one foot so that only its toe rested on the ground, then shifted to the next foot, and then the next, slowly rotating all four to rest them as she slept.

Sick at heart, his every thought around Laureal, John gazed into the glade that adjoined his camp. The moon was out. Not quite full, it cast the glade in the grayscale of night, making it appear somewhat like a pond in the woods. Behind it, the woods stood like a dark wall with a serrated top set against the bright night sky. John drew a breath so fresh, it seemed as though nature had used the cold snap to clean the air in anticipation of a newly arrived Indian summer.

Chapter 3

Indian Summer though it be, the nights were cold and the frigid morning air made steam clouds of Laureal's every breath. Her grandmother had protested when she left the longhouse just fifteen minutes earlier with only a cloak. Laureal had assured Emma that she'd be fine in expectation of fast-rising temperatures. Emma had sent Laureal into the wood to tap a favorite maple tree. The Matriarch knew that warm autumn days and cold nights meant the sap inside the tree would flow, not as sugary as in the springtime but flowing nonetheless and should be taken advantage of. If the sap did not contain too much niter, Laureal was to tap several more favored trees. These were old-growth maples of the 31st century, against which maples of the 21st century might appear somewhat wispy.

To fabricate a maple tap, Laureal began by trimming a small piece off an elderberry branch. She used a small stone knife her father had made for her. Sharper than a steel razor, the knife's replaceable flint blade sat in a handle of polished elk horn. Its hand-tooled leather case depicted a swan in flight. Using the knife, Laureal next stripped the bark from a tiny oak branch to make a ramrod the size of a Japanese hairpin. She then used the ramrod to push the cold but pliable center out of the elderberry branch. She carved the ends of the elderberry to bevel the tap. In her strong desire to complete her tasks, she did not take time to warm her hands. As a result, her bare fingers, having been exposed too long in icy air, became so cold she could scarcely use them.

"Oh gosh," sheathing her knife and pulling her hands to her chest, rubbing them together, blowing into them, hunching her shoulders and feeling cold all over. Meanwhile down at her feet, Chewy had set to growling the way dogs do before getting worked up, low growls, very nearly inaudible. Then came the unmistakable sound of crushing twigs, leaves, and small branches. Something of tremendous size was coming through the wood, and Laureal knew exactly what it was.

"Crush, crush, crush." Each step getting louder, "Crush, crush, crush!"

Forgetting her hands, Laureal turned around, her eyes at once fearful and enthralled. The giant, alone without its rider, stood directly before her. Three times the size of a bull moose, clouds of steam flowed from Ellie's nostrils like a dragon, her fantastic blue eye locked on Laureal's own.

Chewy leaped forward, barking and growling. Down came the massive head with ears pinned back. A glaring eye, dark as night, and a mighty snort drove the canine back. Then, having issued fair warning, Ellie showed not a trifle of concern more over Chewy. Instead, she turned to focus on Laureal with every atom of her being. The giant displayed not one hint of aggression but rather, begging and imploring, forced the girl back with a friendly nudge from a nose only slightly smaller than a medieval battering ram. Chewy, still growling and barking, mustered his courage and went for the giant's front leg only to be warned away with a stomp that seemed to shake the very earth.

Laureal, trying to step back, stumbled on a tree root but managed to keep her balance. She backed up further, yet the giant matched her step for step, nudging all the way to her torso with some wholly mysterious and overly friendly interest.

"Oh, ah, no." Laureal was nearly to turn and run when Summerfield came stepping fast through the wood, "ELLIE!"

Ellie snapped to attention.

"Are you injured, miss?" (with utmost concern).

Laureal, having backed off a few steps more and only mildly in shock, shook her head.

"Please accept my apology if my horse has caused you any trouble. I assure you she meant you no harm."

Laureal made no reply but stood gazing at John with great uncertainty.

Also uncertain, John gazed back. Then, taking in the scene before him, he saw the basket hanging from Laureal's arm and there was Ellie, a picture of hope with ears perked. John's lips turned up at the corners, "Miss," returning his eyes to hers, "it would appear my horse has picked up the scent of something in your basket."

At once Laureal animated as if to say, *"Oh! I should have known!"*

But of course Laureal couldn't have known that horses liked sugary things, although it made for a good guess. She and her mother had made the basket for collecting maple sap. Made of birch bark, the basket didn't have anything in it at that moment other than a few tools and smaller leakproof catch baskets used for collecting maple sap and temporarily storing maple syrup and butter after processing. All were well-used and permeated with a sweet scent that attracted the giant like a bear to a honeycomb. In fact some horses like sweets so much, there exists at least one 21st century account of a horse getting its head stuck in a beehive after semi-climbing a tree to get at the honey, whereupon it had to be cut free with a chainsaw. Fortunately, both animal and bees came away without serious injury. And the tree, albeit damaged, survived to repair itself.

John turned a stern eye on the barking dog, "Sit and be quiet!" Chewy obeyed immediately, having already accepted Summerfield as the new alpha male.

John turned back to Laureal, "Miss, with your permission, I would like to explain something."

Her caution turning to curiosity, Laureal gave a nod and John continued, "You see, Ellie here is a sweet girl but she does not recognize you as having a place above her in the pecking order. She sees you as below her. And we, that would be you and I, would do well to show her at once that you are to be respected."

Reaching into his coat pocket, John fished out a piece of licorice root, "In place of your basket, we can use this." And casting a stern glance at Ellie, he closed his fist around the licorice, "We will hold it back from her until she respects and obeys your command."

Returning his eyes to Laureal, John's smile spoke to his comfort around horses, "Don't worry. This will be easy as pie."

In the silence that followed, the lovers stood but eight feet apart on a well-worn path amid giant tree roots and ferns browned by the cold snap. The maples, some nearly four hundred years in age, spread their limbs out in great umbrella-like lattices.

Holding the licorice out, John took several steps in Ellie's and Laureal's direction, "All you need to do is hide this in one hand and with your other hand push against her chest and say 'back' like you mean it. Push there," pointing, "not there [on her old wound]. If she doesn't take a step back at once, push harder and say 'back' like you intend to swat her if she does not obey. She'll step back. Then you can give her her reward. And when you do, hold it in your hand like this." John held his palm flat to show how. "After this, if ever she gets in your way, you'll know what to do. Just push on her chest and say, 'Back.'"

Moving a step closer, John extended his hand to offer Laureal the licorice. Only then did he notice how she shivered. At once the smile ran away from his face, and he silently chided himself for being obtuse. He stuffed the licorice back in his pocket—

"It's still very cold this morning, miss."

Laureal nodded, her lips pursed tight.

"Sometimes the chill finds its way into us before we even know it has."

"Indeed, sir, this morning I fear that it has done exactly that," mustering a painful little smile.

John extended his hand, "If you would trust me…Ellie and I have a cure for that."

Laureal searched John's eyes. Not one atom of malice could she detect. Not one atom of deceit. Her thoughts went to days past. A dozen times she had questioned her sanity for thinking there might be some good in him. She had seen handsome men before, powerful bright-eyed men, but she had never seen a man like him. Now he stood directly before her, his hand outstretched. A stranger from far away in the west, a horseman come by happenstance of circumstance most tragic and terrible.

John lifted his eyebrows and pursed a smile as if to ask, *"Well, are you going to trust me or not?"*

Slowly, Laureal drew one hand from her cloak and placed it in John's. No sooner had she done so than he extended his other hand, that she might accept it also.

Slowly, John drew Laureal towards Ellie.

It's okay, she won't harm you," and with two steps more they stood directly at Ellie's side, hand in hand, holding one another's gaze while some unseen force took hold and compelled them to maintain their grasp. Eye to eye in an exchange that overthrew anything and everything that shouted of wrong, no matter how loud, it fell in the span of a few seconds. And fleeting though it be, it would always be remembered as the moment their time on earth together began, be it long or short.

"Here's what we're going to do," John explained. "We're going to take your cloak off, but don't worry! I promise you that in less than a minute, you'll be warmer than any coat could make you. You'll see. First, we have to get you up on Ellie. So I'm going to make a step with my hands," and he demonstrated as he spoke, "and you're going to put your foot in it so I can boost you up on her. You can put your hand on my shoulder to steady yourself as I boost you up, and as you go up, swing your right leg over her. Then, when you're atop her...well, I will show you."

Taking Laureal's basket, John noted its contents as he set it out of harm's way. Moving quick and easy, he took Laureal's cloak and hung it carefully on a limb. He then got into position beside Ellie and made a step with his hands, "Okay, put one hand on my shoulder, and your foot in there."

Laureal did as John ordered.

"This will be easy as climbing a tree. Are you ready?"

If ever there was a prize for looking uncertain but nodding 'yes' anyway, Laureal would have won it. She nodded, John boosted her strong but smooth and up she went swinging her leg over Ellie's back.

The next thing Laureal knew, there she sat atop the giant!

High above the forest floor, Laureal appeared a picture of joyful surprise and John delighted in seeing it. He also knew she was losing body heat, although she might not realize it in her present state of exhilaration.

"Lean forward," looking up and motioning from the ground with his hands, "all the way onto your stomach. That's it. Ellie's so broad, you can scarcely fall off but if you like, you can hold onto her mane...it won't hurt her."

Removing his wolverine long coat, Summerfield gave Ellie a reassuring look, "Just think of this as your buffalo cloak," and he swung it up to cover Laureal like a blanket. He then watched and waited, and, within moments...

"Oh my gosh," said Laureal, "she's so warm!"

"She's a big ol' stove," John laughed.

Laureal closed her eyes and sighed in relief, "Ah—."

"You won't be able to take it for long," Summerfield declared laughingly. Then, with a happy but serious air, he continued, "You'll want to sit up after a bit. Otherwise, you'll start sweating, and then, when you come down, you'll be twice as cold as before."

Suddenly worried, Laureal asked, "But sir, what about you? Are you not cold without your coat?"

"Not with all this," gesturing to his under-layers, pushing his chest out. "Heck, I don't even know why I bothered to put that coat on this morning."

Laureal could not help but smile, lying though she suspected he was.

"If I may ask, miss, what brings you into the woods this morning? Have you come to tap a maple, this time of year?"

"I came to tap that tree," nodding to the maple. "Grandma said it would flow."

"This one?" John asked.

"Yes."

"Do you mind if I do the honors?"

"No," gazing, smiling through pursed lips.

John picked up Laureal's basket, took out her drill, and admired its design. A hardwood speed wrench, it had a flint cutting bore affixed to its end with sinew thread and glue made from the sap of evergreens.

Laureal sat up and, comfortably cloaked in John's long coat, watched as he stepped to the maple with drill in hand.

"Here?" he asked, pointing to the trunk with an inquisitive look.

"A little higher."

"Here?"

"Yes."

"Are you sure?" playfully.

"Yes," laughing.

Summerfield placed the drill to the tree and, feeling her eyes on his every move, he told himself, *"Whatever you do, John, don't screw this up. This has to be perfect in front of her."*

As the horseman drilled, Laureal looked on as would a lady watch a suitor in a test.

Having completed his test, John read the affirmation in Laureal's gaze, and so powerfully beautiful were her emerald eyes, he had to look away, down into her basket where he found a tap, the one she had made only minutes before.

"Did you make this?" he asked, returning his eyes to her with wonder.

"Yes."

"This is a good tap," in complete earnest.

Seeing his candor, Laureal took it to heart, for such abilities were measures of value in her world.

Drawing a large steel knife from his belt, John intended to finalize the tap so that it would fit the hole exactly when, suddenly pausing, he looked up at Laureal, "I'm sure your [stone] knife would work perfectly well," referring to one of the tools in her basket, "and I would like to try it someday, but I don't want to push my luck this morning."

Laureal beamed even as she reserved comment. John's unspoken meaning was not lost on her. He valued their fledgling success and wished to preserve it.

Using the butt of his knife, John tapped the tap into the maple tree. Next he hung one of the little catch baskets on the tap so that the sap might drip into it.

"Grandma said it would start flowing this afternoon," said Laureal, herself having never tapped a tree so late in the season.

Setting Laureal's large basket at the base of the maple, John took her drill in one hand and her knife in the other. "These are finely made tools!"

My grandfather made the drill," forgetting her sorrow if only for the moment. "My mother and I made the baskets. And for my birthday two summers ago, my father made the knife, and my big brother made its sheath." Laureal smiled to herself, her thoughts on happy times.

John lifted his eyes from the tools and Laureal realized at once, her every word had been a stone placed upon his chest.

Like cold rain, the tragedy of it all came down and washed away Laureal's happiness, leaving her lost again, having lost so much. Wishing to run and hide, she slid out of John's coat and down Ellie's side to land on her feet but, unlike her usual self, she fell to the ground.

"Are you hurt?" asked John, stepping forward quickly.

"My mother and grandmother will be worried." Donning her cloak, Laureal took her tools from John's hands.

John opened his mouth to speak but he could find no words.

Laureal turned and ran away.

Heartsick, John watched as she vanished into the woods.

That night, Laureal lay sleepless in bed. Unable to get comfortable, she rolled from one side to the other; her stomach, her back—nothing seemed to work. At one point, rolling to her side again, she saw her little brother also lying awake. From his bed, he looked at her from under his covers. The fire in the hearth still had a flicker, just enough to show his face. He was saying something to her without sound, and reading his lips, she saw him say, *"I hate your guts!"*

Laureal rolled to her other side. She missed her father terribly. She missed her big brother, grandfather, and cousin terribly. She had cried so many tears. She felt desperately fortunate to still have her mother, grandmother, cousin, and little brother too. She thought about John Summerfield and what had happened, not that day but on the day of the disaster. A storm had swept in from nowhere and left her standing in a wreckage she had once called home. She could scarcely wonder what the future held.

She remembered listening to her grandmother when she was a little girl. There at the hearth, sitting in the firelight, Emma had told the children the Kasskatchen Spirit Story. Every Kasskatchen knew the story. Deep within every soul there roamed two packs of wolves. One pack was good, the other evil. The good wolves ran in green glades filled with sunlight and flowers. The bad wolves lurked in shadows that hung like twilight along the edge of the wood. Seven good wolves and seven bad wolves within the contours of the human soul, locked in a territorial war. The good wolves were of the realm of light and were ever faithful to the Lord of Truth. The bad wolves were of the realm of darkness and were manipulated by the Master of Deception. Every Kasskatchen child knew the ghost wolves by name, for they were the virtues and vices of humanity, and whichever ones the girl fed with her thoughts, feelings, and actions were the ones that would grow strong and decide the battle that raged within.

Laureal remembered how when Grandma told the story in the firelight, she seemed to grow bigger and bigger in the child's eyes until she was the size of a bear! Back then, the story had elevated her awareness to such a degree, she didn't want to feed those evil old wolves so much as a scrap! Now half her world had been blown away, and the other half teetered on the edge of a precipice. And for the life of her, she could not know if it was some kind of terrible confusion that gripped her or a deeper truth that drew her. For the thing she feared the most, was to wake on the morrow only to find that John Summerfield had moved on.

Chapter 4

To become a Seeker, a young man had to clear a series of academic hurdles. More importantly, he had to master what the Order called the three basics: Killing, Courtesy, and Horsemanship. Unfortunately, learning how to survive on what nature provides, as in survivalist training, was not given the same importance. As a result, John survived by learning as he went from outpost to outpost, and still, in comparison to the savages, he was sorely ignorant. The pocket of civilization from which he'd come had, in large part, escaped nature's hard side; a move they could not be faulted for even as their separation created a paradox that contributed to their failure to locate the Data Block. Now however, in an unintended stroke of good fortune, the magnitude of which John Summerfield remained unaware, he stood as the first Seeker to establish peaceful relations with a group of savages in the wild north.

So John had struck it rich, and still one would not know it by observing him on this particular morning. His mood ill, he sat atop a chest-like storage box, flipping his large knife in the air, alternately catching it by its handle and blade. Not a fancy knife but a deadly weapon custom-made for the Seeker's own hands. Suddenly he stood up and threw it, sticking it in a nearby tree.

John looked around his campsite. It was a fine site, located on the south side of a lovely little glade with a carpet of grass and a brook running along its edge. Next to his tent, he'd made a lean-to that sheltered his kitchen. A bleached-out log, nice and smooth, served as both a bench and a border for a living area that included a few storage boxes currently serving as seats.

"What the hell am I doing?" John thought, surveying it all. *"I must...I absolutely must get on with my mission!"*

Although cold, the morning promised yet another sunny afternoon with temperatures in the mid to upper fifties (in Fahrenheit). John walked out into the glade where Ellie stood munching what little grass she had not already eaten. Fortunately for Ellie, there were many glades and openings along the river for her to graze. Fortunately for John, she always returned after visiting them.

"Stay, girl," John ordered, holding his hand up, signaling her to stay put. Then, with fast-running steps, he leaped and, sliding across her back on his stomach, swung his leg over to sit up in one smooth motion.

Ellie, having scarcely flinched, may have been the ideal place for a young man to get his head on straight. There in the midst of nature, sitting on a trusted mount in a sunlit glade. John knew he was dangerously close to breaking his oath to his Order. He could not get Laureal out of his heart and mind. He could not forget the feeling of holding her hands in his. And since then, his feelings had only grown stronger. And to his thinking, it seemed that Laureal felt the same, for in the days that followed, both made certain to cross paths every chance they got, and although he had not touched her, he always came away deeper in than before. It was wonderful, and it was terrible, for any Seeker who broke his vow of celibacy or misused the assets entrusted to his care by the Order could be put to death. Of the few Seekers that had broken their oaths and were caught, all had been made examples of. It was not pretty, but the Order deemed it necessary for maintaining the sacrosanct nature of the quest.

"Girly girl," patting Ellie's neck, "we've got to get off this runaway wagon."

With no small intent, Summerfield swung his leg over Ellie's neck and slid down to the ground. He had made up his mind. He would break camp that very morning and move on.

That same morning, on the gravelly beach at the base of the small cliff below their summer home, Emma and her grandson Cody sat on smooth boulders while wisps of steam rose from the little river.

"You should be hearing this from your grandfather," Emma said to the boy, "but today I will speak to you for him. Cody, you know that a battle is being waged in each of us. You know that…

"Ghost wolves are fighting for my soul," quipped the boy, shaking his head, "I knew this was coming."

Emma's eyes grew large and, for a moment she was of a mind to give the boy a good switching. She was still big and strong enough to do so. She refrained in the knowledge that her youngest grandchild was heartbroken.

"Cody…you and I, your mother and sister and cousin, we are all that is left. And I know you want to do your part to save our family. But right now, the shadow wolves see you as their best opportunity to finish us off."

Taken aback, the boy gazed at his grandmother in silence.

"It's true," she said, leaning in. "I know because I've seen it before. I lived through the tragedy at the river crossing. Your mother and I both saw how it affected our kin. Some of us made our way to fulfillment and happiness in life even after we had lost so much. But Cody, there were others who couldn't let go of what happened. They clung to it so tightly that…they missed their opportunity for a happy life. And ultimately, they had no one to blame but themselves."

The Matriarch took a softer tone even as she remained somber, "Cody, your pain is terrible because your love was great. But as bad as that pain is, you mustn't allow it to destroy your ability to think clearly. You mustn't let the shadow wolves use your pain to get the upper hand and blind you to the needs of those you love…and Cody, right now, we need John's help."

Emma laid her hand on Cody's shoulder, "Your grandfather, father, brother, and cousin Norman intended to capture John and bring him here. That is what you told me, Cody. You said your father and grandfather feared that John might be an advanced scout for a clan that warred on horse giants. But Cody, if things had worked out differently and we'd brought John here, we would have discovered that he was not a

48

marauder, but on a vision quest. And knowing that, we may have decided that he had been sent to us. And had that been the case, I believe your grandfather and I would have made an exception. We would have spared John's life. We may even have adopted him. And Cody…if we'd done that, well then, you and John would have become brothers."

Emma drew a deep breath, "You and I, your mother and sister and cousin…this is on our shoulders now. We must carry on and rebuild our family for those who will follow. But we cannot build anything if our hearts are consumed with rage. You know the story…a shadow wolf will carry the heart of its victim in its stomach to the den of its dark master, and any heart that is twice devoured is seldom recovered. Feed the good wolves instead, Cody. Feed the good wolves, and help your mother and I, your sister and cousin. Help us save what is left of our family."

From the corner of her eye, Emma spotted Laureal heading out of camp with Chewy, walking the river trail atop the cliff, "Granddaughter," she called, "where are you going?"

"To gather walnuts, Grandma."

"Wait right there for a moment. Your brother is going with you."

"I don't need his help!"

Emma turned back to Cody, "My grandfather passed down a story to my brother, and I know your grandfather would have passed that same story down to you. So I will tell it to you for him. Your great-great-grandfather was a renowned warrior, loved and feared throughout the realm. The story he told my brother was made specially for a warrior's heart. And many a young man that took it to heart, grew up to become a great warrior. I will tell you tonight. But right now, I need you to go with your sister."

Left alone, Emma took the rare luxury of lingering on her beach, soaking up sunshine in the beauty of an Indian summer while gathering her thoughts and fighting off despair. She had been in a decades-long endeavor to rebuild the family since the disaster at the river crossing. Now, having been knocked down by yet another tragic disaster, she felt crushed and broken. She wanted to give up. Just give up! That or, like a drowning person, grab hold of whatever rebuilding material she could get her hands on.

"Excuse me, Ma'am."

Emma turned to see Summerfield standing atop the cliff twelve feet above. *"Speak of the devil,"* she silently thought.

"Might this be a good time to discuss your offer?"

"I thought you'd never ask," replied Emma.

"Might I join you, then?" smiling at her jest.

"You may."

As Summerfield descended the steps, Emma asked, "Have you seen my granddaughter and grandson this morning?"

"No ma'am, I have not," and looking concerned, "Is there reason for worry?"

"No, no worries. They're collecting walnuts and hunting squirrels. I thought you may have seen them."

"No ma'am, not this morning," taking a seat beside her.

Perhaps in all the world there existed no better place to talk. The sun had brought up the temperature, and the little river, pretty though it had been in its early morning shroud of steam, now awakened in glittering swaths as though to welcome the breeze that had come from the south. Then, with a lull in the breeze, the surface calmed to that of a slow-moving mirror, reflecting a crystal blue sky dotted with white cloud puffs.

Seemingly out of nowhere, a white-headed eagle appeared, gliding effortlessly above the treetops, following the path of the river.

Watching the raptor fly, John felt the gravity of his quest pulling at his overthrown heart. For he truly believed that men had once risen to fly faster, farther, and even higher than the eagles.

The Matriarch saw the eagle as a sign. Passing overhead, it turned its head one way and then the other as it surveyed both sides of the river. She had seen enough of John to decide him an extraordinary young man. His Order had not given him that wolverine cap for nothing. And she could not help but wonder if John had come not to destroy but because he'd been asked for, except that sadly, tragically, they had screwed things up, all of them, John included.

Emma turned her eyes to John. She knew he and Laureal had been speaking in the woods. She had not discouraged it.

"Sir, before we discuss our business, there is a matter of great importance that I must address."

"Ma'am, you have my undivided attention."

"My granddaughter, Laureal, as you may have noticed, is an exceptional young woman." And with a nod of acknowledgment, "I admit to my bias. Still, we all saw it in her from early childhood. She harbored an abundant measure of natural happiness. And particularly now, when she has been crushed, her resilience gives me great hope. But that is only the half of it. She has always been quick to grasp, sharply focused, and determined. Put together, such attributes could be too much for the average young man, as she might run circles around him. But for the right man, well, I believe such a union would hold great promise for the future of our family."

"Ma'am, I could not possibly find fault in your granddaughter, not after she put herself in harm's way for me," and grimacing, he averted his eyes to the river, "In light of what has taken place, I would be hard pressed to find such consideration."

"Well, with regard to what has taken place, we women have had a talk. We've had several talks. And we have decided that, although our men had the right to kill you in defense of the territory on which we depend, we also agreed that we cannot fault you for defending your life. We have also decided that, reality being what it is, we are glad you are a gentleman and not a brute, or worse, a gang of brutes that might take particular interest in my dear granddaughter. And my granddaughter, perhaps more than any of us, has taken these things to heart.

51

But of course, that is not to say she is not caught up in a terribly confused situation."

Keenly attuned but not entirely certain, John spoke slowly, "I think…I follow your meaning."

"If I may continue, I believe you will understand my meaning completely. You see, we arranged a marriage for Laureal years ago. Laureal and the young man had not yet had the opportunity to meet and the final decision would be theirs of course but in reality, Kasskatchen children rarely go against the wishes of their families. Anyway, to make a long story short, there was a growing divide between our family and his due to a situation in which, well, they had become involved with a certain faction in the east that was particularly skilled when it came to taking advantage of, shall we say, 'low-hanging fruit.' And that is why, a year ago, we terminated our contract with them."

Pausing to glance out over the river, Emma continued, "Laureal was born at a time when we desperately needed to rebuild our clan after the disaster at the river crossing. And that is why we never planned to send her off to live with another clan. Instead, we felt that based on our good family name and the quality of our young woman, we would find a young man of high quality to come and join us. And towards that end, we had some good offers. Still, we decided to hold out for one more year in the belief that we could do even better. And now, here we are, and my poor granddaughter is nineteen!

"What I am trying to tell you, sir, is that Mother Nature has had time to stoke quite a fire in Laureal's heart, and Laureal has had no means of quenching it. She is so ready to begin her journey that, had you been a witless dope, she may have settled for you anyway. Except you are not a witless dope, and she has gone over the moon, but due to extraordinary circumstances, she is flying over the moon upside down."

"Ma'am," visibly bound up inside, "what would you have me do?"

"If you have fallen in love with my granddaughter, then I would have you be the man we hoped to find. By the abilities you have shown, there is much for you to gain here, not only from our love, but from our wealth and reputation which are still considerable. On the other hand, if you do not love my granddaughter, then you must keep her at arm's length."

At war within, John gazed into space. "I have given an oath of fidelity to my Order." Shaking his head, he struggled in confusion as his brain overthrew his heart, "As a matter of sacred honor," turning his eyes to Emma, "I must not fall in love with your granddaughter."

Emma looked sideways at John. "Sir, if I may be forgiven for pressing, I am an old woman and I have seen much in my life. I have seen the way you look at my granddaughter, and I have seen the way she looks at you. Are you certain that the answer you are giving me, is the same answer that the voice in your heart is giving you?"

Looking out over the river, John poured his energy into thought like a man who, having gotten lost in a wood, sits down to retrace his steps. At last when he spoke, he seemed to be talking as much to himself as to Emma, "To abandon my mission would be to betray those that spent no small portion of their lives training me for it. It was their great hope. They entrusted me with it. And I accepted it in the understanding that I was to give it nothing less than my all, which necessitates celibacy, for which I took an oath to last until my mission is completed, or, until my death."

When John had finished his speech, he turned to Emma with certainty.

"Then we have reached an agreement," stated the Matriarch, making no effort to hide her disappointment. "You will keep my granddaughter at arm's length based on your oath to your Order, and, on your word to me."

"Yes, ma'am."

They sat gazing out over the river. The beauty of the day, holding such promise only an hour before, seemed to have fallen into the shadow of an invisible cloud, blocking the sun and bringing a chill.

At last, Emma broke the silence, "So, things being as they are, let us move to the business of building a wall and stocking up stores for winter… and the trading of information."

Sick at heart, John nevertheless got down to business, "I will build you a wall. And I will help you stock up for winter. I will complete the wall no matter what, but with regard to helping you stock up for winter, I will assist you only until the river freezes well enough for my horse and I to travel, or until the wall is complete, whichever comes first. In return, I want to compile information as we work regarding routes north, which will require me to take notes and make charts. Of course, this will require you to trust in my promise not to depart prematurely but at the agreed time I have proposed."

"As Matriarch of this clan, I accept your offer."

"All right then, I would like to get started at once. I have scouted a stand of aspens along the river. They are very straight. I will cut the poles and drag them here using my horse."

"I would like the north section of the wall to be built permanent," Emma stated, "there is no need for a wall along the cliff, and concerning the rest, I would like it built to be taken down after the family gets back on its feet. And also, there should be at least two gates."

"Very well, ma'am. Tonight or tomorrow, when I arrive with the first poles, we can work out the details of the structure based on what you want."

John rose from his seat, "With your permission, I will get started."

Emma nodded glumly, "Good day, sir."

Crossing the beach, Summerfield had only begun the stairs when, unbeknownst to him, Laureal, having returned to see Ellie grazing nearby, came to check if John might be on the beach below. Thus, she took her lover by surprise—

"Good day, sir," perched at the top of the stairs.

"Good day, miss," coming up the steps, his manner businesslike. "Your grandmother and I have just reached an agreement," and reaching the top step, "I am to build a wall," tipping his cap as he walked past.

Chapter 5

That same day at midmorning, Emma made a last-minute change of plan. Woman's intuition amplified by long life led her to roll the dice. Instead of sending Cody to assist Mr. Summerfield with the work in the aspen grove, Emma decided to send Laureal.

"Granddaughter," she called to the girl.

"Yes, Grandmother."

"Let us put a picnic basket together, that Mr. Summerfield may remain strong while he works."

In the aspen grove, John arrived with his horse and a few tools, foremost being his hatchet. He did not feel confident letting Ellie loose there because, while she would initially stay around due to the good grass, the falling trees would spook her. It was important though, that she keep eating to build her fat stores for the coming journey north. Therefore John led her upriver and left her in a grassy area where she would not be frightened by his work. He knew she would slowly make her way back to him and, in the process, get accustomed to what he was doing.

To get started, it should be known that, due to Summerfield's upbringing, he could not fathom building a flimsy structure. Honor demanded he cut down a fair number of large poles to serve as sturdy corners and intermediaries in a strong wall.

Selecting the first tree, John set to chopping with his hatchet, a tool that many would call an ax. In the hands of a man like John Summerfield, however, it was merely a hatchet. An ax would have been more efficient, and he regretted not having one. He had a bucksaw for cutting firewood but having only one remaining blade, and it being so important to his quest, he left it at his camp, daring not to risk breaking it by foolishly misusing it in an attempt to fell trees. So he had his hatchet, and it took a fair piece of chopping to fell the first tree.

Having removed everything except his buckskin pants and short-sleeved tunic of white cotton, John chopped and dropped a second tree. Pausing not and wet with sweat, he set to chopping a third tree.

Felling the third tree, John paused at last to wipe perspiration from his brow, "If only I had an ax!"

"Mr. Summerfield," came a calling voice, a voice he knew well.

Yet some distance away, Laureal stood in a patch of sunlight on the edge of the aspen grove. She had come down the trail that ran along the river.

"Good morning, miss," John hollered, beginning towards her, pausing only to set down his hatchet.

"Good morning, sir."

As Summerfield came through the trees, Laureal could not help noticing how his tunic clung to his chest, shoulders, and arms. Specially made just for him, the tunic not only fit John perfectly but also had a simple elegance about it, with subtly embroidered chest panels divided by three buttons that ran from neck to solar plexus. The white cotton tunic, soaked with perspiration, revealed him not only tall but broad-shouldered and extraordinarily well-sculpted. He was narrow at the hip and, as he walked, long powerful leg muscles shown in the telltale outlines of his buckskins. Drawing nearer, his face of 21 years, at once boyish and ruggedly handsome, possessed a countenance that softened his piercing dark eyes. But what Laureal noticed more than anything else was the genuine warmth of his smile, for it spoke to his heartfelt happiness in seeing her.

Coming directly before Laureal, John's expression changed to one of surprise, for she had brought the very tool he needed—an ax, but not just any ax—an ax fit for a king.

"Oh, Miss, that is just what I need," and quickly he added, "second to your company, of course."

Immediately wishing to have his last few words back, John silently rebuked himself. For scarcely had three sentences been spoken between them and he had already violated the agreement he had made with Laureal's honorable grandmother.

"It needs new binding," lifting the heavy ax with both hands for John to see.

Taking the ax in hand, John could not help but admire it. A long heavy handle of polished oak, crowned with a great head of jasper which, being highly polished, very nearly looked like jade. An awesome tool and work of art all together in one, the axe's only flaw was its leather binding which, having aged and weathered, required replacement.

"I have new binding in my basket," said Laureal. "If you would like to use it, we can wrap and tighten it over a fire."

"Yes miss, that would be perfect."

"I'll get a fire started while you gather wood."

"I can start a fire, miss. You don't need to trouble yourself."

"What would I do then?"

"You have already brightened my day, not to mention bringing the very tool I need. Just make yourself comfortable."

"Sir, if my grandmother were to come along and see me making myself comfortable while you worked, she would thrash me with a switch."

"Oh," taken aback, himself having no prior experience with savages outside of killing them. Women in his renaissance world were not expected to start fires, at least not in the wild. Still, John was not completely obtuse to the fact that he'd entered another culture and, to his credit, he gave a befuddled nod, "I will get our wood."

That he might bring Laureal the best possible firewood and not just any dead stuff that breaks easily over a knee but doesn't produce any real heat, John retrieved his hatchet and went straight to work. Laureal, meanwhile, took the new rawhide binding from her basket and put it under a rock in the river so that it might soak and become pliable. Next she chose a picnic site amid a group of boulders above the river. Flat, pebbly, and dried out by days of sunshine, the site sat sheltered from the breeze. For fire fodder, she gathered birch bark, twigs, and feathery tips of dry grass. Then, taking a bow drill from her basket, she got a flame started to which she quickly added more fodder, twigs, and sticks.

John returned with quality firewood and soon they had a nice little fire going in the corner of several small boulders like a natural hearth, built in such a way that the breeze carried the smoke away between the rocks so as not to ruin their picnic. Made for shrinking rawhide, the fire also created a pleasant atmosphere in the cool of an Indian summer. And being beside the river, the lovers enjoyed the sound of water slowly rolling around roots and rocks. The crisp autumn air, so fresh in their nostrils, bore the gentle musk of decaying leaves. And with the opening that the river cut through the forest, their little nook appeared to sit in a natural hall. A great hall lined with aspen and birch, naked of leaves, their limbs extended as though in praise of clear blue heaven.

Sitting cross-legged on the gravelly floor, the lovers had backrests at their disposal in the form of smooth boulders if they felt so inclined. Presently, Laureal watched as John cut off the old rawhide binding, being careful not to damage the wooden handle.

"So far so good," said he, cutting away the last of it. Then rising to his knees, he planted the hilt firmly in the pebbly gravel before him so that it stuck straight up with the massive stone ax head at the top, still secured to its wooden handle via an elongated hole in the wood into which a narrowed portion of the stone fit exactly.

"Can you hold it there, Miss?"

Laureal rose to her knees facing John and took hold of the handle to steady it while John, with a long string of moist rawhide, began binding the two together, ax and handle, wrapping and wrapping, copying the pattern he had observed while removing the old binding. And when his hand incidentally brushed hers, as it did every so often, both felt the

59

electricity, like a surge in a powerline between a pair of young hearts.

Having finished the binding with a knot, John took the ax and held it like a giant marshmallow over a campfire, turning it slowly to dry and shrink the rawhide tight to wood and stone.

Beside him, Laureal sat back in silence and relaxed. Cozy in her hooded cloak, she watched him counter the leverage of the axe by remaining on his knees, bringing his entire body into play, gripping the axe with both hands—one hand at the back of its wooden handle and the other halfway to the flame.

"That should do it," said John, examining the bindings. And turning to his lover,

"Shall we give it a try?"

"Would you like something to eat first?"

"Thank you, Laureal. I do feel hungry now that you mention it."

Smiling sweetly, Laureal turned to her basket and, pausing there, turned back to him with a pouty look, "John, please put your coat on. Otherwise, I fear you may catch your death of cold."

John opened his mouth to protest but stopped himself in the realization that Laureal was right. It was a bit chilly and he was still moist with sweat. So he went to fetch his coat in the aspen grove. Not his long coat but a thin undercoat made of wool.

When John returned, he found Laureal had laid out a picnic on a mat of woven reed grass. There were smoked trout, fresh bread cakes, hazelnuts, and apple slices for dessert. So it was that the lovers settled in for their picnic. Reclined against smooth boulders with their lunch laid out in between, they had no bottle of wine but only that special something in nature that intoxicates young hearts. They didn't speak much while eating, as they were too busy stealing glances and trading smiles. John did compliment Laureal on the excellent food, and Laureal took credit, as she should, for making the cakes, even as she confessed they were only leftovers from breakfast.

A few sticks yet lie beside the fire, and, putting one in the flame, John sat back and returned his eyes to Laureal's. He didn't say a word but simply felt a happiness unlike anything he'd known.

"John."

"Yes."

"Tell me about your home."

"My home," his thoughts traveling back, his eyes slowly filling with recollection. "My home lies far away, between mountains and ocean."

"I've never seen a mountain or an ocean."

"Well...the mountains are like this riverbank, except they continue rising from the river until they are above the clouds, and on the way up, there are more rivers and more forests, with giant trees, and tiny brooks running through flower-filled meadows. Below the mountains, the ocean is like a lake, only it is so vast that one cannot see to the end of it. In fact, no one knows where the end of it is. They say a man could walk its shore for a lifetime and never come back to where he began. And because the ocean lies to the west, the sun sets over it and creates a beautiful sight almost every evening.

"Between ocean and mountains," John continued, "there lies a great valley. It is broad and fertile with a river running through it. My home lies in that valley."

"It sounds so wonderful. I could scarcely dream of such a place." Then, after a brief silence, "John, tell me about your father and mother, brothers and sisters."

"Well, there's not much to tell. I hardly know them."

"You hardly know them?" visibly bewildered. "Why?"

"I was separated from them when I was six...five and a half."

"Why?" gazing with empathy beyond her years, "What happened?"

"I was taken into the Order. It was a great honor for my family. And I did get to see them, once, sometimes twice a year."

61

"But in reality," Laureal said sadly, "you never got to have a family of your own."

"The Order is my family," as if to correct her.

"And the Order, they trained you to be who you are today, a Seeker?"

"Yes."

John offered no more, and perhaps wisely, Laureal only said, "Thank you, John."

"For what, Laureal?"

"For telling me about your home," and rolling up the reed mat, she shyly added, "I'd very much like to know more if, sometime, you are of a mind to tell."

Putting the reed mat in her basket, Laureal produced a small towel of leather, soft and thin like a chamois. "Grandma told me that, once on one of her and Grandpa's [rare] journeys to the big village, they met a family from the east, and that family knew another family from further east, who knew a family from very far away where it was said people eat with tools made of silver and gold. And as it was told to Grandma, the faraway people had very specific customs around eating. Some food was to be eaten with the tiny tools, and other food was to be eaten with fingers. And if one were to be successful in life, it was very important to know which was which. And it was especially important that, when conducting some business crucial to one's future, one must never have a bit of food on their face while eating with the tiny tools."

John could not help but laugh, himself coming from a renaissance.

Laureal continued, "As grandma was told, the tiny tools were used with such precision and skill that there was scarcely a need to wipe one's mouth or face. But just in case, a towel was always at hand."

"Yes," said John, gesturing to the small towel in Laureal's hands, "we use a towel like that but made of cotton or linen, like my shirt, and we call it a napkin."

Napkin was the term used on the West Coast of the continent. Serviette was the term used on the East Coast. Both coasts had pockets of renaissance that had recently made transcontinental contact, although extremely limited by way of a sea route through the Gulf of Mexico, followed by a treacherous overland route where if the desert didn't get you, the 'salvajes' would.

"Is it your custom?" asked Laureal, still holding the leather napkin.

"Yes, but out here, if I need to, I just wipe my mouth on the back of my hand."

"Can you show me how it's done?"

"Yes, of course," and taking the napkin, "you keep it out of sight in your lap, like this. And when you need it, you bring it out like this." Lifting the napkin to his mouth, John daintily dabbed his lips.

"That's interesting," smiling as though it were all very funny. Then, taking the napkin, Laureal placed her lips exactly where John's lips had been. And as she pressed it there, peering over its top like a veil, John thought he saw the inclination of a bad girl in her emerald green eyes.

Just then, as that mysterious force in nature would have it, a ground squirrel leapt atop a boulder beside them, stood up on its hind legs, and scolded them for invading its territory.

"Sounds like someone is telling us to get back to work," laughed Summerfield.

Having put the napkin away, Laureal hopped like a cat from rock to rock down to the river's edge where she cleaned her teeth with a hardwood toothbrush, its one end frayed, its other end sharp like a pick.

John took the ax and headed into the aspen grove.

Laureal quickly caught up, "You should clean your teeth after you eat, John Summerfield. That way, when you grow old, you will still be fit for a picnic."

"I clean them every night," shaking his head as he laughed.

"That's not enough."

John stopped, turned to Laureal, and nodded to a good-sized tree, "What do you think, boss?"

"I think I'm not your boss, but, it looks good to me."

"Well then," said John, stepping up to the tree, "here goes nothing," and putting ax head to tree, he slowly traced the arc of a swing. Then for real, winding up hard, he took a mighty swing, an uppercut that went deep into the trunk. Then, with a powerful downward swing, he knocked out a tremendous chunk. It tumbled across the ground before them. And lifting their eyes from it, the lovers shared a look like there was nothing in the world they could not accomplish.

"This, is a fine ax!" holding it up as though showing off a prize, but no sooner had John spoken than a shadow crept into his expression. A darkness overcame him, and he lowered ax and eyes alike—

"Did your father make this tool?"

"My grandfather," softly.

"Well then," studying it so that he might avoid her gaze, "your grandfather, and your father, were skilled tool makers."

"Thank you," watching as John sank under an unseen weight. And fearing for him, Laureal added, "I know my father and grandfather are watching, and they see you helping us."

John lifted his gaze. His eyes were glassy, his lips pursed, his smile was small, uncertain, and yet, wholly sincere. "We will put their skills to good use today."

Chapter 6

The women of the clan, being without their men, had moved from their huts into the longhouse to better organize for the challenges of the coming winter. It was no small job, but they got it done in good order and eased their loneliness in the process.

First to rise that morning, Emma stood on the longhouse deck, wrapped in a robe of woodland caribou. The first hint of dawn revealed the little river below, its dull silvery sheen visible under drifting whiffs of steam. Above the river, the dark outline of the forest stood out against the awakening sky. From the silence, a warbler called out to herald the birth of a new day. A second warbler answered from beyond the northern edge of camp where, in the creeping light, a large shadow revealed itself to be a section of wall. Piles of dirt, a log pole here and there, all part of a construction site that would soon come to life.

Sipping hot tea and listening to the birds, the Matriarch filled her mind with pleasant recollections of days past. She could see John and Laureal in her mind's eye. They were guiding the giant that dragged the poles up the river trail. They were working like a couple that belonged together, clearing obstacles in natural concert so as not to get snagged. Emma had watched them from the deck, and later, from inside the longhouse, she had listened to their voices drifting in through the open window. They had agreed to dig all the post holes first while the weather held. They dug for days, John and Laureal, and Cody also, digging together, down through roots and rocks. Those days had left them covered in dirt, and the day's end had been a comedy in and of itself, brought about by strict protocol around bathing in the presence of the opposite sex. After that, the family always gathered for supper at the long table. Then with bedtime approaching and temperatures falling, they stoked the hearth, wrapped themselves in caribou robes, and worked with John, drawing maps and sharing valuable information regarding the land to the north. For fun in the flickering firelight, Laureal had shown John the traditional dance of the Kasskatchen people, a waltzing type of trot in which the dancers intermittently paused to do a form of Zumba. Emma couldn't help but smile. The thought of John and Laureal lingering in the starlight on the edge of camp, bidding one another farewell at day's end, completely out of words, all tuckered out, and yet neither wanting to part from the other's company. And so it was that the Matriarch had to ask herself, was it only wishful thinking or did the young pair, despite their tragic beginning, have the makings of a partnership strong enough to someday restore the House of Emerson to its former glory? If only Mr Summerfield would let it be.

At present, just enough daylight spilled over the trees to reveal the silhouette of a man sitting on a log bench gazing out over the water below. Curious to know what young Summerfield was about, Emma gathered her robe close around her and proceeded down the porch steps.

"Good morning, sir."

"Good morning, ma'am," standing and removing his cap.

"You are up early."

"Yes, ma'am," both haggard and urgent, like he hadn't slept a wink, "I very much need to speak with you."

"Oh really."

"Yes, ma'am," his hat still in hand, "I'm hoping we can renegotiate our contract."

"Oh, how so?"

"Ma'am, I was not honest with you in our last meeting." And with a forlorn glance over flowing water, "I was not honest with myself."

"Mr. Summerfield," breaking the silence, "are you in love with my granddaughter?"

"Yes, ma'am, I am," returning his eyes to her, he appeared all but hopeless, "I am desperately in love with her."

Emma nearly laughed, "There are worse things than being desperately in love."

"Agreed," the smile kindling on his face, a testament to the promise of youth.

"Before we begin anew," said the Matriarch, "I must confess, I failed to tell you one small thing about my grand-daughter when last we spoke. Her father and grandfather are to blame. With her being so beautiful from birth, they couldn't help but spoil her. I'm only telling you this because I want you to understand...she'll boss you if you let her."

Breaking into a grin, John nodded like one who has cast his lot.

"Your decision brings me great hope, John Summerfield. However, I do hold out some reservations, considering that, as impressed as we are, we have only known you a short time and, yourself having wandered so far from home, you are yet something of a mystery."

John narrowed his eyes even as he kept a smile, "I would not say I have 'wandered.' I am on a mission. It has taken me far afield. There's a difference."

Emma appeared contemplative. "Perhaps you are search-ing for something either way and now is the time to ask yourself...would you be happy if you found nothing more?"

Slowly, John nodded. "Yes."

Returning to the longhouse, Emma found Jessie and Laureal busy at the hearth. "Good morning."

"Good morning."

"That smells good."

"It's for John," Laureal stated.

"May I have a little?" feigning humbleness.

"Of course! I apologize, Grandma! I'm not thinking."

"Laureal and John are going to picnic in the aspen grove today," Jessie chimed, shooting a smile at her mother.

"I see," said Emma, opening a shutter on a window overlooking the river, letting fresh air mix with the air of the house. Then, turning from window to daughter, "The man we spoke of, the man we found to be a good match for Laureal...I have spoken with him again. He has asked for Laureal's hand. And myself believing you would approve, I have granted it. He and Laureal are to be wed."

Stopped dead in her tracks, Laureal gazed at them in shock and horror.

"That would be Mr. Summerfield?" Jessie asked, quick to catch her mother's ruse.

"Yes, of course," replied Emma, breaking into a smile, "Mr. Summerfield and Laureal are to be married, providing of course, Laureal accepts."

"I accept!" cried Laureal, looking like she'd been led to the edge of a cliff, given a push and lost her balance only to be drawn back a moment before falling to her death. Her mouth, still partly agape, slowly gave way to a joyous smile. Her eyes wide with questions, she glanced back and forth between her mother and grandmother, "When did you speak with John? How long have you known?"

"I just spoke with him this morning, in the yard, above the river."

Laureal strode quickly to the window.

"He's gone to the aspen grove, dear. He knew that you and your mother and I would need to talk. This is not a cut-and-dried thing."

"'Not cut and dried?'" Laureal echoed, suddenly worried, "What do you mean, Grandmother?"

"I will tell you...after you finish your business at the hearth."

Difficult as it was for Laureal to wait, they first ate breakfast and prepared a special picnic basket. Only then did the three women sit for a talk by the hearth.

"Mr. Summerfield has asked for your hand," Emma began, "and you have accepted. However, you are not to be married until he returns from his quest in the north."

"But Grandma, he doesn't need to go...not anymore. He can stay here with us," and after a moment's more thought, "John and I can cut poles for our house today!"

"Laureal," Emma knowingly began, "just as you have been raised to rebuild our family, so has John been trained to carry out a mission. We cannot take that away from him any more than we can take what belongs to you."

"But we can compromise," Laureal's mother added.

"Yes, we can," Emma agreed. "And we can support one another."

The Matriarch fell silent, her eyes turned to the fire, and seeing the change in her countenance, Laureal and her mother traded looks of concern.

"Grandmother, is something wrong?"

Emma drew a heavy breath, "Mr. Summerfield and I spoke for some time, and he conducted himself with courtesy as always. But even when he laughed, I could see he carried a burden of great weight. I knew what it was even though he did not want to tell me. I implored him to do so. He said it could destroy your love for him. He fought to hold it in but, such was his burden, he was struggling so, I could not help but beseech him, that he might get it out and be done with it. And through tears, he told me."

"Grandma...what did he tell you?" asked Laureal, her eyes welling up.

"He confirmed what we already know. He didn't know that Cody had seen and told us what happened that day between your brother Cory and John." Then with a trembling voice, "John gave his account of Cory's final moments, and his story matched what Cody has told us."

Jessie leaned forward in her seat. Her head went down into her hands and she began to weep.

"Mom," cried Laureal, leaning in, wrapping arms and pressing together, their tears falling to the wood-planked floor like the first drops of a gully washer in a rainy season.

Wiping at tears, Emma placed one hand on her daughter's shoulder, the other on her granddaughter's shoulder, and waited until the time was right to speak. And when at last it was right, she spoke soft and sincere, "Jessie, I know your heart is broken. Laureal, I know your heart is broken. We are all broken. And, if I am to be fair, I must acknowledge that John's heart is also broken. For even though he may never say so, it is because of his love for you, Laureal, that his heart breaks for what you have lost."

Taking a moment to steady herself, Emma continued, "I could never have agreed to this if John hadn't proven himself to be the young man we've been hoping for. Crazy though it may be, I know that Engel, my own dear husband who led the attack on John, would have loved him like a son."

Emma let out a belated sigh. "What gives me pause is not John's decision to defend himself but the terrible consequence of his decision that haunts my hope for your future, Laureal. You and John will face difficult trials, all couples do, and my concern is that these dreadful circumstances could worsen those trials."

In the silence that followed, it was Jessie's weeping that most stung Emma's heart. Alas, trying to speak, the Matriarch choked up, her eyes flooding with tears, "I thank God that, amid the battle, the Spirit touched John's heart, that we might keep our Cody!"

Having been drawn into the arms of her daughter and granddaughter, and also Mia who had come to huddle with them, Emma calmed and concluded with steadied voice, "Laureal, I know you have made your decision, and your family stands behind you. But we can never change the dreadful circumstances that surround John. And however fond I have become of John, however good a match I believe you and he could be outside of our reality, I cannot help but worry that these dreadful circumstances will amplify the challenges that all couples must face. Laureal, now is the time to ask yourself one last time…can you live with this?"

Laureal lifted her head from her mother's shoulder and, with reddened eyes, gave her solemn reply, "Yes, Grandmother, I can live with it." Then, speaking to them all, "Our men were protecting what we need to survive. John was protecting what he needs to survive. And that's the end of it!"

Laureal turned her eyes to the Matriarch, and for the first time, Emma saw the full woman coming through in her granddaughter.

"Let the future be what it will," Laureal continued. "I will not ruin it with misplaced blame and resentment. Nor will I live in an unending state of confusion. I love John, that is all I know!"

The silence that followed was broken only by the sounds of a new day coming to life. The crackle of the breakfast fire. The birds singing their morning songs. The water in the little river, making its way around snags. The last hoot of an owl, retiring until the dark of night once again returned.

"We should be happy," Jessie stated, rising as if to pull them out of a hole, wiping tears from her cheeks and eyes.

"Yes we should," Emma seconded, also rising.

"I must go to him," putting on her cloak, taking basket in hand.

"Daughter."

"Yes Mother," turning from the open doorway.

"You and John take the day off. We love you. We are happy for you, and we are behind you. So remember us, remember how you were raised, and honor us. Be home before bedtime. And remember, you are not yet married, and under no circumstance whatsoever are you to do as married couples do. Do you understand me, dear?"

"Yes, Mother, I understand. And thank you, thank you all! I don't know what I would do without you! I love you so much!" spoken like a young woman who knows she is cherished and cared for. And in the next instant, she was gone.

As Laureal neared the aspen grove, she heard no sounds of a man at work. No chopping, no dragging or tossing of branches onto the brush pile they had made. No sound whatsoever except for the rattle of dead leaves, still clinging in the autumn breeze, high up in the oaks.

Upon reaching the grove, she found it empty. No sign of John Summerfield. No coat hanging from a limb, no horse, no tools. A moment of panic gripped her as she glanced about, and then, at last, she spotted him. Two long stone throws ahead, John sat on a log overlooking the river, his elbows on his knees, his head turned to the ground.

"John!" Laureal called.

John sprang to his feet, his eyes fast to find Laureal coming up the path. She was walking with intent, then striding, and at last, setting her basket down, she broke into a run.

Straight into his arms she ran, straight into the open front of his wolverine long coat. Her hood fell back as she lifted her face to his, "I love you, John," tears streaming from her eyes, "that's all I know. I love you."

"And I love you, Laureal," wrapping his arms around her, bringing his lips to her ear, speaking soft but strong, "I love you with all my heart."

How long they remained in each other's arms cannot be known. Maybe five minutes, maybe a half hour. At such times, time cannot be measured. They did not get hot and heavy but simply held on to one another like they would never let go.

Chapter 7

Before John was chosen to be a "Seeker," he had been a graduate of the Order, an automatic social pass among the elite of the Golden Coast. A tall, wonderfully handsome, smartly dressed young officer, he would have made a fine catch for any blue-blooded daughter of the renaissance. He had attended the grand balls. He had walked the red carpet and danced with the beautiful young ladies, their hair in great braided crowns adorned with jewels. Their dresses richly embroidered, the soft scent of perfume all around their uncovered shoulders, their eyes painted with such skill as to be art. Their efforts had not been wasted on John Summerfield and his entourage of young officer companions. But our hero had only gotten a taste of that seemingly ample world when, much to the chagrin and disappointment of many a hopeful young lady, the Order chose him to go in search of the Data Block, their 'paradise lost.'

Laureal Emerson's world was no paradise, particularly in winter but also in summer when swarms of blood-sucking mosquitoes emerged from the bogs. Not to forget the wolf packs that roamed the forest, always eager to eat an ill-prepared human alive. Despite this, Laureal's life had been good thanks in large part to what her mother and grandmother called the "art of living." The art of living included the ability to start a fire even when snow and ice covered the ground. It included being able to build snares to catch rabbits in the dead of winter, and catching fish even when one had to chop a hole in the ice and push a net down into the river below. It included digging up caches of tasty and nutritious seeds buried by chipmunks. It was understanding how to prepare a wide variety of game meat, fowl, and fish. It was knowing how to harvest, process, and store wild wheat and rice, walnuts, hazelnuts, acorns, berries, apples and pears. It was harvesting, processing, and storing an array of spices and herbs from the forest. And there was more. With Emerson family knowledge, skill, and mastery of the forest realm, one could fill a market stall with fine fare both healthy and delicious. With their expertise, one could stock a small pharmacy with effective medicines. One could forecast the weather by looking at the sky, feeling the wind and humidity on their skin, and observing the behavior of birds and other animals. With Kasskatchen knowledge, one could build a house from the materials that surrounded them. A home to withstand wind, rain, and snow, its roof of birch bark and sod able to last a lifetime. From willow, Laureal could weave a basket so tight it would hold water. Using the skills and knowledge of her people; her mother, grandmother, and cousin crafted boots that surpassed even the best modern synthetic gear of the 21st century. From forest plants and animals, Laureal could make thread, rope, and nets. She knew how to make clay-fired pots. Her brother knew how to make wooden plates. They could produce all these items from the natural world around them. It was their survival, their art, and their entertainment. And in their art, there was more art—at times realistic, at times abstract—brought to life with natural paints and dyes in wall hangings, pottery, and basketry. Animal figurines crafted from ivory and onyx, some with jewels for eyes. And not to forget hand-tooled leather. And of course there was storytelling. Rich sagas skillfully told by animated storytellers around campfires. Kasskatchen poets captivated their audiences with tales that conveyed lessons of life with heartfelt gratitude for all of the above because, as we shall see, they looked upon all of it as gifts from the hands of their Creator.

Receiving and giving soft kisses, Laureal beamed up at John, "Mom suggested we take the day off."

"That, would be wonderful," also beaming.

Pursing her lips in a contemplative manner, Laureal shifted her eyes away before returning them to her lover, "Mom also gave a stern warning, which I believe I am to pass on to you."

"Oh, and what would that be," suddenly concerned.

"We are not yet married, and therefore, we are not to do as wedded couples do."

Although not the way of the renaissance, John nodded with a sincere countenance, "Yes, of course."

"I brought lunch," enthusiastically, "I know a special place I'd like to show you. We could take your horse. That is, if you don't mind?"

"I would like nothing more."

Laureal turned to look back down the trail, "That basket is big and clumsy, but if you would help me, we can make a little basket to fit on my back in no time, just enough to carry what we need."

John could only smile in wonderment.

"What?" asked Laureal, "Am I doing something wrong?"

"No, not at all! I mean, I should not feel unhorsed simply because you've thought ahead." And smiling, "I like your plan."

"I'm glad you like it," and giving him a happy little kiss, "I'll get my basket."

Having fetched her basket, Laureal sat down cross-legged and, as per her instructions, John cut and brought willow branches which she wove together as quickly and easily as a kid who masters shoelaces. She used her stone knife to trim the ends as she worked.

Having supplied enough branches, John sat to watch Laureal's progress and, finding the repetition of the weave somewhat hypnotic; he drifted in his mind to their first day working together in the aspen grove: *He had scarcely gotten started with the big ax when, hearing a chopping sound, he turned to see Laureal hacking a branch off the first tree he had felled. She had found his hatchet. He attempted to take it away, worried that she might injure herself. She refused to surrender it. It had been their first standoff. He with an ax, she with a hatchet. A significant size disadvantage and still she managed to disarm him by explaining how, if he took the hatchet away, he would dishonor her in her world because, although most tasks were divided between men and women, building large structures was shared work and,*

75

like all work, viewed as proof of value regardless of gender. He had reluctantly acquiesced even as he kept an eye on her, and the impression she made remained vivid in his mind. She had removed her cloak and was working away hacking branches from poles. Her breeches and blouse, tailored by her own hands, were made of thin yet sturdy doe skin, soft and well-fitted. It was her everyday garb, her only outfit outside of one doeskin dress, each a compromise between a young woman's desire to let the world know she'd arrived, her mother's discerning eye, and her grandmother's utilitarianism. Their combined efforts had produced, for lack of a better term, the classic savage look and Laureal modeled it to perfection with her long legs and natural feminine curves. Her blond hair was in a copious braid as usual. Her lips were full, her cheekbones high. Her emerald eyes, being large and well-spaced, were animated with natural happiness.

Having seen his share of beauties, John doubted that Laureal knew just how beautiful she was. In his eyes, she outshined them all. And best of all, she was his.

"All finished," said Laureal, gazing lovingly at her fiancé. What had been a willow bush along the river now lay transformed into something entirely new—a wicker papoose, just there in her lap. It would serve as a backpack for their current needs, quick-made but functional nonetheless.

While Laureal transferred their lunch, John retrieved his horse from down the way and brought it alongside a modest boulder where they could easily mount up. Ellie had done what horse people refer to as 'furring-up,' meaning her coat had filled out for winter. Her riders, already in a state of bliss, found her wonderfully soft and warm.

Riding bareback, they made a brief detour to John's camp where they picked up Ellie's buffalo cloak (that John had hung there to air out). The cloak was more than big enough for them both, and would also serve as their picnic blanket in the warm midday sun.

76

Snug atop Ellie, Laureal held onto John and gave directions on the way ahead. At the far end of the glade, they entered a northern enclave of giant maple and ash trees. No undergrowth blocked their way. No path lay there, just a thick carpet of fallen leaves formerly buried beneath snow, now melted away. The leaves, clean and pressed flat by the weight of the snow, appeared a smooth mosaic of faded red and gold akin to the floor of an ancient temple—a floor made not from a million pieces of colored glass or stone, but from the lingering magic of autumn's glory, reborn in an Indian summer. The phenomenon stretched out and away amid the roots and trunks of deciduous giants while, near and far, shafts of sunlight angled down from the canopy above as though cast by an unseen hand to complete a spell. Further heightening the enchantment, a sweet, musky aroma rose from the decaying leaves to mildly intoxicate the lovers. Forest-dwelling animals, seemingly set free from fear, came out of hiding. A pair of red squirrels scrambled out on a limb, eager perhaps to get the best seats possible, that they might see the young lovers off on their journey through life together. A pair of owls, their feathers white as snow, glided in without sound. They lit in an oak and slowly turned their heads to follow the giant's every step. Out of nowhere, a great stag appeared in their path, its rack unquestionably that of an animal king. It gave way to them, trotting aside but a stone's toss before turning to watch as they passed. The young lovers shared few words but rather, they soaked it in together. And as they did, Ellie carried them with her smooth easy gait, her head held high with ears straight up, majestic queen of horses, proud walking, sure-footed, eyes brightly lit by the animal spirit within.

Resting her head on the back of John's shoulder, Laureal wrapped her arms a little tighter around his torso and softly sighed while the rhythmic motion of the she-beast carried them deeper and deeper into the wood. For hours they traveled in a state of enchantment until at last the land dropped away into a shallow ravine. A crystal clear stream flowed there, no more than a few feet deep and nearly narrow enough to jump with a running start. Once across the stream, the riders picked up an animal trail along the base of a rock cliff approximately thirty feet in height. Through a gaping split in the cliff, they continued between worn walls of limestone up to a switchback above the cliff where a broad hillside lay covered in deciduous and coniferous trees. Further up they went until at last they emerged in a natural saddle. From there, looking back through breaks in the trees, they could see the forest they had just come through, stretching out for miles.

Proceeding through the natural saddle, husband and wife-to-be exited the wood to find themselves on high grassy slopes overlooking the old Saskatchewan River valley. Bathed in sunshine, the "Big River," as the family called it, shone like a great silver ribbon stretching to the distant north.

"There it is, my darling," pointing to a grassy flat nestled atop a prominent outcrop, a natural balcony that overlooked the river valley, "my most favorite place in all the world."

"Sweetheart," turning to smile at her with delight, "it's perfect."

Having turned Ellie loose to graze the hillside, the lovers laid their buffalo cloak out in the sun. And being made from two hides sewn together, it measured big as a king-sized bed.

"Are you hungry, darling?" Laureal asked.

"Oh yes!" and turning to her, fearing perhaps he had spoken too soon, "Are you?"

"I am," smiling.

Laureal sent John with a leather canteen to fetch water from a spring some seventy yards distant. Upon his return, John saw their lunch laid out nicely on a reed mat the size of a large platter. The main course, smoked filets of Atlantic Salmon from the little river, the legacy of a 21st century accident in which salmon genetically engineered to survive a warming climate had escaped into the local ecosystem to make spawning runs in the little river a thousand years later. To explain, genetically modified farm salmon had been legal in 21st century

Canada and had escaped before the fall of civilization at several places, including the local Diefenbaker Reservoir where fishery nets had failed, thus releasing unknown numbers of the salmon into the massive reservoir. There the species had remained nearly undetectable for decades, their only known documentation coming from fishermen. The population grew slowly but surely over time and, after the fall of civilization, when the manmade dams failed due to lack of maintenance, the salmon easily found their way to Lake Winnipeg where they multiplied. Centuries later they made fantastic spawning runs every fall up the big river and its tributaries including the little river. Of course, this is not to make a case for or against such salmon but only to explain the world that John and Laureal lived in.

Also on the lunch menu was smoked tenderloin of wild boar, another invasive species from a thousand years prior when feral pigs had nearly overrun the province of Saskatchewan. The pigs were only brought under control when, after the fall of civilization, wolves moved down from the north.

Rounding out the menu were fresh breadcakes made from climate-resistant wheat, engineered through careful cross-breeding ten centuries before. The wheat, like many other species, had survived the fall of civilization and, over the course of centuries, established itself in the wild. For dessert, a pair of pears and a handful of dried haskap berries—the berries, of all the foods in their lunch, possibly being the most native.

Blissfully ignorant of the above, our 31st century lovers settled in for lunch. It was just past noon. The midday sun felt cozy, the autumn air mild and fresh, the breeze light, and no insects to bother them.

Sampling a bread cake, John shielded his mouth in order to get his thoughts out at once, "I've never tasted cake this good!"

Laureal broke into a smile, "My mother and I made them this morning."

"They're the best!"

"They're my grandmother's special recipe."

"I must thank your grandmother, and mother, when I see them next."

"How about tomorrow evening? We've made such good progress, we could quit work early and have our first family supper together as husband and wife-to-be."

Lifting his cake as if to make a toast, "I'm in! Tomorrow evening it is!"

Beaming, Laureal harkened back in memory to a girl of fourteen, lying in her bed at night, imagining herself there in her favorite place with the man of her dreams. Things hadn't worked out the way she'd imagined. John had not come out of a dream but a nightmare, and still, there they were and she could not help but love him.

"This is so good," his expression that of savory delight.

Contemplating, Laureal watched as he finished his cake, "Darling?"

"Yes, sweetheart."

"Now that we women have moved into the longhouse, would you like to move into one of our huts? I think it would be much more comfortable for you. We could do your cooking for you. It would only be fair, what with you helping us."

Summerfield shifted his eyes away, apparently lost in uncertainty.

"It was only a thought," Laureal quickly added.

"It is a very kind thought," spoken earnestly, reaching for a piece of smoked pork. Then, lifting his eyes to her, "How about this? I will move into one of the huts providing it is okay with everyone. And I will continue to make my breakfasts. And if you would be so kind as to continue making our lunches, then all of us can sup together like we do most nights at the long table."

"I would like that so very much! And I am certain it will be okay," and pausing in thought, "Having you in our camp will be especially good for Cody now that he's accepted you."

When they had finished their meal, Laureal took her toothbrush and headed for the spring. No sooner had she started than she turned to walk backward and asked, "Are you going to clean your teeth, John Summerfield?"

"Yes," he replied, "when I retire to my camp tonight."

"Okay, have it your way," and turning to walk away, "just don't expect any more kisses today."

Summerfield shook his head in disbelief. Then, slowly rising from their blanket, he followed her to the spring. "May I use your brush?"

"I brought one for you," placing it in his hand.

To make them a nice pillow, John folded the end of the buffalo blanket atop a few flat rocks he had selected. He then lay down on the blanket with his head propped up on the makeshift pillow. Undoing her braid, Laureal shook her hair out and rested her head on his shoulder, her eyes turned up to his.

Sharing kisses, they spoke few words there on their natural balcony above a vista so vast as to reveal the very curve of the earth itself.

The mild autumn sunshine was naturally accommodating and, as natural feelings grew warm between them, their kisses grew deeper. Finally, John rolled up on his side and, with Laureal on her back directly beneath, set to kissing her neck. Her breathing grew heavy. His hand on her side, his fingers slowly inched up her torso until he felt her hand close around his wrist—

"John," said Laureal, her normally sweet voice somewhat stressed.

"I apologize," rolling onto his back with a sigh. "I don't know what came over me."

"It's okay," laying her head on his shoulder, "it came over me too. We just can't...not yet."

As they lay together, the silence played on Laureal's mind, "John, are you okay?" And receiving no reply, her chest tightened until, at last, she could scarcely breathe, "John, I would do anything to make you happy."

He turned to her with pained eyes, "You did exactly as you should…and I am happy you did."

Holding on to one another, a feeling crept over them both—a feeling that said they were going to be okay. And when John spoke, his voice carried a reflective tone, traveling back in time to a place he knew well.

"Before I became a Seeker, I was a Graduate, and before that, a Cadet. And all along the way, we boys were brought up on a Code of Conduct. It was not the way of the world around us. There was no might or might not. There was no maybe or maybe not. Rather, doing what one should not do always ended the same…with the rod. And when we reached our teenage years, that included what one should and should not do in the presence of young ladies. And now that I'm older, it seems funny but…I'm only now coming to understand why they thought it necessary to pound those rules into our heads."

"I know what you mean," lifting her head from his shoulder, her expression only a little painful. "In my world, the tool of choice was a willow switch."

John's lips turned up at the corners.

Smiling back at him with unanimity, Laureal returned her head to his shoulder and together they gazed out at the vast world before them.

Still thinking about rules, John thought of his quest and how he had broken one rule after another until alas, he'd lost control and gone into a tailspin. He accepted it. He would not give up his love for Laureal. He would rather break his oath to the Order and face death.

"John."

"Yes," realizing she'd been watching him.

"What are you thinking?"

Searching for words, "I was thinking that I love you."

"Really? You seemed so far away."

"I was thinking about my quest, and that I love you."

"I love you too," warmly. And fiddling with his collar, "John, I don't want to be selfish. I want to do all I can to help you in your quest."

"Thank you, sweetheart. That means a lot to me. But we don't have to talk about it today."

"Let me say one thing, and then I'll be quiet. Okay?"

"Okay."

"Please promise me you'll use our summer home. It's like our place here but bigger. We call it our summer home, but it's built for year-round living. You can use it going and coming. You can fall back on it in an emergency. It has a really big hearth. And I know I've already told you, but you can build a fire and get warm. And you can sleep off your exhaustion, which I fear may be terrible."

John cupped Laureal's cheek in the palm of his hand, "I promise I will."

Although by no means ungrateful, John Summerfield had no idea how fortunate he was in comparison to other Seekers regarding his odds for success, thanks to the savage girl and her family. Nor did he understand that if he succeeded in his quest, the odds were strong that the only world Laureal had ever known would come to an end. And yet, there is reason to take heart, for their world, like ours, was not without heroes and heroines.

"You made me a promise," a smile brightening her face.

"I *will* come back to you!"

"Well yes, you'd better!" And sitting up, she pushed her hair from her eyes, "But that's not the promise I'm thinking of."

"Oh?"

"Mr Summerfield, I showed you how Kasskatchen people dance. And you promised to show me how the people of the Golden Coast dance, except you are yet to keep your end of the bargain."

"I haven't had the chance," John protested.

"Well, you have now. Unless, of course, you wish to renege."

"Me...renege?" sitting up. "Not on my life." And taking her hand, he helped her to her feet.

Leading Laureal off their blanket and onto the grass, John placed her hand on his arm at the shoulder, "Hold on to me there. That's good." Next, placing his hand on the small of her back, he took her free hand in his and drew it to his chest, "We're going to wing it, but don't worry," a reassuring smile in his eyes, "I'll lead and," extending his hand and hers to promenade, "we'll do what comes naturally.

"First, let's take one step forward," leading her. "Good. Now two more. Good. Now three steps: left, right, left, and you turn like this," helping her with his hands.

Giggling, Laureal spun to face him.

"You're a natural!"

Winging it, they promenaded about in a circle atop the natural balcony. And as they went, John sang a ditty, "Ah, da-da-da. Ah, da-da-da. Oh, I once had a girl and she was good, but one of her legs was made of wood."

"That's awful!" dancing and giggling.

Smiling, he shrugged his shoulders as they promenaded, "Ah, da, da, da. A turkey in the straw. A turkey in the hay. A turkey in the straw. Hey! What did you say?"

Laughing and dancing, Laureal joined in, "Ah, da-da-da. Ah, da-da-da...!"

Sprite as a pair of kids on stick ponies, laughing, promenading and spinning they went atop the grassy balcony, a dance floor in the midst of a crystal blue sky. And below, all the world they could ever want or need stretching out to forever in a magnificent river valley.

They fell into one another's arms upon their picnic blanket, her giggling, him chuckling. Then, almost unconsciously, he gathered up a handful of her hair and, lifting it to his face, inhaled her scent. She turned and, pressing her lips to his neck, began a line of gentle kisses, slowly moving toward his ear.

John closed his eyes and let out a low masculine sigh. It was nearly more than he could bear. After a while, not very long at all, they once again had to restrain themselves. Then, as before, they lay in one another's arms, looking out over the valley below.

Ellie came lumbering and, stopping before them, lowered her massive head, sniffed their feet, then continued on to graze a short distance away.

"Was she checking on us?" asked Laureal.

"Yep," John replied.

"Probably thinks we've gone mad."

"Probably," chuckling.

"She's so majestic."

"Everybody loves Ellie."

"Especially you?"

"Well, yeah. I've gotten mighty close to that girl."

"And she loves you."

"I'm not sure that horses can love us. They're different from dogs. But I know this for certain, they know if we love them."

John turned his eyes to Laureal, "Ellie and I have been partners for so long now, I can take her ropes off and she'll follow me anywhere." And chuckling, he added, "Until she sees a patch of clover, or another horse...then she's gone."

"That's funny," giggling. And turning to watch the big draft graze, "It's surprising how smooth and easy she is to ride on."

"Everybody gets Ellie wrong."

"Oh, why do you say that?"

"Everyone assumes that because she's so big, she's also slow and cumbersome. But they're dead wrong. From a standstill, she can launch so hard and fast as to throw an unsuspecting rider off the back. And her agility can be equally surprising, if not downright astounding."

As John continued, he became more and more animated, "She loves to run, and when she does, she just flies, doesn't hold anything back. She'll make the wind whistle in your ears, and the only other sound you'll hear is the thunder of her hooves pounding the ground! And yet, up on her back, crazy as it is, with over three thousand pounds of muscle going wild beneath, everything goes smooth and…it's just pure joy! And in the dark of night with all the stars above, it's like flying through space!"

Laureal felt like she was flying—not because of a horse story but because John was so full of life—absolutely full of life. She buried her cheek in his chest and held tight, "John Summerfield, I love you so!"

"And I love you, Laureal. I love you with all my heart!"

Unable to see Laureal's face, John leaned forward a bit, "Sweetheart, are you okay?

"Yes…I'm just, really happy right now."

"Well, if you like, when I get back from my quest, I'll teach you to ride."

"Oh darling, would you please!" lifting her head.

"Yes, I will," kissing her. "I'm already looking forward to it." And thinking further, "We'll get one or two more horses. And they'll bear us wherever we go. And come winter, we'll build a sleigh, like a dog sled but pulled by horses, with rows of seats for a whole family. On sunny winter days, we'll go sleighing on the frozen river like our own personal highway in a winter wonderland!"

"Oh, John! That sounds almost too good to be true!"

"Almost, but I am certain we can make it come true."

"Yes, John, I believe we can."

Chapter 8

Perhaps Indian summers are so special because the days come like unsuspected gifts that never have to be repaid. Or so it seemed for John and Laureal. Whatever the future held, their Indian summer would be cherished forever by both. And what a long Indian summer it had been. One almost had to wonder if winter would come. But of course old man winter had not forgotten that he had a job to do. And so the day arrived when the north wind rose, the sky grew dark, the snow flew, and the river froze over. It was not all bad, though. The cold made the hearth all the warmer. And with ample firewood and food stores, there was cause for celebration. The family had accomplished the critical work necessary to see them through. They would be safe in their longhouse even as blizzards howled at their door. And so it was that they gave thanks to their God, whom they called 'the Great Spirit.'

John celebrated with them even though he believed, as a renaissance man, that every tribe had its own God, and, once the Data Block was found, primitive people everywhere would trade their superstition for enlightenment. On the other hand, the forest-dwellers believed John to be on a vision quest that would lead him to the Great Spirit. Fortunate for them all and despite their differing beliefs, their juxtaposition had come together like a well-made dovetail joint due to the family's overriding need for survival and the Seekers' overriding need for the knowledge the family possessed. Like a dovetail joint glued with love, they had repaired a tragedy even if somewhat inadvertently. And as Emma would say, that was how the Great Spirit worked. Still, culture clash was not a thing to sneeze at. There would be ramifications. But let us continue with our story, for as we shall see, the following days would bring about one major turn of events after another.

The arrival of snow naturally energized our hero and heroine's dream of riding in a horse-drawn sleigh, especially when their very own personal highway in a winter wonderland waited just outside! They already had a horse. All they needed was a sleigh. And so it was with precious few days remaining before John's planned departure, they set out to chase their dream and all the wonderful fun they could have, even if only for a day or two.

Aided by the seemingly inexhaustible energy of youth, our groom and bride-to-be walked frozen river with horse and packsaddle in tow for a distance of three miles before arriving at their destination: a fallen ash tree, the source of materials from which they hoped to build a sleigh and bring their dream to life.

Upon arrival, they began by setting up a work camp. And this is a good place to note that John no longer wore his wolverine long coat. Instead, he wore a suit of caribou pants, coat, hood, boots, and mitts—a wardrobe handed down through tragedy. Laureal had talked him into it, that he might have the best protection from the elements on his journey north. And in fact, clothing made from caribou offered more protection than all other materials including high-tech synthetics of the 21st century. As a result, husband and wife-to-be appeared a matched set.

Sheltered in their camp by surrounding woods, the pair went to work on the fallen ash tree. Dead but well-preserved, the tree lay suspended at an incline like that of a wheelchair ramp. Working up and down its trunk, John used hatchet and knife to strip desired branches of small limbs and bark. Laureal followed with John's bucksaw, which worked well for square-cutting branches of a diameter right for their needs. Once the branches were removed from the tree, Laureal topped them and John stripped any remaining bark. Working together, they had six poles readied by midmorning.

To permanently bend the poles, the couple built a hot water trough by first placing two logs of modest diameter parallel on the ground. They also used rocks selected from a rocky area along the river, several stone throws from camp. To haul the rocks, they placed them in a leather hide made from a large grizzly bear and then carried it like a hammock back to camp. They made several trips, as they needed rocks both for completing the trough and also for heating the water. It was not easy work, but easier than digging a trench in frozen ground. The completed trough measured about five feet in length.

After building the trough, they lined it with the bear hide, which was thick, strong, and heavily oiled. By midday, being further along than they'd planned, they decided to race the daylight and see if they could get the poles bent before dark. To fill the trough, they chopped ice and drew water from the river. They then heated the water with rocks from the fire. As rocks cooled in the water, they returned them to the fire to reheat before returning them to the water. Laureal exchanged and managed rocks constantly. John cut firewood constantly and added it to the fire, for they would need a great many hot coals to complete the final leg of their bending and shaping project, as we shall now see.

Breathing clouds of steam, John brought an armload of firewood with a smile. And dumping it beside the fire, he turned back to the surrounding woods.

"Stay and warm yourself, darling," worrying because he had removed his coat.

Obeying, John removed his mitts and held his hands towards the flames, "How's our sleigh runners coming along?"

"There's so much steam, I can't see them, but at least the water is good and hot." As she spoke, Laureal used John's small camp shovel to scoop a blistering hot rock the size of a softball from the fire. Then, lowering the shovel into the trough, she let the rock into the water even as she kept the shovel between it and the leather liner. The rock hissed loudly, sending up a plume of steam.

Six ash poles, each about 2 ½ inches in diameter and ten feet long lie with half their length submerged in the steaming trough. Neither John nor Laureal had experience shaping wood poles, although Laureal had seen the men of her clan employ the process while making frames for snowshoes.

Putting his mitts back on, John grasped one of the poles by its dry end and withdrew it from the water. He then put his weight on it. "Well, would you look at that!" surprised that it bent with ease.

"That didn't take long!"

Looking up from the pole, "Are you ready, sweetheart?"

"Yes."

"Let's hope for beginner's luck," carrying the pole to the fallen ash tree.

"There's no such thing as luck," following along with a roll of twine.

"Well then, we'll just hope for the best," kneeling to position himself, that he might bend the pole around the tree trunk.

"You're a good man for putting up with us, John," referring to the difference in their beliefs and how winter had cloistered them together in the longhouse.

"I don't know about that. Maybe it's the other way around."

"No, it's not the other way around. After yesterday, there can be no doubt. I know it wasn't easy for you, what with my family getting in the spirit, and you never having seen anything like that before."

"Thank you for being my protector," and jokingly he added, "in the spirit realm."

"The Great Spirit is our protector in all realms," with a corrective air, sorting out the twine. "I'd like to think he used me yesterday, not as a protector but as a buffer, but I don't mean to go there. Not today. You deserve a break."

"I'd love a break," stopping what he was doing to look up at her, "but first I want to know why your 'Great Spirit' would use you to buffer me from himself?"

"Did I say that?"

"I don't know. Is there a difference between buffering me from your family and buffering me from him?"

Shifting her eyes away, Laureal pursed her lips in thought. Then returning her eyes to John, "Perhaps I did not make myself clear. I meant to say He used me to facilitate things so you would not be overwhelmed, like a parent guides a child when they are learning to walk, so they don't stumble and fall. You know, like the way he brought us to where we are today, together beside this tree, building our sleigh."

For all of his lover's great beauty and natural persuasion; her reference to him as a child being guided by her, and her acting on behalf of a superior being, but alas, for John it was a bridge too far—

"Tell me," his tone more irritated than amused, "exactly how did he bring us here, together, by this tree?"

Having quarreled with John before, rarely, but a time or two, Laureal lost her smile, "Darling, maybe we should take that break I spoke of."

"No," John said adamantly, "I want to know."

"Are you sure?"

"Yes. You have me curious," flexing the pole against the tree trunk, bending it to see if it would hold together or crack.

Holding half of the how and why in her heart and mind already and then seeing the rest fall into place as if meant to be, Laureal put aside her reservations because, deep down, she very much wanted to share it with John—

"Well...darling, it's like, on that wonderful day when we went on our picnic above the big river, and the Great Spirit was watching over us. He saw our love was true, and he was pleased because he had made us to be together. He did not make us to come together the way we did...that was our doing, but our doings do not change his intent. So, when he heard us dreaming about having a horse-drawn sleigh and taking our future family for rides, he was of a mind to help. And so he led you to this tree, and he spoke to your heart. I don't know what he said exactly, but something like, 'I heard your dream. Here is one of my trees. I'm giving it to you to build your dream.'"

Laureal then concluded, "That's how I know this is going to work, because he brought us here. This is part of his plan for us. He wants us to have a happy life together."

Still kneeling at his work with pole in hand, John turned his head down to the fallen tree trunk like a knight of old who prays with his lance at an altar. But he was not praying. As he saw it, the divine plan of which his wife spoke excluded the mission he'd trained his entire life for. The very meaning of his life had fallen into a stream of spiritualism where his actions came back like reflections, weighed, measured, and defined in an alternate dimension overseen by a clan of zealots deep in the sticks with whom he had somehow become bonded beyond any hope of escape honorable or otherwise because, reason as he may, he was too much in love with Laureal to ever leave her.

"John?" Laureal asked. And fearing he might be weeping, she drew close to his side, "Darling, are you all right?"

As an alternative to weeping, John laughed quietly, "This is just crazy."

"John?" in an injured tone.

Leaving the pole to lean against the fallen tree, John stood up with a pained look. He tried to take Laureal's shoulders in his hands but she stepped back and away. Still, he stepped towards her, and she backed further away. Then, with a burst of speed, he caught her even as she spun quick as a cat to get away, "You are the prettiest little poison I've ever known!"

"John! What a terrible thing to say!"

"Okay, you're the prettiest thing I've ever known, and the rest is what it is."

"I am who I am!" trying to break free.

"Oh! I know that!" getting her fully wrapped up in his arms, "I don't know where you come up with half this stuff, but you live and breathe it." And holding her as she struggled, "Until yesterday I was slow to see where all of this 'Great Spirit' stuff was going, but now, well, it appears I'm either going to get used to it or go insane."

"It's not insane!" Laureal chided, struggling, feeling hurt and more than a little annoyed about being held against her will.

"If you really want me to, I'll let you go."

"Yes, please! Let - me - go!"

Set free, Laureal spun round, took a quick step back, and pointed her finger at John, "You said it yourself! You said you saw this tree and you instantly knew it was our sleigh!" And taking a breath, composing herself, she continued, "John, the Great Spirit obviously led you here and spoke to your heart."

"I didn't hear anything."

"John, you asked me how he brought us here. And I gave you my answer. I told you how I see it. It's how I was brought up to see it. It's who I am!"

"I understand that! I'm not saying you're bad, or even wrong."

"Really?" suspicious, but also hopeful.

"Yes, really…I mean, it's not easy putting my mission off. I get frustrated, but that doesn't mean I don't like what you said about how we got here. I do like what you said. At least, I mean, it's wonderful, and sweet, but Laureal, I need a break. I feel like I'm being pulled into an alternate universe, and it's looking like the end of my world. We need to make an arrangement. You lighten up, and I won't laugh, or cry, or go out of my mind."

"John——," pleadingly. "I wasn't pushing! You asked, and I answered! And I know yesterday wasn't easy for you, but…I did all I could."

"I know you did," and taking a more conciliatory tone, "Sweetheart, I appreciated that, I really do. But yesterday your family seemed to have gone crazy, especially your mom. I mean, don't get me wrong, there's been good reason for celebration, and I know she was only being kind…but still!"

"John," stepping to him and taking his hand, "Mom wouldn't have bothered if she didn't love you and want you to feel a part of our family." Caressing his hand, Laureal gazed up with soft eyes beseeching, "Please John, let's not fight."

Glancing away to avoid her eyes, John thought of how Jessie seemed a window-in-time through which he could see Laureal twenty years into their future. He could not imagine her or any of them fitting into the renaissance world he had known, except perhaps as quaint novelties to be shown off in the parlors of the rich and powerful. Perhaps in the beginning he had been drawn to them by his great desire for information, second only to the guilt he felt on hearing their cries coming through the woods the day of the disaster. And maybe on their part, their acceptance of him had started as a matter of basic survival. But regardless of what seeded their relationship, it had sprouted into something only a fool would throw away. His eyes came back to Laureal, "You are not poison. You're the best thing that ever happened to me."

"And you're the best thing that ever happened to me," and seeing his surprise that she would say such a thing, "Yes John, it's true because, if we are to be together, I cannot feel any other way."

Holding John's gaze, Laureal continued, "John, it's like grandmother says...if I believe the Great Spirit made us to come together as one, then you must be the best one for me. But please, darling, don't ever grab me like that again."

"I won't...I promise," visibly moved.

Laureal placed her hand on John's heart, "I apologize for being a pushy girl and for not acknowledging what's important to you. I didn't mean to be arrogant, but if I was, I apologize."

"Apology accepted. And...I didn't mean to make fun of your 'spirit realm,' but if I did, I apologize."

"Apology accepted."

Still holding hands, Laureal leaned into John, "What you said about sweet poison," flashing a sheepish little grin, "Grandma says we have to take the bad to get the good."

John chuckled.

"Are we okay?"

"Yes," kissing her on the lips.

"Good," kissing him back.

The lovers shared kisses, kisses that brought reassurance, kisses that brought smiles of happiness and joy until at last, John stopped kissing and said, "We're burning daylight."

Opening her mouth to speak, Laureal abruptly paused, then said, "I guess we'd better get back to it." She had initially intended to say, *"That pair of hands that is ever working in the dark tried to get us, but fortunately for us, the Great Spirit..."*

Returning to the business at hand, John took the pole that had cooled and exchanged it for a hot one. Laureal shoveled a few cooled rocks from trough to fire, and a few hot rocks from fire to trough. Then with twine in hand, she stepped to the ash's trunk to assist her partner.

With a steaming pole in hand, John knelt at a point where the fallen tree trunk lay approximately eighteen inches above the ground. Laureal gave John the twine, then stepped over the trunk and turned so that she faced him with the tree trunk between them. John then tied the cord to a small notch at the hot end of the pole. Next he passed the cool dry end of the pole under the tree trunk to Laureal so that it lay on the ground on her side of the trunk. John then pulled his end of the pole straight up with his hands, using his strength to bend the pliable wood, whereupon he pinned it against the tree trunk with his body. Laureal then squatted and, grasping the dry end of the pole with both hands, used her leg strength to pull it up off the ground and into John's reach. John then reached over the trunk and grasped the dry end of the pole with both hands while simultaneously using his hip and stomach to keep the opposite end of the pole pinned to the tree trunk. He then used his considerable upper body strength to pull the dry end of the pole towards him, all the while anchoring his body against the trunk. Once he had bent the pole halfway around the tree trunk, Laureal took the twine and looped it around the pole on her side, then stepped over to John's side, put her foot against the tree trunk and pulled the twine tight while looping it around the notch on John's side. She then took the string back to the opposite side and tied it to the dry end of the pole. She smiled as she put her mitts back on. The once straight pole, now wrapped around the trunk, had the shape of a candy cane standing straight up, somewhat like the letter **J**.

On his hands and knees, John craned to see under the trunk of the fallen ash tree. By such means, he inspected the wet section of the pole, which was now wrapped around the bottom of the tree trunk and still yet steaming in the cold air.

On the other side of the trunk, Laureal also looked to see how the pole had fared.

"Looks good so far!" looking under the trunk at his lover, her face framed in fur.

In short order, John and Laureal secured all six poles side by side around the fallen tree trunk. Small notches cut in either side of the trunk restrained the poles from slipping and angling sideways.

John next used a large wooden shovel with a broad flat blade to scoop and dump copious amounts of coals under the trunk. He did this not to catch the trunk on fire or burn the poles but rather to radiate heat up and around the trunk and slowly dry the bent poles. He and Laureal then draped the tree trunk with fir boughs which trapped the heat while allowing the fire coals to breathe. John then went to gather more firewood.

While John gathered firewood, Laureal built a small fire ring of rocks and used a shovel full of coals to begin a cookfire. She then used John's steel grill and other cooking gear to prepare their supper, the main entree, ribeye of elk. Before she put the steaks on, she melted snow in a pair of pots on the grill, one pot for a hot vegetable stew made from tubers and herbs, the other pot for hot wintergreen tea to be enjoyed after their meal along with bread cakes, lightly toasted over the coals.

96

John returned and put another load of wood on the fire so that it would burn down into another batch of coals that could be shoveled under the tree trunk just before they departed for the night.

"Mr Summerfield," said Laureal.

"At your service, Miss Emerson," turning to her.

"Would you please split two large shingles, for dinner plates?"

"You got it."

With daylight waning and fire blazing, the groom and bride-to-be supped side-by-side on a log, speaking few words, for both were exhausted but also thoroughly relaxed and pleased with the excellent progress they'd made. Finishing their supper, they cleaned their pots, piled all remaining coals under the bent poles, and, with plans to return in the morning, trekked home on the frozen river.

Back at the compound, John took care of Ellie while Laureal kindled a fire in his hut. The two lovers then met in the courtyard formed by the walls they had built, presently under a fantastic star dome.

"Darling, would you like to come in the longhouse until your hut warms up?" her lovely face turned up to his, her soft eyes shining in starlight.

"They're asleep," he whispered.

"Wait here and I'll check."

"Laureal, wait," he called lowly after her.

Pausing at the door, Laureal glanced back with a smile, "I'll be right back."

John did not have long to wait. The big door creaked open just enough for Laureal to slip out. Down the steps and directly to him she came, "Mom said it would be okay for you to come in and get warmed up, but they're all in bed now so we have to be quiet."

"Laureal…I feel strange about this."

"It's not strange, it's my home. And it's your home too. And besides, I told Mom that we'd been in the cold all day and we were tired, and I was worried for you because your hut is ice cold, and we had only just gotten the fire going in there and it needed time to warm up."

"Your mom put a stack of caribou blankets in my hut…she knows I won't suffer."

"Well, if you don't want to come in, okay, but now she's going to think something's gone wrong."

"I didn't say I don't want to come in."

"Do you want to come in, or not?"

"I want to come in. It just feels, well…weird."

"Darling, it's alright. There's a perfectly good reason for it." And tugging on him, "Come on, everything will be fine."

Try as they may, it was impossible to open the big door without it creaking. Fortunately, the noise was masked by the crackling fire, which, having been stoked just before bedtime, threw dancing shadows all about.

Laureal left John standing sheepishly by the hearth, only to return directly with an armload of caribou blankets. Then, with coats and outer layers removed, they made a bed of blankets before the hearth and were soon snug as a pair of bugs in a rug.

"Sweetheart?"

"Yes, darling?"

"Are you warm enough?" he whispered low and soft.

"I'm good," snug against him, spooned up in his excellent form.

"What about you?" turning her head back to his, sensing the closeness of his lips in the pitch of their tiny cocoon. "Are you warm enough, darling?"

"Yes, I'm good," and moving his lips but an inch, he found hers and they joined in a gentle kiss, "If you get cold, just say so."

"As long as you're here with me, I'll be fine," caressing his cheek, pushing her fingers into his thick mane.

Knowing how she held her head turned back and up to him, John put his hand behind her, that she might have his palm as a pillow to rest her head. And as she relaxed into it, they shared a few more kisses.

"I'm excited about our sleigh," said Laureal, rallying, albeit only a step ahead of sleep.

"So am I," tenderly kissing her brows, "It's going to be so much fun."

Half asleep, half kissing him back, "I can hardly wait," her voice fading as though traveling away, her eyelids closing for the night. Then, as she opened sleep's door in his arms and the tangible world melted away, her body twitched and then relaxed, whereupon a faraway whisper escaped her lips, softly beckoning, "John, I will love you forever."

"I love you too," he whispered, unaware that she'd spoken from a dream. And within the minute he joined her in deep restful sleep.

Chapter 9

The clouds moved in overnight, causing the morning sky to loom low, dreary, and gray. From the longhouse chimney, a trail of smoke carried the scent of the hearth into the snow-covered forest, a silent reminder of home in the nostrils of our hero and heroine. Up the river they went with Ellie in tow, their stomachs full, their bodies rested, a pair of youths chasing a dream.

"If we were married," Laureal began, putting her arm in John's, "we could camp and stay the night."

"This time of year? I would think you'd prefer the comfort of a hut."

"I would, but we have to get married first," smiling.

Up ahead, where the river disappeared around a bend, a tall cutbank of dark earth and roots stood under a crown of snow cornices. Directly above the cornices, a grove of maple with bare limbs juxtaposed against a low blanket of clouds created a black-and-white simplicity relaxing to the eye.

"John, I would be happy even if all we had to begin with was a tent."

"Oh yeah? I wonder how long that would last?"

"Hey you," stopping and turning to him. "I've spent as much time in a tent as you have."

"I doubt that."

Laureal placed her hands on her hips, "When the men of our clan go hunting in the north, we women go with them. It's a special time of year, and I always look forward to it."

Having learned which skills belonged to men and which to women in Laureal's world, John knew that building wickiups was women's work. Laureal, therefore, had a point. While the men hunted, the women built the hunting camps.

"I guess it makes sense that you would team up for extended hunts," he acquiesced. "Still, you're talking about summer. It's winter now."

"I know that!"

"I know you know. I'm just saying, it's a different story when it's winter, and your spit freezes before it hits the ground."

Laureal appeared surprised, "Have you been on the trail when it's that cold?"

"Close enough to know it was damn cold!"

"John! Don't curse!"

"Sorry. I apologize...again."

"Apology accepted," and smiling up at him suggestively, "You didn't have a partner in your tent to help you stay warm."

"Well, to be perfectly honest, I did."

Laureal stepped back, "I did not need to hear that!"

"It was only a small dog...not very helpful."

"John!"

(Laughing.)

"That wasn't funny!" and turning away, she proceeded as if to leave him behind, even as she went towards their camp.

"Oh, come on," walking after her.

They walked on in silence.

"Miss Emerson."

"What?"

"May I please have your arm back?"

"You may not," feigning indifference.

They continued walking.

"Here's an idea," said John. "When we get married, the aspen grove sits in a natural windbreak from the north. We can try our luck there some winter night, and if it gets too cold, we'd only be a mile from home."

"It's an idea," as though she could take it or leave it.

"When we get married," he reiterated, carefully getting her arm in his.

Walking in a winter wonderland, being good medicine, helped our lovers get back on track. And that was good, for upon arriving at their work camp, they were all the more happy to find that none of the ash poles had cracked during the drying process. Wisely perhaps, John refrained from calling it

101

beginner's luck, and Laureal refrained from claiming it part of a divine plan.

They chose the best two poles to serve as the sleigh's runners. The four remaining ash poles, two on either side of the sleigh, would be turned with candy-cane ends facing down to fasten atop the ski runners. This would make an oval track shape when viewed from either side (like tracks on a bulldozer). The straight sections of the four curved poles would form the right and left rails of the sleigh's floorboard. John planned to use a pair of straight poles to serve as shafts to attach horse and sleigh, including an evener. More straight poles would be cut for cross members. They only needed to build a functioning frame, the bare basics for having fun. Later, on John's return, they could add a wicker seat, birch bark splashboard, side aprons, and rear panel. That was their plan at least. Presently, they shaved the candy cane poles at their mating surfaces, drilled them, and secured them with tapered dowel pins coated in hot pine glue, a method of bonding superior in strength to 21st century screws.

Next they cut the crossmembers which they planned to notch, drill, pin, and hot glue. They made the notches using bucksaw and hatchet. The hatchet served as a wood chisel. A piece of ash firewood was used as a hammer with which to strike the chisel. In their excitement, they made great progress so that by nightfall they had both sides assembled with cross members made and ready to install. Almost a bare-bones sleigh, save for a pair of shafts and an evener.

Leaving their camp intact, the lovers headed for home atop Ellie. Before them, the river gently curved through the forest, a silvery ribbon of snow glistening below a blanket of stars. And because the clouds had moved out, the night promised to be cold.

Ellie was sure-footed as always. Her huge cleated shoes provided her excellent traction on the ice while not gripping so much as to injure her. Her cleats were not spikes, but rather, each shoe had very small squared-edged chunks of steel forge-brazed with bronze to its bottom. It was very effective, "Crush, crush, crush."

Tired but satisfied, the lovers planned to take a day off from the bitter cold. By their calculations, they hoped to have a usable sleigh in one more workday, and both were anticipating great fun. But then again, things do not always go as planned.

That same evening, it was nearly bedtime when Laureal came breathing heavily through the longhouse door, shed her coat, boots and over pants, then crossed the floor, climbed the ladder to the loft, and fell into her bed where she lay weeping.

Below, Emma looked to Jessie, "She's your daughter."

Jessie went to the bottom of the ladder, "Sweetheart, what's wrong?"

"Mom," came a pathetic whimper.

Climbing the ladder, Jessie came to her daughter's bedside, "Did you and John have an argument?"

"Yes."

"Would you like to talk about it?" taking a seat on the edge of the bed, her face softly illuminated by a single oil lamp.

Nodding, Laureal whipped at tears, "All I did was suggest that because we women plan to go to our summer home in spring, I thought John and I should get married now. That way, come spring, we could all go north together."

"And what did John say?"

"He said he cannot marry until he completes his mission. He said we should wait here until his return. He thinks it's unsafe for us to travel alone. I didn't want to push him, so I tried to explain how it would be better for us all if we went north together. We could help one another. It would be safer for us all. Then he'd have a base much further north than we are now. It would increase his odds for success, even if it meant putting his mission off until next winter. When I said that, he got testy, and that made Ellie antsy. We dismounted and argued on the ice. He lost his temper and began to shout. Ellie spooked, and John spun to catch her, but she got away and disappeared into the forest. John chased her, and I was so upset, I climbed up the opposite bank and ran for home."

"Where is he now?"

"I guess he went to find Ellie. He shouted for me to come back, but home was just around the bend, and I kept running."

"Sweetheart, I think it would be best if you went out there and helped him."

"Mom," beginning to cry all over again, "before I ran away, John shouted that he'd have been better off if we'd hung him up by his feet," the implication being that John would have been better off if the men had captured him, dragged him back to camp, and tortured him to death.

"He said that?"

"Yes," squeaking.

"Well, I'm sure he didn't mean it." And with a sigh, "Sometimes, when lovers get angry, they say stupid things."

"I never heard Dad shout at you like that."

"Oh, your father and I had our shouting matches. We just managed to do our yelling out of earshot, thanks to the wisdom of your grandparents."

"I never knew that."

"Someday,' half-smiling, "you and John will leave your kids with me so you can go off in the woods and shout at one another."

"Mom, that's awful."

"You and John will have more good times than bad, but there will be bad, and sweetheart, you know you have to take the bad to get the good."

"I know that," and, musing in thought, "I can take the bad...so long as it's not too bad."

"John shouldn't have shouted at you, but these things happen. He'll probably apologize before this night is over. And sweetheart, you have a part to play. There's a reason he shouted. He's frustrated. He has put his mission off repeatedly. You don't want him to go, I understand that, but crazy as it

104

may seem, you may be making him feel like he has no value. Perhaps you could improve the situation by making him something that will be useful in his mission."

"I want to support him, Mom. I helped him with his maps before we got engaged, or at least I helped as best I could," knowing her grandmother had done most of the mapping work with John. And thinking further, "We gave him Dad's furs. Other than that, I don't know what I could make him. You've seen his stuff, he has everything." And with a sigh, "I know, I'm making excuses. I'll think of something. But Mom, right now I just honestly believe it would be better for us all if we went north together. And if we're going to do that, then John would be putting his mission off until next winter, so, we may as well get married now."

"Well, I think you're right."

"Really?"

"Yes, but after you suggest it, give him time to mull it over."

Holding hands, mother and child shared a moment of silence while their minds wandered through past, present, and future. Then, from recollection, a smile crept upon Jessie's lips, "Has Grandma ever told you the story of Brant and Freya?"

"No, not that I recall."

"Brant was hung by his feet after the men of our clan captured him trespassing in our territory. But as things turned out, according to the story anyway, Brant and your great-great-great aunt Freya had a long and happy life together."

"Really? He wasn't killed?"

"No, the clan adopted him. It rarely happens, but it did with Brant. Ask Grandma, she knows the whole story."

"They cut him down on my great-grandmother's orders," said Emma, who having quietly come up the ladder, leaned comfortably against the wide rail of the loft, observing the exchange between her girls.

"I was only a small girl. My memory of it is vague," coming to sit on the edge of the bed, "but I know this: our men captured Brant and brought him to camp where they hung him up by his feet. My great-grandmother was Matriarch, and when she saw how handsome and well-made Brant was, and, more importantly, how he never let out a peep, never showed any pain or discomfort during all the poking and taunting but would throw a wicked punch at anyone that got near...she was so impressed, she ordered him to be cut down and tied to a post."

"What happened then, Grandma?" sitting up with interest.

"My great-grandmother assigned your great-great-great aunt Freya to take care of Brant. Freya was a comely and well-mannered young lady near your age. She fed Brant, kept him company, and showed him kindness. Of course, being high-spirited, Brant tried to chew through his sinew tether, but the men would only add more. Eventually, Brant had to make a choice. He could either chew sinew all day or relax, be civil, and speak with dear Freya. They spoke for days. They got to know one another. In fact, the last few days, Freya slept out there. Not within Brant's reach, of course, as that would have been terribly inappropriate. Anyway, when the men cut Brant free, he ran off. But he came back several days later, hungry, cold, and longing for his Freya. He and Freya were married, and they lived happily ever after."

"If only we could have adopted John like that," Laureal sighed wistfully. "Dad and Cory, Grandpa, and cousin Norm would all be here with us. We'd be one big happy family."

"Indeed," Emma agreed, "I am certain John would have been spared if our men could have taken him alive. He would have fallen in love with you. Of that I can have no doubt. But, things didn't work out that way."

Jessie stroked her daughter's hair, "We live in an imperfect world."

"Far from perfect," Emma seconded, 'but when one door closes, our Creator always opens another."

"Yes, and sweetheart, hard as it may be to understand, any door the Creator opens will always lead to something better than can be imagined. And whomever he opens it for will walk through, unless talked out of it by the voice that speaks from the dark."

"That doesn't mean what we had was bad," Emma clarified. "We cannot know why the Great Spirit allowed disaster to befall us. Except that he gives us free will, and, well, here we are. We can still be grateful for what we had, and for what we still have. We have their memory and legacy. We have one another. We have our home. And what your mother says is true. The door that stands open leads to a life that is bigger and better than we can imagine. And even though we cannot see through to what lies beyond, here we are, poised on its threshold."

Laureal started out of bed, "I need to go and help John."

"No, dear," Emma ordered softly. "We can't have you wandering the woods at night, especially in this bitter cold. John will find Ellie. He'll have light to see his way, what with the snow reflecting the starlight."

"What should I do?"

"Go to his cabin, build a fire, then come back here and wait for him," said Jessie. "He'll find Ellie and come home to you, I'm sure."

"I hope so!"

"He'll come home."

"Is everything okay?" asked Mia, coming up the ladder, having just put the twins to bed.

"Yes, dear," replied Emma, "just a lover's spat."

"Been there, done that," said Mia, cautiously smiling.

"John's coming," said Cody from below, sitting by the hearth, listening to the women while carving a fish hook from the wishbone of a grouse.

Everyone listened, and in the silence, the sound of Ellie's hooves came through the night, "Crush, crush, crush..." drawing nearer until, entering the courtyard, they could hear John's footsteps as well. Next came the sound of his cabin door being opened and, after a moment, closing. Then, only silence.

"I need to go to him," said Laureal, getting up and heading for the ladder, but no more had she got to the edge of the loft than the door opened and John stepped into the longhouse.

"Hello, Cody."

"Hi, John."

"Is Laureal here?"

Cody nodded to the loft. And John, looking up, saw Laureal, her face illuminated by firelight, stricken with a mixture of hope and anxiety.

"Laureal, I apologize for shouting. Can you forgive me?"

"Yes, John, I can," her countenance changed to one of great hope. Yet, with lingering anxiety, she asked, "Can you forgive me? I'm so afraid I will push you away."

"You're not going to push me away," he replied as if the very thought were ridiculous. Then, pushing his hood back, "I've been thinking about what you said, and I think you might be right. I might lose a season, but if I were to spend the hunting season among your kinfolk in an advanced base of operation…well, it stands to reason that I would have an opportunity to gather information that might prove invaluable. Plus I would have a base of operation closer to my objective. Such things could make the difference between success and failure."

Laureal could hardly believe her ears, "John…do you really feel that way?"

"Yes, I do."

"Oh, thank God! Now we can be together so much longer! And John, your mission is important to me, and I promise to help you in any way I can!"

"Thank you, sweetheart. It means a lot to hear you say that."

Jessie appeared beside Laureal at the rail, "John, this is wonderful news! We will feel so much safer with you along!"

"I'm glad to know you feel that way, Jessie. I thought about that very thing while out in the woods." Then, lifting his hand to signal for quiet even as he smiled, "I'll be right back. I've got to get Ellie taken care of. Oh, and I'm going to light a fire in my cabin so it can be warming up in there," and turning for the door, "I'll be back."

"I'll take care of the fire, darling," said Laureal, hurrying down the ladder. "You see to Ellie. And we'll meet back here."

"Sounds like a plan," and through the door he went with Laureal close behind, herself carrying a clay vessel in which she had stowed a few fire coals.

At the bottom of the longhouse steps, Laureal came alongside John, "Mr Summerfield, I love you so much!"

"I'm glad you do," smiling.

Laureal held the smoldering vessel clear as she leaned in to kiss him. They were always kissing, occasionally fighting, but then, they were young and in love.

"Laureal."

"Yes, John."

"There's something I need to tell you."

"What?" at once curious, and a little worried.

"It's nothing to worry about. It's just that, before I got here, when I had gone to track Ellie down, I saw something. Something happened in the forest."

"What did you see? Tell me!"

"I'll tell you after I take care of Ellie. But you have to promise not to tell," and with a kiss he pulled away and went to take care of his horse.

Laureal entered John's cabin where she lit the hearth, lit an oil lamp, and arranged the caribou blankets on his bed. She then sat beside the fire, waiting and thinking until he came through the door.

"John, darling," standing to meet him, "I want you to know that whatever comes, I am already so very happy, I can scarcely believe that you will be coming north with us."

"It's the right thing to do."

109

"Is it what *you* want to do, John?"

"Yes," affirmatively.

"Then it is a prayer answered," her emerald eyes shining in firelight.

Seated together by the fire, Laureal lay her head on John's chest. The fur of his caribou coat, so cool, and yet silky soft to the touch. She could feel the fire warming them. The pleasant crackling of fire logs. The aroma of the hearth, mixed with the fragrance of the spruce boughs. She closed her eyes, the warm traces of firelight dancing on her eyelids.

Nearly falling asleep, Laureal lifted her head to see John's eyes were closed, his jaw slacked—the upturned corners of his lips spoke to contentment.

"John?" she whispered.

He smiled fondly.

"Darling, does your decision to come with us have something to do with what you saw in the forest tonight?"

"I'm not sure," turning his face to hers, "but it certainly got me thinking."

"Well...are you going to tell me about it?"

"Yes, I just feel...well, I mean, here I've asked you to let up on the spiritual stuff, and you agreed. And now here I am about to put fuel on the fire."

Laureal let out a sweet little laugh, "There's no need to feel that way. Just forget about all of that and tell me what happened."

"Well," pulling himself up a bit, "when I saw you run around the bend, I knew you were only a few steps from being safe at home, so I went to find Ellie."

"I shouldn't have run away," frowning. "John, I'm so sorry."

"I don't blame you. I would have run away too."

"No, you wouldn't have, but thank you for trying to make me feel better about it."

"I shouldn't have yelled at you."

"True, but it all worked out, and here we are," nestling to make herself comfortable, smiling in anticipation.

Drawing silent, John looked back a mere stone's toss in time. His eyes filled with recollection. His broad chest rose up and fell like the changing of a tide—

"Ellie didn't go far into the woods. I tracked her through the snow. When first I saw her standing amid the trees, I felt relieved and, I stopped and looked up. I don't know why I looked up, I just did. I happened to be in a birch grove. All the limbs were bare, of course. Anyway, I was struck because the stars backlit the lattice to such a degree that, what would otherwise have gone unnoticed appeared boldly pronounced, and...well, I'm certain that what came next was only an illusion. I had become mesmerized. My eyes played tricks on me. The stars no longer appeared up in the sky, but were as leaves in the trees. I was caught up in it, and I got this sixth sense kinda feeling, like something more was there. My eyes couldn't see it, and yet, it was as crisp as the air.

"Ellie nickered and I snapped out of it. She was watching me. She wasn't going anywhere. I looked back up to see the stars had returned to the sky, but whatever it was that I'd sensed remained. I can't explain it, but I'm sure there's an explanation. Some phenomena yet to be discovered. Anyway, I started home with Ellie and my thoughts turned to what you said. I was trying to figure out what to do. And all the while, this thing was there, in the silence of the forest, in the river beneath the ice. It was flowing under my feet, and up in the sky too. I felt like I was walking in the eye of a hurricane, on a winter's night, just as calm and still as could be."

John shook his head, "I know I must sound crazy."

The Seeker could not know that the night had only seemed perfectly still when, in fact, the earth and its forests spun with tremendous force while simultaneously flying with the moon and stars through space at well over a million miles per hour. Even in the rocks, seemingly so stoic under the stars, electrons in orbitals raced around atoms at well over a million miles per hour according to the best and brightest scientific minds of the 20th and 21st centuries.

"You're not crazy," said Laureal, thinking on an entirely different level.

"You think not?"

"I'm certain of it." And with a knowing smile, "You had a vision."

"You think so?"

"Yes. Grandma has them all the time."

Chapter 10

The weather turned on the following night and forbade the lovers, if only temporarily, from chasing their dream of a horse-drawn sleigh. When the snow and wind ended three days later, and what with their new reality being that of extended time, it was only natural for Laureal to put first things first according to the desires of her heart. Thus in the days that followed, she sought to reshuffle their plans, and in doing so, proved her determination equal to John's even though their focuses were not one and the same. Nor were their means of approaching their objectives the same. Nevertheless, both were of a nature that bound them to getting their way. A nearly impossible situation. And yet, we all know what they say about challenges. So without further ado, let us return to our hero and heroine and let the chips fall where they may.

John Summerfield stood clean-shaven in buckskin pants and the better of his two shirts. His shirt, a white cotton tunic reserved for formalities, had long sleeves with a partial button-down front and richly embroidered chest panels. And being specially tailored to the Seeker, his bride thought her groom appeared particularly handsome in it.

Laureal Emerson wore a great crown of golden braids upon her head, wreathed in tiny maroon leaves of ripened wintergreen, laced with the white feathers of the snowy owl. Her simple wedding dress, made of the finest doeskin, was white as snow. Her dress and crown, being custom tailored with love, went hand in hand with her radiant countenance, all of which had such an effect on her groom that, her image, standing there before him, would forever be the most beautiful in all his many memories.

Gazing solemnly into his bride's eyes, John extended his hands with his large steel knife laid flat across his palms.

"Thank you, darling," speaking lowly as she accepted his knife for all to see. The meaning being that, in the event the warrior fell, his widow would give their firstborn son the symbolic knife entrusted to his mother by his father on the night of their union. This was the way of a Kasskatchen warrior, and under normal circumstances, the knife would become a heirloom passed from generation to generation. As things stood, Laureal would give the knife back to John for the time being, as he presently had no way to replace it and would need it for his mission.

Having accepted John's knife, it was Laureal's turn. With trusting countenance, she extended her hands palms up and presented him with her small stone knife. The symbolism meaning that she was bringing the skills and knowledge of her clan into their marriage. John would entrust the heirloom back into Laureal's care after the ceremony, even as they would share all their possessions from that day forth.

The thick walls of the longhouse muzzled the wind while, holding hands, the bride and groom turned to the Matriarch who then recited a passage reaching so far back in time as to be of unknown origin:

> "Love is patient, love is kind. Love does not envy,
> it does not boast, it is not arrogant or rude. Love
> is not self-seeking, it is not easily angered, it
> keeps no record of wrongs. Love does not
> delight in evil but rejoices with the truth.
> Love always protects, always trusts,
> always hopes, always perseveres."

Turning face-to-face before the hearth, John took Laureal's hands in his. And here again, John and Laureal knew not the origins of their vows but only that they had been passed down by oral traditions reaching many centuries into the past. The lexicon had changed somewhat but the meaning remained the same.

"I, John Summerfield," holding his bride in his eyes, "take you, Laureal Emerson, to be my lawfully wedded wife, to have and to hold from this day forth, for better or worse, for richer or poorer, in sickness and in health, to love and to cherish, till death do us part."

"I, Laureal Emerson," beaming, "take you, John Summerfield, to be my lawfully wedded husband, to have and to hold from this day forth, for better or worse, for richer or poorer, in sickness and in health, to love and to cherish, till death do us part."

John and Laureal shared their first kiss as husband and wife, a picture of youth and all its promise, backlit by the glowing hearth.

Jessie leaned in and whispered to her mother, "To overcome such a start…they have been given something truly rare."

Nodding, Emma wiped a tear, "They're going to rebuild our family."

Clasping and rubbing his hands together, John spoke to Laureal under his breath, "Now for the good part."

"Oh," somewhat confused, "what would that be?"

"The food!"

"Oh! You!" biting her lip, leaning into him with a pained smile.

The wedding feast, laid out on the long table, centered around a spit-roasted boar. Not a big two-hundred-pound behemoth but a young succulent boar of about seventy pounds before dressing. Basted with a mix of herbs and maple syrup, it had been slow-cooked until the meat was ready to fall off the bone. A little further down the table, there rose a delicious aroma from a large clay-fired pot, a steaming stew something like potato soup made from vegetables of the wood—a mix of roots and tubers spiced with herbs. Also on the table, laid out on a wood platter, rainbow trout from the river. Not smoked like dry picnic food but freshly baked in a stone oven. And there was wild rice with herbs in a clay-fired bowl. And in a bowl woven from reeds, walnuts. And in another woven bowl, baked hazelnuts and beechnuts. And finally, freshly picked wintergreen berries in an oak bowl. For drink, two clay pitchers of water, easily refilled. And finally, an oak vase of blueberry wine, semi-sweet, intense and deep, not for drinking in quantity but to be sipped like a desert, although not for the bride and groom. By Kasskatchen tradition, anything that could alter the bride and groom's natural state was forbidden on their wedding day.

Had the wedding taken place in the hunting season at the clan's summer home, there would have been extended family members such as Emma's younger sister's family, Mia's brother's family, and Jessie's in-laws. For although nowhere near as numerous as they had once been, the clan still came together in the rich hunting grounds of the north every summer to cooperate in hunts of forest caribou and woodland buffalo. At season's end they returned to their homes to the southeast, Laureal's family being the exception. Long being the strongest of the families, they had managed to hold on to a significant swath of territory on the far western reach of the realm. Nowhere near the strength they had once been, their reputation nonetheless lived on as a people willing to defend their territory without compromise.

Presently at table, the surviving family members were as follows. The newlyweds, John and Laureal; the Matriarch, Emma; Jessie, Emma's daughter and Laureal's mother; Cody, Jessie's youngest and Laureal's little brother; Mia, Emma's nephew's widow, and Mia's two young children, the twins Noah and Sophie. Well-behaved were the twins because, in their world, their survival depended on it.

To begin the feast, Emma rose and raised her glass for a toast, "John, Laureal, you had a big project to complete, and you got it done in good order. Then, while you were still set up for it, you used your giant to drag dead trees here and, as a result, we have firewood for two winters. John, you and Cody hunted and brought game meat to smoke and dry. We scraped and stored hides, that we may have them later to make clothes and blankets. Laureal, you and your mother and Mia went from glade to glade, digging roots and tubers, and caches of seeds and nuts. What we did not store whole, we dried at the hearth and ground into cereal...and Noah and Sophie helped me with that. We took the canoes to the backwaters and harvested wild rice. We did whatever needed to be done. Everyone did their part. No one complained. The weather turned against us. At times we did not agree on how to proceed. A few times, as is perfectly normal, young lovers became annoyed with one another, but you always showed up, you always worked hard, and we did what needed to be done. Now we are ready for winter. Our food stocks are good. The longhouse is well chinked."

Emma paused to restrain her tears, "You have given me hope for the future of our family."

In the silence that followed, John's sincerity gave his voice a certain softness, "Thank you, Emma. It's been like you said, a team effort."

"Yes, it has," Laureal seconded. "Thank you, Grandma."

Emma next turned to Jessie, "Daughter, would you like to say a few words?"

Standing, Jessie turned to the newlyweds. "John, Laureal, with the freedom entrusted to you, you could have taken a very different path. You could have taken the path of self-gratification and burned past your opportunity to find true happiness in your hearts. But you kept to the hard path, and by that path, you earned your heart's reward."

"Thank you, Mom. I'm glad we remained faithful to your wishes."

"I'm glad too, sweetie," gazing fondly at her daughter.

"It wasn't easy," spoken like a daughter who shares pretty much everything with her mom. Then, upon further thought, Laureal quickly added, "I didn't mean that to sound like I was having to fend John off...I was as bad as he was."

John put his head down in his hands as if looking for a place to hide.

"We don't need to know the details," Emma interjected, laughing to herself. Then, turning to the groom, "John, would you like to say a few words?"

Lifting his head, John stood up and, abandoning his planned speech, spoke off the cuff, "Laureal and I have been very fortunate because…we have all of you. Any success we've had is because of you. So thank you, truly, for all you have done."

Then, turning to his beloved, "Laureal, thank you for being who you are. I am so very happy to know we will spend our life together. I love you, sweetheart. I love you with all my heart."

Trying to keep her tears from escaping, Laureal gazed up into John's eyes, "I love you too, John. So very much!" And rising from her seat, "That day in the woods when you put me on Ellie, I saw something in you, something that…well, I can't find words to explain, except to say I knew that with you was where I truly wanted to be."

"Can we eat now?" asked Cody, his tone being of humble impatience.

"Yes, Cody, we can eat," John replied, chuckling.

John carved the hog. Laureal and Mia filled and delivered steaming cups of soup. Jessie took the platter of trout and doled out helpings around the table. Cody filled their water cups. And in short order, as the food fueled them, the joy of the occasion inspired them, and sipping wine, they found themselves engaged in animated conversation. Emma told a family story involving a bear in which no one got hurt but there were plenty of antics from all, including the bear.

Afterward, and still laughing along with everyone, the bride spoke loudly, her face aglow, "John and I have a bear story!"

"We've heard it," said Cody.

"No, you haven't," Laureal rebutted, "not the best part."

"Laureal," John beseeched as if to ask her not to tell.

"Darling, there's no need to be embarrassed."

"Easy for you to say."

"Oh come on," pleadingly. "Let me tell them."

"No."

"Darling...it was only a cub, freshly weaned from its mother," and with an irresistible smile, "We're all family here."

Under assault from numerous entreaties, John sighed in resignation, "Oh—all right."

"From the beginning," Emma ordered with a grin.

Laureal shot John a reassuring smile. Then, speaking to everyone, she told about their second "special day off," a micro-vacation in which she and John had canoed the little river to its confluence with the big river.

"The weather was perfect that day, but it was cold early that morning when we set out. John had thin wool underlayers beneath his buckskins. He paddled strong all the way there, and by late morning when we reached the confluence, he was all sweaty. So he went to take his underlayers off. I said I wouldn't look, but he wouldn't trust me."

"I trusted her not to look," John interjected, "but she had an ornery look in her eyes, like she might steal my pants and run off down the beach or something."

Offering neither denial nor confirmation, Laureal simply continued, "We were on the beach across from the sandbar island, and...

John interrupted, "She has that look in her eye right now!"

With "that look" in her eye, Laureal continued, "We were on the beach at the confluence. John set out walking up the hill there. Not the big wooded hill but the grassy knoll that flattens out on its top. He was going to get out of his underlayers up there, out of sight. I waited by the canoe. So, I'm standing there looking across the water to the big sandbar island on the confluence where we planned to picnic. It was so beautiful," drifting back in her mind, "not a cloud in the sky. The sun warmed the sand. And all around us, the water was sparkling."

Dreamily, she turned to John, "Darling, that was such a day. One of the best days of my life," and she fell silent.

"What happened next?" Mia implored.

"I can't tell."

"You have to tell now!" Cody exclaimed.

"I'm sorry. It's hysterical, but, it's between John and I."

Cody turned to the groom, "John, will you tell?"

"Definitely not."

"Well heck!"

John saved face with a story about a mother deer and her fawns, "I was scolded by a young mother deer once. She came right to my camp. She knew I was there. She came there looking for me, and as soon as she saw me, she started in on me, read me the riot act I tell you...she was just out-and-out screaming at me."

"No way!" cried Cody, staring at John in disbelief.

"I'm telling the truth! It really happened...just like that. One of the craziest things I ever saw."

"What had you done to upset her so?" Emma asked.

"Well," John began, "I just happened to have some time on my hands when I spotted this young doe on a hill. The hill was smooth but sharply pronounced and mostly covered in prairie grass, except its top where it had a crown of trees. Fifty yards from the base of the hill lay a heavily wooded ravine. I was downwind of the doe. She had her fawns nearby, a pair of them. Twins," glancing at Noah and Sophie. "They had to be her first. She was very young and inexperienced. She'd found herself a choice patch of grass on that hilltop. Under the eave of the trees, she was in the shade and breeze, away from the bugs. She must have been very hungry, as small as she was to be nursing a pair of fawns. Anyway, while she ate I crept up on her carefully. Every time she lifted her head to look around, I would freeze. Didn't matter if I had one foot off the ground, I froze and did not move until she returned to eating. Little by little, I inched up on her with my spear at the ready. Then, when I had closed the distance between us to less than thirty feet, a bluebird landed on a sapling between us and sounded the alarm. That little bird was really carrying on, *Run missus deer! You are in deadly danger! Run!*"

Aware that Noah and Sophie had become infatuated, John focused his dark eyes on them, "Now, missus deer certainly did hear that little bird's warning all right. She lifted her head and looked right at me, but I was frozen in place like a tree. And all the while that little bluebird was doing all it could to save the young mother deer's life. *That's him! Right there! Can't you see him? Oh my gosh, you're looking right at him! Run missus deer! Run!*' But being so young, missus deer did not understand the dangers of the world. She was tired, and that shade and breeze with no bugs to bite her felt so good! And all that lush green grass, and she was oh so hungry! She just thrust her nose back down in all that wonderful deliciousness. And as soon as she did, I took another step towards her...slowly! Ever so slow and quiet! Then, after another step, that bluebird flew away because I'd gotten close enough to wring its little tattletale neck.

"Now, there wasn't even ten paces between that deer and I. But just then the matriarch of the deer herd came up the hill. She had heard the bluebird's warnings. And she saw me! So, being old and wise, she veered and came up on the opposite side of the young mother deer. She got right beside her and tried to get her to move off, *'Move your tail, missy! Move!*' But the young deer would not listen to her elder, *'No!*' said she, insolently, *'I'm hungry, and here's all this delicious grass. My children have worn me out, and here I've found all this wonderful food, and shade, and breeze. So, I'm not going anywhere!*'

"Now while the matriarch and young mother deer were arguing, I inched closer and closer. The matriarch saw my every step, and finally, knowing that she had others in her herd that depended on her, well, she gave up hope on the young doe and trotted off. Now, at last, I was so close that, with one quick step, I could thrust my spear into the young doe's heart!"

John fell silent, fearing he may have taken things too far, such was the look in Sophie's eyes.

"Don't stop now!" Cody pleaded, "Tell us about the kill!"

"John," said Laureal, looking up into his eyes, "tell us what happened."

"Well, I wasn't starving. In fact, I had more food than I needed. So I just looked at that deer and said, 'You really should be more careful.' She jumped straight up in the air six feet! She then bolted down the hill. Her fawns were some distance off and, seeing her run, they bolted also. All three went down into the wooded ravine. I returned to my camp, and later that same day, that young mother deer came and gave me a piece of her mind!"

Laureal searched John's eyes, "Is that a true story?"

"Yes, it is. It happened just exactly as I told it," replied John in all earnest, and in fact it was true.

"I believe you," nestling against him like an affectionate cat, her contented expression suggesting that something in his story had special meaning to her.

"John, tell us another story," Jessie beseeched. "We've heard all our own stories, but your stories are new."

"I can't think of any stories I haven't told you," searching his memory.

"Tell about the time you were trimming Ellie's feet and you fell under her," Laureal suggested, "you haven't told that one."

"Oh…yeah. Well, you've all seen me taking care of Ellie's hooves, lifting them up, holding them between my legs, cleaning them out, checking them, and trimming them if needed. Well, I was needing to trim her one day and I saw this branch that looked like a three-legged stool. So I thought to myself, *That would make a good hoof stand. I could cut it and notch it, then I could set Ellie's hoof on it, and it'd be easier for me to trim her.* So I got my hatchet and bucksaw, and I soon had me a tripod hoof stand. I started with Ellie's front left hoof. She helped me lift it up and put it on the stand. So I'm trimming away and, somehow, I got my foot caught in the legs of the stand and fell underneath Ellie. The hoof stand toppled off to the side. I lay flat on my back looking up at Ellie, and she was looking down at me. She was holding her hoof up with nowhere to put it because my head was in the way. She had her neck turned to the side so she could get a visual on me, not turned a lot though, I guess because she would have lost her balance. Anyway, she ever so carefully lowered her hoof, all the while keeping an eye on me until her huge foot came down gently beside my head. I crawled out from under her and got up. I was so impressed, I didn't know what to say. So I just said, 'Thank you, Ellie.' No more had I said it then she brought her mussel over and put it on my heart. She rested it there for a few moments before returning to her previous stance, ready to continue with the trimming."

"It was the Great Spirit," Laureal said knowingly, looking round the table.

"It sure was," Jessie seconded. Then, speaking directly to John, "The Great Spirit touched your heart through your horse. He can do that. He can come in a sunrise. He can come in the eyes of a newborn child. He came through your horse to knock on the door of your heart."

Smiling at John, Laureal nodded as if to say, *"You see, I told you so."*

John only smiled. He knew they thought him to be on some kind of vision-quest but he didn't give much weight to the idea. As a Seeker, his mission was to find the data trove that would lift the world to a better place by way of the advancements contained therein. It was the hope of all believers. John could see them in his mind's eye, just a stone's toss across the untold miles, parading through the dusty ruins of old LA. He could almost hear their cheers as he rode out into the desert. And as their hopeful voices faded, it struck him how, back then, he could never have imagined where his quest would take him. And coming back to his new family, he could not help but notice Emma. She was gazing at him, a knowing look in her eye.

Presently, Mia told a story that her Father had told when she was a child, a legend about a race of people that lived at the top of the world. As utterly unbelievable as it sounded, the "snow people" lived in houses made of snow. Of course, everyone laughed in the knowledge that, outside of a child, not even the most gullible adult would actually believe that there were people who lived in houses made of snow.

Emma then told how her great-grandmother and great-grandfather met, not by the traditional way of arranged marriage but by divine plan. The pair had fallen in love during a feud between their two clans. It was a story of hardship and victory through the power of love. A story the family never grew tired of hearing.

Her head on her husband's shoulder, the bride slid her hand to the inside of his thigh, about halfway to the knee. As she did, she turned her face up to him and smiled warmly into his eyes.

With love and desire on his lips, the groom leaned and whispered in his wife's ear, "I'm ready if you are."

Laureal nodded, and John lifted his eyes to the family. "If we may be excused, we will retire to our cabin now."

"Yes, of course," said Emma, rising from her seat, as did everyone.

Jessie, who had recently returned from stepping outside momentarily with Mia to light candles and stoke the hearth in the wedding hut, hugged her daughter tight, "I'm so happy for you!"

"Thank you, Mom! Thank you for all you've done!" Then turning to the family, "Thank you. You've made this the best day of my life!"

Emma stepped forward and hugged Laureal, "None of us has done more to make this day what it is than you and John, dear. You've earned this."

"Thank you, Grandma."

"Don't worry about Ellie tonight or in the morning, John," said Cody. "I'll make sure she has plenty hay and water."

"Thank you, Cody," clasping hands with the boy, knowing he would take good care of his other girl. And in fact Ellie was in good shape, there in the shelter of the wall with the dogs. John and Cody had brought hay across the river using the canoes. Good hay, for although cut and dried late, it came from excellent quality fall grass that still had good nutrition in it.

As the family members spoke, they shuffled slowly, randomly towards the heavy door of the longhouse where they would see the bride and groom off on their short walk to the honeymoon cabin.

A billow of snow came gliding in as John opened the big door. And looking into the night, all could see how the courtyard very nearly appeared a snow globe, what with the snow glancing off the newly built wall to float all about. A snow globe complete with courtyard and handsome wedding hut, lacking only its bride and groom.

As the newlyweds crossed the courtyard, the family looked on from the deck of the longhouse. Halfway to the wedding hut, the groom picked the bride up in his arms. Then, at the stoop of the wedding hut, for reasons unknown even to him, he turned to the family one last time. Perhaps to say a silent thank you, perhaps to become part of an oral tradition; a story of lovers told at the hearth, of the lovely picture they had made with the snow gently swirling around them. He in his buckskins and embroidered cotton tunic, she in her simple white wedding gown, a crown of golden braids upon her head, wreathed in tiny maroon leaves laced with white feathers.

In the next moment, John turned to the door. Laureal turned the latch with her free hand. The door opened, the groom carried the bride across the threshold, and the warm light of the hearth enveloped them.

Chapter 11

Not too early the following morning, there came a knock at the door of the wedding hut.

"Come in," said John.

Jessie poked her head in to see the newlyweds wrapped in a large quilt made from hides of forest caribou. They were not in bed but cuddled up on an elk rug before a granite hearth constructed in the shape of an arch—the centerpiece of the hut. The floor beneath them, unlike the wood-planked floor of the longhouse that had rugs of bear, moose, and elk, instead began with a base of clay, sand, and straw that had been mixed together wet and laid down to dry like concrete. It was more forgiving on the feet than concrete, even while it remained rigid and durable. Atop it, a tender layer of spruce boughs served as an underlayment for elk rugs, creating a soft cushion with a fresh mild scent that mixed well with the scent of wood burning in the fireplace.

Alongside the hearth stood the sleeping platform, an elevated floor made of hardwood planks atop which the young lovers slept on a surprisingly comfortable mattress of dry hay grass contained in a wood frame, richly covered with animal pelts.

Presently, the newlyweds appeared somewhat disheveled, not because they'd spent the night swinging from chandeliers, so to speak, but rather because they simply had a glow at once peaceful and happy.

"Good morning," said Jessie, stepping in and shutting the door behind her.

"Good morning," they answered in unison.

With a quick glance, Jessie determined they had eaten all the treats that she and Mia had laid out for them the night before.

"Would you like some breakfast?"

"Yes, please!" again nearly in unison, both of them smiling.

John's eyes shifted briefly to the elevated floor where his trousers lay beside the bed.

Noticing, Jessie said, "There's no need for you to get up. I can bring you breakfast in a few minutes. Would you like that?"

"Oh yes! Thank you, Jessie."

"Thank you, Mom!"

"You're most welcome!" And opening the door to step out, "I'll be right back."

As Jessie came through the longhouse door, Emma turned from the hearth, "How's our kids?

"Never better," with a smile.

The Matriarch and her daughter, being aware of Laureal's cycle, had made certain the wedding fell on such a date as to waste no time beginning the process of rebuilding the family. Jessie hung her coat by the door and, crossing the floor, came to her mother's side at the hearth, "It stopped snowing."

Emma peered into the oven to check the breadcakes. "We need to keep them in there for a few days."

"I don't think that will be a problem."

"No, neither do I," using a stone slab to close the oven, "Last night I dreamed their union produced a handsome boy."

"Boy or girl, it would do John good to hold their child in his arms before he goes."

"It would sober him," and lowering her voice so the twins would not hear, "and perhaps, save his life."

"Save his life?" struck by the change in her mother's tone. "You mean like, bring him around…right?"

"Yes, and no. A few weeks ago, before he decided to come north with us, John asked to speak with me. He wanted me to know that if he had not returned in a year, to know that he had died. He promised to be careful. He promised that everything would be fine and he was only confiding in me as a matter of protocol. Of course, this is never to reach Laureal's ears, unless, heaven forbid, a time comes when she must be told."

"He will return to us," as if it were a fact.

"He will have every intention. Of that, at least I am certain." And pausing in thought, "I imagine that, when a boy is taken from his mother and father at six years of age, it creates a kind of need, a type of desperation really. A desperation that, in the hands of experienced trainers, produces a warrior as determined as humanly possible. And that worries me because, regardless of what John says, I fear he will not be able to surrender his quest in the face of the impossible. Have you noticed he never talks about the other Seekers, like perhaps he doesn't want us to know that none survive."

"Mom," pleadingly, her tone that of a little girl who resists bad news.

"I'm only seeing what's before me, dear," contritely. "John's Order did not give him that wolverine cap for nothing. But more than that, I think John was meant to come here, not to kill...that was not the Great Spirit's intent. A door has been opened in John's heart since coming here, and, even if only a little, it is no small thing."

"I've seen it!" regaining hope. "And I've seen it in Laureal also. In her soul, every day, she becomes more a woman."

Nodding, "We have more reason for hope than not." And pausing in thought, Emma shook her head, "All my life I have seen signs, but I have never seen so many signs as I do around those two. Even before they were wedded and I was only considering their union, a white-headed eagle appeared at the moment of critical thought, and it was following the course of the river! And another time, a snow-white owl glid out of the forest, landed on a limb, and gazed into my eyes. Another time, on the heels of a prayer, a gentle breeze came from nowhere to caress my cheek. And once, before the freeze, as the two of them walked the river trail, I saw a bright reflection of light following them in the water, and despite my many worries, I could not help but believe that they were being protected."

"I also have seen signs," her countenance animated. "Just last night, while they were yet here in the longhouse, I went out to check the wedding cabin to make sure the hearth was stoked and the lamps were lit. So I went through the door twice," (glancing to the big door of the longhouse), "and I saw nothing unusual. But then, only a short while later, when John opened the door and stood before it with Laureal at his side, a light came from the hearth like a fire log had flared, and the way before them suddenly illuminated. It made the snow shimmer across the floor and out the door…and as they crossed the threshold to begin their journey, they appeared to walk on a path laid down by a hand from heaven!"

"Oh!" cried Emma. "Listen to us!"

"Maybe we are," laughing, "just a couple of loony old women." Then, quieting down, relaxing, and thinking, Jessie added, "Mom, something good has come in this season of disaster, and it is around those two kids, and it is not bound to this world."

"Yes dear, what you say is true." And smiling with hope, "Let us pray it leads our family to a new beginning."

A short time later in the wedding hut, John and Laureal sat snug in fur quilts before the hearth, enjoying a breakfast cooked just for them. And suffice to say, it was special. When they had finished, John arose and went to the window where, pushing a hanging fur aside, he opened a shutter just enough to peer out and check on Ellie.

"How is she?" Laureal asked.

"She's fine," closing the shutter and turning to her, "You have a wonderful family."

"We are *your* family now, darling."

A playful grin came over him, "It sure feels good," coming back to her, "getting breakfast in bed and not having to do anything at all."

He brought his nose to her neck, under her ear, not kissing but nuzzling like a happy pup.

Laureal cringed and let out a gleeful squeak.

Yet nuzzling, John whispered, "I don't suppose you care at all for this married stuff."

"Nah," cringing, squeaking.

"Ellie," he called lowly, turning away.

"Hey," grabbing his arm, "get back here!"

Gently pushing her hair to uncover her glowing face, he admired her. Then, easing his hands under the large quilt, he lifted and carried her to their bed and laid her down. He then laid down beside her, on his side, his head propped while hers lay on fur pillows.

Laureal ran her hand over John's powerful chest, then up his neck to his jaw, and onto his cheek, touching and caressing his face, gazing into his eyes, "When you go…I'm going to miss you something terrible, John Summerfield."

"I'm going to miss you too," softly stroking her hair, "but that's a year off, and when I return, we will never again be parted."

Overcome with worry, Laureal dropped her gaze.

"Sweetheart…everything will be alright."

Visibly struggling with her thoughts, full well remembering her mother's warning about being overbearing; Laureal just could not keep herself from it, "John, I have such fear for you in my heart," lifting her troubled eyes to his, "I have something I must tell you, and, it's going to hurt you, but, in my heart, I know it must be said."

Suddenly confused, "What, Laureal? What must be said?"

"John, after that day we met in the woods and you put me up on Ellie, I would look for any excuse to go into the woods in hope of finding you."

"And I was always looking for you," unable to understand what the problem was, "I was always hoping to find you. And when I found you and we would talk…and afterward, even though I felt I shouldn't, I could not stop thinking about you."

"You felt you shouldn't think about me because of your quest, and you struggled with that?"

"Yes, but…

"John, wait. Please, hear me out."

His mouth open to speak, John fell silent even as his expression spoke to his confusion.

Laureal continued, "I also had reasons to struggle and feel that I shouldn't think of you."

She pushed her hand into his, "John, stay with me," pleading, reading his pained expression. "I couldn't stop thinking about you either. But, early on, I struggled with my thoughts and feelings. And yet, whenever we met and I saw your smile, any bad feelings I may have had melted away. I wanted them to melt away, and you always made them melt away. We learned to avoid talk that might bring us pain...we avoided what happened to us that first day under the maple. But then one day, fairly early on, while on my way to dig seeds in a glade, I was missing my father, brother, and grandfather so much that my pain was terrible. I felt completely lost. I became confused in my mind, and...I began to blame you, and hate you, all over again."

Laureal drew a heavy breath, "What I am about to tell you may sound crazy, but this is what happened that day. As I came into a glade, I saw a lone dove in a leafless tree. It was not a big tree but medium to smallish. As I passed under its eave, the dove and I held one another's gaze. There was something immediately obvious about it. The dove was not unnatural in physical form, yet something about it was wholly unnatural. Strange as it was, it would have captivated me, except I was in so much pain that it only partly distracted me from my thoughts. Anyway, I put my basket down and started to dig for seeds in a squirrel hole. I was on my hands and knees. Then, when I turned to look back, that dove was perched on the handle of my basket not five feet away, and it was staring into my eyes. John, you know how birds naturally keep a sharp eye out for predators, especially when on the ground. They nervously turn their heads this way and that. Well, this dove never looked anywhere but into my eyes. I asked it what it was doing but of course it made no reply. I tried to return to digging but couldn't help turning to look. And always it was there, just gazing at me. And the look it gave me! It was like, fearless serenity. This went on for a good while. Finally, I turned to look, and it was gone. I had scarcely realized it but the darkness in me had faded. The shadow wolves had lost their grip on me. And only then did I realize what had happened. The Great Spirit saw that the seven deadly shadows had ambushed me in the glade. They had surrounded my heart! But the Great Spirit, in his mercy, sent a dove to touch my heart. He turned my eyes from evil just enough, and I saw that I could spend my life in the shadow of a tragedy, or I could walk out into His light and be free. And realizing that he had opened my eyes, that I might know the one from the other, I broke down in tears."

"Laureal, you don't have to…

"Yes I do!" cutting him off, wiping tears with one hand, unconsciously squeezing his hand with the other. "My grandfather had a name for the master of the shadow wolves." And pausing in thought, "It was more of a reference, really. Grandpa would say, 'That pair of hands that is ever working in the dark.' And grandma, she called him, 'The Master of Deception.' Mia told me that her grandmother, who came from a family far away to the east, called him 'Lucifer.' I've heard that some folks call him 'Darth Vader,' or 'Sauron.' I don't know what he or it is exactly, but I know this. If I had continued feeding the wolves that lurk in the shadows of my soul…then when you and I next met, you would not have recognized me. You would have looked into my eyes, but you would not have found me. You would have seen a different woman, a woman given over to darkness. And lest I somehow freed myself from the shadows within, which only get stronger once a person starts feeding them, they would have devoured my opportunity for happiness in life."

"Laureal, I…

"John please! Let me finish," drying her cheeks, "My family and I, we believe the Great Spirit is calling you even though you do not believe in him. He is using you for something, something bigger than yourself. He proved it when you put your quest aside to help us. He touched your heart, John. He had already given you a powerful body...and in your mind, he gave you focus and determination. Your mentors saw all of this, and they chose you from many to wear the wolverine cap. But John, even with all that, you do not stand a chance alone against the Master of the Seven Shadows. John...oh John, I have felt such fear for you. I fear I will lose you!"

Laureal looked awful, her fearful expression framed in a tangle of hair from which gazed reddened eyes, "John, I had a dream...no, not a dream...a nightmare. I dreamed the lord of darkness got to you. He got to you in a way I could never have imagined. He presented himself to you as being the very thing you seek. He deceived you into thinking him the master of all that is good, pure, and beautiful. A shining white wolf, sitting on a polished boulder of onyx. He offered you the world and you accepted because you thought it was good. And when you returned here in victory, I could not find you. I looked into your eyes but I was not able to find you. You walked and talked, but inside, you were dead and gone."

Laureal broke down completely, "I'm sorry, John," she sobbed, "but I had to tell you."

Shocked by Laureal's state, John took her into his arms and pulled her close, "It was just a dream, a nightmare. It wasn't real. It's not going to happen!"

"Maybe not as I dreamed it, but John, no matter how brave and strong and smart you are...without the Great Spirit to protect you, you haven't a chance against the one that lurks in the shadows!"

"Laureal." John looked her straight in the eyes, "Everything is going to be alright. You'll see," stroking her hair, "I'll come back to you, and I will still be me, and you will be you, and we will spend our lives together."

With his wife's cheek pressed to his heart, her tears running down his chest; John recalled the words of one of his instructors, a married man who came to work one day and made an offhand remark about life, *'Marry the prettiest package you can, boys, because they're all nuts inside.'* In his mind, Summerfield could not help wondering if, having been happily married not even a day, the other shoe had already dropped and dropped hard. And yet, in his heart, another voice spoke up, saying, *'Listen to her, John. She moved a mountain to love you. But she did not move it by herself.'*

Too many thoughts to list was John Summerfield thinking. Glancing at his wife, he realized she had fallen asleep, having poured herself out. He had never seen her looking bad but there she was, drooling. He laid his head back, closed his eyes, and thought of the story she had told him about the dove. There had to be a logical explanation. Perhaps the bird, being migratory, had a human friend to the south. A kind old savage woman who hand-fed it. And when it saw Laureal gathering seeds, it simply landed on her basket handle because it was a familiar perch from which to beg. He smiled because he knew what Laureal would say about his explanation. She would say that that was exactly how the Great Spirit worked. Whatever the case, he had no reason to doubt her story. He figured most renaissance men would find his story about the bluebird hard enough to believe, or that an angry young doe had actually sought him out and scolded him. But because the Order had given him the wolverine cap and thrown him out into nature, he had seen the unexplainable with his own eyes, and little by little, it had changed him. He knew it wasn't a simple matter of visiting nature and feeling the presence of something bigger than oneself, something beyond what is visible. Rather, he had been out in nature long-term with no backup and no retreat, and it had forced a brutal kind of honesty on him because, on a day-to-day basis, his very life depended on his every behavior. He could not lie to himself and live. He could no longer observe nature as a beautiful painting in an art gallery. He could not because, he was in the painting. And mysterious though it be, a real connection existed between him and whatever it was that wielded the paintbrush. Not a static painting but flowing and swirling like a river, sweeping him into depths where his hard-driving need for self-preservation might outweigh his soul and drag him down unless, some greater truth were there to save him.

Deep in thought, John knew good and well that it had not been his decision to put his quest aside for Laureal and her family. Rather, he had done so by stumbling along and finding himself there after the fact. And so he could not help but wonder if some invisible force was at work. Had the same force that tumbles and polishes a rock in a stream, brought him to where he was? A force that could not be explained even as one felt a mysterious connection to it. Not an evil force. Not a pair of hands to pull a man into the dark but, insomuch as his limited ability to understand could couch it, the hands of a craftsman, performing his labor of love to shape a stone in a stream, a tree in a forest, or a man in a family.

John Summerfield could no longer discount the possibility that there could be something beyond the visible at work in all that he saw. And deciding it couldn't hurt, being that he had nothing to lose and perhaps, something to gain—

"I'm not a praying man," his voice low, his eyes closed, "I wouldn't know where to begin. But, if there is some kind of entity that can actually hear me, and, if all of this is your doing…well then, I guess I should start by thanking you for my life, and for this woman at my side. And, well, if you have some control over how all of this works, or if you know how to make it work, then if you could work it out so that whatever I may find out there, I return home no worse a man than I was when I left, I would greatly appreciate it."

John opened his eyes only to discover his wife Laureal, gazing at him, the joy in her expression like a simple summer sunrise.

Chapter 12

It was the kind of thing one might expect to see in a magical music box. The longhouse and wedding hut bedecked in white with courtyard between. Wispy pillars of smoke rising from stone chimneys on a windless day. The surrounding forest and frozen river, a lost highway in a winter wonderland—all set to music. The feathered musicians, twenty to thirty goldfinches known as a charm. They sang for the newlyweds and the promise of new life. Or so it seemed as their voices rose to a crescendo and spilled over the courtyard walls, bearing the enchantment of the forest into the dwelling of the humans.

In the courtyard, Jessie's lone figure could have been mistaken for Laureal at first glance. Dressed in doeskins and caribou cloak, she had come to check on the honeymooners. On the stoop, she lifted her hand to knock and ask if they would like a late lunch. Pausing instead, she cocked her head and, with a look of uncertainty, put her ear near the door, whereupon she turned around and went back to the longhouse.

"That was quick," Emma said as Jessie came through the longhouse door.

"They're busy," said Jessie.

With a knowing smile, Mia continued her business at the long table, working to prepare a hide, scraping it extra thin for the making of summer clothes that would be altogether light, airy, and resilient.

Emma kept to her sewing work, "We'll check on them later."

While the hearth crackled and popped, the three women worked at their long table factory, all the while telling stories of their own honeymoons. Without keeping track of time but having allowed a portion to pass, Jessie decided she would try again to check on the newlyweds. But she had only put down her work when Laureal came through the door.

"Good heavens, child!" Emma cried in shock, "Save some of yourself for later!"

"It's not like you're thinking, Grandma," on a beeline to the hearth where she served herself a cup of porridge from the pot.

"I could have brought you that, dear," said Jessie.

"Thanks, Mom, but I'm really hungry."

"What about John? Isn't he hungry?"

"He's conked out," and sipping the stew, "Oh, good grief this is good!" Then pausing, looking over her soup cup at them, "What's so funny?"

"Nothing dear. We just love you, that's all. Oh, and for your information, we made that stew special for you and John."

"Thank you. Thank you for pampering us!" And pausing in thought, "Mom, could you bring some of this to the hut in a few hours, please?"

"Yes dear, I would be happy to."

Spent though she be, Laureal made for a picture of joy, "I came to share some wonderful news!"

"Oh, and what would that be?" asked Emma.

"John has accepted the Great Spirit into his heart!"

"Truly?"

"Yes, well…at least, he kind of said a prayer, and he acknowledged the possibility of the Great Spirit's existence. And he asked for his help!"

The women shared looks of amazement. "This truly is wonderful news!"

"I've got to get back," said Laureal, dumping the last of her stew back in the pot.

"Laureal!" Jessie cried, standing up swiftly, "You know better than that!"

"Oh gosh, Mom. I'm sorry!" exclaimed Laureal, surprised at herself.

"Go get some sleep!" Emma ordered, unable to keep a smile from her face regarding the news about John and the infectious antics of her love-drunk granddaughter.

"Laureal, take my cloak," said Jessie, bringing it to the girl. "You could catch your death of cold going out in nothing but your doeskins." And wrapping her cloak around her daughter, she lowered her voice, "You're going to get some sleep now…right?"

"Yes, Mom," gazing happily at her.

Stepping to the door, Laureal paused to look back at them, "Mom, Grandma, Mia, Noah, Sophie, and Cody also, wherever he is…I love you!"

Chapter 13

John and Laureal's honeymoon, spent in a cozy and well-prepared wedding hut, would forever be remembered by both. And yet, wonderful as it had been, it was only natural that our young hero and heroine return to their dream of a horse-drawn sleigh. Thus talking it over, they planned to resume work the very next day. And yet, as we have already learned, things do not always go as planned.

It was just after supper in the longhouse when Emma, her mind at work on possibilities yet unknown to anyone except Jessie, struck up a conversation, "John, back when you were building our wall, I watched that giant of yours pulling logs, and I must say, her strength would be hard to believe if I had not witnessed it with my own eyes."

"It truly is a thing to see," nodding in agreement, "I know I've said this before, but Ellie is equivalent in weight and strength to fifteen men. That's a lot!" And turning to his wife, "With Ellie, we could easily plant a crop along the river, from which we could reap a fine harvest."

Emma appeared doubtful, "Forgive me John, but with regard to this thing you call farming, why on earth should we go through all the trouble of plowing and planting when the Creator has already planted everything we need exactly where it grows best?"

"Well, as I have said before," John countered, "it is a way to ensure against starvation. From a good harvest, one can store grain away to eat in a bad year."

"Are we not able to store wild rice and wheat?"

"Yes," laughing because he'd anticipated the question.

"So, John, whose plan is better...man's, or the Creator's?"

Gazing at Emma for a moment, John replied, "The creator's, or depending on how one views it, nature's plan is better than man's plan. But I see no reason why any plan should not include agriculture. Moreover, the stability it provides opens doors to greater advancement. I've seen it myself."

"I have heard of the 'advancement' to which you speak," referring to stories she'd heard from those who had traveled far to the east, beyond the Five Seas. And smiling in earnest, "John, I know your desire to build a better way is well-intended. I just don't believe it's possible. The way I see it, you could build and build and build, and you'd never build anything better than what's just outside our door."

"What about those things outside the door yet to be discovered? Could they not make our lives better?"

"Well, perhaps you have something there. Then again," (thinking of the Niths), "perhaps they would lead to our undoing."

"Grandmother!" Laureal protested.

Turning her eyes to her granddaughter, "You and John are young and full of life, which means you have much to learn. But to be fair, I am old and set in my ways. Therefore, as you have always shown me respect, I promise not to close my mind to your ideas." And moving her eyes around the table, "Be our ways new or old, like these over here, or those over there, we must always look to the Great Spirit. Otherwise, it matters not how our food grows or how much we have, as it will only be a matter of time before we consume ourselves in an attempt to relieve our starvation."

Emma rose from the table, "Tomorrow, after breakfast, I have a proposal to make, a plan that goes to the heart of our family's survival."

"What would that be, Grandmother?"

"In the morning, we will discuss it in the morning."

Trading looks of curiosity and confusion, Mia, Laureal, John, and Cody set about the work of cleaning up after dinner, stoking the hearth, bringing in firewood, feeding and watering the animals, etc.

Chapter 14

"Good morning, darling," looking on as John came to consciousness.

"Good morning," groggily, his eyes half open, the slumber of night like a mask not yet removed from his face.

"I've been watching you sleep."

"Oh really," still looking out through slits. "Have you been up long?"

"Long enough to stoke the fire," her eyes bright, her long hair falling all about while, in her mouth, she chewed some unidentified fruit.

"What are you eating?"

"Here, I have one for you," taking a tiny object from her palm, holding it between her fingers.

"Wait," trying to resist, not yet fully awake.

"It's only a berry," giggling, pushing it into his mouth.

Chewing, John tasted the creamy, sweet, cool, minty flavor of wintergreen, and suspecting his wife's intention, a smile came to the corners of his lips.

"Just one left," said Laureal, placing it on her tongue. Then, with a gleam in her eye, she pressed her lips to John's, and he took it from her mouth.

In the longhouse, the rest of the family, having finished their breakfast, made use of their time while waiting for the newlyweds to arrive.

"See how straight the stitch is," Emma pointed out to Sophie. The child knelt on the bench at the long table, directly beside the Matriarch, that she may watch and help the women put finishing touches on clothing made for the coming summer. "See how evenly it rounds the corner," Emma continued. "That stitch tells a story about the person who made it. It is good work, and all who see it know that good work comes from good hands, and good hands tell of the good intent in one's heart and mind. Do you know who made that stitch?"

"My mommy!"

Noah, meanwhile, sat down the way beside Cody where he watched and helped the teen make fish hooks from the breast bones of grouse.

Pausing, Cody looked to Emma, "Grandma?"

"Yes, dear."

"Shall I summon the rabbits?"

"Cody!" Jessie chided.

Cody only shrugged, evidently to grant his own pardon based on grounds of honesty.

Mia grinned but said nothing.

Emma only shook her head, a silent reply that meant, *"No."*

"What rabbits?" asked Noah.

Not ten minutes later, Laureal came through the door, "Good morning, everyone!"

"Good morning," came their replies.

Having hung her coat, Laureal went to the hearth where taking ladle in hand, she fetched herself a bowl of hot cereal. Then seating herself at the long table, she smiled at them, her eyes glazed with a blissful afterglow.

"Where's John?"

"He's checking on Ellie."

"I already made sure she has hay and water," said Cody.

John came through the door, "Good morning, all!"

"Good morning, John."

"Good morning."

"Thank you, Cody, for haying and watering Ellie."

"You're welcome. I was already out there anyway, feeding the dogs."

While John removed his coat and over pants, Laureal fetched him a bowl of hot cereal and met him at the table, "Thank you, sweetheart."

"You're welcome, darling."

Leaning over his steaming cereal, John savored the aroma of stoneground wild wheat. He added honey from a clay-fired jar, sprinkled in a handful of walnuts and picked up his wooden spoon in anticipation.

Mia passed a saucer containing sundried wedges of apple and pear. Laureal returned with two steaming mugs of tea, a mild blend of forest herbs sweetened with a dash of honey. It didn't take long for the lovers to finish their breakfast, whereupon Laureal cleaned up while John brought in an armload of firewood.

Emma waited until the newlyweds were reseated. Then, looking from one family member to the next, "We all share the same desire...we want to hold on to what we love. We want the best for those we love. We want to keep the land on which we all depend. We want to preserve our way of life. And to do this, we need to find worthy replacements for the men we have lost. And as you all know, I intended to enlist the help of our cousins and friends when we meet in our northern hunting grounds this summer. They would help us, but of course this would reveal our vulnerability and, at least to a degree, make us reliant on charity and, willing to settle for what we can get. Therefore, I would like to adopt an entirely new plan. A plan that previously crossed my mind but, until this recent change of plans regarding John and his giant Ellie, seemed out of the question."

The Matriarch paused for a sip of tea. Then, setting her cup down, "This is going to take some time to explain, so bear with me. I will begin by saying that Jessie, Mia, and I have spoken and agreed we are ready to rebuild. We know that if we are to meet the challenges of living in these woods, we must have high-quality men. And I know, we women can laugh and joke about what that means, but when it comes down to the nitty-gritty...we know. We know that if we are to be free from the whims of those that would claim dominion over us, we need men who possess the courage and skill to defend our territory and way of life. We need right-thinking men so that together

143

we avoid mistakes that lead to downfall and sorrow. And if we are to foster what is most near and dear to our hearts, we need men that fully invest their hearts."

Turning to her fellow widows, Emma continued, "Nearly six months have passed since disaster changed the course of our lives...all our lives," nodding to John with an inclusive tone. "Summer will be here before we know it. Our isolation will be at an end. News of our loss will take foot and run quickly ahead of us. Fast down the trails it will go, through summer hunting grounds and camps until it is known far and wide that the strongest family in the House of Emerson has fallen. Our kin will do what they can for us, but as I have said, our clan is only a shadow of what it once was. Still, there is much good-heartedness among our people. Pressed though they may be, some will step forward and offer their time. Many will express their sympathy. There will be encouraging gestures. Sadly though, there will be others that see us as 'ripe for the picking.' With their eyes on our land, they will come with false smiles and insincere condolences. Worse yet, in these times of weakness, it is possible we might find ourselves caught up in a fight with a rival clan."

Sober looks went around the table. Their faces, illuminated by oil lamps, cast shadows like thoughts to dance in place on surrounding walls. And perhaps if those walls could talk, they would not say a word but only listen, that they may one day tell of a fateful morning when a fellowship formed at the threshold of the unknown, beyond which awaited a journey that none could imagine.

Emma turned to the youngest widow, "Mia, you have two small children in tow, and that could present a problem for finding a husband, as it is a man's nature to invest in his own blood. However, you are the widow of a warrior who fell in battle, a champion of the House of Emerson, synonymous with courage and valor. Honor, respect, and wealth come as a package with you. And you are young, just twenty-five, and beautiful with fine figure and determined nature. Therefore, I think it safe to assume our prospects are bright for finding you a deserving husband."

Mia thanked Emma, and as she did, the shape of her well-formed lips signaled resolve. The look in her eyes, like deep dark pools, told of her desire to live. She was ready, and Emma wasted no time.

"Jessie, it stands to reason that you would have more difficulty finding a man than Mia, and I would have greater difficulty yet. But then again, it stood to reason that we would not survive the winter, and yet, here we are with every reason to go forward. I am proud of you, daughter. You have raised three children. You know what marriage requires. You have the gift of thirty-seven years. You survived the disaster at the river crossing as a young wife. You then threw yourself into the challenge, that our family may not vanish altogether. The fact that you have such a résumé at this place and time cannot be a coincidence. And you are yet young! You may find an honorable widower of your age, perhaps with children like you. A man looking for a woman like you. A man old enough to know a good thing, and still youthful enough to know what to do with it. A man only now coming into his true prime. For you are only now coming into yours."

"Thank you, Mother." The flickering firelight on Jessie's face seemed to ally itself with her physical constitution, making for such a deception—she could scarcely be taken for thirty-seven. On closer look, however, one might gaze into those large emerald eyes and gleam a life's story worth knowing. Presently looking from one family member to the next, her tone was decided, "Our Maker would not have seen us this far if he did not mean to see us all the way."

"He will, Mother. I am certain of it!"

Reaching out, Jessie took Laureal's hand and, without words, shared feelings of hope and optimism. A subtle smile revealed Mia's dimples as she looked to the tiny table just off the hearth where the twins busied themselves. Cody pushed a batch of fish hooks across the long table and John nodded in approval. Emma read the signs before her, and she knew the family had gotten over a mountain. It was a special moment in time, made all the sweeter when mother and daughter met one another gaze to share their sacred bond.

It ended too soon. A sudden sadness overtook the younger and, her eyes fell to the table. Fleeting though it be, Emma knew the current business had touched an old wound. A wound known only to the two of them. Years before when Jessie had come of age, she had given her heart to a young man with great hope and enthusiasm. Then, in an eleventh-hour decision, the family chose another for her. And though it seemed the end of the world for the girl, in the end she accepted the will and guidance of her elders. To Jessie's credit, she and her husband not only learned to love but built a happy family. And so it seemed in Emma's thinking that no good could come from rehashing the old question as to whether she should have sided with her daughter in the ordeal. She alone knew how Jessie had cried.

Steeling herself as duty demanded, Emma proceeded, "Jessie, Mia, it would be all too easy for us to find a family looking to expand their scope of power through marriage, as in they offer us security in trade for our land. So I will say this just once. I will not consider any deal of that sort! We have one another. We have faith. We know the value of hard work and honesty. We know how to weather the little storms that sometimes erupt between us. We have the basics on which great families are built. We only need men that feel as we do."

Listening to the Matriarch, John Summerfield pondered his role. His eyes, having moved from one family member to the next, wandered away to the longhouse wall where several sets of snowshoes hung just inside the heavy oak door. The frames of the snowshoes had been made by the men. The netted decks that filled the frames were made by the women. Everyone had a role to play. Also on the wall hung a good many spears, bows, arrows, and a few hatchets. Tools and weapons made by the men. On the same wall but on the other side of the door hung a row of heavy fur coats and pants, winter armor made by the women. No small fortune hung on that wall. In fact, the fruits of the family's labor were to be found high and low throughout the longhouse. Fortunes spun from nature. Spun from knowledge passed on and refined from one generation to the next, combined with skill derived from countless hours of labor. Too many riches to count, to mention nothing of what the women wore for house clothes: sable, mink, ermine, fox, and lynx. Still, all their belongings were but a pittance in comparison to the value of the territory they held. And because John had come to know them, he understood that all their holdings put together amounted to nothing when compared to the value they placed on their freedom. Perfect it was not, but it was their way of life, and without it, living meant nothing to them.

John returned his eyes to the Matriarch. Sitting upright at the end of the long table, Emma's entire being told of stubborn will and hope. Her long experience, etched into the lines of her face, gave her a different kind of beauty than that of her youth. A different kind of beauty, framed by large gray braids mixed with free-flowing locks falling down like silver on shoulders clad in sable. She could easily have been an old Viking queen who, in the aftermath of a battle lost, must take the helm with a singular focus, being the survival of her people.

"As I said," Emma continued, "I once thought we had but one path before us. I planned to use our connections with cousins and friends in our summer hunting grounds. But now, knowing that John and his giant will be coming with us, and having seen what his giant is capable of, and what we ourselves are capable of…I believe I can disregard my old plan in favor of the plan that, if successful, will net us the finest men to be found anywhere."

Jessie and Mia exchanged looks while fire logs cracked and popped in the hearth.

Emma turned to the Seeker, "John, as you know by the maps we made at this table, our summer hunting ground is located north across the two great rivers that meet and flow east as one. You also know that if anyone were to continue north from there, far north, to the edge of the Kasskatchen realm, they would come to a hunting ground on the shores of a vast lake that few of our people have laid eyes on."

"Roderick's Grounds," said John.

"It is said to be of such bounty as to have no rival!" Cody interjected.

Smiling at the boy, John added, "And it takes its name from the most famous hunter in all of Kasskatchen history, Roderick the Wolf!"

John Summerfield had learned several of the Roderick tales. Roderick and the Golden Eagle. Roderick and the White Bear. Roderick and the Storm King. The very name was synonymous with Kasskatchen legend stories. Popular fireside tales, most containing instructive lessons for children and adults alike.

Aiming to keep the family on the business at hand, Emma had only opened her mouth to continue when Mia suddenly chimed in, "Roderick and the Shadow is my favorite." Then, looking between Seeker and Matriarch and seeing a certain kind of smile on Emma's lips, Mia became sheepish, "I didn't mean to interrupt."

"Roderick and the Shadow?" asked John. "Sounds eerie. Is it good?"

With a little nod, Emma gave Mia her blessing.

"The whole story?" Mia asked, somewhat confused.

"No, no," chuckling in the knowledge of a very long tale. "Only the gist for now, if you would."

Mia turned to John, "Well…in the story, Roderick pursues the rarest creature in all the forest. For many days and nights, through thickets and torrents…"

"…he chased after the beast," Cody jumped in excitedly. "Then at last, with his spear at the ready, he stood on the threshold of his greatest victory ever…for he had run down the most elusive creature in all of nature! The very shadow of the forest itself!"

"Cody!" Jessie chided. "You interrupted your cousin."

"And you jumped to the end of the story," Laureal scolded, echoing her mother's stern tone.

"Sorry," quipped the boy, glancing about in hope of a supportive look, of which there were none.

"What happened?" John asked, turning back to Mia, his curiosity piqued.

"Well, in the story, Roderick pursues his prey not for food or clothing but on account of its uniqueness. Its pelt alone was worth a kingdom. But more, if Roderick could eat of its flesh, he would gain magic power as promised to the hunter by a wood nymph. The nymph never appears to Roderick in plain view but beguiles him with its enchanting voice and eyes, gazing out from the openings of hollow logs, abandoned animal burrows, rocky overhangs, and shadowy thickets. Egged on by the nymph, Roderick's moment of truth comes when, having run his quarry down after a great chase, a ray of moonlight pierces the forest canopy like a spear thrown down from heaven to stick in the ground before him. In the shaft of moonlight, Roderick sees all the gifts that have already been placed in his possession by the hand of his Creator, and he spares the beast."

"What beast?" asked John.

"A black stag."

John's eyes went wide, "A black stag?" chuckling. "I've heard tales of white stags. But a black stag?" And laughing all the more, "There's no such thing...is there?" suddenly falling silent, glancing around the table.

"In a hunter's lifetime," Emma began, "it is doubtful he will ever see a white stag, the ghost of the forest. But a black stag, the shadow of the forest, is even more rare...far more rare. A hunter could live a dozen lifetimes and never see one, and yet they do exist. It is said that the hunter who eats the flesh of the shadow stag will know the secrets of the forest.

Henceforth, he will know the location of every burrow, nest, and den, every food cache, everything. No prey shall evade him. No predator shall overtake him. However, his newfound power comes at a terrible price. But let us get back to the business at hand.

"John, as you know, Roderick's Grounds is a well-known place. That is, every Kasskatchen knows of its existence same as they know the Roderick legends, but only a few have actually been there. This is because to get there a man must make a voyage through what is known as 'The Gauntlet of the North.' But again, you already know all of this. Except that now I am not speaking to your quest alone but to this family's quest to rebuild. For it certainly seems to me that our quests have come together, not as a coincidence, but by the work of the Great Spirit come down into these woods with all the heavens in tow. And, if as I believe, this is indeed the case, then his will is our destiny, and we need only keep putting one foot before the other in…"

Pausing, Emma cocked her head, "John, are you alright?"

His eyes addressing potent thoughts, John nevertheless nodded, "Yes, I'm fine."

"Are you sure, darling?" asked his wife. And leaning in to whisper, "Do you want to tell Grandma what you saw in the woods?"

John shook his head. Then turning to Emma, "I'm good."

"If there is something you need to tell us John, then by all means tell us. Otherwise, let us proceed, for if we are to succeed at what I propose, time is of the essence."

John, gazing at Emma, "There is nothing I need to tell, save that, so far, I'm all in."

"Good," said the Matriarch, "very good indeed!" And continuing with gravity, "As we all know, any man that makes it to Roderick's Grounds and back returns rich in the eyes of his fellow warriors and hunters. He earns the subtitle of 'Riddare äv Vatten.' It is a rite of passage achieved by only a handful. There are greater subtitles a man can earn. There are greater tests and rites of passage. But becoming a 'Knight of the Water' is highly valued, and it bodes well for a young warrior's future, that he add it to his resume. In this very house, going back through our long history, I can name many warriors that made the journey, including my own husband, Engel Emerson."

"Father ran the gauntlet to win Mother's heart," Jessie interceded with a touch of pride.

"And," Emma began with a wry smile, "to buy his way into the House of Emerson."

To clear up John's confusion, Emma took a moment to explain, "John, you know my husband made the journey. I told you that much. I did not tell you that his last name was Askelson. He changed it to Emerson, not because he had to but because he was an unknown and, back in those days, the Emerson name brought him instant recognition and respect throughout the realm." Emma shook her head even as she smiled in fond recollection, "Engel could be calculating. He was handsome, and good at getting his way with words and a smile, but not one to back down from a fight. A natural diplomat with the muscle to back it up."

Her expression shifting from fond recollection to grim reality, Emma continued, "Judging from the accounts of Engel and others, we can only imagine the Gauntlet of the North. I have no intention of entering it. Its existence, however, is pivotal to my plan. Surviving it requires many skills, including the expert handling of a canoe. Also, to get one through, a certain kind of genius is required that applies to the wild. And perhaps most important of all, natural toughness, not in size or strength but...grit.

"It is said that, on entering the gauntlet, a man might find himself paddling a lake calm as glass, its water reflecting such beauty as to be heaven come to earth. Then, without warning, he is plunged into deadly rapids and fights for his life. And if that were not bad enough, the portages are grueling. The forest through which they pass are haunted by packs of wolves that know no fear of men. The bears are highly territorial, highly aggressive, and enormous in size. And perhaps worst of all are the black clouds of mosquitoes, inescapable except when far out from shore.

"Many men turn back. A few simply vanish. But a handful make it each summer and gather at what is said to be the location of Roderick's famous camp. These men of Roderick are the best of the best, possessing the brawn, the brains, and the heart to get themselves there and back before winter comes and transforms the lakes and rivers into a frozen waste. They range in age from around 20 to 50. The young bucks, driven as they are, willing to risk all that they may build a resume and make something of themselves. And the mature bucks, already with big racks and little to prove, nevertheless taking on all comers. If we could be so fortunate as to choose from this pool of potential husbands, I believe we can rebuild the House of Emerson."

The family members exchanged looks of wonder, hope, excitement, and uncertainty. No doubt in their minds that Emma was going for broke, for to suggest the House of Emerson could once again realize its illustrious past was a great claim indeed!

"It is not a given that such men will possess the substance of good husbandry," the Matriarch warningly continued. "No doubt a few would fail miserably. A few will already be married. But the majority, I strongly suspect on the basis of my sixty-four years, will be the best in the realm.

"Now, to the crux of my plan: we know that these men use a stopover camp before entering the gauntlet, and when they return they also stop there to rest and regroup before continuing home. We also know that for some of our people the stopover camp has become a summer destination for hunting, fishing, and, most recently, a rendezvous for the making and trading of goods. And in its new capacity, the rendezvous has become rather popular since its inception seven years ago. But regardless, be it used as a stopover or rendezvous, it is known by one name, the Lake of the Swans. And it is there, before the campers come for the summer, that the men of which I speak will stop for only a short time early in the season, perhaps three or four days, in which they will make final preparations before entering the Gauntlet of the North."

Emma rose from the table and went to the hearth where she refilled her mug before turning to John, "The ancient land trail beyond our summer hunting grounds to the Lake of the Swans is not used anymore, not beyond the old crossing of the River Montreal where my mother and father drowned. We did send Cory across the river last summer, however, to check the trail. He reported it used only by animals and, although in need of work, was yet passable. At that time, we were looking for a new resource for trade among other things. We are old fashioned people and, with so many of our people adopting the ways of those that live in the land beyond the Five Seas, we were considering the summer rendezvous at the Lake of the Swans as an alternative."

Emma remained standing for her summation. "I propose we get to Lake of the Swans early, that we may have our 'fishing' nets ready when the finest bachelors in the world come though on their way to Roderick's Grounds. Young and old, we can invite them to sup with us in our camp. Indeed, if we can precede their arrival by some weeks, then we can build an impressive camp with which to welcome and assist them in their quest. And if presented with the opportunity, we will mend their clothes. We will show them our many skills. We will put our best foot forward, that they may evaluate us, and we will evaluate them. We will never implore but will be candid in telling why we came. We will speak from the heart about our beliefs. And when, as I believe the Spirit that speaks to us all will see to it, that the right men come forward with proposals of marriage...we will await their return from Roderick's Grounds," and in jest, she added, "when they are rich, respected, and worthy of membership in our family."

Around the table, the younger members broke into smiles and laughter, but not Jessie, for she understood what was coming.

"There is a catch," Emma added, losing her smile entirely, "To get there in time, we would have to leave here...now."

How quickly their smiles ran away from their faces, replaced by grave looks going round the table. To do what Emma proposed, the family would have to make a wilderness trek deep into winter's grip. They would, in a very real manner of speaking, have to run a gauntlet of their own. Even John was stunned, for it was one thing for him to travel alone in winter and something else entirely to travel with a family that included both the old and the very young.

"I know what you're thinking," said Emma, "but with John along, and with the great strength of his giant, we can make good time traveling north on the big river. On windy days we can use the trail in the trees along the river. We have the right gear and supplies. And when we reach our summer home, we can rest and regroup before continuing north up the River Montreal. From the old river crossing it is only three or four days more to the Lake of the Swans."

Fixing her eyes on the Seeker, the Matriarch continued, "John, my plan would greatly advance your plan. It would put your base camp even further north, closer to your objective. Better still, it would put you in contact with a rare handful of men that know the far north like no others."

Mia raised her voice, "It is very cold to be traveling with small children, especially when Noah and Sophie are too big for a papoose but too small to walk and keep up on their own." Her tone expressed the depth of her concern.

Sitting between the two, Jessie shared her cousin's apprehension, "Mia is right, Mother."

"She is, and that is why we would have the children ride on a sled, pulled by John's giant. And if necessary to keep them warm, we'll bundle a dog or two in with them. It wouldn't be the first time that was done."

"I have an idea," John put in, the wheels in his head turning. "Ellie's packsaddle, as you know, carries three packs on either side. Each pack is an oak chest made so that it can be taken off and carried on the back of a man. We can modify two of those chests into child seats for Noah and Sophie. They can sit side-by-side while riding on Ellie's back. And we can blanket them up in a way that traps Ellie's body heat to keep them warm."

"Ellie's gait is gentle," Laureal added, "She will not jostle the children."

John used his hands to help in his description, "You have seen how the packs fit in the packsaddle's frame, side by side, top to bottom, at an incline, with hinged lids like chests. We can make them into seats, slightly reclined and open at the top, with leg openings cut into the bottom of the lids, and opening on the sides for their arms if they so choose. That way we can set the children in and latch the modified doors like gates. The kids won't be able to fall out, but they won't be squished in either. Besides serving to protect their bodies from passing branches, their seats can be overlaid with Ellie's buffalo cloak like a tent to hold in her body heat. We can modify her cloak for that purpose. And while we're at it, we can add hooded openings, like on a coat so the children can see out. And of course, we would keep a close watch on them as we travel."

"Mia," said Emma, "we are going to vote on this. Not now, but tomorrow after we've had a chance to sleep on it. And you have the right to veto, in which case we will find another way to get the men we need."

Mia looked first to Emma, then to John, then back to Emma, "I vote to go."

"What about you, Mother?" asked Jessie.

"I can make the journey," somewhat offended by her daughter's concern. Then, setting her jaw as she sat, "I have plenty fight left in me."

"I vote to go!" Cody put in.

John turned to Laureal, his enthusiasm heightened, "Instead of giving our sleigh a wide body as planned, we can make narrow cross-members to join the two sides. Then we'd have a horse-drawn dogsled, narrow enough for river paths."

"I was going to ask you about that," Emma interjected.

Laureal turned to her grandmother, "Just this morning John said the snow depth is perfect," referring to the approximate six inches of snowfall presently on the ground.

"We can put our gear and provisions on the sled," John seamlessly added, "Ellie can pull it, and the children can ride in her pack saddle. One of us can ride on the back of the sled, the same as on a dog sled. And with less for us to carry on our persons, we should be able to cover a fair piece of ground each day."

Jessie gazed at her daughter and son-in-law. "What a wonderful thing your project has turned out to be! I'm so proud of you...both of you."

"Thanks, Mom. But like I said, we just thought it would be great fun." And turning to John, taking his hand under the table, "Now we see how the Great Spirit has been guiding our steps. All along, he's had our best interest at heart."

Chapter 15

Never before had the family left their winter home unoccupied, but there it stood, alone on its cliff above the snowy river. Laureal looked back one final time. The white roof of the longhouse, now barely visible behind gentle veils of falling snow, passed from sight.

Using the river as a highway, the family traveled north, walking in single file through a world covered in ice and snow. Not only the river, the trees, and the forest floor, but the tall grasses and shrubs that grew along the shores were bent and blanketed. Young evergreens stooped like old men under winter's white weight, the occasional patch of boulders lay transformed into abstract groups of moguls—a beautiful world to behold, a deadly world to anyone without the knowledge and skill to survive it. Beneath the family, the ice measured over a foot thick. Strong enough to support a 21st century delivery truck. Still, our travelers never forgot they were on a frozen river. For example, they kept to the inside track of every bend in the river not only because it was the shortest route but because the river's main channel naturally flowed to the outside of each bend and thus, by avoiding the main channel, the trekkers walked where the river was shallowest. If they did fall through, the river was unlikely to be over waist deep. Keeping a protective eye on them all, John Summerfield walked twenty paces behind and slightly off to one side. And keeping an eye on John, Laureal glanced back so often that scarcely twenty paces passed from one affirmation to the next.

Excluding John, the family column from back to front started with Laureal. Mia walked seven paces ahead of Laureal. Ahead of Mia, Emma rode on the sled platform just as one would ride on the back of a dog sled. Ellie pulled the sled. The twins rode in Ellie's packsaddle. Cody guided the beast with lead rope in hand, his main concern, as John had warned, was to make sure the giant didn't get directly behind him and step on his heel. Jessie walked ten paces out on point. And just ahead of her, Yike, Nemo, and Chewy walked like dogs do when outings begin, wagging their tails and tussling happily with one another.

The humans were clad head-to-toe in fur, and all were armed with spears and bows. The need for weaponry did not come from rival clans. Nor did it come from grizzly bears which were in hibernation. It came from wolves. Late winter was that time of year when wolves came together in packs to run down creatures weakened by long months of winter cold. As for wolves attacking humans, people living outside the protective insulation of modern technology could not afford to discount the danger. This we can know thanks in part to good record-keeping in pre-industrial Europe, which can also help us understand why wolves were once feared and hated even as we love them today. As recently as February 16, 1917, the New York Times reported that wolf attacks on wounded soldiers could not be stopped even with machine guns and hand grenades. In fact the attacks became so bad, the commanders of the opposing sides declared a temporary armistice, whereby the two sides joined forces to drive the wolves from the theater of battle. Not to be too hard on the wolves here, as they were almost certainly starving, themselves being victims of war. We can also assume that the men, having driven the wolves off, were then able to get back to the business of maiming and killing each other.

Thanks to good record keeping, we can also know that in the winter of 1437, after the residents of Paris (population 220,000) over-hunted the local deer and wild boar population, starving wolves began to enter the city through areas of wall in disrepair. At first it was one wolf pack, then more packs came in search of food. Soon, wolves were roaming the city, killing and eating three people a day! A fight for control of the city ensued. Finally, the citizens dragged slaughtered cattle through the streets, leaving blood trails to draw the wolves into an ambush at the center of town where the citizens threw up barricades to trap the feasting wolves. Trapped in a makeshift corral, the wolves were stoned and speared to death.

Today, in our 21st century, the largest subspecies of wolf is the Canadian Timber Wolf, and in particular those living in and around a 700,000 square mile area of wilderness known as the Mackenzie River Basin. These wolves average 175 pounds, with the largest ever recorded at 235 pounds. Moreover, their brains are 30 percent larger than domestic dogs. And larger where it counts, in the cerebral cortex, that part of the brain associated with thinking and planning.

Besides their impressive size and cunning intelligence, these wolves have a sense of smell 100 times greater than a human's. Their eyesight is twenty times sharper than ours. They have superior night vision. And uncanny though it be, their hearing is so acute, they can listen to their prey's heartbeat from ten feet away. They are impossible to hide from. And when they find their prey, each wolf can exert a bite force greater than a tiger or great white shark. With such force, they gang up and rip their prey apart. Each can gulp down more than twenty pounds of meat at one feasting.

Fortunately for those of us living comfortably outside the hard realities of nature, we will never run through the woods with a pack of ravenous wolves on our tail, or send our children walking miles to school through a countryside roamed by wolves. On the other hand, our hero and heroine were already on the periphery of the Mackenzie Valley wolf territory and walking deeper in with every step. That said, odds were highly unlikely that wolves would attack an armed group of humans. There was easier prey in the forest, though it should be noted that the long Indian summer had shortened the winter, resulting in fewer vulnerable animals for wolves to catch and eat. Nevertheless, the humans were armed to the teeth. And they had Ellie, a giant in the prime of her life with huge steel cleat shoes, a terrible force to reckon with. Additionally, the dogs, Yike, Nemo, and Chewy were big dogs with strong bonds of loyalty to the family. In the event of a wolf attack, they would fight to the death, and all three sported heavy leather collars specifically to protect their necks. They wore packs that would hinder them in a fight, but the packs could be quickly and easily removed.

While understanding how wolves in certain situations, for example, when they are starving, can be extremely dangerous to humans, it does not hurt to remember that somewhere in the not-so-distant past, wolves allied themselves with humans, which is how man got his best friend.

Wolves and thin ice duly considered, the real and present danger came from the unrelenting cold. The family could not run away from it, nor could they hide from it. And again, they were only going deeper into it. Thankfully the little river, with its banks nestled in dense forest, sheltered the family from the wrath of the north wind. Thus they traveled in relative calm even while old man winter occasionally threatened, blowing snow from boughs high above, sending snowy cascades down through the evergreens. The temperature was ten degrees, not bad for being warm-dressed and on the move. Snow fell steadily but not heavily.

Two miles into their journey, Laureal purposely dropped back to walk beside her groom, "You look so happy back here all by yourself."

"I am happy."

"Because you're finally going north?"

"Because of a fine-figured woman walking ahead of me."

"Oh, you liar!"

"No, truly!"

Playfully, Laureal gestured to her bulky furs, "And what figure could you possibly see with all this."

"The one that's underneath," and he grabbed her bottom.

"John!" Laureal shrieked, jumping away. Then animated, glaring with eyes wide, "You really are feeling good this morning!"

"Yes, I am."

"I'm feeling good too," coming back with such enthusiasm as to crash into his side, whereupon they got tangled up and, laughing, nearly fell together in the snow.

Having recovered, John spoke lowly, "Your grandmother is watching."

"Then be careful what you say and do sir," whispering back, "For I assure you, she has the eyes and ears of an eagle."

"Then you had better go back up there."

"Nah, I'll stay back here with you."

"No."

"Why not?"

"Because it's my duty to keep watch, and you're distracting me."

"Just pretend I'm not here."

"Yeah right, like that's going to work."

"John—" pleading musically.

"No." And nodding forward, "Go on. Get!"

"John Summerfield!" suddenly fire-eyed, 'don't you shoo me like a dog!"

"I'm not shooing you like a dog," his voice going high like that of a boy, "I'm shooing you because I have to."

"Laureal," came Emma's call.

Laureal gave John a pouty look. Then, obeying the Matriarch, she returned to the rear of the family column where looking back, she made a face to show her displeasure with him. It was only a game. As proof, before the passing of another mile, she smiled over her shoulder. And when she exaggeratedly sashayed, they both laughed.

At noon the party stopped long enough to pass out helpings of venison chunks that had been stored in the packsaddle where they would not freeze. Hard on the outside and soft on the inside, the cold chunks were previously seared and smoked in flames, then quickly cooled to keep the meat inside fresh and moist. Each chunk amounted to three or four bites. Also from the packsaddle, the family passed a leather water bag between them. John used an ice chisel to chop a hole in the ice so Ellie and the dogs could drink, and everyone laughed when Ellie lowered her nose and snorted like a dragon to frighten the dogs, letting them know who would be drinking first. Mia and Laureal took care of the twins. Jessie covertly checked on her mother. They all checked on one another, and, satisfied that all was well, the family proceeded with chunks of fresh venison in their purse-like pouches of leather, eating while they walked in daylight too brief and valuable to waste.

Frigid and lifeless as it seemed, the surrounding forest harbored an abundance of life. Even as snowfall covered the evidence, the river served as a record of animal activity that morning—an important source of information for the family. Many animals were in their dens but not in hibernation. They would be out and about. Bobcats, weasels, and wolverines were alive and well, albeit no tracks were to be seen that morning. Still, there were deer tracks, fox tracks, and even rabbit tracks where the shoreline was gentle. Red squirrels were snug in their nest with stashes of nuts stored below. Flying squirrels slept in nests holding up to fifty animals. Active in winter, they came out to fly at night. Plus there were always various bird tracks on the river. And finally, late that afternoon, when the family had gotten far from home, they encountered a single set of wolf tracks.

Immediately after seeing the tracks, the family rounded a bend to see the confluence of the two rivers. Just two hundred yards ahead, it appeared a semi-luminous opening at the far end of a forest hallway. One hundred yards nearer, and it appeared a natural motion picture in a large forest opening—a scene in which the big river appeared to crawl like a serpent, the result of blowing spindrift snaking this way and that across its frozen surface. Drawing closer still, the travelers heard the voice of the wind: an eerie whistling ever-changing in tone, rising and falling as if to give fair warning—

"Turn back! Turn back while you can!"

It was not a blizzard per se, but an average day on the big river where one had no protection from the north wind. It was not an unexpected sight or sound. And still, it drove home the reality before them.

Yet in the protection of the forest hallway, Jessie stopped and, while looking back at John, gestured to the bank of the little river. John then came forward while the tiny column stood at rest.

"We made good progress today," said he, obviously well pleased, handing his rifle to Jessie who had come back to meet him. Jessie then proceeded up the bank to have a look-see and, providing all was well, stand guard while the family negotiated the snowy bank.

Pausing only briefly, John took measure of the big river, its spectacle yet a safe distance away. Then, turning to the family, he pushed his hood back and smiled assuredly, "It'll be calm come dawn."

Emma looked to Laureal, "Dear, help your cousin take the twins out of the packsaddle, please."

Nodding, Laureal turned to do as tasked.

"You seem to be doing well," said John to Emma. He had been watching her more than the others.

Emma responded with a slang term she'd learned from John, "This ain't my first rodeo." It was not exactly the same as the 21st century term but a successor translated here for the reader.

"I saw how you divide your time between walking and riding."

"Yes, well, I'm glad you were watching." And with a coy grin, "Hopefully, I have taught you something you can use when you grow old."

Chuckling, "I believe you have."

Walking on, John went around the young ladies who were just then using a simple step stool to take the children down from the packsaddle. Then, coming before Cody, he asked, "How's our girl doing?"

"She's doing fine," stroking the giant's massive shoulder.

From the bank above, Jessie called down, "Looks good up here."

Surveying the bank with his eyes, John knew of an easier place to go up, a gentle shore leading to a grassy knoll. He and Laureal had been there once before. Still, the bank directly before him lay sheltered from the wind. "I'll take her up," turning and taking the lead rope from Cody's hand.

"I can do it, John."

"I know you can, Cody. And you will, but first, you and Ellie need to get more time working together."

Just then, Laureal and Mia came alongside, "Should we unhook the sled and remove her packsaddle?" Laureal had seen John take Ellie up moderate inclines before.

"No, I think we can manage this one." And turning to Emma, "If you would remain here with Cody and the twins, this won't take but a minute." Then turning back to Laureal and Mia, "I need you to steady the sled as I take Ellie up. Steady it from the rear corners. Do not get alongside it! That way, if it tries to tip over, you can drive against it with your leg strength to keep it upright, and if it tips anyway, you won't get caught beneath it."

"What should I do?" asked Cody.

"Load your bow and keep watch. Protect your grandmother and the twins. Between you and your mother, you can lay down a crossfire to protect them from any would-be predators."

John knew the chances of a predatory attack were slim to none. He also knew that, empty as a wilderness may seem, there were always eyes on the lookout—moving through the woods, searching for the vulnerable, the lame, the sick, the very young and old.

Leading the giant several paces to the base of the embankment, the horseman put one foot on the bank and spoke like it was all in a day's work, "Okay girl," extending his arm with lead rope in hand, he made a 'come-along-with-me' gesture, "let's go."

164

As the incline increased, Ellie began to rear and jump. Not rearing like in a 20ᵗʰ century cowboy movie but rearing just high enough to lift and throw her front hooves forward while driving with her powerful hindquarters, repeatedly launching herself in violent increments—

"Easy," came the voice of her master. "Easy," as chunks of snow and ice exploded from her hooves.

John fell hard against the snowy bank, sprang back up, scrambled mightily with arms and legs, and somehow managed to keep up with the giant's progress. Laureal and Mia drove hard with their legs to keep the sled upright until Ellie reached the top and jerked it away, whereupon the girls fell against the snow-covered bank.

Emma and the twins watched in awe from the river below. It was over in a matter of seconds. Ellie stood at the top, and save for the heaving of her ribcage and the clouds of steam that flowed from her dragon-like nostrils, it was obvious it hadn't been her first rodeo. Her packsaddle sat slightly off kilter. The sled was fine, being somewhat overbuilt, its cargo jostled but intact.

Stroking Ellie's neck, John spoke through huffs and puffs, "Good job, Ellie."

Jessie marveled at the power she'd just witnessed.

Laureal and Mia lie in the snow just shy of the top, laughing at it all.

Having brushed the snow from his pants and coat, John brought out a few pieces of rock candy made from honey and maple syrup. He gave one to Ellie. Then, looking to the river below, "Noah, Sophie, whoever gets up here first gets a piece of candy!"

The race was on! Noah took the lead, but Laureal, yet lying on the incline, grabbed him.

"Let me go!" cried the boy, just inches from the top. "Laureal! Let me go!"

Then came Sophie, crawling fast, trying to get past, but Laureal, having dug her boots into the snowy bank for support, caught her also, "I'm not letting either of you go," laughing, "not until you agree to share the candy."

"Deal!" Noah cried. And set free, both scrambled to the top like fur-clad monkeys.

The children got their candy while Mia and Laureal helped Emma up the steepest part of the bank. Cody came up last. Jessie remained on guard until all were together at the top.

Fortunately for the family, the confluence, being an excellent fishing and hunting spot, had a permanent winter campsite. Sheltered from the north wind by dense forest, it came complete with a substantial lean-to. The family would not sleep in the lean-to but would use it as a cook kitchen and dining room.

Being off trail for the day, John returned leadership of the clan to Emma, "With your permission ma'am, I will unpack our horse and tend to her needs."

"Yes, and thank you, John. And you too, Ellie," said the Matriarch, running her hand over the giant's shoulder like a boulder worth its weight in gold.

Emma next turned to the others, "Cody, take the shovel and clear snow from our campsite. Laureal, build a fire, but before you gather wood, remove the dog packs, take the dogs with you, and feed them only when you've finished. Jessie and Mia, put the tent up." Then, turning to the twins, "Noah, help Cody clear snow until Laureal brings an armload of firewood. Then, while she's out gathering more, you can break off and sort the sticks in one pile and twigs in another. Sophie, you and I are going to make supper."

While John unhooked the sled and removed Ellie's pack-saddle, the giant grazed by uncovering grass with front hooves like shovels. And being that the grass was plentiful there, John left Ellie to graze on the edge of camp, which suited Ellie just fine. Next, John took a spear-like icebreaker from the sled. He also took a basket so expertly woven that water could not leak from it. The basket, being deeper than broad, had a shape like

166

that indispensable marvel of the 21ˢᵗ century: the 5-gallon plastic bucket.

Gathering firewood with her dogs, Laureal paused momentarily to watch her husband chopping ice on the little river below. And he, spying her from the corner of his eye, suddenly thrust his arm into the air, holding the spear-like ice chisel up in a gesture of victory.

Laureal laughed, then, falling silent, gazed on him fondly.

Having gathered a good many pine boughs, Jessie and Mia laid them out where Cody had cleared the snow. Then, taking a set of willow poles and a family-sized tent made of caribou hides from the sled, they set about erecting their shelter for the night. Beneath the tent, the thick layer of pine boughs would serve as padding for comfortable sleeping and help insulate the family's temporary abode from the frozen ground.

Soon, the scent of hot stew filled the lean-to: a wonderful-smelling blend of game meat, tubers, wild grains, and forest herbs.

So it was that as the temperature dropped in waning light, the family sat around a crackling campfire, warming themselves with hot food and that relaxed kind of conversation that comes at the end of a successful workday.

As they spoke, Emma cast her eyes beyond the edge of camp where Ellie grazed with natural efficiency; using her hooves to uncover the grass, eating it, then taking another slow calculating step, uncovering more grass, and so on—

"John, I must say, the value of your horse giant is not a thing to be measured."

"Think if we all had horses, Grandma." Laureal's eyes, although tired, were nonetheless filled with optimism, "We could ride into a whole new dimension."

"I rather like our dimension as it is," smiling, "but Ellie is wonderful."

Mia gazed at the giant with admiration, "I have never known a more majestic animal."

"I have never met anyone who did not fall in love with Ellie," John affirmed. And turning to watch his mare, "A good horse really does take a man into a new dimension, or a woman, or a family, or for that matter, a nation."

Before them, the giant had lifted her head to full height. Grass hung from her mouth. Her big white face stood out in the twilight. Her ears perked straight as pikes, she gazed back at the family. Then, after a moment of silent observation, she returned to grazing.

"I know Ellie so well. And still, she's something of a mystery to me."

"And how would that be, John?" asked Jessie

"Well," John began, "Ellie does not see us as members of a herd like our dogs see us as members of a pack. Whereas our dogs show extreme attachment to us, Ellie sees herself as autonomous. She is independent of us, and yet, she would work herself to death for us, and from what I've seen, it would not be dumb animal stupidity. And therein is the first half of the mystery. The other half has to do with her split personality. One side for humans, one side for horses. With other horses, her first response is to subdue all comers. If she is not restrained by a human, she will go directly to any horse in her scope, and if it does not submit to her at once, she will attack it. As soon as it submits, she will accept it as one of her subjects. But if it does not submit, she will dispatch it, viciously, as if its life were nothing to her."

"John—" Jessie uttered in horror.

Mia eyed John from within her fox-lined hood, "John, I have trusted you with the lives of my children!"

"And they are perfectly safe!" on the defensive, realizing he had upset them. "I swear it! Ellie is the opposite with us. That's the mystery!"

After a brief silence, John softened his tone, "Mia, they really are safe...or at least a lot safer than they would be without Ellie. Truly, time and time again on the trail I have witnessed her behavior. And you will too. And yes, she is a highly trained horse, but there is a limit to what humans can take credit for or explain regarding the behavior of a horse. And this leaves the mystery unanswered. It's an enigma that I wouldn't have thought twice about had I not come through the wild with her. But I did come through the wild with her. And I think I have to take it for what it is. She holds herself apart, and she could easily set herself free, and yet, she gives us her all."

Emma turned to look at the giant. Tired from pulling the sled, Ellie stood motionless, teetering on sleep. A glimmer in her heavy eyes somehow seemed more than only a reflection from the fire—

"I think I understand, John. There is, as you say, a mystery. And then again, there is not."

"Oh really? And how could that be?"

"Well, while we cannot understand everything about Ellie's nature, we can simply know what we have seen with our own eyes. Ellie, is a gift."

"Amen!" exclaimed Jessie. And looking around the fire, she nodded to the giant, "Just look at her."

In silence they gazed upon the beast. Standing on the edge of camp, Ellie had drifted off to sleep.

"Now look at us," Jessie continued. "We could have fallen by the wayside. We did not. We drew together and made a new beginning. And Ellie had a big part in it, lest we forget how she labored dragging those heavy logs…and now, our sled."

The firelight burned hot in Jessie's emerald eyes, "The Great Spirit is working through Ellie to help us along because, He has a plan for us!"

Laureal felt trails of goosebumps running up her arms, "Grandmother, we have gone through that door you spoke of."

"We certainly have," said the Matriarch, her face illuminated by the flames.

Chapter 16

Laureal awoke to John's voice whispering in her ear, "Laureal...sweetheart."

Opening her eyes, she saw his smile.

"Did you sleep well?" he asked.

"Yes," groggily, "did you?"

"Yes."

"I was worried because you were on the end where it might be cold."

"I wasn't cold," giving her a little kiss.

"Really?"

"Yes." And sitting up, "Time to rise and shine."

At the opposite end of the tent, Jessie poked her head out from under the covers. Then, still wrapped in covers but leaning forward, she reached just past her feet and grasped her caribou coat and trousers before disappearing back under the covers. Unseen, she put on her inner layer of caribou clothing with fur facing her skin. Then emerging, she donned her outer caribou coat and trousers with fur facing out. Her double layer of arctic attire made her look bulky, like a bear, though it would keep her warm no matter how cold the outside temperature. In fact, the inner layer would soon become too warm and, with the exception of brutally cold days, she would have to exchange it for doeskins.

Emma poked her head out, and Mia too.

"Good morning."

"Good morning."

Like a sleeping clutch of quail, the family had spent a restful night in their dome-shaped tent despite the winter cold. The tent, constructed of willow poles covered in high-grade caribou skins, was weathertight and strong enough to hold up under heavy snowfall. Presently, the light of dawn filtered in through a translucent window made from bear intestine sewn in above the tent door. The door consisted of a heavy flap made from grizzly bear hide. Beneath the occupants, an underlayer of unscraped bull caribou hides lay covered by a top layer of young bull fall caribou hides. Atop that, the family's blankets were of cow caribou hides, specially tanned for softness and warmth. The family had also brought a few possum blankets. The continent's only marsupials were not native to the north but had migrated there over the millennia, and that was good because possum fur was not only extremely soft and warm but possessed therapeutic qualities that helped to prevent winter skin conditions like eczema. Of course, the Kasskatchens did not understand the science, but they had discovered the benefit. Finally, as previously mentioned, a mat of spruce boughs between the tent and the ground served both as padding and insulation against the cold.

First out of the tent and into the dawn, John slung bow and quiver onto his back and set out on a quick scout of the immediate area. He went on foot, which allowed Ellie to graze at camp. And he left his air rifle behind with the family, that they may have it to protect themselves in an emergency.

Laureal got a fire going, gathered more wood, and gave the dogs passed-over chunks of game meat. Jessie and Mia packed up the tent and its contents. Cody used the snow shovel to expose an area of thick grass the size of a driveway above the shoreline and, by such means, Ellie did not have to spend time shoveling with her feet but simply ate one mouthful after another. Emma and the twins prepared breakfast in the lean-to, into which the cook fire radiated its warmth.

John returned to camp without any game which was not a problem at that time, "Nothing much moving around out there."

"Everything is holed up in this cold," said Cody.

"Did you see any wolves?" Mia asked, suspecting, as did they all, that wolves had been watching since late the day before. Not watching constantly but rather monitoring as wolves do. Wolves monitor the different animals and animal groups in their territory to see if there are any old, young, or injured animals to be had for dinner. By such means, wolves keep tabs and howl to signal what they find. And the family had heard a wolf howling the night before.

"Only a single set of tracks," John replied. And casually he added, "Probably a scout that checked us out and moved on."

Emma sat stirring the breakfast porridge, "They're more worried about us than we are about them." Then, turning a warning eye on the children, "That isn't to say they wouldn't take the opportunity if presented, for they most certainly would!"

Nodding in agreement, John eyed the twins, "Wolves love to eat children, and, they doubly love to eat twins!"

"John!" Laureal chided.

Seating himself next to his wife, John widened his eyes at Noah and Sophie while making low growling sounds.

Laureal poked her fingers sharply into John's ribs but to no avail, his heavy clothing having blunted her effort. Responding, John lifted his hands and, holding his fingers like claws, made fake growls as he pretended to maul Laureal playfully, supposedly like a wolf eating a child. Not having it, Laureal fended him off. Then, eying him with disdain, she rejected him when he tried to give her a peck on the cheek.

Noah and Sophie, having been distracted by Emma, passed out wooden bowls and spoons, after which the family took turns ladling steaming helpings of porridge.

"Oh! This is good!"

"It certainly is!"

"Thank you," said Emma, herself well pleased with it.

Fueled with hot porridge, John and Cody fetched Ellie, checked her hooves, loaded her packsaddle, and led her down the river bank. Simultaneously, the women cleaned dishes and packed cooking gear away. The family then lowered the sled down the bank.

Mia and Laureal loaded the twins into their seats, then secured Ellie's buffalo cloak. Mia and Emma had previously

172

modified the cloak to keep the children warm while simultaneously keeping the giant from overheating.

John secured Ellie to her sled and, with everything set to go, took a moment to speak with his wooly companion, "Little girl, if need be, we'll make you a pulling collar," stroking her neck, visually examining the breast strap he had modified for her, its purpose to spread the load evenly across her massive chest as she pulled the sled.

Next, John handed the lead rope to Cody, then turned to the twins, "How are you guys doing?" he asked, looking up at them.

"We're good," said Noah, sitting side by side with his sister, each of them looking out from hooded openings sewn into Ellie's buffalo cloak like a pair of gables on the side of a hut. Around each of the hooded openings, a fox fur ruff would function to disrupt the wind and help to create a calm boundary around their little faces.

"Sophie, are you good?"

"Yes."

"Are you sure? You weren't so sure when we started out yesterday."

"I'm okay now."

"Do you think that maybe riding on Ellie could be fun?"

"Not for her," quipped Noah, "she's a scaredy-cat."

"No I'm not!" Sophie rebutted.

"Be nice to your sister," warned Mia, looking sternly at Noah. Then glancing at John, she rolled her eyes with a smile.

"Mom, are you ready?" asked Jessie, standing at the lead with spear in hand.

"We're ready!" Laureal replied, as impatient as she was enthusiastic.

"Lead on," ordered the Matriarch.

And they were off! But no more had they gotten underway when Emma called out to her daughter, "Jessie."

"Yes," turning to look even as she continued on.

"Stay sharp!"

Jessie understood her mother's warning all too well. The source of it had been permanently etched into her mind. The terrible suddenness with which disaster could strike, be it a flash flood, a shootout, or a fall through the ice. Thin spots in the ice, though far and few between, existed, and her job was to keep a sharp eye and ear out for danger.

Out in front of Jessie, Yike and Nemo who, unlike Chewy were young dogs, wagged their tails and tussled like pups even as they wore backpacks. Apparently oblivious to danger, they loved to travel and they knew the way.

A short distance behind Jessie, Mia had taken her new position for travel on the big river. Walking with a coil of rope on her shoulder and spear in hand, her job on the big river would be to act as a second pair of eyes and ears before the truly heavy part of the column came along, being that of the giant, bearing the children, pulling the sled, accompanied front and back by Cody and Emma.

At the tail end of the column, John fell back a short distance to give himself a broader view of the family and their surroundings. To further advantage his field of view, he walked to one side, the same as he had the day before.

Emerging from the protection of the forest, the family exited the little river to enter the confluence. From there the big river appeared a winter superhighway of fresh fallen snow. It stretched north to the horizon beneath a low cloud ceiling sharply defined by countless sagging bulges in near-perfect symmetry. It was familiar territory. It was their territory, and still, it seemed like entering a different world. Meanwhile and unbeknownst to them, a young she-wolf watched from the land point of the confluence.

Hidden in the shadow of a black spruce, the wolf had looped around them to approach from downwind because the air, even in the morning calm, had a nearly indiscernible movement from north to south. Her position on a shelf predominantly of balsam firs served to mask her own scent in the strong piney odor of the firs. The dogs never knew of her.

174

John, however, ever scanning his surroundings, spotted her as he walked. And the wolf, knowing he had spotted her, did not run and hide but simply stared back.

Only a few days before, Summerfield would have shot any wolf for the sake of protecting the family, especially the children. Presently entering the wolf's home turf and thinking they posed no serious threat, John saw no need to kill the animal which would only diminish his limited supply of ammunition. Still, he kept an eye on it and, seeing it look away, he followed its gaze to the distant shore where a second wolf stood in a stand of aspens. A big alpha male, it possessed a natural aura that spoke to strength and power. John could see and sense it even at a distance.

The two counterparts stared dead on at one another, neither showing an ounce of fear.

Suddenly, Laureal appeared like a young doe that springs from the bushes, "What are you looking at?"

John jolted, then sighed in relief, "Damn...you scared me."

"John! Don't curse!" Then turning towards the aspens, "What were you looking at?"

"A wolf," and seeing that the wolf had vanished, he turned to the land point only to see that the other wolf had also vanished. He then turned to Laureal, "What are you doing back here?"

"Saying 'hi' to you," happily as they set to walking. "We've scarcely gotten two minutes alone since we left home."

"The day is yet young."

"Yes, it is! And here we are, walking side by side."

"You should be up there," nodding to the tiny column.

"John, I want to stay back here with you."

"No, you can't," shaking his head. "You're distracting me."

"Then stop looking at me, and I'll help you keep watch."

"No."

"John—," pleadingly.

In silence they walked on until, at last, picking up her pace, Laureal began towards the others.

"Laureal," John called after her. And getting no reply, "Sweetheart, I'm sorry."

"That's alright John," said Laureal, not bothering to look back. "I know when I'm not wanted."

"It's not like that and you know it!"

Laureal made no reply.

Exasperated, John glanced to the sky as though to ask why things couldn't just be easy. But in truth, the low cloud blanket kept the temperature from dropping below zero. No wind blew. No snow fell. And the snow on the river lie dry, powdery, and easy to walk through. John Summerfield could scarcely have asked for better conditions.

John picked up his pace and, coming alongside his wife, "If you really want to…you can walk with me."

Walking along, Laureal glanced at John with hurt eyes.

Doing his best to think things through, John tried again, "Laureal, I'd like you to come back and walk with me, provided we do not allow ourselves to get distracted from watching over the family."

"Do you promise to be nice?"

"Yes, I promise."

"Four eyes are better than two," mustering a little smile.

"Not in this case," said Emma.

"Grandmother," Laureal uttered, taken by surprise, as was John, for the old woman had closed on them with surprising speed.

"Come with me," said Emma.

"But Grandma, I…

"Do not 'but grandma' me!" came the sharp retort. "Granddaughter, what if there was an emergency and the twins needed unloading at once? Where would you be? You'd be in the wrong place! That's where you'd be!"

Laureal, somewhat shaken, "I'm sorry, Grandmother."

"Apology accepted. Now go back to your station."

With a long-faced glance at John, Laureal picked up her pace and returned to her place in the column.

Emma remained briefly walking with John, "My granddaughter is a wonderful young woman, and while I am immensely proud of her, I also know she is somewhat spoiled and, highly persuasive. She gets it from her mother, the persuasive part, that is. Her grandfather and father are to blame for spoiling her." Then, having walked a bit further in silence, Emma turned her piercing eyes on John, "Sir, you are our guard out here on the trail…we must be able to depend on you."

"I apologize," contritely, "I let my guard down."

"Apology accepted." Then, walking a bit further, "Don't be afraid to say 'no' to your wife," and she went on ahead to her place at the back of the sled.

Chapter 17

Stepping through the snow behind Laureal, John slipped his hands under her arms and around her front to cover her tummy, "How we doing in there?"

"We're good!" pulling her hood back, craning to beam up at him.

Jessie stood at the lead with spear in hand, "Are you ready, Mom?"

"Why are you always asking me if I'm ready?" half annoyed, standing on the sled platform. "Next time, ask someone else."

"We're ready!" Laureal announced.

So began the family's third day of travel. Like the day before, dawn broke calmly on the big river with wind expected by midday. Unlike the day before, a freezing fog had set in overnight. Temperatures were slightly warmer, hovering around eighteen degrees Fahrenheit.

Step by step, the family advanced north through the frozen pall. They went with scarcely a word between, and with every mile, the forest slowly changed, becoming less deciduous and more coniferous, although birch, poplar, and aspen remained prevalent along the river. Presently on the near shore, a grove of poplars stood frosted in white and would have been a lovely sight on another day in Laureal's eyes, but not on this day. Not in a murky soup that fractured what little light got through the clouds, blurring her surroundings into shapeless forms until even the evergreens seemed to lose their color.

"Grandma," said Laureal, breaking the silence.

"Yes, dear."

"I'm sorry about yesterday."

Turning to look behind, Emma pushed her hood to one side, that she may smile on the girl, "Yesterday's behind us dear, and so are our mistakes."

Laureal followed along and, after a few more steps, "It would be nice to see the sun."

"It certainly would," stepping off the sled, that she may walk for a spell.

The tracks left by the beast and sled made a path wide enough for two, and so it was that grandmother and granddaughter walked side by side, sharing an occasional glance, both comfortable in the silence. The younger, being disciplined by the unspoken will of the older, refrained from needless words in the knowledge that all things had their place and, in the formula of human wellbeing, most days would leave enough energy for words to play their part around the campfire.

"Momma," came Sophie's little voice. Then louder and more urgent than before, "Momma!"

Mia stepped aside and waited for Cody to pass. Then, walking alongside the giant, "What is it?"

"I need to potty."

"As soon as we get in the woods, we'll stop and have something to eat. Can you wait till then?"

"I need to go now," pleadingly.

"Grandma," Laureal said lowly, "I need to go too."

Emma stepped out to look around the giant, "Cody, we need to stop." Then looking past her grandson, she called to her daughter, "Jessie."

Noah protested as Mia and Laureal took him down from the packsaddle, "I don't need to go."

"You're going to go anyway," Mia stated matter-of-factly.

Cody held the giant while Laureal and Mia brought the twins down. A few feet away, his grandmother stood looking to the south, and as she turned back to the way ahead, he could not help but notice her troubled expression—

"Grandma, what's wrong?"

"I'm not sure," looking into the gloom, "I can't see a thing in this mess."

Just then, John came forward, "What's up?"

"I'm not sure, except that we're taking a pit stop," replied Emma. "Girls to the right side of the giant, boys to the left.

And boys, please keep your backs turned until I give the all-clear."

As they set out to do what countless families had once ritualized in 20th century interstate rest stops across the continent, John paused and turned to the ladies, "Hey Noah, where are you going?"

"With my mommy," Noah replied.

John, who had started his own training at Noah's age, motioned to the boy with his hand, "You're with Cody and I."

Noah looked to his mother.

"It's okay," Mia reassured. And nodding towards the men, "You go with them."

A short time later, while Laureal and Mia loaded the twins into the packsaddle, Emma turned to her daughter, "Jessie, find us a place to exit the river."

"Mom…we have a few hours yet before the wind comes up."

"Perhaps, but, I just have a feeling," glancing into the murk before returning her eyes to her daughter, "we need to get off this river."

If only a little puzzled, Jessie returned to the point position intent on finding an exit along the east shore. Unfortunately, no exit existed due to the continuity of the cutbank, a vertical wall of tangled earth and roots topped with curling snow cornices.

A half mile further, the dirt cutbank gave way to a lime-stone shelf. Itself part of an ancient seabed, the stone shelf afforded no exit either. At last, the shoreline transitioned to a pitch of approximately thirty degrees and while it appeared quite challenging due to a wall of foliage weighted with snow, Jessie soon spotted what she sought: a narrow opening marked by various animal tracks.

"Can the giant get through that?" asked Mia, coming up behind.

"Let's hope so," Jessie replied. Then, using her spear to knock snow from limbs, she entered the tunnel-like opening and, having disappeared into the forest, quickly found what she sought—

"Laureal, Mia," Jessie called from the river trail above, "bring your hatchets."

Taking advantage of the stop, John chopped a hole in the ice only to watch as Ellie refused to drink. He knew there was nothing wrong with the water. Ellie was simply being a horse. The dogs at least took the opportunity to fill up.

Laureal and Mia returned, and having knocked much snow loose while chopping branches, they stopped to brush snow from one another's clothes. Jessie also emerged and joined them.

"John," Emma began, "would you be so kind as to take the twins down?"

"Yes, ma'am."

Very much alive with blood pumping from chopping ice, John walked around the other side of the giant. "Who wants to fly like a bird?" smiling up at Noah and Sophie.

"I do!" cried Noah.

"Well alright then," using his long reach to throw the buffalo cloak up and back. Then, as he lifted Sophie out and over his head in an arch, he spoke like a boxing ring announcer that welcomes a princess to a grand ball, "And—it's ladiiieeesss first!"

Returning for Noah, John lifted the boy high and flew him about exaggeratedly above his head, "There he goes! Up in the sky! Soaring like an eagle! Swoosh! Swoosh!"

No more had Noah got his feet on the ground than he went charging about, "Woohoo! Woohoo!"

Mia spun and scolded him, "I told you never to run around the horse!"

"It's my fault," John interceded, coming forward, running his mitt along Ellie's side to comfort her. Then, kneeling down to Noah's level, "You're excused this time, little buddy, but remember, what your mother said is true. Never run around a horse."

With the twins turned over to the women, John went to have a look at the deer trail. Upon his return, he spoke to Cody, "Do you want to take Ellie up?"

"Yes," as certain as he was anxious.

"All right then. It's not very steep, so she shouldn't lurch as long as you don't allow her to get in a hurry. Otherwise, she might get away from you. But that's not going to happen because she's already gotten used to following you, and she's going to watch to see how you lead out. All you need do is be calm but firm. Make eye contact and say, *'Okay Ellie, we're going to take this nice and easy.'* Then lead out with your arm the way I showed you. Remember, she reads your body as much as your words. Move steadily and deliberately. If you slip, that's okay. She's seen me slip and fall a dozen times. If she starts to get ahead of you, say *'Easy girl.'* If she doesn't respond, bark and turn into her. Your will must be bigger than hers!"

Breaking into a smile, John added, "I know she's big, and it's a lot to do, but don't worry, I'll be right there with you."

John then turned to Jessie, "If you would trade me places," redundantly offering his rifle.

Jessie accepted the weapon, "John…take care of my little boy!"

The Seeker opened his mouth to speak but he never got the chance …

"Mom—!" Cody musically protested.

"Just be careful," looking on with motherly concern before turning to take her position as rear guard.

Emma took the twins a safe distance to the rear. Her intent was simple, stay out of harm's way should the giant become claustrophobic and try to back out of the natural chute.

Laureal, on her way to take up her position with Mia at the back of the sled, ran her mitten along the sleeve of John's coat as she passed. He alone could see into her hood, and seeing the look in her eyes, he uttered a few words under his breath which in turn caused Laureal to come back directly—

"What did you say?" eying him with suspicion.

182

John leaned forward and whispered into her hood, "I said, you're such a naughty girl."

"You misinterpret me, sir."

"Oh really? How so?"

"I saw you with Noah and Sophie, and Cody too, and I was thinking what a wonderful father you will be."

Taken off guard, John could find no words even as his eyes spoke volumes.

"But if I'm a bad girl…then lucky for you," and she spun away.

"As I recall, you don't believe in luck," John called after her.

"Can we please just get on with it!" Cody protested.

All went smoothly, and the humans proceeded on the river path, gnawing chunks of pemmican as they went. Jessie walked at the point followed by Cody leading Ellie. The twins rode in the packsaddle. Emma both rode on the back of the sled and walked behind depending on the condition of the path. Laureal and Mia manned the rear corners to make certain the sled remained upright. John brought up the rear as always.

Not a half mile further had they progressed when a sudden gust swayed the treetops, dislodging snow on the uppermost boughs, sending it down in a chain reaction from branch to branch to become waterfalls of dry white powder. It poured down all around, ending in billows of snow dust rolling like fog over the ground until, settling and dissipating, the forest once again stood dead still.

"Looks like you were right, Grandmother."

No more had Laureal spoken than the sled ran up on a branch buried beneath the snow, whereupon the young woman responded at once, driving with her legs to counter the imbalance.

Walking behind the sled, Emma's eyes spoke to the intuition that dogged her. The frozen fog was dissipating but that was to be expected. There had been no shift in wind direction. No big change in air temperature. Nothing to warn of the warm air mass that had pushed up from the south. And yet the warm air was there, directly above them at 30,000 feet. It had collided with the cold arctic air and rolled atop as a great atmospheric wave, pulling air down from the north, growing rapidly even as it lay hidden like a crouching tiger.

"Cody, we need to stop."

"What is it, Grandma?"

"I'm not sure, dear," shaking her head. Then, turning to the Seeker, "John."

"Yes, ma'am."

"I hate to ask, but would you please find a place where you can access the river? Go out on the ice where you can get an unobstructed view and see if you can see anything in the sky to the south."

So cryptic was Emma's countenance, John asked no question but immediately passed the rifle to Laureal and started down the path in the direction they'd come.

"Jessie," Emma called.

Jessie came around the giant, "What's the matter, Mom?"

"I fear a storm has found us."

Jessie followed her mother's eyes to the canopy where, lo and behold, the highest boughs began to sway. No more had Jessie seen the warning than a flock of wobblers swept across the path and into the deeper wood where they took shelter under a fir.

"Let us proceed slowly," said the Matriarch, "that we do not get too far ahead of John," her intent that they not become separated in the event of a whiteout.

Back on point, Jessie acted at her mother's behest and kept an eye out for a naturally sheltered campsite. Meanwhile at the rear, Laureal glanced back continually in anticipation of John's return, and catching sight of him, she knew something was terribly wrong—

"Grandma! John is coming!"

At a full run, John slowed only to avoid spooking his horse. Then approaching with some semblance of calm, he came breathing heavily, "A storm approaches from the south. It draws in the gloom and rides high into the sky like a wave."

"What color is it?"

"Black as night."

"John," Laureal uttered, her tone a mix of dread and disbelief.

The Seeker turned to the Matriarch, his eyes burning with intent, "With your permission, I will lead us into the deeper forest."

"We haven't a moment to waste."

John turned to Jessie, "If you would trade me places?"

Laureal passed the rifle to her mother who in turn took the rear guard position.

Taking point, John signaled for Cody to bring Ellie along as he left the path and headed away from the river and into the shelter of the forest.

Laureal and Mia had to work hard, for although the ground lay mostly flat, dead branches buried beneath the snow caused the sled to rock side to side, a few being large enough to cause a rollover if not counteracted. Emma did not ride but walked behind. The dogs walked directly behind Emma, having been ordered to do so. And Jessie brought up the rear.

Ahead of the giant, John turned to Cody, "Follow my tracks. Come along as quickly as you can, but not too fast. You do not want to wreck the sled!"

John then vanished, trotting into the trees. On the heels of his departure, the north wind rushed through the treetops, dislodging the snow that clung there, causing it to pour down from bough to bough, cascading like waterfalls to obliterate the Seeker's tracks.

"John!" called Cody.

"I'm here," came his voice, already at some distance.

"Where? I've lost your tacks!"

A second gust stronger than before sent down a series of snow bombs—one a direct hit on Ellie—her giant head, like a bug-eyed wraith, was all to be seen above billows of snow dust.

Ellie lunged to the left in an attempt to bolt, only to crash into a tree branch and break it. The children shrieked as the giant swung right and left. Trapped as though in a cage by the dense wood, she pulled Cody side to side like a rag doll—

"WHOA!" holding to the rope for all his worth, himself covered in snow dust, "WHOA! WHOA!"

"MOMMY!" howled the twins, their little faces visible at last, caked in white powder, "MOMMY!"

"I'M HERE!" cried Mia, who, having run up on the right, found herself locked in a panicky dance with the giant.

"Mia, wait!" Cody implored, unable to bring Ellie under control.

Mia appeared to make things worse when in reality she inadvertently blocked the giant's only escape path. Hemmed in elsewhere by the forest, Ellie had only stopped for fear of running over Mia. And still the giant danced! The twins shrieked! And the boy cried, "WHOA! WHOA!"

Emma came forward on a beeline, snatched the lead rope between boy and beast, and without shouting came face-to-face with Ellie, *"Settle down!"*

Ellie stammered, her great head taken aback as far as her massive neck could hold it. Her huge eyes, bulging with fright, remained fixed on the Matriarch.

Emma glanced at the girls, "Bring them out!" she ordered, her tone urgent in the knowledge that, due to the giant's warmth, the powdery snow that had gotten into every crack and crevice would quickly melt, in which case the children would become perilously wet.

Ellie remained in place even as she fussed about with nervous little steps which, due to her great size, caused no small difficulty. Still, the girls managed to get the twins out and down. They then removed the children's coats and pants, brushed away snow from inner layers, and quickly bundled the children back up again.

Jessie remained at her post on her mother's orders. Orders based on knowledge, or at least on knowledge of an account as old and far-reaching as the trail itself: A half-dozen wolves had rushed in on an unsuspecting family with perfect timing and, amid the chaos, vanished just as quickly with a small child.

Much to everyone's relief, John came trotting back, "What's happened?"

"We got dumped on," Cody replied, brushing snow dust from his coat and pants.

John swept snow from Ellie's neck and shoulder while stepping around her side where, seeing the empty child seats filled with white powder, he took them down and quickly cleaned them out before returning them to the packsaddle.

The wind and snow continued to rise as Mia and Laureal returned the twins to their seats. At the same time, John reported to Emma and Jessie—

"A grove of cedars lies 200 paces ahead," referring to eastern red cedars—stalwart little trees, dense and bushy enough to deny passage to strong winds. Originally planted by the thousands as windbreaks around northern homesteads of the 20th century, the invasive species had found its niche in the forest.

"We must go…now," John enjoined.

"It's here," Emma uttered, gazing north with dreadful foreboding. "We've no time left."

"We have time," John rebutted, but no more had he spoken than a mighty gust gathered up snow from forest floor and tree limbs alike. Filled with ice crystals, it blasted their eyes as it rushed through the trees. Ice-cold air pulled down from the north—like an undertow in a powerful surf, it blasted them again and again. And so it was, the storm fell upon them as would a ravenous lion spring on its prey.

Scarcely able to see, John put his hand on Cody's shoulder and shouted into his hood, "I'll lead Ellie…you help your grandmother!" Then with a wave of his arm and shoulder, he motioned to the others, "THIS WAY!"

Falling back on instinct, Ellie tried to hunker down, that she might weather the storm. Having none of it, John pulled her lead and barked over the wind, "Come on, Ellie! COME ON, DAMMIT!" Then, as he lifted his arm to bring the lead rope down on her tail like a whip, she jumped into a spirited walk.

Deadly as their fortune had turned, the family was not entirely at the storm's mercy. Stout and in the prime of life, John plowed at the point with resolute determination. And because they headed east, the windows of Ellie's buffalo cloak faced south, protecting the twins from the slicing wind. Laureal and Mia, also in the prime of life, kept the sled upright. Grandmother and grandson followed directly behind, holding to one another on the path cut by beast and sled. Jessie brought up the rear and, albeit in a blurry whiteout, could easily see the giant's form at the front of the column. The dogs, woolly creatures of hardy northern origins, stayed near as loyalty and instinct demanded.

Exposed as they were, they wouldn't last long without shelter, and presently Laureal got the worst of it. Her position at the sled's back corner on the south side meant she could not turn from the gales as she struggled to keep the rig upright. To make matters worse, every time a buried obstacle tossed the sled her way, the wind caught the rig like a sail and threatened to roll it over on her. Stubbornly she pushed back, fighting with every atom of her being, driving with her legs, at times going to her knees but quickly scrambling up again. The fierce wind bit her cheeks. Driving ice crystals stung her eyes. Her lashes became heavily crusted with snow and ice until, alas, semi-blinded, she scarcely heard Mia's shouts above the deafening roar—

"Trade me places!" Mia cried, her voice lost to the storm until she came across the runners and, getting hold of Laureal, screamed, "TRADE ME PLACES!"

Taking her turn in the grinder so to speak, Mia drove against the gales with powerful legs, her lower center of gravity being advantageous.

For all their stalwart nature, our little band of hunter-gatherers were run through with fear, so dreadful had their situation become.

"Lord, help us!" cried Emma, her voice drowned out, save that the one mortal soul close enough to hear took it to heart and doubled down on helping his grandmother along.

Old but not so old as to require the boy's assistance, Emma clutched Cody all the more dearly to her side.

Meanwhile at the front, the cedar grove came into view; a shadow in a whiteout, robust trees standing like soldiers in a phalanx, holding their ground in the withering chaos of battle. Eastern red cedars, about fifteen feet in height and semi-conical in form, their thick bushy bases began on the ground, leaving no room for the enemy to come cutting even from underneath.

As John closed the yards, the grove rose before him like a great hedge. A few lone cedars appeared as outliers, behind which stood a nearly impenetrable wall.

With no other choice, the Seeker pressed into the snow-laden branches. As he did, he pulled at the lead and his faithful giant followed. Instinctually, the twins curled up in their boxes beneath the buffalo cloak, shielding themselves as best they could from the branches that dragged against the giant's sides. It was a situation tolerable only because the snow that came in on them did not come with the momentum of before.

Directly behind the giant, Laureal and Mia stumbled and struggled mightily against the dragging branches but were at least spared from icy blankets of snow because man and beast had already knocked most of it away.

Emma and Cody came next. *"Thank you, Lord,"* said the Matriarch, for no more had she and Cody pressed in ten feet than the wind fell off. Just behind them, Jessie made sure the elder dog Chewy got in. She then turned for a final look back before slipping between the boughs.

Pressing through to better fortune, the travelers found an opening near the heart of the grove. Roughly twenty-five feet at its widest point, the tiny clearing had been invaded when a large black spruce fell into the grove years before. Only the skeleton of the spruce remained, engulfed by the cedars except for that part of it that lay in the clear.

As a campsite it didn't look like much, what with broken bits and pieces of spruce branches cluttering its makeup. Still, the family recognized it for what it was—their mortal salvation.

John parallel parked Ellie along the inside wall of the opening with the twins facing inward, "You did good, girl," brushing snow from Ellie's face. "You can sleep now. Sleep all you want."

Even with sharp ears, Ellie didn't hear John so much as she read his lips and facial expression, such was the roar of the wind in the trees. She understood he was commending her. She knew they had reached safety.

"Oh John," Laureal cried, coming forward, shocked to see him caked from head to toe.

Turning to her, he gripped her by the shoulders and, if only for a moment, they held one another's gaze, hood to hood, exchanging such a look as to share their entire lives in a single glance.

"Look after the twins," was all he said, his voice raised only that she might hear, for although the cedars blocked the wind, the storm yet roared in a great continuous blast, thundering throughout the forest. And even in that protected enclave, snow-filled drafts came dancing like specters over the hedge-like walls.

Jessie came forward, a special tool in hand, taken from the sled; she used it to paddle and comb the heaviest snow quickly from John. She then stripped off his coat, shaking and beating it out while John and Laureal hurriedly brushed off his underlayers. The twins underwent a similar process, after which they were re-bundled and returned to the packsaddle, their place of warmth and safety for the time being.

"John," Emma called from just five feet away. And getting his attention, she made a sweeping motion with her hand as she shouted, "Can you clear this area?"

The Seeker nodded and gave a thumbs-up with his mitt. Then, fetching ax from sled, he set to chopping dead branches from the fallen spruce, carving out an area for their tent.

Emma turned to Cody, shouting as she must, "Clear the ground, pile the dead wood here!" Then addressing Jessie, "Take Laureal and chop out a den," pointing to cedars on the south side of the opening.

Jessie and Laureal used spears to knock snow from boughs, then forced their way between the branches and set to sawing and chopping with bucksaw and hatchets. The work was down low, tight, and difficult but became easier as they opened up a natural den. John finished his ax work and joined Cody in clearing the ground and piling firewood. Mia and Emma gathered boughs from where Laureal and Jessie had tossed them, and continuing together with help from John and Cody, they trimmed and laid out the boughs and erected the tent on top, its door facing the opening to the den that had been carved from the hedge, a supply of firewood piled to one side.

Ellie hunkered down and slept in a standing stupor. The dogs curled up in the snow like huskies. The humans entered their den by crouching under the boughs and crawling onto a carpet of caribou blankets. Old blankets, not fit for the tent, dog beds almost but still thicker than thin, lain atop fir boughs. Humble it was, and yet, what with such a crazy change of fortune, great feelings of relief and hope prevailed as everyone gathered in like a huddle of football players, the wind playing the role of a roaring crowd—

"I could not have foreseen this," Emma began with enthusiasm, "but here we are with the opportunity for a hot meal." And continuing somewhat loudly as necessary, "Cody, bring some firewood in. Laureal, get a small cook fire going here," pointing to the center of the floor. "Jessie and Mia, retrieve what we need from the sled to make an early supper.

John, if you would please, cut several large pieces of wood to ring our fire and lay your grill across. Laureal and Mia, once the fire is going, bring the twins in. Okay, now let's all join hands. And Jessie, if you would please?"

With heads bowed, Jessie lifted her voice so that all may hear heartfelt words of thanks.

Thanks to good preparations, Laureal did not have to search for fire fodder in a blizzard but instead used from emergency stores. Soon a fire was going, and not long after, hot porridge warmed their cores. Close around their little fire, they sat in their makeshift den. Stray snowflakes, no bigger than gnats, floated about, having filtered down from above. The small cook fire didn't produce much heat, but hot porridge and, most importantly, the quality of their winter armor went a long way in keeping the family alive.

"How did you find this place?" Cody asked, looking at John.

"I just stumbled on it."

"One does not stumble on a place like this with only hours to live," Mia countered, gazing at the horseman before lowering her eye to the children gathered close at her sides. Then returning her eyes to John, "The hand of God brought you here."

"Could be, I suppose." And moving his eyes to the twins, "So what was it like being buried in an avalanche?"

"What's an avalanche?" asked Noah, his fur-lined face a picture of puzzlement.

"An avalanche," with eyes growing wide, "is when a whole bunch of snow falls off the side of a mountain, or a tree in this case, and it buries you alive!"

"It was terrible!" Sophie exclaimed, her eyes also growing large.

"And freezing cold!" Noah added.

"You weren't completely buried," Mia interjected.

192

"And thank goodness they weren't," nodding in exaggeration, his gaze fixed on the twins, "Just think, we may never have found you!"

"Oh good grief!" cried Cody. "There wasn't that much snow, although, it was terrible."

Happy to be alive they were! And with nothing more to do, Emma called it a day even though daylight remained. Before entering the tent, they used a long paddle with a comb-like edge, helping one another to beat and comb any remaining snow and ice from fur coats, trousers, and boots, which could then be removed just inside the tent door.

In they went one at a time, each removing their outer clothes and, while still in their underlayers, crawling under caribou blankets. The storm roared as if the world would end and, oddly perhaps, as they closed their eyes, their dry tent and warm beds never felt better.

Chapter 18

Dawn arrived in drab gray monotone, and still, the white snowfall gave testimony to nature's beauty. John was first out of the tent as always. And seeing him stand up, Ellie lifted her head and nickered.

"Good morning, Ellie."

Grazing what grass she could dig, the queen of horses wore a white mantel of snow over her dark fur coat.

Day five would be one of slow but steady travel, bland, gray, and non-eventful. The added snow depth did not warrant snowshoes. Snowshoes were cumbersome, ate up loads of human energy, and were to be avoided except when truly necessary. And they were almost never necessary on the river because the afternoon wind swept the ice daily, limiting snow cover to several inches, except in places along the shores where drifts accumulated. Presently, light snow fell off and on but the wind, having exhausted itself the day before, came late, and even then, never packed a punch. Not a pretty day but a decent day for progress, especially when compared to the day before, especially in the knowledge that some blizzards last a day, and some last three or four.

Late the following morning, the sun appeared through a small gap in the clouds, and as the cloud blanket continued to fracture, John assumed the afternoon wind would bring clear skies even as it forced the family to leave the river.

To gain the forest trail, Jessie kept an eye out for a friendly exit in an otherwise hostile environment. Walking at the front of the column, her thought process was that of a natural accountant, one whose goal was to make the most of the river before the wind came and then pay as little tax as possible while gaining the forest trail. She had not been looking long when, from the ice under her feet, a strange sound like a tap on an otherworldly drum froze her in place—

"Stop!" lifting her hand to signal a halt.

Cautiously taking another step, Jessie once again heard the warning—a haunting drumbeat followed by a series of growls traveling up and down the way.

Oblivious to the danger, Yike and Nemo came back to encourage her onward, "Go away! Go away!"

Stepping quickly from the sled, Emma called out, "Yike, Nemo...come! Come!"

While Emma leashed Yike and Nemo behind the sled with Chewy, Mia tossed a length of rope to Jessie, and John came forward from the back.

"You're our rear guard," said John, handing his rifle to Laureal, scarcely missing a step on his way to the front.

"Be careful."

"Will do," speaking over his shoulder while proceeding to the front where he stopped a stone's toss shy of Jessie's position, "Thin ice, huh?"

"Yes."

Standing halfway between Jessie and Ellie, John turned to Mia, "Let's get the belay hooked up."

Knowing the drill, Mia fed the rope through the belay that had been permanently secured to Ellie's breast strap. She then took up the slack.

John then motioned for Jessie to step towards him.

Carefully, Jessie took a step, then froze in place as the ice weakened under her weight.

John grimaced as the ice cracked, "If you fall through, I know at least one thing that will happen real fast."

"What would that be?" her voice filled with dread.

"We'll have you bundled up in front of a fire before you know it."

"Oh, John!" letting out a nervous laugh.

John encouraged Jessie to proceed, and with each step, the creaking and groaning diminished until, at last, she reached the safety of stable ice.

"We'll go around it," said John, looking at Jessie and the others, unaware that a hot spring (not common to the region but not unheard of either) had opened up on the river bottom. And because the spring happened to come up in a large eddy, the warm water was not carried away directly but rose to rotate in a wide circle below the frozen surface.

Stepping to the sled, John had only taken out the ice chisel when the small voice of a child asked, "Are we going to fall through the ice?"

"No, we are not," turning to Sophie.

"Are you sure?" peering from her fury dormer like a little bird.

"Yes, I'm certain," standing with ice chisel in hand.

"How can you be certain?"

"Well…I tell ya what. You watch what I do, and then you will know."

And Sophie could watch because her seat, along with Noah's, faced the forest trail on the east side of the river, the side John planned to take around the thin ice. She needed only to do a little craning, which she did at once, intensely focused as John returned to the front.

"Be careful," said Jessie, looking on while John tied a quick-release knot around his waist.

John smiled as he took the chisel from her hands, "Stay fifteen paces behind me."

As John proceeded, Cody brought Ellie along fifty feet behind. Mia managed the slack via the belay, and Jessie managed the rope between.

Walking to the right and wide of where Jessie had been, John intended to pass on the side closest to the river trail when once again the ice sounded off in protest. Baffled that the ice could be thin in such a large area, he glanced back and shook his head as if to say, *This is odd.*

Laureal watched as snow disturbed by John's boots snaked away in a ghostly finger of spindrift. One small finger, like a little snake that runs away and quickly vanishes. A telltale warning, the afternoon winds were coming.

Lifting the ice chisel, John struck the ice once, twice, and again, raising the tool to strike a third time, he paused in surprise as traces of water appeared. With only a few more chops, he produced a football-sized hole.

It would have been surprising to see only three inches of ice, but there John stood on scarcely two inches—thick enough to support him but only just barely. A more cautious scout may have backed away. Instead, John probed to gauge the river's depth with his chisel. Then, setting his chisel aside, he turned to Jessie, "Toss me your spear."

The spear shaft extended John's reach several feet and still he was unable to find the bottom. He did not know the river bed lay in the shape of a cauldron. The water that flowed beneath the ice fell into the cauldron and swirled in an eddy warmed by a hot spring. Knowing that deep water should mean deep ice, John was momentarily caught up in wonder. He was yet to withdraw the spear when Jessie suddenly cried out—

"JOHN! YOU'RE SINKING!"

Glancing around himself, the Seeker saw the snow darkening like a shadow. It could mean only one thing, the ice sheet was sagging under his weight, forcing water up out of the hole where the snow quickly absorbed it like a sponge.

Rising up, John spread his feet to distribute his weight. Then looking to Jessie, he tossed her the spear, then the chisel. The idea being to remove any chance of losing critically important tools.

Hoping for the same luck as Jessie, John's first step produced a low drumbeat which, if not for several inches of snow cover, would have been louder and all the more alarming. Another careful step and another drumbeat, accompanied by low groans running out in a radius.

"John."

"Yeah," looking to his mother-in-law.

"If you fall through…we really will have you wrapped up and before a fire in no time."

"Thank you, Jessie," standing perfectly still, the ice around him groaning, the shadow of wet snow spreading.

Her heart in her throat, Laureal wanted to run to John's aid but Jessie, Mia, and Cody were doing that, and she'd have the devil to pay if she abandoned her post.

No matter how unlikely, Summerfield wondered if the family had blundered onto a field of thin ice. In fact they had, and in his mind's eye, be it normal or paranormal, he saw them falling through, and the vision of it struck him like a punch in the gut—

"Tie off my belay!" he suddenly shouted, his voice filled with urgency, "Take the twins down. Unhook the sled and drag it back the way we came!"

They gazed at him, their expressions a mixture of confusion and uncertainty.

"Go!" he shouted, "Go now!"

Laureal leapt into action. Passing the air rifle to Emma, she worked fast. Jessie, Mia, and Cody joined in. A knot was tied on the belay. The twins were brought down. The sled was disconnected. And as they worked, no one asked why perhaps because John's outburst had been completely and utterly removed from his normal character.

At John's behest, Emma, Cody, and the twins backtracked up the river. At the same time, Laureal, Jessie, and Mia discovered just how badly the sled could hang up when pulled backward because the sled's builders, being young and inexperienced, had not built it to be pulled backward.

While they struggled, John tried another step only to have the ice under his feet warn so sternly of disaster, he scarcely dared to move.

"This isn't working," and jumping to the front of the sled, Laureal tugged sideways on the runners, "We have to turn it around first!"

Jessie and Mia joined in, tugging mightily but despite their powerful legs, the sled's runners only dug in.

Realizing that Ellie had to be moved out of the way, Laureal got hold of the giant's lead rope but had only led her several steps forward when John shouted, "Don't take her any farther!"

"Okay!" somewhat on the defensive, rushing back to the sled where, having made enough room to get past the giant's tail end, she, her mother, and cousin pulled for all their worth.

Having retreated eighty paces with Cody and the twins, Emma took the rifle back which she had only just given to her grandson, "Go and help them."

Cody took off at once, running as fast as he could.

"Is John going to fall through the ice?" Sophie asked, clutching Emma's pant leg.

"Let us pray not, but if he does, we know what to do." And placing a hand on the child, she comforted her even while worriedly watching the struggle unfold. She wanted to go and help but she could not leave the twins on their own, as the woods were home to watchful eyes, ever searching for an easy meal.

Having turned the sled around, Jessie, Mia, Laureal, and Cody struggled to tow it back the way they'd come.

Pulling for all his worth, Cody looked at Yike, Nemo, and Chewy, still tied to the back of the sled, coming along behind, wagging their tails in confusion. "Mom," looking to his mother, "can we use the dogs?"

"We certainly can!" suddenly looking as though she should bop herself in the forehead.

Hodgepodge though it be, the dog's backpack harnesses became pulling harnesses, and the sled team of humans and canines from bloodlines naturally inclined to pull began to make headway. Then, with less than half the distance remaining to reach Emma, Laureal suddenly broke off and dashed away.

With the sled out of the way and the family moved off to safety, John had only begun backing Ellie with verbal commands, taking the slack out of the rope when he saw Laureal coming on at a full run. "Laureal, stop! Stop!"

As close as she dared, Laureal looked on in horror. John stood in a large area of wet snow. She could see it darkening as the river came up out of the hole.

"John, if you fall through, hold on to the rope…I'll back Ellie for you."

"Forget about that!" And gesturing towards the shore, "Go over there!"

Seemingly defiant, Laureal remained where she was. A few seconds of hesitation, it seemed like forever while fingers of spindrift appeared and disappeared in the rising wind.

"Laureal," John implored, "if Ellie falls through, the ice between her and I could break up."

Laureal glanced back at Ellie.

"Laureal!"

"Yes," turning back to John.

"You have to get out from between us!"

"Will she pull you out without anyone to manage her?"

"Yes," and gesturing towards the safety of shore, "Please! Go over there!"

Reluctantly, Laureal moved towards the shoreline.

John then turned his attention back to Ellie, "Back girl, back."

As the mare took a step back, John took a step forward, and as he did, the ice sank so much under his weight, as to give way any second.

Eighty yards upriver, Emma knew exactly what must be done. A fire had to be built quickly. It would not be the first time she had saved a family member who had fallen into a frozen river. Thus, she visually scoured the shoreline, looking for access to the forest no matter how difficult. Her eyes were no longer those of a young woman, and still, she had gained an intuition that could give one the impression of perfect vision. And just then, gazing into the shadowy wood, she felt a warning voice rise within her.

"Mommy! Mommy!" cried the twins, "Mommy!" running to Mia as she, Jessie, Cody, and the dogs came towing the sled like beasts of burden.

"I'll go and help them," said Cody, spinning away towards John and Laureal.

"Wait!" Emma ordered, and stepping to the boy, knowing his sharp eyes made him a good shot, she handed him the rifle, "We have trouble," nodding to the woods.

Following his grandmother's gaze, Cody saw two, then three, and finally four large wolves in the trees along the shore. They were not hiding but simply watching from the shadows. Unfortunately, a snow-filled gust pelted Cody's eyes like frozen sand. Then, as his blurred vision cleared—

"Where'd they go?"

Meanwhile downriver, Laureal turned her face to the sky, "Please, Lord, don't let him fall through."

"Back girl," said John to Ellie, taking another step and sinking until, feeling the weakness of the ice under his feet, he looked at the growing slush pond around himself and knew his chances of escape had slipped away.

Eighty yards away, Emma took a spear from the sled, "Make no mistake, they know we're in trouble, and they know we have small children."

Spear in hand, Jessie scanned the woods while Mia took a tomahawk from the sled and stuffed it into her belt.

"We have to take the shoreline," said Emma. We'll leave the sled here for now. Stay close together and keep the children between us. We have John's rifle, and we have our weapons. We've got to get a fire going, a big fire. John's life may soon depend on it."

"Fire will keep the wolves at bay," Cody added, aiming the rifle into the woods, searching for a target as they went forward together.

Nearing the shore, Emma took another look downriver where, to her horror, she saw the figure of her granddaughter not ten paces from the shoreline, standing alone with her back to the shadowy forest.

"LAUREAL!" Emma called out.

Focused on the dilemma before her, Laureal did not hear her grandmother's voice in the wind.

"LAUREAL!" they called. "LAUREAL!"

Hearing their shouts at last, Laureal turned to see them waving their arms. Unable to make out their words above the wind, she looked on in confusion.

"She can't hear us," said Emma, and going down to her knees, she set to unstrapping Yike's pack. Jessie and Mia followed her lead and at once the dogs were free of their backpacks and harnesses, leaving nothing except their heavy leather collars.

"Sic' em Yike!" Emma ordered, "Sic' em!"

Reading the Matriarch's gesture, the big alpha dog bolted downriver with Nemo and Chewy close behind.

With the last of the ice giving way, John lifted his eyes to tell his wife he was going down. Instead, he cried out, "LAUREAL, BEHIND YOU!"

Laureal's turned to see the shadows coming through the trees. Timberwolves, two in the lead and five more just behind. They crashed through snow laden undergrowth and leapt down the steep riverbank with blistering speed.

Stumbling backward in shock and horror, Laureal turned and ran for the open river.

With a spinning leap, Ellie bolted in panic and John, seeing as much, held tight to the rope and, as it snapped taught, he leaped for all his worth.

Catapulted forward literally as the ice beneath him fell way, how John did not break through the ice on landing his next step cannot be known, save that his weight, no longer a strong downward force, meant the ice held just enough, allowing him to take one more flying leap as Ellie put on a burst of speed.

Every atom of strength she possessed, Laureal poured into saving herself. A flood of adrenaline energized long strong legs and, if only she hadn't been encumbered by heavy furs, she would have accelerated like track star.

Out of the blue, Yike, Nemo, and Chewy crashed into the wolfpack's flank. Vicious fights erupted in which the dogs were unfortunately disadvantaged against the superior size, strength, and intelligence of the wolves.

The lead wolves remained on Laureal's tail, three of them, one of which veered towards John who came at an angle, charging headlong with knife in hand. The wolf aptly dodged John and then tried a swift attack from behind only to have John spin like a cat and nick its face with his blade, surprising the beast and causing it to take pause. John scarcely broke stride but continued to spin around and charge straight for the alpha male—

"YOU SON OF A BITCH!" bearing down to force the alpha off his attack just moments before it caught Laureal from behind.

"OH JOHN!" as the wolves encircled them, her voice a crazy mix of terror and relief.

"Use your bow as a club," putting his back against hers, knowing it was their best defense. But Summerfield wasn't thinking of defense. His mind didn't work that way. Charged with adrenaline, he had his favorite weapon in hand and, importantly, he had years and years of training with it. He also had his bow and quiver of arrows, although so fast had the attack come upon them, there'd been no time, no opportunity, no way to string an arrow in close-quarters combat, and the wolves were just that close.

Baring large fangs, the wolves juked with terrifying speed as they aimed to land a devastating bite. Hunger drove them to abandon their usual strategy of cautious bluffing meant to panic their prey, to separate and cause it to run, whereupon it could be chased to exhaustion and eaten alive.

"Keep your back to mine," John barked over his shoulder. "Don't let them drive us apart."

Again and again the wolves tried to land a bite even as they jumped and juked to avoid blade and bow. It was not a bluff meant to separate the young couple. Rather, it was desperation driven by starvation.

"John?" speaking over her shoulder, her voice high and breaking only to suddenly scream out as she swung her bow, striking at incoming jaws.

"Don't take your eyes off them! Not even for a moment!"

No more had John spoken than the alpha male leapt on him. Colliding head-on, man and beast bounced off one another like a pair of fighting rams. The big wolf just did dodge John's blade, and John just did dodge the wolf's fangs.

Husband and wife kept back-to-back as the wolves pressed their attack—pressed for an opening to land a crippling bite.

Thinking of Laureal's knife, John knew it to be fantastically sharp. Flint is five hundred times sharper than the finest steel scalpel according to the AMA. In fact, having used her blade on occasion, John had been astonished by it even as Laureal saw it as nothing more than normal in her world.

"Laureal," he began, the rhythm of his speech bouncing with the movement of the wolves, "I have to throw my knife. When I do, I'm going to lose it. And I'm going to need your knife to kill the next one before they can regroup. Leave your knife in its sheath so we can make a safe pass. And whatever happens, keep your back to mine."

"Are you ready?" John asked.

"John…please, don't let them get me."

"I won't." And in his next breath, "Are you ready?"

"Ready," her voice filled with fear and yet, resolved.

John flipped his big steel knife and caught it by its blade. He did it in one quick snap without the need to look. By such means, he did not avert his eyes and give opportunity to the wolves as they juked and circled. Then, at the ready, the right moment came at once, and John threw his blade. It penetrated to its hilt, just behind the shoulder as the beast jumped to avoid it too late. Mortally wounded, the unfortunate wolf turned and bolted for shore.

"Your knife," said John, and no more had Laureal pressed it into his palm than he drew it from its sheath and lunged for the alpha male. But the beast jumped away in a state of confusion and uncertainty. The strongest of his offspring, the prince of the pack, had just turned tail and run. Leaving a trail of blood, it attempted to climb the bank only to tumble to the bottom where it lay motionless.

"Come on!" barked the Seeker, his dark eyes like cold steel, his flint blade at the ready.

The alpha turned and ran for the forest with the rest of the pack breaking off the attack and following his lead. Laureal shouted for Yike and Nemo to heel. She did not see Chewy lying motionless in the snow. The attack, which hadn't lasted but a minute, was over.

Laureal let out a great sigh as John wrapped her up in his arms. Cheek to cheek, their fur hoods long since fallen back, the lovers scarcely felt the wind and cold in the aftermath of their intense exertion.

"You okay?" he asked.

"Yeah," breathlessly. "Are you?"

"Yes," his chest heaving. Then, pulling back just enough to look into her eyes, he broke into a smile.

High as a kite on adrenaline, Laureal smiled back, and John again pulled her close.

Alas, opening her eyes to look over John's shoulder, Laureal saw her little brother down on his knees beside Chewy, the oldest of their three dogs, the one they had grown up with—

"Oh no!"

Crying, the boy looked up as John and Laureal approached, "I wanted to shoot but I couldn't get a clear shot."

Laureal knelt and embraced her brother while John checked for signs of life. Then, sure that Chewy was dead, John spoke with certainty, "Cody, with them tangled up, and the snow thrown up in this wind…there was too much risk. You could have hit one of the dogs, or one of us. Instead, you did the right thing and pulled up."

"They double-teamed him," wept the boy.

John put his hand on Cody's shoulder, "Chewy gave his life so that we could live. And from now on, every time we remember him, we will be better for it because we will be reminded of what true honor is."

John Summerfield was not old enough for wisdom but had been mentored by old warriors who passed on simple sets of codes. The Seeker ran his hand over his wife's shoulder as he stood up to acknowledge Emma and the family on the approach. They were keeping close, protecting the children, moving as a unit with spears at the ready. Meanwhile, out on the river and well away from danger, Ellie trotted two and fro, throwing her head and snorting.

"How we doing?" asked John.

"We're okay," replied Jessie. *"What about you?"*

"We're alright," John replied, "except…we lost Chewy."

Emma turned to her grandchildren, yet down in the snow with the lifeless dog. Many times she had watched them as kids, frolicking with the big happy pup. She had only taken a step in their direction when a sudden windblast forced her to the immediate reality and, shielding her face, she turned back to John, "We need to get off this river."

John nodded in agreement, "I'll get the horse and meet you at the sled."

"John."

"Yes," turning back.

Emma glanced over to the broken ice, "Is it possible to put Chewy in the river? I don't want to just leave him there, and I don't want you to take any unnecessary risks, but could you use a tent pole or something to push Chewy across the ice and into the water?"

The Matriarch understood that putting dead animals into a river was unhealthy business, but it was Chewy, it was winter, the family was in a fix, and they did not drink from the big river anyway, not to mention their animals were immune.

"A tent pole will flex too much," Mia interjected, thinking of the difficulty they'd experienced while trying to pull the sled backward. She knew that when they tried to push the carcass, the snow would pile up ahead of it.

"I could chop a hole in the ice right here," John began, "but it might be quicker and safer to lash a pair of tent poles side-by-side." And glancing at Mia, he added, "Then we can push him in, and we can use a rope for safety."

While John went to fetch Ellie, Emma turned to her grandchildren, "Kids, I am so sorry!"

Laureal stood up and hugged her grandmother.

"Chewy, old friend, we're going to miss you," said Emma, and feeling her granddaughter shudder, she patted and spoke softly, "Now, now, Chewy had a good long life, and no dog ever died with more honor."

Still holding Laureal, Emma could not help but notice the dead wolf. She knew time was of the essence. They needed to get off the river. And still, such a beautiful pelt would be recognized by all as a symbol of a hunter's prowess and, by extension, a family's status. Thus for the sake of rebuilding the family, she pulled back to look into Laureal's eyes, "Dear, are you up to taking that wolf's coat?"

"Would you like me to, Grandma?" wiping her eyes, her tone uncertain even as she read her grandmother's look.

"If you're up to it?"

Glancing at the wolf, Laureal turned back to her grandmother, "I'm up to it."

"Very well. Work fast but keep your focus. Take Cody with you. Before you begin, drag the carcass away from the shoreline. Bring it over here. From here, Cody can stand guard over us all."

"Are we going to put the wolf in the river with Chewy?"

The Matriarch nodded in affirmation, "Chewy and the wolf died honorably, fighting for the sake of their own."

With her grandchildren off to task, Emma joined Jessie and Mia. John came, and a conference began among the four: the Seeker with his horse, the savage women with spears in hand, and a pair of small children clinging about their legs, seeking shelter in the rising wind.

"It will be very cold tonight," Emma said gravely, glancing at the clearing sky. "This wind may not die down until late, if at all. We need a well-sheltered campsite, one we can defend."

"Agreed," said John. "The likelihood of a second attack will depend on how we fare."

Searching her memory, the Matriarch spoke her thoughts aloud, "A flat below the south face of an abandoned cutbank would be ideal, but I cannot recall any such place, at least nothing we could reach before nightfall."

"There would be shelter in the Nith," Jessie offered, referring to the ruin of Saskatoon, which the family had planned to pass that very afternoon.

A Nith, as John understood it, was a ruin, and entering one was taboo. In the entire territory of the Kasskatchen people only a handful of ruins survived. There was the ruin of Regina, the ruin of Prince Albert, Saskatoon, and the largest being the ruin of Winnipeg. All were seen as dwellings of a bygone race that had come to no good end. Emma, and folks like her that lived out on the frontier, believed Niths to be haunted by the spirits of the damned. And that being the case, Emma gazed at her daughter in disbelief—

"Have you lost your mind?" recovering from the initial shock.

"I do not see how we have a choice," Jessie rebutted.

Looking from one family member to the next, John felt himself once again facing a patch of thin ice albeit of a different nature. Nevertheless, he offered his two cents, "As you all know, I have taken shelter in such places. I have even explored them."

"You are more fortunate than you know," stated Emma. "The Great Spirit who made you, Himself having a plan for you, has obviously seen to your protection. We, on the other hand, know of the evil, and therefore, we must not test our God."

"I have taken shelter in a Nith," Jessie rejoined.

"Certainly you have not!"

"I have...long ago."

"Where?"

"It was in the summer. Myself and three friends. We snuck out and spent the night on a dare," referring to the ruin of Prince Albert, located in their northern hunting grounds.

Within her hood, Emma searched her memory and it all came clear. The summer her daughter turned sixteen. A lanky, strong-made boy, just as handsome as they came. All of seventeen, cocky and a real daredevil among youths. Jessie had fallen head-over-heels for him. And for the next two years, they were ever seeking one another's company.

"Harley Sanders," Emma said like it could be no other.

Jessie made no reply but John saw a distant sadness in her eyes even as the corners of her mouth turned up ever so slightly.

Shaking her head, Emma lowered her eyes.

"I know, Mother. I could have brought a taint upon our family. A stigma from which we may never have recovered. And for that I am sorry."

Stung and astounded, "Thank God this has remained a secret."

"Yes Mother, thank God. But isn't that just it? If the One who gives us freewill found it in his heart to protect a pair of wayward kids, then would he not also protect us? Did he not open a door for us, in spite of ourselves? And since we stepped through it, has he not delivered us, twice now? And in light of that, could it even be an accident that the shelter of the Nith lies so near?"

At that moment, a powerful gust struck them like a swat to their bottoms, leaving them to exchange potent looks.

"Mommy, I'm cold," came a little voice.

"We have to move," Mia asserted, looking first to Emma, then to John who responded at once—

"Return the children to the packsaddle," looking to Mia and Jessie. Then turning to Emma, "If you could sort and lay out the rope for me, please." And lastly, calling out, "Cody, go to the sled. Get two tent poles, lash them together, and bring them here."

The river had awakened like a sleeping serpent. Beautiful but deadly, its body writhed with the illusion of spindrift. Under passing clouds, it shifted in and out of shadow while Laureal, down on her knees beside the wolf carcass, huddled with her back to the wind, that she might gather up her warmth within her caribou armor. Then, seeing John on the approach, she stood to meet him.

"Is this not the most beautiful you've ever seen?" holding the wolf pelt for him to see, her expression solemn.

John nodded but spoke no words. Moving quickly, concerned about getting off the river as he should be, he bent to take the carcass away only to pause, whereupon leaving it lie, he rose and embraced his wife.

"I'm going to make you a vest," she said as they held tight.

John pulled back just enough to look into Laureal's eyes. He'd come so close to losing her, but there she was, safe in his arms.

Chapter 19

With the bodies of the canines put in the river, the family retreated to where they'd left the sled. They did not hook up the sled due to the steep incline of the riverbank, and for the same reason, Ellie's packsaddle was removed. John then went about the hairy business of riding Ellie up the bank. A rope was then used to pull the sled up via the giant's great strength. The packsaddle and its box-packs were brought up by hand. There was no shortage of hard work. The family burned up precious energy and daylight—neither of which they could afford to lose, for as faithful as they were—they were also keenly aware of nature's indifference.

At last, with everything moved to the forest trail, the family and their animals got a much-needed reprieve from the wind. John tied Ellie to a tree where she would remain until after the sled and packsaddle were secured and the twins were loaded. Once untied, her master would not leave her, as the path ahead was laden with wolf tracks, and the scent of the predators had the giant in a state manageable only by an experienced horseman.

While they made ready, John did not have to think hard to know that the winter season, usually a time of plenty for wolves, had been just the opposite. The long Indian summer meant animals otherwise vulnerable due to long winter months had remained healthy and thus capable of escaping the jaws of their predators. In the knowledge of this and having seen their desperation firsthand, it was easy for John to surmise that, with every passing hour, the wolves might pose all the more danger.

When the women had finished, John looked to Jessie, "Ellie and I will be right behind you."

"I can lead her," said Cody. "That way you'll be free to man the rifle."

"I know you can, Cody. And under normal circumstances you would, but if the wolves try to come in on us, I'm the only one that can control her."

Sophie poked her head out from the side of the giant, "Are you sure you can control her?" her little face stricken with worry.

"Yes, I'm sure."

"That's what you said about the ice, and you almost got us killed."

John put his hands on his hips, his lips pursed tight, his eyes vexed.

Sophie pressed the issue, "We wouldn't be in this mess if you hadn't gone so far out on the ice."

"Well, maybe you're right," acquiescing even as he addressed her like a child, "I'll try and be more careful next time."

Sophie's little face contorted and, turning to her mother, she began to weep, "Mommy, I want to go home."

As Mia came forward, Noah spoke to his sister from within the confines of their own little world, there inside the buffalo cloak, "You're gonna get a whippin'."

Mia spoke from below, "Sophie, we are going home. We're going to our summer home."

"That's not what I mean and you know it!" weeping all the louder.

Mia pushed her hood back, "Sophie, this is no time for fussing, and you know it!"

"You're gonna get a whippin'," Noah warned.

Taking the footstool from the sled, Emma got up and looked into the hooded opening, that she might be eye to eye with the distraught child.

"Sophie, I'm afraid same as you. It's only natural, after all. Our fear can keep us alive, but, it can also keep us from fixing what's been broken. You are too young to know, but I am old and have seen many things. And you can trust me when I tell you that, once we have fixed what's been broken, you will be glad we did not turn back."

"I want to go home," weeping.

212

"Sophie," somewhat firmly, "I know you love us, and you don't want us to be sad and all alone...do you?"

"No," sobbing lowly.

"Of course you don't, and we don't have to go home and be sad and alone...we don't have to because the wolves are the ones running home, not us. So you can be brave. Otherwise, the wolves will hear you crying, and that will encourage them to turn around and come back on us, and I know you don't want to be the cause of that...do you?"

Fighting back tears, Sophie shook her little head.

Reaching in, Emma gently squeezed the child's shoulder while speaking in a reassuring tone, "Everything will be okay Sophie, you'll see. And you'll be happy we stuck it out and fixed our broken hearts." Then turning to Noah, "Little man, you take good care of your sister for me, okay?"

"I'll take care of her," Noah said, taking Sophie's hand in his, just as earnest as could be, having listened to Emmy's every word. The Matriarch then got down and put the stool back on the sled—

"Okay John...as you were saying?"

Looking dire, John used a hand signal to bring everyone to the front. Then speaking lowly so the children would not hear, "If the wolves come, I cannot guarantee that I will be able to hold Ellie. I should be able to, but...I cannot guarantee it."

John shook his head apologetically, "Things might not go well."

Emma was first to speak, "I think we all understand, there's no safe plan right now."

"Could we put Noah and Sophie on the sled?" asked Mia.

"We could, with some rearranging," John replied. "It'd slow us down, but worse, the sled would still be attached to the giant, and, they might be thrown off in an attack."

Visibly upset, Mia gazed into space.

Laureal put her hand on her cousin's shoulder, "We have to go."

Mia only nodded, and Laureal turned her eyes to John.

213

John turned to Cody who, although only thirteen, had proven himself capable with the rifle, "Bring up the rear and stay close. And when I say close, I mean not more than a pace behind! Wolves like to approach their prey from behind, so that will be your sole focus. If you see them, say so, and we'll continue moving as long as they keep their distance. If they start dogging us, trying to get us in a panic, we'll keep our cool. And when they get within range, we'll hit them with a volley of arrows.

"Laureal and Mia," John continued, "keep the sled upright same as always. Keep your spears within reach and your bows and quivers on your back. Emma, continue to do as you have, alternating between standing on the platform and walking behind it. Keep the dogs tethered to the back of the sled. Do not cut them loose unless you absolutely must."

"They're injured," Cody put in.

"You'll be right there with them. If either of them falter, call a halt and we'll make room for them on the sled, somehow. But Cody, the dogs are not your concern. Your grandmother can keep an eye on them. You, are our rear guard!"

Cody only nodded, his expression telling of a young mind in high gear.

As they took their positions, Jessie remained at the front with John, her expression a picture of worry, "John, I should take the rear guard position."

"No," firmly, "we need you on point."

"John," her emotion rising even as she lowered her tone, that's my little boy back there."

"Boy or not," also keeping his voice low, "he's the best shot we got. And he'll have Laureal and Mia backing him with arrows and spears."

There was nothing more to be done except to go forward. John stepped out to look around Ellie's massive body, "Are we ready?"

"Yes!" Laureal replied, gently stamping her feet in the cold, her every exhale an icy cloud of steam.

At once their pace was all business, for all knew a defendable position must be reached before nightfall. And even though the day had turned bright without a cloud in the sky, the sun cast tree shadows like the hands of clocks to warn the travelers—long shadows meant time was short, but at least the river path would not go dark as quickly as the rest of the forest, thanks to the great clearing created by the river immediately to their west, which allowed sunlight in to lighten an otherwise dark situation.

The methodical sound of the clan's progress created a marching cadence with Ellie crushing snow beneath her mighty weight, the sled runners cutting through snow, and the humans treading in unison like a chorus. The children were mostly silent, occasionally speaking lowly between themselves, as did the adults. The dogs kept up. The forest, being solid trees to the north, did a fair job of blocking the wind. All seemed to be going well when from up ahead, there came a bone-chilling cry—

"ARH-WOOOOOOOOO!"

Jessie, despite a life lived in the wild, appeared pierced through and through.

"Keep moving," John said quietly.

"That came from the Nith!" looking back at him.

At once the cry was answered by another, roughly the same distance ahead. Unmistakable in tone, anguish in its rawest form, unfiltered by any intellect that might dilute it with words. The second cry was answered by a third and a fourth. The wolf prince was dead. And that such grieving could come from the bosoms of beasts seemed impossible, "ARH-WOOOOOOOO!"

Astonished, Jessie shot a look over her shoulder.

John acknowledged with a solitary nod even as he kept his focus on Ellie, lest the giant lose her cool, "Easy, girl. You're safe with me."

The cries only elevated Ellie's fear level. For however sorrowful they were, they came from a predator so deadly and ancient—it had its own dwelling in the very instinct of her species. The giant would have run away if only her master would let her. But he would not let her, and therefore, she did as good horses do when upset; she went towards danger in spring-loaded steps just as fast as John would allow. And that being the case, the family picked up their pace and made good time

Arriving at a fork in the trail, Jessie gestured to the path that turned away from the river. "We normally take this path," she explained to John. "It goes around the Nith. Stays well clear of it before coming back to the river on the far side." Then, with a grim countenance, she turned to the other path, an animal trail dominated by wolf tracks, "That, goes into the Nith."

Laureal came forward at John's request, and together with Jessie, the two women used spears and hatchets to knock snow from low branches and remove them when necessary so the family might make their way into the Nith.

John kept close behind even as he had no choice but to keep hold of Ellie.

The wolves had fallen quiet for better or worse. And looking through an opening in the trees, John noted out loud how the wind yet swept the river but, having chased the clouds away, might soon abate. The path there began a mild upward incline while, in lowlands across the river, the sun hovered over the forest. Not a summer sun, not a large orange globe but a small white orb shining like a diamond above a landscape clad in ice and snow.

Straight away the family came to the remains of what once been a large concrete bridge. Centuries of floods had swept everything away except for the east abutment. Meanwhile, looking across the river, a floodplain of shrub trees and bogs lay where the towers of the business district had once stood. The towers had fallen victim to the river after Gardiner Dam failed in the first century of abandonment, followed by a thousand years of repeated floods. Very little of anything remained above the silt.

The east side of the river told a different story. On rolling heights above shoreline bluffs, a group of structures survived due to two factors: their elevation and their stone construction. A clutch of lonely skeletons, they were all that remained of the University of Saskatchewan's original buildings, constructed during the Gothic Revival of the Victorian Era. Made of granite, marble, and limestone, they crowned the heights in the cast of medieval castles and monasteries, complete with lance-shaped arches and castle-like ramparts.

Standing before the ruins, Laureal turned to John and, without words, shared her feelings in a single look. Feelings of wonderment mixed with a tinge of fear. Never before had Laureal seen such structures up close. Never before had she seen such haunting beauty. For just there amid the evergreens, the ruins stood aglow in those brief moments when the sun's final light has no angle but flows parallel to the earth like water, flowing under snow-laden eves, illuminating marble-framed doorways and windows where shadowy voids appeared all that remained of a mysterious past.

Hearing her name, Jessie looked back to see John nodding to an opening between a pair of walls. "There," was all the horseman added. The rest was self-explanatory. The ground between the two structures lay flat, a passage wide enough for a party of humans with horse and sled. And so it was that they veered into the ruin.

As curiosity got the better of her, Laureal unconsciously went ahead of her mother, and having passed between adjacent walls to round a corner, she looked into an opening the size of a small sports field with a prominent wall along its north end.

"This is perfect," said she as Jessie came alongside.

Lesser walls in various states of ruin stood here and there on the east and west peripheries. Fallen stones lie strewn about individually or in piles of rubble, not rugged but smoothed by the centuries into grassy mounds presently covered with snow. Only a few trees grew in the opening, as would be found in a glade, with ample grass under the snow. And most importantly, the family would have both a defendable position and excellent protection from the wind.

Taking stock of the family, Emma read their faces and postures. And seeing great hope even as only a pittance of their strength remained, she called them into a prayer circle to give thanks and ask for protection.

Immediately thereafter, their weary eyes were drawn to where the gentle heights dropped to the river below. For just there amid snow-laden boughs, a row of windows in a lone wall backlit by the sunset appeared as natural portals to a realm of heavenly light.

"The Creator has sent us a sign." Jessie's voice, softened by exhaustion, gave her elation a beauty all its own.

"He has heard our prayer," Emma seconded.

Together they beheld that which, at least to them, seemed a sign from heaven. It lasted but a fleeting moment. Then, as it faded to darkness, Emma brought her eyes about slowly as if expecting to spy an incubus or two lurking in the shadows of the Nith.

John tiredly laughed to himself.

Seeing his subtle grin, Laureal scowled at him, albeit only mildly.

Mia, young mother that she be, appeared greatly relieved, "The Great Spirit has delivered us."

The Matriarch assigned work tasks while John took basket and chisel to fetch water from the river, not for the humans but for Ellie. The giant could eat snow and, in fact, horses in the wild often did, but having worked all day, Ellie needed a solid shot of water. At least five gallons all at once, and she was too big to easily negotiate the snowy bluffs.

Meanwhile in camp, precautions were taken that the twins be well guarded, and with the exception of John, no one went off alone to gather firewood or spruce boughs. It took more time, but the tent went up in relatively good order. The campfire grew large and illuminated a portion of limestone wall directly behind their camp, making it glow dull orange, ever-changing in hue, pulsing this way and that to keep beat with the dancing flames. The wounded dogs were tended to and, having eaten well, scratched out their beds and fell asleep. The family sat together around the fire, filling their stomachs with hot food, their faces illuminated by firelight. No one spoke much except for a few words paying tribute to Chewy. And still, despite everything, they traded looks with something extra in their eyes. They were alive, and it was good. The giant, having satisfied her hunger as best her strength would allow, laid down to sleep. Smoke from the fire rose straight up to vanish in the inky darkness of outer space. The Milky Way shone like a glittering brush stroke across the sky. The night air, although cold, seemed the very essence of purity in the nostrils and lungs. No guards were posted. The dogs and giant would suffice. Thus with fire well stoked, the weary travelers crawled into their tent where nothing felt so good as the earth they lay on. Within minutes, all were deep asleep.

Chapter 20

Coming into consciousness at first light, "Good morning."

"Good morning," tired but relaxed.

"Good morning," echoing the same.

"Good morning," making it unanimous.

Cody, having lain awake for the past half hour, spoke from under the covers, "Chewy came in the tent last night."

"You mean he came in a dream?" Jessie redundantly inquired.

"Yeah, I guess, but he seemed so real." The boy remained under the covers, fearful of becoming emotional in front of the others, "He was wagging his tail so much, his whole body swayed."

Emma chimed in, "He came to visit you in the spirit realm Cody, so that you would know and could tell us that he is okay."

"That would be just like Chewy," Jessie fondly seconded, donning her caribou furs. "He must be happy because," her voice suddenly going squeaky, "he's with Cory now."

In the silence that followed, Sophie's little voice seemed almost birdlike, "Mommy, I wish Daddy could come to visit."

"I do too." Taken off guard, Mia did her best to recover while helping the child into her furs, "But you know, today we can be happy because, before Chewy went to be with Daddy in the forever, he came running back to tell us that they're all okay."

"Are they in glades of sunshine now, Mommy?"

"Yes, dear. They walk through flowered glades. They hang their cloaks on sunbeams, and take their seats at a great feast…a banquet table as long as a river!"

Laureal rolled and pushed her face into John's chest. Her tiredness elevated her emotions, and as she began to shudder, John wrapped his arms around her.

Noah began to cry out loud. Sophie followed suit. Then Cody joined in, followed by Laureal until at last all except John shed tears in a group wailing where, in the din, it nearly seemed Chewy was there with them, going from one human to the next same as a thousand times before, wagging his tail so broadly that his entire body swayed.

Exiting the tent under a pale blue sunrise, John came face to face with Ellie. The giant, having heard the cries of the humans, had come to investigate. Her troubled look was one of seventeen discrete facial expressions horses were said to possess according to 21st century science. Also discovered by 21st century science, horses and dogs were capable of reading an impressive range of human expressions in large part because they'd been walking side by side with humans for many thousands of years—an interspecies relationship with a language all its own. Of course, it could not have been discovered without first being lost.

At breakfast, storage boxes from Ellie's packsaddle once again served as seats around the campfire. Also, a suitable log had been carried to camp to serve as a bench on which John, Laureal, and Cody sat. They had positioned their camp to catch the earliest possible sunlight and presently benefited from its distant warmth. Steaming hot porridge also helped to ward off the cold. Noah asked Emma if dogs were allowed into heaven or if that was just something nice people said. The Matriarch assured the children that the Creator would not have made such a loving animal as Chewy if not to eventually bring him home. Thus started an impromptu tribute in which family members told happy stories of the old dog. Meanwhile, Yike and Nemo, hearing Chewy's name, lifted their ears and looked about as if expecting him to show up at any moment.

As they finished their breakfast, John looked from one set of tired eyes to another, Emma's in particular. And when he spoke, it was to her, "We are in no condition to travel today."

Having agreed, Emma sighed and looked skyward, "I am grateful, Lord. But of all the places to take refuge…a Nith, really?"

And so it was decided they would remain for two days. The first day would be spent in rest, performing limited chores like cooking and caring for their animals. The day after would be one of maintaining gear, hunting, and, as we shall see, unexpected discovery.

The following morning John retrieved an oil stone from his gear and, returning to the campfire, sat sharpening his knife in preparation for a hunt.

"Is that a big knife where you come from?" Cody asked, sitting down beside him.

"The biggest," grinning and sharpening.

"Are all knives made of steel where you come from?"

"Pretty much."

"Did you make it?"

"Nooo," his tone low and musical as if to say, *I could not hope to achieve such skill.*

"Do you know who did?"

"Yes," and pausing, John passed the blade to the boy. "It's one of a kind, made by a renowned metalsmith."

"Did you trade many furs for it? "admiring the knife as only a boy could.

"My Order commissioned its making, and paid for it in gold," said John.

Happy to see John and Cody spending time together, Laureal shot a smile over the campfire, and John smiled back.

Cody didn't notice their silent exchange. His eyes were fixed on the knife, but hearing John's reply, he nodded in the knowledge of what gold was. Then, turning to John with a measure of bewilderment, "So they gave gold for it, and then what…they just gave it to you?"

"That, and my spear, my bow, my rifle, all my gear, my clothes, and my horse too."

Astounded, the boy asked, "They just gave all of that to you?"

"Well…yes. They invested it in me, along with many hours of their lives, and in turn, I vowed to carry out the mission they gave me."

Having grown up on fireside sagas that told of great trials and hard-won victories, the boy looked on the Seeker with an expectant perspective, "Your deeds must have been great to earn such trust."

"I did what they asked," dropping his eyes in the knowledge that he had broken his vows to his Order.

"What does this mean?" pointing to a symbol stamped into the base of the blade.

"Those are the initials of the metalsmith: JH."

"Initials?"

"Yes." And rising up, "Come," gesturing for Cody to follow, "I'll show you."

The two went to a patch of untrodden ground where, squatting down, John drew the initials C.E. in the snow. "These are your initials. They stand for Cody Emerson." John then spelled Cody's name out in the snow, "Your initials are the first letters of your first and last name." Then pointing from one letter to the next, he sounded out, "C. O. D. Y…Cody, and then, "E. M. E. R. S. O. N…Emerson."

"Can you draw my father's initials? I want to put them on my bow."

"Of course," and while he drew, he asked, "Did your father help you make your bow?"

"He made it, and I helped."

Having finished the initials, John sounded them out, "O.W., for Orm Westergaard." Actually, Ormskirk Westergaard, of the House of Westergaard, but having married into a more powerful clan, and taking up with that clan, he had become Ormskirk Westergaard of the house of Emerson, known to most as Orm Emerson.

"My grandfather helped too."

John spoke the initials as he drew them, "E.E., for Engle Emerson." Originally Engle Askelson, but having married into the Emerson Clan, he had chosen the name Engle Emerson which, regardless of his prior poverty, immediately advanced and advantaged him, but only because, as a young man, he was shrewd, bold, and handsome. His granddaughter, Laureal, in marrying John, had become Laureal Summerfield of the House of Emerson, but being from the Emerson clan, her everyday name would remain Laureal Emerson, for it was the practice of her culture that the name of powerful clans be attached to their members as recognition of their bond to said clan.

Returning to the campfire, the young man and boy seated themselves on the log bench. "It's balanced," said Cody, offering his bow so that John might examine it.

"Indeed it is," taking its measure and nodding in approval.

"If you would scribe the initial marks for me, I can do the carving."

"I suppose you want them small and precise?"

"Yes."

"Where would you like them?"

"Here," pointing.

John used a bone punch to scribe the initials, "Your bow is smaller than mine but of no lesser quality," carefully scribing the final initial, "and my bow is the work of a renowned craftsman to whom my Order paid a small fortune." Then handing the bow back to Cody, "I take it your father was held in high regard among craftsmen."

"My Father was a good craftsman. Everyone knows that. But perhaps it is also true that everyone in your homeland knows your Order has lots of gold."

John barked a pained laugh.

Unaware of the humor, Cody continued in earnest, "My father told me that an arrow can be made to fly straight and true. And anything we make such, if it be a labor of love, will bring us closer to our Creator because the rocks and trees, and the plants and animals, and everything we make our lives from, are His labor of love for us."

Gazing at Cody with no small impression, John scarcely thought before speaking, "I would like to have known your Father."

"I think he would have liked to have known you."

On the opposite side of the campfire, Jessie held Nemo while Emma checked and tended to his wounds. Neither dog had suffered life-threatening injuries. Just a few yards away, Mia instructed her children, laying out rules for play in the snow. The rules were simple; stay within certain parameters or get a whipping, a far better fate than being disemboweled by starving wolves.

Scraping the wolf hide, Laureal paused to look up at her groom. He had returned to sharpening his knife. Catching his eye, she smiled affectionately, and he, holding her gaze, smiled back. Meanwhile, beyond the walls of the ruin, the forest seemed deep asleep, for the day was yet very young and no air stirred to wake the trees.

John sheathed his knife, put two more logs on the fire, fetched his spear, and set to sharpening its steel head. Like his knife, his spear had been custom-made for him. Not bejeweled or banded with gold but the same as his knife, strongly made and perfectly balanced.

Across the campfire, the women continued working, occasionally speaking between themselves. The twins, both pictures of good health, enjoyed being children, playing under Mia's watchful eye, safely hemmed in by the walls of the ruin as well as the family camp. Noah, having gotten close enough to touch the giant's leg while she grazed, was trying to talk Sophie into doing the same. Cody, having finished carving the second set of initials and feeling good about the job he'd done, turned his thoughts to the air rifle with which he had become proficient—

"Your rifle puts these weapons to shame."

"Like hell it does," musically, very nearly laughing.

Cody appeared taken aback, and all eyes were suddenly on John.

"John, it's bad enough that you curse, but must you now teach your bad habit to my little brother?"

"I apologize," feeling the weight of their stares.

Gathering his thoughts, John slowly brought the rifle from his back to his front. Only the day before, he had disassembled and cleaned it thoroughly, "Cody," his tone both easy and earnest, "this is an awesome weapon, and as I was told, it is both a design of genius, and a work of exacting craftsmanship. But even with all that, it cannot put these other weapons to shame."

The Seeker returned the rifle to its place without another word and went back to sharpening his spear. As he worked, he lost himself in a distant memory. A smile creased his lips, and he spoke lowly to himself, "What man sharpens here, he dulls over there. He devises to go straight ahead, only to come full circle. So carry on, boys, and let the torpedoes be damned."

Laureal glanced up from her work, "John!"

"I'm not cursing...I'm quoting," examining the spearhead, well satisfied with the edge he had put on it.

"Where did you hear that?" Cody asked.

"From an old Seeker, in a tavern, just moments before he fell off a table. My friends and I were green cadets. We weren't supposed to be there. Could have gotten into a lot of trouble!" Summerfield chuckled even as he shook his head, "Anyway, he left quite an impression on us. For weeks we mimicked him and had good laughs at his expense. But that was long ago. Now, with what I've come to know, I think that washed-up old drunkard may have known a thing or two."

"Why do you say that?"

John took on a covert air. He glanced toward the women as if to make sure they were not listening. They were engrossed in their work. He then brought his rifle from his back to his lap and, somewhat playacting, spoke in low tones to share knowledge meant for elite warriors only, "In my homeland, from the time I was a small boy, I was taught that a new breed of man had risen, and it was my great fortune to be born into their world. I was to follow in their footsteps. I was to do things in their new and better way. This meant I was not a raider of tombs but a seeker of knowledge for the betterment of humanity."

The Seeker, somewhat facetiously, took his spear in one hand and his rifle in the other, "This," gesturing with the spear, "is the old way." And gesturing with the rifle, "This, is the new and improved way."

"Truly, it is a great weapon," visibly impressed, although confused by the jest.

"Someday, not all that far from now, it will be produced in enough quantity to outfit a standing army. Then my people will expand their domain, for they truly believe that their ways are best, and all people should live accordingly."

As his words trailed off, John fell into silent thought, his eyes fixed on the rifle.

"How could anything be better than this?" Cody asked, gesturing to their surroundings.

"I'm not sure, not anymore," drifting back in his mind, retracing his steps. "I'll never forget the day I learned about this rifle. I had only just become a Seeker. I was taken aside by my superiors. They escorted me to a closed carriage, itself heavily guarded by mounted riders. I climbed in alone. And there, to my great surprise, sat none other than the Grand Master of our Order! A legend in his own time, he was seldom seen in public, being greatly aged. The most I ever saw of him was at my graduation when he gave a brief speech. Later, when I was chosen as 'Seeker,' we shook hands and shared a few words in a formal ceremony. It may only have been protocol, done countless times before, but for me, it was the pinnacle of my career. Still, with all that, I never imagined sitting face-to-face with him, having a private meeting. But there we were. He began with a few niceties. He seemed to know everything about me. He said it had been decided I was to be outfitted with a new weapon and, with it, I would be greatly advantaged in my quest. He spoke at length about the Data Block. He spoke of 'the lost age.' He spoke of towers that rose into the sky, of men that flew above the clouds, and even walked on the moon. I had heard the stories before. I'd heard them all my life. And I believed them. I still believe them.

"Anyway, we hadn't gone far when our carriage rolled through the gates of our armory. We went inside, through guarded doors, into a special chamber where this weapon was placed in my hands. It seemed so foreign and complex, I could not help but wonder, *'How will I master this strange device in such short order?'* For I was soon to depart on my mission. But as it turned out, it was easy to master. Or at least it seemed a piece of cake when compared to, say, throwing a hatchet and hitting a bull's-eye while riding bareback at full gallop."

"That's why you chafed."

"Yes. And I don't know, but sometimes I find myself wondering if…even as this augmentation increases my ability, my improvement is, in reality, an illusion. And, well, I think that was his meaning, the washed-up old Seeker, I mean."

Breaking into a grin, John repeated the quote, "'What man sharpens here, he dulls over there. So carry on boys, and let the torpedoes be damned.'"

Cody stared in confusion.

Anyway," said John, pursing his lips into a contrite smile, "I apologize for chafing."

"Apology accepted."

Lifting his rifle, John pointed it in a safe direction and gazed through its sights, "In my homeland, before my time, battles were fought that blackened the sky with arrows, and still the world survived." Then, lowering the weapon, he turned to Cody with a solemn expression, "A new kind of power is rising in the world outside this forest, a power derived from knowledge brought up from ruins that dwarf this place. And I think that, if by chance those that seek power were to suddenly find a great trove of knowledge in the palm of their hand…well, I fear they would sweep this family's way of life

228

away before they could see clearly enough to recognize the value of what they destroyed."

Struck silent, Cody gazed at John.

"There's no good to be found in worrying about it," John quickly added. "Besides, the changes I speak of are far off. You may never see them in your lifetime. But I have seen enough to know they are coming. And when they come, we won't be able to stop them any more than we could turn back a river in flood."

"There must be something we can do."

"Carry on…and let the torpedoes be damned." Rising up, the Seeker passed his rifle to the boy, slung his bow and quiver on his back, and took up his spear, "Look after the family."

"Hey," starting after John.

"Yeah," turning around.

"What does this mean?" pointing to a medallion inlaid on the stock of the rifle. Cody had seen the symbol on John's knife and spear, and even embroidered on his shirt. The medallion, being the size of a large coin but not round in shape, had a face divided into four tiny panels, each a detailed engraving. And presently, Cody could not help but wonder if the engraved pictures told of the world beyond the forest and the flood of change that John spoke of.

"That's the insignia of my Order," John replied. "No one knows its true origin, but it is believed to come from 'the lost age.'"

The Seeker pointed to the panel in the upper right corner of the medallion where a man-at-arms was engraved charging on horseback, "This panel stands for courage, most valued of all possessions." Then, pointing to the upper left where a man of science stood at a lectern with an open book, "This panel stands for knowledge, second most valued of all possessions." Then pointing to the lower right where a blacksmith worked at his forge, "This stands for dedication and application of skill, through which men of courage and knowledge forge assets for the betterment of all humankind." And finally, pointing to the lower left where a ship sailed on an ocean, "This stands for man's natural desire to discover what lies beyond the horizon, his journey into the unknown."

Cody seemed confused, "If these panels represent the changes you speak of, then this does not seem all that bad."

"They are ideals," said John, his tone and expression saying, *"Don't count on men to follow them."*

"What about this symbol? Does it bring the ideals together?"

"What symbol?"

"Right there," pointing to the center of the insignia as though it were obvious. "It looks like one of the symbols you drew in the snow."

"Oh that," said John, "that's no symbol...well, it could be a '✝' in lower case, but that's not what it is. It's only a border to divide the panels. It doesn't mean anything."

Chapter 21

Far away in John's homeland, the search for lost knowledge burned like a fever in the mines. The knowledge did not come in the form of writing because nothing in the 21st century had been written in stone, clay tablets, or parchment. It had been digital, wonderfully faster, easier, cheaper and lighter than the wind—and gone with the wind in the year 3011. And yet, the knowledge survived. For example, stainless steel deteriorates and is gone in a thousand years; however, under favorable conditions, a stainless steel DeLorean automobile might survive deep underground, its body crushed from the weight of the ruins above it and badly decayed but nonetheless intact. Men could quickly ascertain that it had wheels and seats, and the wheels were connected to drive axles, and so on. The renaissance was picking up steam. The new breed of men John spoke of had plenty of fodder for their fires, waiting for them deep in the mines.

Laureal walked with John to the edge of the surrounding ruins. Normally, several men would set out together on a hunt but under the circumstances, he was the only one.

"John, please be careful."

"I will."

"Promise?"

"I promise," giving her a kiss. "Are you and Jessie going for firewood?"

"Yes."

"Take spears and bows along with your hatchets."

"We know to do that."

"I know you do. Take Yike and Nemo with you also, but keep him tethered. Don't let him run after anything."

"Will do," giving another kiss.

John pushed a few strands of hair from Laureal's face, "You're so pretty."

"You're so handsome," smiling.

John glanced towards camp, "Cody and Mia can watch over your grandmother and the twins. Cody has the rifle, so they should be fine."

Laureal could feel the strength of his large hands even through thick layers of fur, "Mr. Summerfield," gazing into his eyes, "I'm dying to spend time alone with you."

"I'm dying to spend time alone with you."

They stood together, alone on the edge of the great wide open. Looking around, John said, "Darn."

"Yeah, darn is right."

"We're out of luck."

"Yep, probably until we get to our summer home."

"Oh, please don't say that!"

Finding pleasure in her husband's pained reaction, Laureal flashed a happy smile.

John set out across the gentle heights where, from his vantage point, he spotted a coyote crossing the river. The canine did not see the Seeker on the bluff above. It moved with purpose, not wandering, not sniffing about for a scent trail but appeared to be following a pair of crows flying to the west. The coyote, having gone straight as an arrow across the river, went up the far bank and vanished in lowland bogs thick with patches of shrubby little trees.

Setting out after the coyote, John focused his every atom as he must, that he not fall on the snowy incline even as he slid here and there, always keeping balance, weaving between trees and jumping over obstacles on his way down the bluff. At the end he nearly skied down the steep riverbank. Then trotting across the frozen expanse, he quickly climbed the far bank and continued at a trot, following the canine's tracks through a scraggy lowland where centuries of floods had washed away all but a trace of the city that once stood there.

For the better part of a mile John followed the coyote's trail until quite suddenly he stopped and froze. The coyote crouched with its back to him not a stone's throw ahead.

Unaware of John's presence, the canine remained intensely focused. Crouched low, it used a cluster of scrubs to conceal itself from that on which it spied. As John crept forward, it startled and dashed away to the side but ran no further than a stone's toss where it stopped abruptly. John watched as the coyote again hunkered down in an effort to conceal its position. Oddly, it wasn't hiding from him, or at least not nearly as much as it was hiding from something else.

"What are you onto?" under his breath. Then turning and stepping cautiously ahead, John craned to get a look for himself, and with a few steps more, peering through a ragged stand of scrubby trees to a clearing beyond, he saw a large bull moose surrounded by a surprisingly large pack of wolves.

Had the winter been longer, the old bull may have been worn down and vulnerable. But that hadn't been the case, and the big old bull was wise. He stood strong, knowing he had little to fear so long as he stood his ground. The wolves would not risk the peril of his deadly hooves. They had already tried that and suffered the consequences. So it was a standoff, one that had been going on for many hours. And the moose was at an advantage in the bog. Having foliage to eat, it could sustain its strength whereas the wolves had nothing.

Turning again to the coyote, John just could see its golden eyes gazing from the snowy thicket. He knew why it was there. As added proof, several more crows glided in and landed in surrounding trees. Scavengers were gathering in hope of getting their share. The word had gone out through the forest.

Judging by the size of the pack, John understood that the cause of their hunger came not only from the Indian Summer but also from sheer numbers. Wolf packs spread out in summer but come together in winter to hunt big game. And being that time of year, John felt certain that an alpha female waited somewhere nearby in a den, pregnant with pups and in great need of food.

Unable to bring the moose down, some of the wolves stood around. Others milled about. A pair of yearlings tussled in the snow. Summerfield quietly stripped down to his buckskins, then hung his coat and trousers on a branch. He needed the cold air after trotting for miles, and getting into it felt like freedom, that is, if freedom had a physical sensation.

With snow in his mouth to hide his breath, John crept forward. He knew he had no chance of harvesting the moose, not with over a dozen wolves to contend with. Still, for the price of a single arrow, he could buy safety for his family. He could tip the balance against the moose and relieve the hunger of the pack. The bull's carcass would keep the wolves feasting for days. If he fired, though, he'd give away his position, and if by chance they came after him, he'd need a quick mind and many more arrows to make the moose their better choice. Such were his thoughts as he inched forward amid the cover of scrubby trees, leafless but thick with crowded branches.

No more had our huntsman gotten in range when the alpha wolf spotted him. Following the alpha's line of sight, two of his underlings set out at once, cautiously trotting John's way while four more stood looking on with interest. John wasted no time. He put an arrow through the moose, straight through both lungs. The beast bolted and the wolves sprang into action. Hot on its tail, they exited the far edge of the clearing. As they did, Summerfield crouched and hurried away into the foliage where he picked up his coat and trousers before trotting on. A few yearlings followed him for sport but their effort was halfhearted and when the Seeker turned to face them, they turned back to get their share of the feast.

A stone's throw beyond the first set of walls that surround the family camp and still very much within the campus ruin, Laureal doggedly struggled to free a modest-sized branch from a cluster of dead branches mixed with loose cones and needles all covered in snow. A cluster of firewood obviously washed together in a spring deluge was too good to pass up. If she could free that one branch, other branches would then come free as well, and from that one pile, she and her mother could gather all the firewood the family needed. Stubbornly she wrenched the branch from side to side while driving with her legs until it broke free, nearly sending her back onto her tail end. Quick to regain her balance, she dragged the branch aside. Then grasping the next branch, she pulled it from the pile with considerably less effort.

"Mom," Laureal called, "there's plenty of good firewood over here."

Jessie arrived only to see Laureal backing away from the pile even as her eyes remained fixed on it.

"Get away from there!" Jessie cried, quick to see the ground sifting away beneath the branches, vanishing into the earth like sand in an hourglass.

The ground stabilized, leaving what appeared an eroded hole visible beneath the branches, the result of erosion from rare occasions when extreme rain created temporary surges of surface water, a portion of which filtered underground on its way to the river.

Laureal stepped forward, squatted down, and grasped another branch.

"Laureal, I don't think you should do that."

"No problem, Mom," and giving the branch a firm tug, the ground gave way and Laureal vanished into the earth.

"LAUREAL!" Jessie scrambled to the edge of what appeared a sinkhole, her heart pounding.

A dozen feet below, Laureal sat on a cushion of snow, dirt, and pine needles. The pile of branches, having come down with her, lay before her.

Greatly surprised, Laureal looked up at her mother, "I'm okay!"

"I'll get a rope."

"I can climb out," observing the walls of the pit, which, although impossible in some places, were favorable in others, being stitched with tree roots. Escaping the pit was not Laureal's first concern, however. For although fearful, her curiosity had been captured entirely, and standing up, she gazed into a large manmade tunnel.

"Laureal, get out of there."

"Toss me my spear," looking into the tunnel, its opening brightly lit by the angle of the morning sun, beyond which lay the dark interior.

"Laureal, you come up here at once!"

"Mom, it's okay! Just toss me my spear. It's leaning against that tree," pointing towards the tree even though she could not see it.

Gripped with worry, Jessie retrieved Laureal's spear, then looked on as her daughter, with bow and quiver still in place on her back, leveled her spear and took several cautious steps into the mouth of the tunnel.

Setting her spear aside, Jessie set to climbing down the wall of the pit.

"Mom, what are you doing?"

Jessie jumped the last several feet, brought her bow from her back and drew an arrow, "You are not going in there alone!"

The women could not know what they had found. The network of tunnels beneath the University of Saskatchewan had been built in the 20th and 21st centuries to protect students from harsh winter weather. An underground world once bustling with students in transit between campus buildings, some having lunch in eateries along the way, others playing games in arcades, browsing in shops, and of course studying in study areas.

Having gone only as far as sunlight allowed, Laureal and her mother stood peering into the pitch, the absolute silence broken only by the whines of Yike and Nemo, both leashed near the top of the pit.

"We need a torch," said Laureal.

Returning from his hunt, John walked into camp, his spear in one hand, his parka and pants under his free arm, "How's everything?"

"Crazy," Emma replied, somewhat vexed.

"Laureal found a tunnel," Cody added, unable to hide his excitement, "and when she and Mom have finished gathering firewood, we're going to explore it."

"We'll see about that," stated Emma.

"A tunnel?" with no small curiosity, laying his parka and trousers aside. Then, taking up Ellie's bridle, "I'd like to see that."

"Your wife is quite excited about it," Emma reported coolly. "She has asked to use from our lard supply, that she may make a torch. And I said no!"

"I'm sure we can sort this out. I'll be glad to help when I get back."

"Where are you going?"

"I shot a mule deer," John replied. "A big one," he added, walking off towards Ellie. And turning to walk backward, "It was luck, really...I just stumbled on it."

"There's no such thing as luck," Mia stated correctively.

John broke into a smile. He was high on endorphins, having trotted back to the river only to then climb the bluff like a long flight of stairs. Along the way, he'd surprised the deer on the far side of the river. The muley had sprung from hiding in a stand of shrubby trees. With a quick draw of his bow, John had hit it on a dead run just behind the front shoulder.

"I hung it up," said the Seeker, still walking backward, "and I gotta get back before any cats or wolverines tear it up."

"John!" Mia exclaimed. "The wolves are certain to be there!"

"Yeah, John!" Cody seconded, "Their tracks are everywhere!"

"I don't think we need to worry about wolves for a few days...not too much anyway. They brought down a bull moose

237

across the river about two miles from here. They're feasting even as we speak, and it's a lot to eat. No doubt they'll be sprawled out around it for several days, eating and sleeping like drunkards."

"Do you know how many?"

"I counted thirteen. And I'd be surprised if they didn't have a pregnant female in a den with one, maybe two guards. So that would make fifteen or sixteen."

"Oh dear," said Emma, "that is a big pack."

With a nod, John turned and went to get Ellie where, after securing her bridle, he mounted and trotted away.

Relieved by the good news regarding the wolves, Emma sent Cody to help gather firewood while she and Mia remained in camp with the kids (and rifle) performing small but important chores of maintenance. Soon all were back in camp where they worked to butcher the big mule deer before it froze rock hard. They would not eat from it right away but would give the meat time to age, that it not be tough but tender. To do this, they made simple wood racks from which they hung pine bough backings. They then hung the meat in the racks near enough to the fire so as not to freeze even as it remained cool. The trick was to keep the temperature as steady as possible. They did not cut any of the meat into jerky at that time.

There was always work to do in camp. In fact, camp work equaled and sometimes exceeded the work of walking ten or twenty miles a day. Like walking, it kept them sharp and healthy so long as they followed what Emma and Jessie called "the art of living." As a result, their vocabulary had no terms such as insomnia, obesity, high blood pressure, colorectal cancer, etc. But as with all things, there was an up and downside. The family simply had a different set of concerns, like deadly predators and brutal natural elements. The trick was in the art of living, and the clan had spent generations perfecting it.

Emma, being against the idea of exploring the Nith, refused to allow lard to be taken from their supply for the making of torches. John explained how it was his duty as a member of the Order to have a look in the tunnel. Laureal conveniently claimed it her duty to follow John because he was her husband, along with the fact that she had found the tunnel. Jessie, being more lenient than Emma with regard to Niths, suggested that torch fuel could be had by gathering frozen droplets of sap wherever bugs had drilled holes in the bark of pine trees. The frozen droplets, of which there were a great many, could then be pushed into branches whose ends had been split in many directions. The torch ends could then be wrapped in birch bark and tied below the flame line with sinew. Emma insisted that, since they were gathering torch fuel, they gather extra pine sap to be stored for later use as an anti-microbial bonding agent (in part to replace what had been used from their supplies to mend the dogs).

And so it was, the youths, their torches made, set out to explore the tunnel. John was first to climb down into the pit, followed by Laureal and Cody. Laureal bought a pocket full of fodder and a few fire coals in a clay jar from which she got a small fire going. John and Cody added sticks broken from the branches that had fallen into the cavity. They lit only the tip ends of their torches, that they may burn from top down like candles.

Laureal lifted her torch to the tunnel opening. No longer illuminated in sunshine, it lay cast in shadow, "I've never done anything like this before."

"I have."

"Really?"

"Yes, as a cadet. I went down into a ruin as part of a class."

"What did you learn?"

"Certainly not what I expected. I was the only one to make it out alive."

"John, that's not funny!"

The Seeker remained stone-faced.

"You're just kidding…right?"

John broke into a smile.

Laureal whacked his arm.

"Hey! That hurt!"

"Would you two just stop it!" Cody chided, himself a picture of restlessness and apprehension.

First to enter the darkness, John pushed his hood back in order to better see and hear. Directly behind him, Laureal did the same.

"Don't catch my hair on fire!" she chided, turning to her little brother.

Their torches illuminated the concrete ceiling while, on the floor below, a small dry water trail wound through centuries of dirt and dust.

Having gone some twenty paces, John stopped and turned to Laureal. The look in her eyes showed that, despite her fear, she was all in. Behind her, Cody appeared a mixture of fear and boyish wonder.

John said, "There doesn't seem to be much here."

"This must lead to something."

"I say we keep going."

"I didn't mean to say we should turn back," somewhat offended. "I was only commenting on the empty state of the place."

Returning to the way ahead, John led on another ten paces before pausing where a side entrance came into view.

"What's that?" Laureal whispered, taking hold of John's arm.

"It's a doorway," Cody replied, his voice way down low.

With two steps more, John held his torch out to it. A dark void, the doorway revealed nothing except to drink up his torch's light as though thirsting for it.

Laureal and Cody remained several steps back as the Seeker pushed his torch into the pitch-black opening, "Now we're getting somewhere," stepping into an arcade, turning one way and then the other, his torch revealing rows of gaming machines along the walls. Covered in heavy layers of dust, the machines had been spared from the ravages of time thanks to an environment in which plastic and glass could last for a millennium. Other machines made of plywood or fiberglass had collapsed and decayed.

"What are they?" Laureal asked, coming alongside John.

"I have no idea."

"Hey, guys…what's this?' Cody held his torch over a pile of rubble. The remains of an arcade machine, its glass screen leaned over its remains like a tombstone.

Passing his torch to his sister, Cody squatted and reached for the glass. It fell straight back, a puff of dust billowing out from beneath.

Leaning forward, Cody picked up the glass, a thin gray plate about two feet square. Filled with curiosity, the boy set to brushing away centuries of dust in hope that some mystery might be revealed. As he did, the flames of the torches appeared to come alive in the glass.

Cody threw the plate down like a hot potato.

"What'd you do that for?" Laureal hissed, seeing it had shattered.

"It had fire in it!"

"It did not!"

Kneeling, John picked up a piece of glass and held it between his fingers, "It's glass." But of course he could not know the difference between glass and safety glass even as he had seen the remnants of both. It was safety glass designed to break into pellet-sized pieces, a preference among arcade machine manufacturers in the 21st century.

"Glass," Laureal echoed, taking the pellet from John's fingers, herself knowing of glass in pellet form. Glass pellets, originally taken from ruins, were sometimes traded in summer camps and used for making art. Glass, unlike wood and steel, can last for a million years. Quartz glass may last three hundred million years. But glass is inherently susceptible to breakage. Precious little of it had survived in unbroken form, which also explains why it was not used in wares like cups and plates. It was delicate, and producing it was labor intensive, requiring a kiln. Wood, being far less fragile, readily available, easy to work with, and lighter to carry, remained the logical choice for daily wares. Also worthy of note, the technology for making plate glass did not yet exist outside a few pockets of civilization such as in John's homeland, and even there only small panes of crude quality were produced at great expense.

"It's exceedingly rare to find it in its original form," replied the Seeker, his dark eyes shining in torchlight.

"Was that piece worth anything?" asked Cody.

"To a frontier trader, maybe twenty caribou hides. But for a perfectly preserved relic of antiquity such as that, the right people, if we were in my homeland, would pay enough gold to buy forty or fifty horses."

Cody stared at John in disbelief.

Immediately and spontaneously, the three set to searching for more glass. And as fortune would have it, finding it was easy as dusting off the machines, of which more than a dozen survived.

"Here's a piece," brushing away dust to see the fire reflecting within.

"Here's another one, darling, over here."

"Look at this one!" cried Cody, "It's huge! John, it must be worth a hundred horses!"

"We've found a treasure trove," John uttered in disbelief, examining the large plate.

"John!" exclaimed Laureal, "We're rich! We're..."

Her words fell away as he turned to her, his eyes filled with ambivalence.

"Darling...what's wrong?"

"I took an oath. I am never to raid a ruin for personal gain, but always to turn all findings over to the Order. For me to use the assets entrusted to me for personal gain would be a grave violation of my oath."

"That hardly seems fair," Cody protested, "after all, Laureal found it, and it's in our territory."

"My people see it differently. They see it as belonging to all humanity, and…they are only its guardians."

"How do you see it, darling?"

His countenance a picture of confliction, John shook his head, "I honestly don't know anymore. I only know that having accepted all that I have been given, I cannot break my oath to my Order with regard to this, at least not with regard to my own personal gain. But, perhaps, for the sake of helping the family recover, I can take myself out of the equation this one time. I can step aside with regard to that part of my oath that pertains to protecting ruins from pillagers."

Laureal spoke in a hurt tone, "Is that how you see us John…as pillagers?"

"No, of course not!" backpedaling.

"I would hope not…I'm your wife, after all!"

"I know that!"

"John, think of what we could do! We could buy the horses we dreamed of!"

Cody looked back and forth between them, his expression speaking to the gravity of it all, "Guys, what if there's ten more rooms like this one?"

Laureal turned to her little brother, "There might be, but even if there's only this one room," and turning back to John, "think of what we could do. We could put every member of our clan on horseback. John, we could rebuild, even better than before the disaster at the river crossing!"

"John!" Cody cried in sudden realization. "We could throw back the flood you spoke of!"

Summerfield glanced from his wife to his brother-in-law and back again. Their torches, having burned half their fuel, were at their brightest. And looking into their eyes, it was impossible to determine which was more determined. At last, thinking fast, he found a way out—

"Let's take this matter to Emma."

Laureal and Cody thought it a good suggestion. And when John proposed they explore a bit further, they were all in. For at least in that moment, their fear of the dark, so very instinctual, had vanished.

Continuing through the arcade, they moved towards a doorway at the far end. Along the way, Laureal held her torch up to a round glass disc recessed into the wall, "What's that?"

"As I understand it," John replied, "it's a device by which people could know if it was morning, afternoon, or nighttime."

"Didn't they have the sun and stars?" Laureal asked, somewhat perplexed.

"They lived underground," Cody stated as if anyone with a brain could figure it out.

"I seriously doubt that!" Laureal scoffed.

"A long-long time ago," Cody began, his imagination running wild, "they were just like us, but then some took to living in burrows, and as the years passed, they became…mole people."

"Cody—" musically expressing her disdain.

"I would think they only came down here in winter," John interceded.

Laureal glanced behind them, into the pitch black, "We've lost sight of the tunnel opening."

"We can follow our tracks out," John said over his shoulder.

"How will we know if it's day or night?" Laureal asked, keeping close behind, having second thoughts.

"We'll ask the mole people," Cody replied.

"Would you please shut up!"

At last the hall emptied into a surprisingly wide area, and walking into the midst of it, John held his torch up high. Laureal and Cody followed suit. Their torches, although impressively made, did little to reveal the extent of their surroundings.

"Looks like this is some kind of central hub," said John, looking to the shadowy openings of connecting tunnels.

Some of the tunnels were small, like narrow halls. Others were quite large. Most prominent was the dust. Layers upon layers lie on everything.

"John, this looks dangerous," seeing that several areas had caved in.

"It's amazing," turning and shooting her a smile.

"John, did you hear me?"

"What?"

"I think we should go back now," worriedly.

Cody, meanwhile, looking about with boyish curiosity, suddenly exclaimed, "John! Look over here! There are symbols, like the ones you drew in the snow!"

The symbols, mostly filled with dirt and dust, had to be cleaned out with knives and fingers. At last, when John and Cody had finished, they stood back to see what they'd uncovered. Someone or some group living untold years before had used hammer and chisel to cut big bold letters deep into the concrete of a prominent wall. Apparently, the authors did not want their message to be overlooked. And sure enough, centuries later, it danced in torchlight before a trio of survivors. The Seeker, like a warrior monk trained in the ancient script, read the verses aloud,

"To those in need of shelter,
may these tunnels protect you.

To those on the hunt for treasure,
look not in tomb nor mine, but to the
life within that consumes the dead.

To those that seek the knowledge,
it has died here but lives on,
forever in the wolves."

Chapter 22

Emma sat in a patch of sunshine amid the pines. Her makeshift bench, the trunk of a fallen tree, offered a clear view of the river and lowlands beyond. Not an hour before, the kids had come back from exploring the tunnel, at which point she had stepped away from camp to be alone. She had done so against the wishes of her daughter. She had not gone far away at least, and in fact when she had made herself comfortable, brushing snow from her log bench and settling in, she turned to look behind only to see Jessie a stone's toss behind with bow in hand.

Emma looked up through snow-laden boughs to a blue sky. The air was crisp and windless, the silence golden. "I wish you were here, Engle. It's such a beautiful day." And tiredly rubbing her face, "It's hard doing this alone. I shouldn't have allowed the kids to go down into the Nith. I'm sure you know they've come back changed."

Jessie watched as Emma got down on her knees to pray. She didn't need to hear the words to know her mother asked for strength and wisdom. The moment had not passed when seemingly from nowhere, a breeze from the south caressed her cheek light as a feather. Quickly but gently building, it swept through the trees as though to let itself be known. And no sooner had it come than it was gone.

Back at camp, Cody used John's bucksaw to cut firewood, "What's taking grandma so long?"

"She's trying to figure out what to do with us," Laureal replied, looking up from scraping her wolf hide.

"Maybe she'll have some insight into those verses." John had put the empty sled up on its side. He was waxing the runners with a brick of bear lard, already having used his bucksaw and knife to round their back edges.

"It takes a lot to impress her," said Laureal, deliberating beyond her nineteen years, "but Ellie has impressed her. And once she gets over her anger with us, I think she will decide we should have at least one or two more horses like Ellie."

"Why not a dozen!" Cody interjected, stacking the pieces of firewood, "I can't stop thinking about it."

"I'm still trying to believe it," said Mia, turning the meat on the racks.

"I swear, Mia, it's true." Cody took up John's hatchet, that he might split the larger pieces. "Whoever built this," gesturing with hatchet to fallen walls, "they hoarded like chipmunks in autumn. And now," looking like a boy that couldn't wait to be a man, "we've struck it rich!"

"We were rich before you went down there," stated the Matriarch, entering camp with her daughter alongside. Everyone stopped their work with the exception of Jessie who had insisted her mother allow her to make supper that evening.

Emma seated herself before the fire, "Has anyone here thought of the time and energy we would spend getting the glass out of the pit without breaking it? Has anyone here thought of how we would transport it miles and miles, again without breaking it? And what are we to say when our people ask how we got it? Are we to tell them we dug it from a Nith? Perhaps we could track down a shady dealer, one that would ask no questions. I know of only one place to find such a man, and there are many such men in that place. But alas, we would have our fortune. And the wrong men would know it. And without our men, how should we expect to make the long trek home without being set upon?"

"Grandma…"

"Cody!" sharply, "I am not finished," and turning to the Seeker, "John, the treasure belongs to this family, of which you are part. We found it, and it is in our territory. However," turning to the others, looking from one to the other, "we have no need of it…at least not presently. In fact, it is a stumbling block between us and that on which we have staked everything. Therefore, I would have us each take an oath of secrecy. For the future of this family, it will be as if this day never happened.

But later, when we have rebuilt, we will hold a full clan council to decide what to do with this treasure that has fallen into our hands. And for my part, I think acquiring horses would be a good beginning."

Looking at John, Laureal felt relieved to see he appeared satisfied.

"If I may," Summerfield began, "I will be first to take the oath. But it must not include the verses, save to guarantee that I never so much as hint that they exist physically, let alone tell of their whereabouts, which would betray the location of our treasure."

"Agreed," said Emma. And reading the others, she could tell all were satisfied. She then turned back to the horseman, "John, I confess, I find the verses to be, well, a bit intriguing. And I believe I see a thing or two. If I may?"

"Please do, for I am wholly confounded."

"Well, the first verse tells of goodwill. It is simple and straightforward, whereas the following verses are enigmatic. Obviously, the three verses make a riddle. And being prominently chiseled in stone, as you have said…well then, the author, or authors, must have wanted it to last a long time and be found. And yet, he, she, or they purposefully hid whatever it tells of in an odd compilation of clues which, according to its beginning at least, are offered in goodwill. So, the question in my mind is, if someone is offering something in goodwill, why would they hide it in a riddle?"

For a brief moment, John and Emma sat staring at one another in silence. Emma then smiled and said, "I wish I could tell you more."

"As do I…but thank you. I appreciate your insight."

By the time they had gone round the campfire with each person giving an oath of secrecy to the family, it was time for supper. Again there was talk of Chewy, talk that remembered his happy character.

In waning light, Jessie and Emma cleaned up and also did some setup for breakfast because it would be cold come morning and therefore easier to do the work at present. John finished waxing the sled runners, set the sled upright, reloaded items, and went to check on Ellie. Cody split wood for the morning fire and put several large logs on for the night. The large logs had not been chopped into pieces, as that would have taken too much valuable time and energy. Instead, they had been carried into camp and laid on the fire to repeatedly burn in half through the afternoon. In such a way, a fair number of large logs could be fit into the fire at bedtime. Noah and Sophie helped their mother put venison into large leather bags to be stored in the tent so as not to freeze. Laureal set her wolf pelt aside and, leaning forward, used a bare stick to stir a small clay-fired pot just off the fire's edge. The pot contained a little water along with the brain of the deer John had shot. In it the savage girl had made a paste for tanning the wolf pelt, a simple formula that would leave the pelt flexible, strong, and velvety soft. Thus reaching into the pot with her fingers, she scooped out the warm brain paste and smeared it evenly over the inside of the hide. She then rolled up the hide and put it in the tent. John came and tethered the dogs the same as the night before so they would not run off after raccoons or other critters and end up in a tangle with wolves.

"Yike, Nemo…you look like you're missing Chewy," said John, squatting and petting one with each hand.

Laureal came and joined in. Then, taking John's hand, "Darling, are we okay?"

"Yes," somewhat surprised that she would ask.

Laureal searched his eyes, "Are you sure?"

"Yes. I'm positive."

"You seem different."

"I'm just full of thoughts, that's all," the firelight illuminating his handsome eyes, shining within his hood. "I mean, I can't explain it, but those verses, they weren't put there for nothing. They lead to something, and it's dogging me." Then, managing a smile, "You had me worried for a while too…you and Cody."

Laureal smiled back, "I guess we did go a little crazy. But I think we're all pleased with Grandma's plan."

"It's a good plan."

"John."

"Yeah."

"You said you felt like those verses were meant to be found."

"Yeah...they must be."

"Well, maybe we were meant to discover those tunnels."

"Well, I..."

"John," cutting him off, "when the time comes and we reach that fork in the path where you go off to hunt for your magic place, maybe, instead of separating and going in different directions, it would be better for us to stay together."

"We're husband and wife. Whatever directions we go in, nothing's going to separate us," reading a mixture of hope and uncertainty in his lover's eyes. "You'll see. We'll have our home. We'll clear a bit of land along the river. Our children will swim and fish there," and smiling fondly, "we'll have our horses, and we'll take sleigh rides in winter."

Taking Laureal's hands in his, John stood and brought her up with him.

Looking towards the tent, Laureal watched as the rest of the family ducked in one member at a time. Mia and the children went in first, followed by Emma. Next Jessie and Cody helped one another with the snow paddle, whereupon Cody went in. Jessie then turned and offered the paddle to Laureal.

Brushing snow from John, Laureal whispered, "I wish we had our own tent."

John knew his little tent was stowed away in one of the packs. It was not practical in their present situation, and yet his wife's words spurred him to action, "Jessie?"

Jessie, who was already inside the tent removing her boots, poked her head out the door flap.

"Laureal and I are going for a short ride."

Caught off guard, Jessie appeared suspended in time.

"Just a little starlit ride," John quickly added. "We'll be back in a jiffy."

Caught between bewilderment and understanding, Jessie gazed up at the young couple. Then, speaking in a low tone, "Okay…but please, don't be gone long. And for heaven's sake, be careful!"

"Will do," taking the snow paddle from Laureal and handing it to Jessie.

There'd been no reason for John to give Jessie the paddle. His mind was elsewhere. Jessie laid it beside the door, after which she disappeared into the tent.

John turned to Laureal, his teeth grit in embarrassment, "I apologize," he whispered, "I should have asked you first. I don't know what came over me. You seemed worried about us, and…well, I just thought it might do us some good. But of course, we don't have to go."

"I want to," smiling.

"I'll fetch Ellie," all at once happy. And setting out, turning to walk backward, "Get some blankets from the sled.

"What for?"

Staring blankly, "Yeah, forget about that…I must be crazy."

"No…no, it's okay! I'll get them."

Only three old caribou blankets remained on the sled and Laureal took them all. John brought Ellie and, with blankets laid over the giant's back, the young lovers mounted via the stepstool. Then sitting on the blankets, they wrapped themselves in Ellie's buffalo cloak.

Inside the tent, the Matriarch spoke lowly, "Daughter, what is going on out there?"

"They're going for a 'starlight ride.'"

Emma sighed in exasperation.

"I know Mother, it worries me too. But they've worked so hard, and they've had no time alone together, and…I think they need this."

251

Emma listened to Ellie's hooves moving away through the snow, vanishing into the dead of night.

Mia broke the silence, "We can say a prayer for their safe return."

Outside, Ellie, having eaten and slept most of the day, walked tall and proud with sure-footed gait. Completing a jog to exit the ruins, the queen of horses carried her riders north between ruins and bluffs. A well-worn animal trail lay there in an ancient stand of giant jack pines above the wide river. The pines were not crowded together but seemed to share the space well, perhaps having come to an agreement after spending centuries fighting for sunlight. Their shadowy forms towered alongside the limestone skeleton of the university and, together with the river, made for a dramatic nightscape set inside a great dome of stars. One could only guess how the builders of the university must have felt upon finding the site: the perfect place, safe from floods, its gentle contours would only add to its character—a character that had grown strangely beautiful in death—like a country cemetery, long forgotten, at rest in eternal peace and quiet.

Just then, a tiny shadow came gliding down from high in the trees. Quickly passing through starlight, it crossed the trail directly before them and caused Ellie to pause, uncertain as to whether she had actually seen something or not. Then, coming on the shadow's heels like a missile, a second shadow, much larger in size, swept right in front of Ellie's face, "SWOOSH!"

Ellie reared up, nearly throwing her riders. The Seeker struggled to gain control, gripping her mane with one hand, reining with the other to counter the giant as she tried to bolt—

"Easy girl! Easy!" using his legs and reins as the giant danced dangerously close to the bluff's edge.

A few more aimless steps taken in near panic, first this way, then the other, and Ellie came to a halt on legs and shoulders tense as spring steel. Her ears straight as pikes, her nostrils blowing mighty puffs of steam, her large eyes bulging to pin down the whereabouts of the phantom wraith!

Only with cat-like agility had Laureal held on without dragging John off Ellie's back. Having recovered her place, she caught the motion of the second shadow, now with wings open over the river.

"Are you okay?" asked John.

"Yeah, I'm good," watching the shadow fly. A Great Horned Owl, somewhat larger than its 21st century forebearers, it glided on a wingspan of seven feet until, flapping its wings at last, it continued west where a crescent moon hung over boggy lowlands.

"We may need to dismount and lead Ellie for a while until she calms."

Not particularly wanting to dismount, both humans set to stroking and speaking soft words to settle the beast. And when she began to smack her lips, a sign that she had gotten over her fright, John steered her back to the path.

Continuing in peace and quiet, John asked, "Was that little thing a flying squirrel?"

"I don't know. I never really saw until it was gone."

"Well, whatever it was, it got away."

"It's probably breathing a sigh of relief…like us."

(Low laughter.)

John mimicked a messenger that gives a report, "They escaped the wolves but, unfortunately were done in by a squirrel."

"A flying squirrel!" squeaking.

"And a hooter!" snorting.

At last, our young hero and heroine laughed so hard they began to slide off their mount.

"John!" shrieking musically.

Calming even as they remained elevated, the riders exited the pines and entered a six or seven acre microcosm of grassland that had originally been the northernmost reach of the Great Plains. The native grasses of the north were not tall like their southern cousins but short and robust and thus completely covered with a smooth blanket of snow. A blanket that stretched out before them, its snow crystals sparkling like diamonds.

Up the gentle rise they went, up to the crest where, looking north over frosty treetops, they saw how the forest stretched into the night without end. Only the star dome dwarfed the wood, and enveloped all the earth.

John looked on in awe, for although Laureal had told him about the northern lights, he had never seen more than traces of them. Now they danced across the breadth of the northern horizon, shimmering green and blue, shifting and swirling between earth and stars.

"They're more beautiful than I imagined."

"They've come out for us," looking over John's shoulder, her arms around him tight.

He turned to her and pushed his hood back, his eyes shining in starlight, "It's a gift."

"Yes, darling. It truly is."

Chapter 23

It is said that in all of nature the top three distance runners are humans, horses, and dogs. Some claim the horse best of the three. Many claim that a human will eventually catch and pass a horse. Others claim dogs to be number one. Men and women from the 21st century might point out that sled dogs ran the 1,000-mile Iditarod in 10 days. Others might point to 2015 when, in the world's longest certified footrace, Pekka Aalto of Finland ran 3,100 miles in 40 days. Perhaps it is too close to call. In any case, it is encouraging to know that in the work of creation or course of evolution, or whatever one chooses to call it, great gains came from countless miles traveled in the sometimes grueling race for survival. And in that race, untold numbers of humans, horses, and dogs formed friendships to which all who came after are indebted.

The next morning, John emerged from the tent only to see Nemo chewing on his tether. Seeing John, Nemo jumped up and began to dance and whine loudly. His big brother Yike was gone, his sinew tether chewed in half.

"Yike! Here boy!" Cody called, having come out of the tent. "Yike!" the boy shouted, casting about, "Here Yike!"

"John," Emma beseeched, "would you please go and find Yike."

Slipping Ellie's bridle on, Summerfield mounted up, and from the high advantage of the giant's back, walked the perimeter until, spotting fresh tracks, he set off at a trot only to stop and dismount not twenty yards further. Then, turning back to the others, he called out, "I see him."

"Where is he?"

"On the river." And with a grin, "It looks like he's found a lady friend."

Laureal and Cody came alongside, followed by Emma who, seeing Yike doing a mating dance with a she-wolf, cried out, "Oh my goodness!"

"Yike!" Cody called, "No Yike! Yike! Yike, no!"

"Good luck with that," John said laughingly, although as Cody continued to call, the female became alarmed and broke off the dance.

"Where are the other wolves?" cried Laureal.

"Passed out drunk at the party."

"John! That's not funny! If they happen along right now, they'll kill Yike!"

"I'll get him," musically reluctant, even as he acquiesced. Then, turning to Ellie, he removed her bridle so that she might return to grazing. He handed said item to his wife, and knowingly winked at her.

"John wait!" Emma exclaimed as he began to descend the bluff. The Matriarch looked back and forth between the young couple, "Laureal, go and get a tether for Yike."

Finally, Emma turned to Cody, "Take the rifle. From here you can cover both river and camp."

John may have spent days exploring the tunnels had his motivation not shifted from that which pushed him to that which pulled him, so to speak. As always, everyone worked hard to complete their tasks. Likewise, when they hit the trail they kept pace. Not double-time but all business.

It would take five more days to reach their summer home. Along the way, it became obvious that Yike and the wolf had a thing going on. Yike chewed through his tether the first two nights, so they gave up on that. Nor could they keep him from sneaking off to feed his lady friend by way of regurgitation, a common practice among wolves and still a powerful instinct in all dogs. The wolf kept her distance from the family, and the family remained focused on their objective. Clouds moved in and brought the return of the snow. At times the flakes fell so perfectly steady it seemed every individual crystal kept to the exact same angle so that, wherever one looked, one saw an even pattern. At other times the flakes were so tiny and light, they floated aimlessly, almost like gnats on a warm summer day. When the big river turned east, the family continued north on a well-worn forest trail. On the fourth day, they crossed the north fork of the old Saskatchewan River near the ruin of Prince Albert. The next day under a darkening sky, they pushed ever northward. The afternoon brought heavy snowfall and, in waning light, they reached their summer home. Needless to say, it came as a great relief to all.

Chapter 24

Built when the Emerson clan was at its zenith, the family's summer home showcased an immense hearth of red granite in which a large fire presently blazed.

At nineteen, Laureal had never known the clan's heyday. Even so, the comfort and familiarity of her childhood summer home saw her wrapped in warm furs, cozy and relaxed, having washed her hair only minutes before. On the long table before her, a steaming bowl of cereal contained stone-ground wild wheat, a legacy of 21st century farming for which Canada and Saskatchewan in particular had won world renown. The red wheat genome, bred to survive cold climates and fully capable of reproducing itself, had gradually moved north with the warming climate to find its niche in forest glades and especially in openings along the rivers and streams.

Presently, John watched Laureal add a copious helping of honey to her bowl as if it were nothing. Honey was abundant due in large part to a 21st century project in which researchers at the University of Saskatchewan collected honeybees from around the world in an attempt to cross-breed and create a super bee. They succeeded, and Saskatchewan became famous as a honey-producing region. The Saskatchewan bees were long-legged, robust, disease-resistant, cold-weather bees that, while docile, worked hard and produced large amounts of honey. A thousand years later and an abundance of woodland bee colonies, combined with the fact that honey, like wheat, can keep for decades and even centuries when stored correctly, was one more resource in thousands enjoyed by the Emerson clan.

Having dowsed her cereal with honey, Laureal lifted her eyes only to see John looking on in amusement. She straightened her back, squared her shoulders, lifted her chin, and narrowed her eyes with an air of superiority to silently tell him that, in that place, she was the princess of the wood, and she could have all the honey she wanted.

Cody looked up from his cereal, "It's crazy how Yike and Nemo have fallen out lately."

John only chuckled, for it seemed one amusement followed another.

"Mommy?" Sophie whispered, casting a sideways glance at the Seeker, "Why do men laugh at sad things?"

"Because they're men," Laureal interjected, turning to John with a scowl, "It's not funny."

"Oh yes it is," John rebutted with a knowing grin. "And I'll tell you why. It's the same old story from the beginning of time and everyone knows it; two fellows become best buddies, and then, along comes a little lady and—pow!"

"Little?" Cody cried through a mouthful of food. "She's bigger than both of them put together!"

"Mommy," asked Noah, "can little doggies marry big doggies?"

"Where there's a will, there's a way," Mia replied, smiling, hiding her eyes in her cereal.

Thus began a breakfast banter among the youth, more in fun than not until, at last, Emma put an end to it, "Laureal," the Matriarch said sternly, her eyes fixed on the girl.

"Yes, Grandmother," suddenly fearful.

"Did you feed that wolf this morning?"

Laureal's eyes went directly to Cody.

"What are you looking at me for?" Cody cried.

"Laureal," Emma pressed, "I asked you a question."

"I only tossed her a little scrap, Grandmother. I…I wanted to get a better look at her."

It was only a white lie, a half-truth, but nonetheless, having a potential for tragic results (like all lies). The truth was, Laureal had been tossing scraps to the she-wolf since their arrival at their summer home. Innocently enough, it had begun with youthful curiosity. Laureal, and to a lesser degree, John and Cody, all wanted to know about Yike's pretty lady friend. It was common knowledge that wolves mate for life, and young female wolves were often driven out of their families to find a mate and start families of their own.

"Laureal," said Emma, "what has gotten into you?"

"I'm sorry, Grandma."

"I told Laureal not to feed it!" Cody burst out, casting a condemning glance at his sister. Then turning to the Seeker, "John and I both did."

John grimaced. And Cody realized his betrayal too late.

Emma looked from one youth to the next, and when she spoke, her tone set her edict, that all may know she was fixing to lay down the law, "I was hoping that wolf would go away on its own, but obviously that's not going to happen now."

Emma then addressed the Seeker specifically, "John, when you have finished your breakfast, take your rifle, and take Cody with you. You know what to do."

"Grandma," Laureal cried out, "I…"

"We have two small children here!" Emma expounded, cutting Laureal off. "Do I need to remind you what that beast will do the first chance it gets?"

"Grandma, she…"

"She's a wolf!" Emma exclaimed. "And that's an end to it!"

In the absence of words, looks went around the table, of which many pages could be written.

"Laureal," Emma finally said, her tone yet firm, "you owe your cousin an apology."

Laureal turned to Mia, "I apologize, Mia. I didn't mean any harm."

Her lips pursed tight, Mia gazed at her cousin. "What were you thinking?"

"Honestly, I don't think she's a threat to us."

"Laureal?" Jessie questioned in disbelief. "Did you not hear your grandmother?"

"She's more afraid of us than we are of her, Mom." And quickly she added, "She never allowed me more than a stone's toss. She never bared her teeth, or even growled. You can ask John, he saw, and Cody did too. And Mom, now that our dog

260

has surely gotten her pregnant, I cannot see what honor there is in us abandoning her."

"Oh, for heaven's sake!" cried Emma, putting her tea down. "I will not entertain any more of this nonsense. Not another word!"

The fire crackled in the great hearth while around the long table, all seemed to withdraw within themselves, eating their breakfast like an unrelished chore.

"John," Emma said at last, "you know what you must do."

John drew a heavy breath, "Laureal, I'm going to need your help."

"*Why?*"

"You know why," John replied, visibly sorry that he had to ask.

"That wolf trusts you," Cody chimed. "It won't show itself for John or I."

"I'd hardly call it trust," Laureal rebutted and, turning to John, "You don't need me."

"She won't show herself to me."

Tortured, Laureal looked from one family member to the next.

"I'll make sure she doesn't suffer," John added.

"Let's get this over with," said Cody, standing up.

"Mom," Laureal pleaded, looking to her mother as a last hope.

"I'm sorry dear, but your grandmother is right. That beast is a danger to the children. And because this is your doing, it is your duty to do your part in its undoing."

Not a word passed between the three youths as they donned their furs there beside the heavy double doors of the longhouse. John spoke lowly as he opened the door for his wife, "Laureal, I'm sorry."

"It's not your fault," stepping over the threshold, her voice so low as to be nearly inaudible.

John, Laureal, and Cody went down the steps, passed between several huts, and continued to the edge of the compound where they passed several more huts that stood long abandoned. Turning south, they walked along the edge of a stream that supplied the family with water, fish, mollusks, and other things, like smooth stones for grinding grain.

At last, they began to call for Yike, and before long, the big dog came bounding up the trail.

Having caught Yike, Laureal turned to her brother, "Take him back."

"No, I'm coming with you."

"No you are not!" upset, but nonetheless gathering herself. "This is something John and I must do alone."

"Laureal's right," John affirmed. And taking a contrite air, "Cody, somehow your sister's made a connection with that wolf, and…this is not going to be easy."

Halfway between a disappointed sigh and a frustrated huff, Cody turned and trudged back towards the longhouse, pulling Yike along with him.

Looking to Laureal, John nodded to the trail on which Yike had come, that she might take the lead and do as she must. He followed several paces behind. The sound of snow crushing beneath their boots broke the quiet of the wood—a cadence of muffled squeaks like so many wet rags being wrung into knots.

Arriving at the edge of a small meadow, Laureal turned to John. Her expression, plain to see by the morning light that entered her hood, was one of grim acceptance. Turning away, she called across the meadow, "Weya," her voice soft and sad, yet tight with self-control, that she may keep from faltering, "Weya. Weya."

No more than a few minutes had passed when from the trees across the way, the she-wolf appeared, obviously hoping for another scrap, that she might stave off the cold. And although humbled by hunger, it just so happened that this particular wolf had been none other than the princess of the pack. And when her brother the prince died in battle, she lost her powerful ally and was subsequently driven out at the behest of her own mother the wolf queen who saw her beautiful daughter as a rival—a traumatic turn of events even for an animal. Presently, she bore a healthy dose of apprehension, and yet, sensing Laureal's sadness, unable to understand the reason behind it, she cocked her head.

Slowly and smoothly, John stepped to the side in order to shoot clear of Laureal, "Don't move," he whispered, lifting his rifle to aim at the canine. The wolf, which Laureal had named Waya, possessed such rare beauty as to be the very icon of nature's untamable majesty. With her bloodline flowing straight from the heart of the Mackenzie Valley, she measured exceptionally large even for a timber wolf. Her coat, being that of light cream, not only gave her contrast against the freshly fallen snow but added warmth to her natural luster. Her green eyes were softly beautiful and yet keenly aware. On her back and shoulders, she wore a faint mantle, a hint of gold that came over her head like a hood.

While Weya sniffed the air with hope, John sighted his rifle square in the middle of her chest. He moved his finger to the trigger and drew a deep breath, then exhaled half of it so that he might be as steady as possible while squeezing the trigger.

Laureal went numb awaiting the irreversible outcome.

Then came the sound of the rifle, "Click."

"Oh this damn thing!" John exclaimed, frustrated by the malfunction.

Laureal turned to her husband, her young face filling with hope, "John...it's a sign!"

Pushing his hood back, the horseman's frustration shifted first to confusion, then to contemplation. He glanced from his wife to the wolf and back again. Then, at last, letting out a cathartic exhale, he shouldered his weapon, "Let's go home."

"John," searching his eyes, "what are you thinking?"

"Let's go home and I'll tell you."

Laureal listened as they walked and when John had finished, she told him what she thought, "It's a wonderful plan but, just so you know, Grandma's probably already considered

263

it, and it's doubtful she will reconsider unless she believes it to be the will of the Great Spirit."

"Well then, let's hope it's his will."

They walked on until Laureal paused and, turning to John, said, "Mr. Summerfield."

"Yes, Mrs. Summerfield."

"I love you."

"I love you too."

"John."

"What?"

"It is important to have the Great Spirit's favor. And that's why it's important that you stop your cursing."

Laughing to himself while shaking his head, John turned to the path ahead. Following along behind, Laureal did not press the issue.

Meanwhile in the longhouse, Emma and Jessie worked at the table organizing and packing food supplies for the next leg of their journey. Nothing was held back. Everything had been put on the table for a well-planned roll of the dice.

Coming in, John and Laureal hung their furs by the door, then proceeded to the long table where John wasted no time getting down to business, "I didn't shoot her."

Stopping her work, Emma turned to John, "Why not?"

"We were given a sign," Laureal interjected.

Emma and Jessie exchanged no small looks of suspicion.

Fearing they might not believe him, John stated only what he thought truly necessary, "My rifle jammed at the critical moment, and while Laureal believes it a sign…you know I'm of a more skeptical nature. Still, we all know that I carefully disassembled, cleaned, oiled, reassembled, and tested my rifle after our arrival here the day before yesterday."

Pausing, John drew a deep breath before proceeding, "With your permission, I would like to make a proposal. Perhaps it is something you have already considered, in which case it is my hope that you will reconsider."

Each in their own thoughts, all stood looking at John, not only Emma and Jessie, but Mia and Cody had also stopped their work to look on.

At last Emma broke the silence, "Well, let's hear it."

"If we may all have a seat?" John suggested. "This won't take long. And then, if you still think we should dispatch the wolf, I will do so."

The Matriarch agreed and with everyone seated, John began, "If allowed to live, that wolf will have pups. And judging from her build and Yike's build, and also taking into consideration the tremendous endurance that wolves possess, and also, Yike's good nature around humans...well, I have to believe that a litter of hybrids from these two animals would make a team of sled dogs as good as could be found."

Seeing that he had gotten their attention, John took heart. But before we proceed, this is a place to note that cross-breeding dogs with wolves might be seen as a perversion by some, while others might argue it is only another experiment in man's long history of experiments, good and bad. No case for either is being made here. Instead, what can be told is this: Nature did not give our hero the luxury of such arguments. Rather, nature forced his hand as a member of a semi-nomadic hunter-gatherer group whose survival depended in no small part on their ability to find advantage in the challenges that nature placed before them.

"Given the wolf's great size," Summerfield continued, "and given Yike's smaller size, she could have a litter large enough to make a full sled team. And given our plan to increase our numbers, I have to think a sled team would be of great value to the family. Now, I admit I have no experience in this, but I know of an account in which wolf pups were taken by softhearted humans in order to save them from extraneous conditions. And although the mother visited her pups when the humans were not around, she did not carry them off but had the intelligence, or love perhaps, to let them remain where they were safe and well cared for. And if that could be our case, well then the children could raise the pups from early on with our careful oversight. This would bond the dogs to the family. Better yet, it would be an opportunity for the children to learn skills and responsibilities that would serve them throughout their lives. And lastly, I have to believe a sled team would not only be of great value to the family but would impress a large measure of respect on anyone that saw us coming."

John was right about status. Arriving at a rendezvous with a large team of high-quality sled dogs in 31st century Saskatchewan was perhaps as impressive as arriving at a grand ball in Victorian England with a carriage and six. On the other hand, perhaps young Summerfield's role could be compared to that of a 21st century grandson-in-law who, best intentions aside, tries to convince grandma that borrowing money for a new Cadillac is part of God's plan for the family.

Emma could not help but come off knowingly, "John, I have already taken into account everything you have said."

John countered with the obvious question, "May I ask what swayed your decision?"

"Aside from the danger of the wolf attacking the children, her pups would be half wolf. But suppose we overcame that with careful rearing. We would then have the expense of feeding not two, but eight, nine, or ten very large dogs. They would eat us out of house and home. And what about the time it would take to train them? Being half wolf, they would require great care in their upbringing, that they may become trustworthy as adults. John, don't get me wrong. I appreciate your good intentions. We both want the same thing. And God willing, we will rebuild our family. But we cannot justify this, not at this point in time...we just are not that far along yet."

Thinking on his feet, John offered an alternative, "We could trade the pups at the rendezvous. Surely they would make good barter as sled dogs, or guard dogs. The family could increase its fortune that way."

Looking at John, Emma was reminded of her own late husband for whom distance had made the heart grow fond. It wasn't that John and Engle were two peas in a pod but rather that John, like Engle, had proven to be a horse to bet on. And there was her granddaughter, sitting beside him with great hope in her eyes. And looking at them both, she could not help reminiscing over a past age and what a good team she and Engle had made. And in that exact moment, she knew that if ever there was hope for the family to regain what it had lost, it was looking her in the eyes. And that, in and of itself, was a sign.

At last, Emma turned to her late nephew's widow, "Mia, what do you think?"

"I have serious concerns," and casting her eyes to her children, she visibly appeared to drift, and seemed not to hear when Emma said, "Take your time, dear."

"They have lost so much," Mia said at last. And returning her attention to the Emma, "Perhaps a litter of pups would be good medicine, something to help fill the void."

"If we traded the pups away," Laureal softly interjected, "we could keep the most gentle one for the children's sake. I have memories of Chewy that I wouldn't trade away for anything." And looking to her brother, "I know Cody does too."

"I suppose," Jessie began, "a litter of pups might serve as a medium for the children, to help them transition from old family to new." And lifting her eyebrows, "Perhaps, a medium for us all."

"Cody, what say you?" John asked.

"I see no reason not to have as many dogs and horses as possible."

"Are you willing to do the extra work required to supply the meat to feed the dogs?" asked Emma, looking from John to Cody, Laureal to Mia. "Are you willing to take on the responsibility of their care and training, and oversee the twins in their learning?"

Seeing all were in agreement, Emma looked to Jessie, and seeing her lips turn up as she gave a little nod, Emma lastly turned to the children, "Noah, Sophie, would you like to have some puppies?"

"Oh yes Emmy, please!"

"Puppies!"

"All right then," said Emma, "as we all agree to do our part, and to spare no diligence in keeping the children safe at all times, the matter is settled…puppies it is."

Chapter 25

Before departing their summer home, the family painted two leather parchments and left them on the long table for their kin to discover. The first parchment served as a pictograph telling of the disaster. The second parchment used paint and pebbles to create a simple diagram showing that the survivors had been there and had continued north towards their planned destination, the Lake of the Swans, located one hundred miles beyond their traditional hunting grounds.

Together in a column with each at their familiar station for ice travel, the family stood ready as John and Cody made minor adjustments to Ellie's sled ties. Having left their summer home, their second day of travel was set to get underway. They had made good progress on their first day before camping in a stand of jack pines at the southern tip of Lake Montreal in central Saskatchewan.

Lake Montreal, having joined with Crean Lake by natural processes centuries before, measured approximately eight miles wide and extended due north for approximately fifty miles. It would serve as a winter highway and, same as when on the river, the family would have the option of a forest trail, this time along the west shore—not as good as the river trail, but an animal trail at least.

While the family waited on John and Cody, Jessie gazed ahead. She had been there many times before. The frozen lake, an expanse of snow stretching for as far as the eye could see, marked the beginning of a change in the land. They were entering a realm of lakes and rivers. It would be gradual until the Lake of the Swans, beyond which the terrain changed so dramatically as to become a world neither of land nor water but something in between.

"Did you get it adjusted?" Laureal asked, watching as John donned his mitts.

"Yep," smiling. And turning to Jessie, he gave a nod.

"Are we ready?" Jessie asked loudly from the front.

"We are ready!" answered Laureal. And away they went through snow rarely more than several inches deep due to the sweeping effect of winds that came across the lake most afternoons. There were occasional snowdrifts, but going around them presented no problem. Only a cloud or two hung in the sky, and no breeze stirred to disrupt the serenity of early morning.

Among the many mysteries of nature, a unique carpet of freshly fallen snow had been laid down overnight. Not deep but thin, not wet but dry, not small flakes but large and wispy. It had fallen so delicately as to remain loose and airy, as though each flake were still semi-suspended in the air, all juxtaposed to one another at countless angles to create an extraordinarily fluffy layer of crystals akin to hoarfrost. Its beauty did not go unnoticed.

Along the shore just a stone's toss away, jack pines rose like snowy white towers set against a sky so deep and blue that a nature-loving soul could very nearly fall into it. A large flock of northern cardinals, having come together for the winter, congregated there in the thickets that lined the shore. And of the 30 or more birds, a brave handful sang songs as crisp as the icy air, perhaps in joyful celebration of the sun that would soon rise over the wood.

Laureal turned to walk backward so that she may check on John, and as she had hoped, there also was Waya following in the family's snow trail an eighth mile behind.

Guessing what Laureal was about, John turned to see the wolf, although as soon as he turned, she stopped only to begin again as soon as he turned back to the way ahead.

Scarcely another mile had passed when Sophie suddenly extended her mitten to the frozen expanse, "Mommy! Looky!"

The sun was rising over the trees, illuminating the surface of the lake. The unique layer of fresh fallen snow, so loosely knit, allowed the sunlight to penetrate deep, momentarily trapping it, reflecting it from one crystal to the next before releasing it, the effect being that the lake sparkled so intensely, it appeared to be filled with stars.

"It's a sign!" Noah cried.

"It surely is," Mia affirmed loudly, that her children might hear even as she kept to her station, a coil of rope on her shoulder some fifteen paces behind Jessie.

"The Great Spirit is with us!" Jessie joyously shouted from the front.

The spectacle lasted but a few precious minutes. Then it was gone, done in by the very thing that had given it beauty. The delicate crystals melted and collapsed in the warmth of the sun even as the snow remained cold, dry, and powdery to the human eye.

The morning sun made a considerable difference for the humans, their animals, and the wildlife also. By midday the temperature had increased to 10 degrees. And as was often the case, layers of clothing had to be removed to keep from overheating. Then, as expected, the arrival of the wind forced the family into the forest where the trail, being only an animal path, presented more difficulty than expected—

"Jessie, Laureal!" called Emma.

Mother and daughter came walking back from the front where they had been clearing the trail, their hatchets in hand.

Emma continued, "We will make camp here today."

Emma did not have to explain. Everyone understood the path was too difficult. They were wasting too much energy.

Laureal glanced at the frozen lake, just visible through the trees. A sea of spindrift bathed in sunlight, the afternoon wind forbade them from traveling there.

"The moon will be near full tonight," said Emma, glancing skyward. "The wind will die out. It will be clear and cold, very cold, but also very calm, and we have good gear. We can return to the lake and make time. And tomorrow when the wind comes up, we will strike camp."

"We couldn't hope for a better place," Cody acknowledged, looking into the wood where, as Emma had seen, a modest opening lay in near-full sunshine, well-sheltered from the north wind. And so it was that the family struck camp in the warmth of the midday sun. Ellie dug snow and grazed. Yike and Chewy meanwhile, seemed to have made peace.

Working to put supper on, Emma turned to her grand-daughter, "Laureal."

"Yes, Grandmother."

"Feed the dogs."

Laureal gave a little nod only to remain in place, gazing at her grandmother with uncertainty, apparently expecting something more.

"And the wolf," Emma added, shaking her head as she returned to her work. Then, taking note of John who appeared momentarily off in thought, "Well, John, are you just going to stand there, or are you going to protect your wife?"

Emma watched as John and Laureal went away down the trail. "Kids," she said to herself, once again returning to her work over the fire, once again shaking her head even as she smiled.

Spear in hand, John followed Laureal down the animal trail in the direction from which they had come. Both dogs remained behind, distracted by their early supper, not to mention neither dared chew its tether in front of Emma.

Having gone approximately one hundred yards, Laureal began to call, "Weya! Weya!"

"She may have gone hunting," scanning the forest, John's eyes came to rest on the lake just visible through the trees. Previously a sea of serenity, the big lake looked like a wind-blown wasteland.

Just then, the wolf appeared on the trail only a stone's toss ahead. Never had they been so close to it, and while impressive enough to see a 100-pound dog like Yike or Nemo, seeing the 200-pound wolf was something altogether wild.

"Set the food down, sweetheart, and we'll back away."

"I will, darling," whispering over her shoulder, "but let's get a bit closer first." And taking several more steps, Laureal softly called to the beast, "Hey there, pretty girl. I brought you some supper."

"That's far enough," John whispered.

"Just a few more steps," yet advancing ever so slowly.

The wolf, scarcely ten paces ahead and visibly apprehensive, lifted its nose to savor the scent of the meat.

Attempting another step, Laureal was unexpectedly drawn back. John had ahold of her coat. She glanced back at him but before she could protest, he whispered, "I'm only protecting you." Gazing into his eyes, a fleeting smile graced her lips. Then, turning back to the wolf, she squatted and set the front shoulder of a mule deer on the trail.

Slowly, the Summerfields backed off a safe distance where they watched as the wolf cautiously came forward. It kept its eyes on them even as it lowered its head to its meal. Then, picking up the deer's shoulder, it turned and vanished into the wood.

On watch for the coming of the calm, Jessie lifted her eyes as a great horned owl glided in to land on a perch just twelve feet above, "Hoo-hoo. Hoo-hoo," turning its head to look at Jessie. "Hoo-hoo. Hooooo! Hooooo!" Its voice was so singular, its look so unique, it left no room for doubt in Jessie's mind. The owl had been sent and the message was obvious: *"Arise. Arise. A way has been prepared for you."*

"Mother," said Jessie, "Mom."

Slowly coming around, "Yes."

"It's time."

A mere stone's throw lie between camp and lake and yet the forest seemed to have gained a dimension beyond regular space and time. Moon shadows cast from trees fell vividly upon the snow while, strangely enough, the very same light that produced such sharp contrasts made for an altogether soft and satiny world. Upon hearing the sounds of Ellie's hooves crushing the snow, and seeing the great clouds of steam emitting from her nostrils, an onlooker might be forgiven for mistaking the giant for a dragon in a ghost realm, accompanied by a cult of hooded necromancers.

No more had the family arrived at the lake's edge when, as though on cue, the last of the wind, having already faded to a light breeze, died completely.

John made a final check of Ellie's riggings and, having found a pair of knots that needed attention, worked to redo them.

Cody, who'd become the horseman's apprentice, looked on while holding the giant's lead rope, "Have you ever noticed how, unless you're looking for them, you might not see small animal trails in daylit meadows, but in the moonlight they practically jump out at you?"

"You mean when there's no snow on the ground?"

"Yeah, like in summertime."

"Yeah," said John, "I've noticed that."

"Why do they jump out?" asked Noah, looking down from his little window.

"I don't know," John replied, rubbing his hands before proceeding. "This strap isn't jumping out, or in, or anything."

Sophie poked her head out, "You are getting them tight, aren't you?"

"Yes, missy, I am."

"I would hope so. I wouldn't want to fall off!"

"Oh," looking up at her and feigning surprise, "you mean the saddle straps. I'm checking the sled straps."

"Have you not checked the saddle straps?"

"Sophie," Laureal intervened, just then coming forward, "don't let John tease you."

"How does moonlight make animal trails jump out?" Noah asked, his little voice insistent, so baffled was he by the mystery.

"Small animal trails," Cody clarified.

Thinking about it, John stipulated, "I suppose it's because they blend in with the grass in the light of day, whereas under the moon, where shadows can be more obvious than real things…well, things just kind of get reversed, I guess, and then, they jump out."

"What does 'rezersed' mean?" Noah asked.

"Reversed," Cody corrected.

"Reversed," John began, "it's, well, like I said, shadows can make small things seem big, and big things seem small, out here, under the moon."

"But I'm still small and you're still big, and we're under the moon."

Cody stared up at Noah, "It only works on certain things."

Fearing himself in over his head, John noticed how the pines cast their shadows along the shore. Then, turning his eyes to the child, "Noah, you can't see them because you're facing the lake but the trees along the shore…well, in the light of day they stand out against the sky, but right now, under the moon, they blend into the sky while their shadows jump from the snow."

Listening to John, Laureal thought of how the moonlit lake had impressed her when first she spied it through the trees, "Snowy lakes jump out of the earth."

"But snowy lakes don't have shadows," Cody stated, somewhat confusedly.

"They still jump out," insistently.

"Snowy lakes have shadows," Sophie chirped, pointing to John and Laureal's shadows, so vivid against the luminous surface.

Hanging Ellie's lead rope on her neck, Cody removed his mittens. Then, holding his hands up in the moonlight, he cast shadows of animal figures on the snow; a fox chasing a rabbit to his thinking. The twins loved it. John and Laureal also began to laugh.

Emma may have cracked the whip on their antics had she not been lost in thought, like a thousand miles away. In reality she stood but a few steps behind the sled. Yike's whines had alerted her and, following his gaze to the trees along the shore, she'd caught sight of the wolf. Weya's eyes shone softly, reflecting the moonlit lake like mirrors. The Matriarch, standing transfixed, saw the riddle of the ruin, its final verse in her mind's eye.

To those that seek the knowledge,
it has died here but lives on,
forever in the wolves.

Realizing the meaning of the passage, a smile came to Emma's lips.

"Are we ready?" Jessie very nearly barked as she came walking back.

"We're ready!" John announced, realizing how completely off track they'd gotten. And then they were off, traveling along the shore of that vast lake. The moon, suspended like a jewel in the star dome—the northern lights, shimmering like magic in the great unknown.

Chapter 26

Perhaps those ancient wolves that chose to come along with man on the long road out of the wild, and who along the way became man's best friend, but alas, perhaps the process of how such a thing happened is not given the attention it deserves. How did that which was most feared become that which is most loved? How valuable is the knowledge, skill, discipline, balance, and dedication needed to evade nature's cruel indifference while retaining the freedom to walk in the midst of its amazing harmony and beauty? Truly a most remarkable feat, which is not to romanticize our primitive past, nor to discount the achievements of modern science, nor to deny the work of a higher power, but simply to stop, realize, and appreciate the wonder of it all.

Fortunate was the family to have a pair of crystal-clear nights one after the other. On the second night, they reached the north end of the lake where they entered the mouth of the River Montreal. Continuing up the medium-sized river, they struck camp at midday, where, seeing how approaching clouds signaled an end to their night travels, Emma sent John out hunting. She did not send him because they were dangerously low on food but rather to avoid such a situation by making the most of the afternoon. Cody was assigned the rifle and kept guard, among other camp chores. The twins were unloaded. The sled was unhooked. Laureal chopped a hole in the frozen river for access to water. The tent went up and a fire crackled to life. John returned with a wolverine weighing about 50 pounds. The elusive animal had not been his choice but what nature offered. Emma, however, was delighted in the knowledge that at that time of year, the wolverine's meat would be sweet and tender—a rare and particularly palatable treat. Laureal helped John skin and butcher it while Mia and Jessie built a simple rack to hang the meat and begin the aging process. The hide was rolled up for a later day.

The river, being modest in size and therefore not too terribly windy, allowed for ice fishing just a stone's toss from camp. Cody and Noah pulled in a stringer of trout destined to become the main course in the evening meal. When done fishing, Cody covered the ice hole under a pile of snow to keep it from refreezing. Sophie helped Emma and Jessie prepare supper. Ellie dug and ate buried grass. And just a hundred yards downriver, the newlyweds fed the wolf, and made out against a quaking aspen.

With chores done and stomachs full, all that remained was to retire to a good night's sleep. Yet no one wanted to do that, for tired though they be, the setting sun had illuminated a vast cloud bank across the river to the west, making for a spectacular sunset. Emma proclaimed it a sign, one in which the hand of their Creator had pulled back the sky like a curtain to reveal the promise of paradise.

In the afterglow that followed, the Matriarch took the opportunity she'd been waiting for—

"John."

"Yes, Ma'am," tired but happy, his arm around Laureal, he smiled across the fire.

"Regarding what you call, 'the riddle of the ruin.'"

"Yes," visibly perking.

"If I may, I believe I have come to understand the final verse."

John looked on in anticipation, as did the entire family.

"As you know," Emma began, "I believe the first verse is intentionally simple and straightforward for a reason. It establishes goodwill. Now, I need to ask you, John, are you certain the first line of the third verse contained the word, 'the,' as in 'the knowledge,' as opposed to simply, 'knowledge'?"

"Yes," John replied, "I am certain of it. The first and second verses did not include the word 'the,' but were simply, 'need of shelter' and 'hunt for treasure,' whereas the third verse was, 'seek the knowledge.'"

With a nod, Emma continued, "That is important to know, seeing as the nature of a riddle requires careful construction. It is safe to assume, then, that the third verse is not referring to just any old knowledge but to the knowledge. Now let's go back to the second verse, 'look not in tomb nor mine.' It tells us that the treasure is not to be found in the realm of the dead or anywhere in the earth, but rather is some mystery related to life; 'the life within that consumes the dead.' I do not understand that line, but I suspect it holds the key to unlocking the mystery.

"Now, let us return to the third verse. To me, it suggests that the knowledge leads to or is somehow connected to the treasure mentioned in the second verse. The third verse tells us that knowledge has died but still lives elsewhere. Not only does it live, it lives forever. 'Forever in the wolves,' it says. So why did the author or authors point us toward the wolves? What did they want us to see?

"Well, let's look at the wolves. Wolves live in family clans, like us. And within their clans they have different roles, like us. They work together, like us. And like us, they have a hierarchy with a patriarch and matriarch. It is their way. And while they may not have the intellect to question what they do, they run for days on end, swim rivers, love, fight, kill, die, and even babysit to live free like us. Vast is the reward for their hard-won success. And in it they go where they please. And when the mighty grizzly comes to take what is theirs, they do not roll over. So, looking at wolves, it would seem they are symbolic of our own hard-won freedom, and, the knowledge necessary to live free had been lost. Whoever wrote that riddle knew their words would not be unearthed without survivors. Without knowing us…he, she, or they knew what we would be."

Pausing, Emma looked from one family member to the next, "We, are the wolves in the riddle."

In silence, they sat exchanging glances. The last of the day's afterglow, having slipped away, left the firelight free to dance on the Matriarch's face.

"The riddle," Emma continued, "says the knowledge lives forever. Well, that which lives forever is not bound to this world. So the knowledge is not bound to this world. And the wolves in which the knowledge lives are not bound to this world. Therefore, if I am reading it right, the riddle tells of a freedom that only our souls can know. And that freedom is the 'treasure' in the second verse."

Leaning forward, Emma pushed the burnt-off end of a log into the fire, "These past two nights, as we traveled the moonlit lake, the riddle played in my mind like a voice that calls across a great expanse of time. And I could not help wondering if finding those verses was meant to be. Then again, perhaps I'm just an old crackpot."

"You're not a crackpot, Grandmother."

Scooting back in her seat, Emma gathered her gray hair, for it had fallen out of her hood, "Thank you, dear." The lines in her face, cast in shadows by firelight, seemed exaggerated, like the keen quality in her large green eyes.

"When I was a little girl, my grandmother, who was Matriarch, told the Spirit Story at the hearth for us children. Now, sitting in her place, I understand the characters in the tale are but symbols of the good and evil inside us all, as seen through the earthly limits of my mind's eye. And yet, with every year I age, the portrayal becomes all the more fitting as my sense of the spiritual battle grows."

Emma again looked to her granddaughter, "Laureal, would you recite the beginning of the Spirit Story for us, please?"

"Of course, Grandmother," and speaking the first verses of an epic poem known to every soul in the realm, Laureal looked from one family member to the next until, at last, her eyes came to rest on John.

"Come forth from the glades of heaven.
Seven wolves ever loyal to the Lord of Light.
Their patriarch and matriarch, Truth and Love.

Leapt out from the black void of hell.
Seven wolves enslaved to the Lord of Darkness.
Their patriarch and matriarch, Hatred and Deceit.

Two wolf clans locked in a territorial war.
Flashes of light, and darting shadows,
deep within the contours of my soul."

"Thank you, dear." Turning her eyes to the fire, Emma gazed cryptically into the flames. "The riddle tells of something lost, but not gone. Something that died and yet, lives on. Something beyond this earth. For within every life, there is something of immeasurable value to be gained…or lost."

In the absence of conversation, the sound of grass being chewed between the giant's teeth seemed louder than one might otherwise expect.

Jessie was first to speak, "So, even though the knowledge in the riddle ultimately speaks to a treasure that's tied to our existence both now and in the beyond…attaining it, as we already know, is within our grasp, providing we seek guidance from The Great Spirit, and feed the right 'wolves.'"

"Yes," replied Emma, "but the riddle suggests there's more to it than that. It's a riddle, after all. Something is hidden in it for a reason. And as we know from the riddle's first verse, it begins with goodwill. So why is it hidden? What is it hiding from? What is opposed to goodwill? The obvious answer is, malice. Perhaps the riddle was written in a time of evil so pervasive that, the treasure it tells of had to be concealed in an enigma."

John, being more scientific-minded and closer to the truth than he knew, spoke from the edge of his seat, "Could there be something actually hidden in the wolves? I mean in the real wolves? Something the authors put inside them?"

Emma only shrugged.

"You mean like some kind of magic?" Mia asked.

Cody's eyes nearly bulged from his hood. "If they put some kind of magic in the wolves, then maybe all we need to do is, drink wolf blood."

"Why on earth would we do that?" Laureal asked, visibly grossed out.

"To get the extra everlasting freedom into us," replied the boy, looking about as if everyone should know it was worth a try.

Jessie, Mia, and even John, all shaking their heads with faces of doubt, nevertheless shrugged at one another like it might be a possibility.

"We are *not* drinking wolf blood!" Laureal forcefully interjected, scowling at her little brother in particular.

"Could it be," John began, "that the author, or authors, sought to safeguard critical knowledge for future generations in a way that treasure hunters could not find and destroy?"

"Perhaps we are reading too much into it," Mia put in. "Perhaps it's only a riddle with some local meaning, and beyond that, it doesn't mean anything."

"All we have to go on, " Jessie began, "is what the author has left us."

Shaking his head, his expression baffled, John echoed the passage, "Look not in tomb nor mine, but in the life within that consumes the dead," and looking round the fire, "What is the life within that consumes the dead? Is it my stomach?"

"I too am stumped by that passage," Emma concurred. "And as I said, I suspect it holds the key to unlocking the riddle. After all, it tells us where to look to find the treasure."

"Could it be," Cody began with trepidation, wondering if he should open his mouth at all even as he put two and two together, but alas, he asked, "Perhaps we should cut a wolf open so grandma can look in its stomach?"

Glaring at Cody with frightful resolve, Laureal spoke in hushed tones, "You so much as touch Weya, and I will cut you open."

"That's enough!" snapped their mother.

"Perhaps we should forget about the riddle," Mia interjected. And with an added measure of gravity, "After all, it came from a Nith…and just look at us."

"It comes from an ancient civilization," Summerfield rebutted.

"A civilization that God destroyed," countered Mia. "And if he has destroyed something, it must have been evil, and we have no business digging around in it."

"If it is as you say," John began, "he still left its pieces scattered in such a way that we cannot walk in any direction without finding them."

"Yes, as a warning."

Looks went around the fire, the flickering flames casting their expressions in ever-changing shadows.

Seeing himself outnumbered, John doubled down, "All right then, let's say it is a warning. Is a warning not also a form of lesson? And is a lesson not part of a formula to build from?"

Crossing her arms, Emma gathered her parka in against the cold that came with the dark, "It has gotten late, and here we are arguing in this remote and unforgiving place. Let us get the rest we need, and agree to take this up at a later date."

Gazing into the flames, John could not let it go. And yet, lifting his eyes, he showed his softer side, "Emma, if I may ask one last thing. Let's say you are right about the Nith, and those verses come from dark times. Would that not add all the more weight to what you yourself have said, being that they were written in goodwill? And could it not then be possible, as you also eluded, that they are a treasure map to lost knowledge? Knowledge that might light the dark?"

When at last the Matriarch replied, her tone reflected the sum of her years, "Well, awful as it seems that we not only entered a Nith but actually dug down into it, I confess, I cannot shake this strange feeling that we were meant to find those verses. That said, we must not allow ourselves to become so distracted that we forget where we are."

"Agreed," concurred the horseman, looking round the fire, "out here, we cannot afford to lose our focus."

"If I may get something off my chest," Mia began, "what if, as we plan to do, we eventually return to the Nith and use the glass treasure to acquire horses. And we put every member of our clan on horseback. And we grow strong, perhaps even stronger than in days of glory past. What if the word then got out that we did so by way of a treasure dug from a Nith? Would our people not say we made a pact with the devil? Would they not turn on us? Would we not end up hated?"

"We had no choice but to take shelter in the Nith," Jessie countered, her large emerald eyes filled with resolve. "Who among us could ever forget that day? Who among us believes that our finding the treasure happened by chance?"

Summerfield raised his mitten albeit only halfway.

Taking his mitten in hers, Laureal smiled as she brought it into her lap. Then, looking around the fire, her countenance turned so severe as to be nearly witchlike, "The treasure is ours! We found it fair and square!"

"Darn straight it's ours!" Cody put in.

"There's a far bigger treasure," retracting his mitten, "a trove of lost knowledge. I am certain of it now more than ever. And I mean to find it."

Sophie's little voice came out of the dark, "Emmy."

"Yes, dear."

"Mommy says that when we lose something…it's often right under our nose."

Chuckles went around the fire.

Chapter 27

The following day saw our travelers continuing north on the River Montreal. Snow fell steadily, but at least the wind did not have the open expanse of a big river or lake to build and become intolerable. Shortly after noon, they arrived at the old river crossing. Eighteen clan members had died there when, as we already know, a tumbling wave filled with debris overtook them. Many of the bodies were never recovered.

A pyramid-shaped pile of boulders and stones stood as a memorial on the shore above the river. Rising to a height of nine feet in the center of a tiny man-made clearing, it had become overgrown. Still, being nicely blanketed in snow, it appeared a natural winter garden too beautiful to tread on.

First ashore, Jessie stood at the edge of the clearing with spear in hand. John came along last as usual, being the rear guard. Emma nodded to the derelict trail that entered the forest there, by which they hoped to gain the Lake of the Swans, "Hopefully, this will not be too difficult."

"At least we won't need to haul loads," said John, referring to how the river banks had become gentle in the changing geology of the region.

"Makes for a good start anyway," Cody added, standing alongside the giant.

While John chopped a hole in the river ice, Laureal handed out brownie-sized cakes of pemmican. Each member stuffed some extra in their pouches to gnaw on the forest trail ahead. Ellie took a long drink, as did the dogs. The humans drank from their water bags, then refilled and placed them back in the packsaddle where they would not freeze.

The children were brought down and the family gathered before the memorial with heads bowed. Emma spoke words honoring the dead, then asked the Great Spirit to watch over and protect the living on the path ahead.

"That's not much of a path," said Laureal, turning to the trace before them. Together with her mother at the front, neither could know they looked upon the once-famous Can-Am Highway.

Presently an animal trail, the path ran through a stand of aspens before vanishing in the deeper wood—a haunted wood, as rumor had it in the aftermath of disaster. In reality, a much older forest had burned there years before, and its demise had contributed to conditions that caused the deadly flood. The forest that sprang up in its place had not yet fully sorted itself out in the battle for light. Thus it stood before them, a dense mix of pine, spruce, tamarack, poplar, birch, and alder draped in white. All that remained of the old growth were a few blackened trunks rising here and there above the snowy canopy, standing alone like charred grave markers against an overcast sky.

That she may help her mother clear trail, Laureal went to get a hatchet from the sled. And pausing there in curiosity, she stepped to the shoreline to look downriver one last time where, as she had hoped, Waya stood only a stone's throw behind.

"She's staying closer today," said John, coming alongside.

"It would appear," Laureal began, turning her eyes to his, "that our rear guard has acquired an assistant."

"I hope that's the case," putting his arm around her, "because from the looks of her, even big Yike must have trembled when first he saw her…that is, even as he turned backflips."

"John," laughing, "sometimes you can be so funny."

"Laureal," Jessie's voice came calling, "I need your help up here."

Proceeding a stone's throw into the forest, Laureal scanned for a trace of trail. Never had she or her little brother been beyond the memorial, and presently, losing all indication of a path, she turned to her mother with concern—

"Mom."

"I haven't been this way since before you were born."

"I thought Cory said the trail was viable?"

"You know how Cory was. He could bust a trail like nobody's business, but he wasn't the world's greatest communicator."

"Mom, how are we supposed to get through this?"

Without a path, the woodland appeared an impenetrable wall of snow perforated with dark openings, none of which appeared open for travel.

"John," Laureal called, "we've got a problem."

John hadn't taken two steps past Emma when the Matriarch said, "John."

"Yes," turning around.

"Where there's a will, there's a way."

"Always." He then continued to the front where a single glance told the tale: there was no trail. Fortunately, the Seeker had drawn a number of charts based on Emma's considerable knowledge of the region. Thus, by his best estimation, the Lake of the Swans lay only thirty-five miles north-by-northeast of their present location.

Looking here and there, John made his way into the woods. He returned Several minutes later, shaking his head, "Damn."

"John, how many times do I have to ask you?"

"I know, I know. I'm sorry, but this ain't good."

"Can we get through?" Cody asked.

"Only if we're willing to cut a trail."

"Surely it's not this thick all the way to the lake?"

"I would hope not!"

John looked to Emma, "Is there another way?"

"Well, providing we can find it, this path is a straight shot to the lake. Otherwise, there are waterways to the north and south. To the north, the river continues from here, winding and curving before turning east to eventually make its way to the northern tip of the lake. It would cost us many extra days of travel. To our southeast, there's a small stream that also leads to the lake. The problem is, it winds like a piece of tread picked up and thrown down by the wind. And the terrain there is unfavorable. By its course, every stone's throw would be multiplied by three or four."

"And beyond the stream is rugged territory," Jessie put in. "Hills that stretch south to our summer hunting grounds. Our only option would be to go around them, and that would be an undertaking."

"That would put us out in this cold for another moon," Mia asserted.

"Yes, I know. I didn't mean to imply we could do that. We would have to hold up at our summer home and then depart after the spring thaw."

Mia turned to Emma, "We would miss our prospects."

"But we would be there when they returned," Laureal put in optimistically.

"That's true, dear," Jessie began, "but in that case, their impression of us might be very different. If we arrive late and therefore can only get a poor location with little time to build better than a paltry camp, and all the while we're expecting to net big fish…who then could blame anyone for seeing us as the sort of people that expect to get something for nothing."

"Mom, I'm not saying we should do that. I'm just looking at our options. The summer crowd that Grandmother spoke of would be there. Surely there would be single men. I would assume some reasonably decent ones around your age."

"Laureal," Mia cut in, somewhat annoyed, "you're not the one looking for a man. I mean, yeah, we'd have the summer crowd, but are we now to give up and settle for something less after all that we've come through?"

"I say we continue with Grandmother's plan," said Cody, getting his two cents in.

Emma turned to John, "Do you think we can get through this?"

"We can give it a shot."

"Mia, what say you?"

"I have not come through snow and ice to get a 'reasonably decent' husband," shooting a look at Laureal.

"Laureal, what say you?"

"I was only trying to be helpful, Mom. You know, look at all our options." Feeling somewhat offended, she looked at Mia, "If this was all about me and I could have what I wanted, then John and I would return to our summer home. We would sell the glass treasure, build our house, and buy horses." And having gotten somewhat worked up, she added, "And I couldn't imagine a better life! But this isn't about me!"

"Is that a yes or a no?" Jessie asked pointedly.

"It's a yes, Mother!" And turning to John as if to assign some measure of blame, "You have the compass, darling."

Struck by their determination and more than a little concerned, John worried particularly for Emma who, being up in her years, suffered most from the wear and tear of their endeavor even as she hid it in a seemingly bottomless well of determination—

"Perhaps," he began, "we should camp here and sleep on it. Then come morning, we can decide."

"How about we give it a try now," Emma proposed. "And come morning, we can decide based on our experience today."

"Very well. Do you mind taking the rear guard position?"

"Whatever it takes."

Handing his rifle to Emma, John turned to Jessie and Mia, "If you would manage the sled, Laureal and I will break trail." And turning to his wife, "I will use my compass to indicate our course. And based on that, if you would look for the path of least resistance and knock snow away with your spear, I will cut branches behind you. And when you aren't knocking snow down, you can help me cut branches."

Turning to Cody, John continued, "If Laureal and I leave a few branches lying on the path, pick them up and move them aside as you lead Ellie."

The Seeker reached into his pouch and brought out his compass. Cased in brass and resembling a locket, its lid bore the insignia of his Order.

"We might have five days of this ahead of us," speaking as he oriented himself, "that is if we decide to continue." Then pocketing the compass, he fetched his hatchet which, as we already know, qualified as a small ax.

Everyone took their positions, whereupon the horseman, standing alongside his wife at the front, pointed his hatchet and said, "We need to go that way."

Laureal, who had picked up a favorable stick, threw it end over end like a tomahawk. It landed in the trees a mere stone's toss before them and the ensuing chain reaction ended in a cloud of snow dust, rapidly dissipating to reveal a snow-free patch in the forest.

Pleasantly surprised, John turned to Laureal, "That was clever!"

"When we were kids, we used to do this for fun. We learned where to throw our sticks to bring down the most snow."`

"It wasn't always fun," Cody remarked from just a few steps behind. "Laureal threw a stick into a snow-bomb above me once. She did it intentionally. The snow came down and got in my windpipe. Cory had to carry me home."

"And after Cody was safe in bed, Laureal took a trip with her father to the wood pile out back," Emma remarked from behind the sled. And thinking back to it, she chuckled even as she shook her head.

So it was with old recollections and new expectations that the family set out on a bushwhack where knocking away walls of snow only left more snow on the ground to plow through. Chopping what branches had to be chopped still left many to negotiate, and clearing away old dead branches still left more of the same buried under the snow to twist an ankle or throw the sled on its side. Alas, it was slow going, and they were not even a mile into it when Laureal paused before yet another fallen tree. A victim of the fire, the old-growth pine lay on its side, its blackened trunk presently topped with snow, could easily last another hundred years before rotting away.

"We'll go over it," said John, as he had been making the call from one fallen log to the next, deciding which were better for Ellie to go over and which were better to go around. Laureal went over the log to clear ground on the opposite side while John used his hatchet to make a narrow flat atop the fallen trunk. Then laying his hatchet well aside, he turned to the business at hand.

"I can do it, John."

"I know you can, Cody. But unless we want Ellie to jump, she is going to need help from both of us."

Sophie poked her little head out, "Do you know what you're doing?"

"I'm pretty sure I do. Although, I've never done this before."

"Are you teasing me again?"

"Yes, but only partly. I want you and Noah to hold tight to your box tops. That way, if Ellie jumps a little, you won't bump your heads."

Knowing the trunk was solid enough to hold Ellie's great weight, John instructed Cody to stand opposite the trunk and directly in front of Ellie, while, at the same time, ordering her to stay (this would prevent her from jumping). The horseman then lifted one of the giant's massive steel cleated hooves as though to clean it, but instead, he placed it atop the log which, being eighteen inches in diameter, had a combined height of approximately 21 inches. The second hoof was the hard part, and John used his considerable strength to help Ellie lift her hoof up onto the log. From there, she carefully stepped down to the other side under John's direction. The process was then repeated with her back hooves. Next it was time to lift the front of the sled up and onto the log. John lifted on one side while Jessie and Mia lifted on the other. It was no light thing but they got elevated enough for Cody to edge Ellie forward, slowly bringing the curved runners up and onto the log. John directed both Cody and Ellie while, one step at a time, they carefully drug the sled fully atop the log so that it balanced like a teeter-totter. The family team then let the front end down as gently as possible. They then repeated the process on the back end, using care to prevent it from suddenly dropping and possibly cracking or breaking under its own weight.

"Perhaps in a day or two we won't have to do this," John remarked while retrieving his ax.

Meanwhile, Jessie had gone back over the log, "Mother, let me help you."

Emma pulled her arm away, "It's only a log, for goodness sake!"

Cody gazed about, taken with the number of rabbit tracks, "There's no shortage of hares in this place."

"That's because we're yet near the river and a good supply of grass.

"Fisher cat tracks as well."

"They're drawn here by the hares."

The travelers hadn't gone a half-mile deeper into the wood when pausing yet again for John to check his compass, Mia turned her eyes to a small opening in the canopy above, "Can't say for sure," craning to get a better view of heavy overcast, "but I doubt we have two hours of light left."

"Where did this day go?" Jessie asked redundantly. "These winter days are so short, it's hard to get half of what one hopes done."

"Maybe we should strike camp now?"

"We could set snares for hares."

"Sounds like a plan. We're going to have to snare them high, though. Otherwise, I doubt we'll have anything left come morning, what with fishers-cats prowling about."

John did not have to say more. Everyone knew the fisher cat's reputation. Notorious cousins of the wolverines, they were not a threat to humans but a terror to all small forest animals.

So it was that the family struck camp (they had to clear a space due to the crowded nature of the forest). The day soon faded, leaving their campfire to illuminate only the surrounding branches like a candle's flame in a starless pitch.

The surrounding wood came to life with the voices of night. It happened abruptly, the otherworldly scream of a fisher cat. Like the cry of a banshee, that ancient spirit of Gaelic folklore whose wail warns a family that one of them would soon perish. Then again, perhaps it was only the fisher cat's ancient enemy the red fox, also known to scream like a woman being murdered in the night. Whatever the case, the hair-raising ruckus prompted a few barks from Weya. Not dog barks but those half barks particular to wolves, used to warn intruders away. This was followed by the hoots of an owl, after which all fell quiet, leaving one to wonder what had been said.

Chapter 28

Day three in the "haunted" wood with no sign of anything but the same—a snowy maze in which one could scarcely see further than a stone's toss. Looking up in hope of visual relief did not reveal an open sky, but only small patches of drab gray between crowded limbs. It seemed very nearly impossible, and yet life went on mostly out of sight. The brown hares had turned white to hide from the lynx. The lynx had changed its color to sneak up on the hare. Each animal had its way. Some made themselves part of the maze. Others burrowed down to ride the winter out. Some stuck it out with pure ferocity like the wolverine, and its equally ferocious cousin the fisher cat.

"I'm sorry we haven't found you much to eat," said John, stroking Ellie's neck to calm her hunger.

Tiredly, Emma came alongside and joined in, "She's proving what you said [about her] to be true, John."

Pursing his lips tight, Summerfield glanced with pained eyes to the path behind—a path they had hacked out one mile at a time. Turning to Emma, he forced a smile, "At least we had a gentle start to winter. Otherwise, she'd have no reserves left at all."

"She's burning through them now," Cody put in worriedly.

Ellie had been losing weight since the beginning of their journey, albeit slowly. Now, with very little grass to eat while pulling the heavy sled through a tangled wood in freezing temperatures, her loss had accelerated to become visibly worrisome.

"If we can find even a small glade for her, it would…" Emma cut her speech short, seeing Jessie, Mia, and Laureal returning with the twins, having taken them for a bathroom break.

Gleaning the conversation, Sophie protested while her mother secured her in her seat, "Horsey shouldn't have to carry us without eating."

"Horsey is still plenty strong," her mother assured. And back to work they went, chopping and hacking, knocking away snow, clearing debris, keeping the sled upright on uneven ground, and crossing fallen logs when necessary.

Without the ability to see distance, John could not use landmarks as directional aids. Thus he brought his compass out on a regular basis, that they may keep their bearing. A few paces ahead of John, Laureal looked for the easiest route based on their bearing. They kept their path as straight as possible even as they wove. Difficult though it be, they continued by way of least resistance until midafternoon when they came to the edge of a rocky crag. Not a ravine but a rift, like a fracture in the earth. It angled down some eighteen or twenty feet through a hodgepodge of rock shelves and bushes under a blanket of snow.

Side-by-side at its edge, the newlyweds could see the crag was more of the same on the opposite side, going up from bottom to top.

"Damn it all," gazing on the daunting obstacle.

"John, please don't curse."

Cody came next, shaking his head, "Damn."

Laureal turned from Cody to John, "You see what you've done, John. He's picked it up from you!"

"I apologize," yet looking into the crag.

"No John, that's not going to work this time. I'm on to your 'I apologize' tactic. If you truly meant it, you would stop doing it."

"It's not a tactic," his tone annoyed.

"I'm not asking that much of you, John. I just…

"You're not asking much?" He turned to her, "Outside of what…all of this?"

"What is that supposed to mean?" angry at being cut off, raising her voice.

"Just what I said!" semi-shouting.

"Oh, so now you're blaming this on me?" And shouting at the top of her lungs, "I never wanted to go this far north!"

"What's the problem up here?"

"I won't tolerate his foul mouth, Mother."

Cody gestured to the crag, "Personally, I can't say I blame him."

"You stay out of this!" Laureal warned.

Emma came next and, looking into the rift, let out a sigh, "Well, at least now I know we're not on the path." And looking up and down the way, "Problem is, I have no idea if the crossing is a stone's throw that way or five stone throws that way."

She then turned to the newlyweds, "It's been a difficult few days. We are tired out. And this wood has us feeling caged. And not to make light of things, but under the circumstances, it is understandable that perhaps this crag appears worse than it is. After all, we should be able to find a place to cross with a little scouting. What say you, John?"

"I concur. I will do the scouting."

"Granddaughter, what say you?"

"Whatever way he goes, I will go the opposite."

"You're not going anywhere," John ordered.

Laureal did not argue, well knowing Emma would not allow her to go scouting alone.

"John, do not go out of earshot," Jessie cautioned, to which Emma added, "In these woods, with all this snow soaking up our voices, I would say no further than four stone throws."

"Agreed."

"While John scouts," Mia began, "we can build a fire. Jessie, Laureal, Cody, and I can hunt in teams for grouse and squirrels, and look for nut stashes."

All understood Mia's thoughts. Without a campfire, they had to keep moving to keep their blood flowing or face the deadly danger of becoming chilled. Not only that, but in such cold they had to consume large amounts of calories to keep from starving. And because they were getting low on food stores, looking for food was only logical for all but Emma who could remain at the fire, guarding the children with rifle and animals.

Emma turned to Laureal, "Granddaughter, I want you to forgive John before he goes. And John, I want you to forgive Laureal. To borrow a term from you, John, the two of you are the same in that you both 'chomp at the bit.' John, you chomp and curse. And Laureal, you chomp and push. Men will be men, and women will be women, and all are only human. So let it go because, in this place, we cannot afford less. And John, not to take sides but, for future reference, it is a better habit to ask help from the One that made all this than to curse what he has laid before you."

Struck by the Matriarch's final words, John looked at Laureal, and she at him. And while neither spoke a word initially, when they forgave one another, the look in their eyes was nothing new to Emma. She had seen enough of life to know that, although currently on one another's nerves, they would get past it.

Chapter 29

Four days after crossing the crag, and the business of bush-whacking in unrelenting cold had taken a heavy toll on the family. Snow fell off and on, sometimes heavy, sometimes light, and not once had the sun shown itself. Even at midday the wood lay in the grip of shadow. And in the starless pitch of night, when on occasion there came a scream so blood-curdling as to startle even the bravest heart, who could blame our travelers for wondering if perhaps some dark power held dominion in that place? After all, death clung there like a stain in the Kasskatchen imagination, for while few had ever been there, most knew the story. Only a handful of survivors knew the true story, however. All those years ago, there had been sharp dissent among the elders of the different families within the clan, and their discord had distracted them. The clan should not have struck camp where they did, and among those who survived, those who were unable to bear the terrible truth claimed it to be the work of evil spirits—and told of other-worldly screams from the woods just before disaster struck. The story had grown legs from there.

Noah and Sophie passed out bowls while Laureal followed behind, doling out rations of hot cereal. The family waited for the children to take their seats. Laureal put snow in an empty pot, set it over the coals, and took her seat.

"Son, would you like to say our prayer this morning?"

"I will if you want, Mom. But, I'm not sure what to say."

"Just give thanks, Cody. Speak what comes to your heart."

All bowed their heads—

"Dear Maker of all things," Cody began, "thank you for bringing us this far. Thank you for this food. And if you could see a way for us, I pray that today we break out into sunlit meadows with lots of deer, moose, elk, and grass for Ellie."

Cody could scarcely have said a more fitting prayer. For they had run out of meat, and worse, the absence of large game tracks confirmed their fears: the wood harbored no grazing animals. Without grass, even rabbits had become scarce in its depths. The dogs had not eaten in three days. And Ellie had become a source of grave concern.

John looked around the fire. Tired and huddled in that unforgiving cold with no stomach for conversation, all understood they had gotten in deep. Emma in particular concerned him. The Matriarch's determination had masked the depth of her exhaustion up until then, but no longer—

"If we do not find the lake today," said he, standing up from the fire, "we will have to do something."

"Do what?" Mia asked, her lips and face, like the others, chapped from the cold."

"We'll cross that bridge when we get there," glancing at the dogs.

"Let's see what this day brings," Jessie uttered. "It may be but a mile more to go for good hunting and fishing."

"We've been saying that for days, and every day ends the same."

Jessie took up the pot and began cleaning it out with a brush which was nothing more than a cluster of pine needles.

"Let me do that," said Emma.

"I got it, Mom."

"I'm not going to sit here like a bump on a log."

"You are not a bump on a log, but you are going to sit there and stay there."

Jessie was not being cruel, and Emma, too worn out to argue with her daughter's good intentions, gathered the twins close to her side before the fire while the packsaddle and sled were secured and loaded. Thus began day eight of the bushwhack.

A downy woodpecker, all but concealed in its hole, looked on as the family passed below. Cody caught its movement with his sharp eyes. It was turning its head to look out the hole with one eye, then the other eye as if to verify what it saw. No doubt it had taken refuge there after hearing the oncoming sounds of hatchets chopping, branches cracking, twigs snapping, and snow crushing under the giant's hooves.

Worried for her mother, Jessie glanced back repeatedly.

"Don't worry, I'm not going anywhere."

"We can stop and rest anytime you like, Mother."

"It's not even mid-morning," trudging painfully slow.

Having listened to every word, Sophie protested, "Emmy's not well, and horsey shouldn't have to carry us!"

"Don't you worry about me," Emma rebuffed, "I'm fine!"

"Sophie," Mia began with a warning tone.

"What?"

"Don't fuss." Even as she spoke, Mia concealed her face within her hood, that no one might see her own distress, for having witnessed the decline of the giant, she had come to understand that its fate and the fate of her children were intertwined.

Ellie, queen of horses with her smooth and rhythmic gait, had been reduced to slow labored steps. Her head, once held high, now low with starvation, her half-empty eyes to the ground. Yike and Nemo, also starving, walked the path just in front of Emma, struggling to carry their packs like the loyal troopers they were.

Jessie and Mia tiredly wrestled the sled to keep it upright over uneven terrain while, at the front of the column, John and Laureal broke trail in deep snow and heavy foliage.

Trying to get through a particularly tight spot with fallen limbs hidden like stumbling blocks under a blanket of snow, Laureal tripped, lost her balance and made a grab at one of many branches crowding in on her. The branch saved her from falling even as it ripped loose from her hand and, whipping through the icy air, caught John in the eye—

"Damn it!" dropping his ax, stooping, lifting his mitts to his face.

"John, are you okay!"

"Don't crowd me!"

"John— please."

He gave no reply except to hold his mitt out to keep her away.

"John."

"I'm all right." And pulling his mitt away from his eye, "Watch what you're doing!"

"May I please look at your eye?"

"I said I'm all right!"

"John," pleadingly!"

Summerfield picked up his ax and, with his free mitt, motioned for her to get back to work.

Laureal returned to knocking snow, chopping branches, and hoping against hope that the next turn or gentle rise would reveal what they sought, for it was no longer just a lake they sought, but their deliverance. Weeping quietly, she had progressed no further than fifteen paces when John's hand came onto her shoulder from behind.

"I'm sorry...can you forgive me?"

She turned around and he drew her into his arms, "It's these woods," he murmured, "they just go on and on."

Several paces back, Cody came into view, "Is everything alright up there?"

"Yes...we're just, trying to get reoriented."

With all the family struggling before her, Emma second-guessed her decision to lead them afield. Failure no longer meant they could simply say they gave it their best and go home. All were aware of it. They were in too deep to turn back. It played upon her mind like a grim reaper with scythe in hand, walking the trail behind, patiently waiting for the first of them to fall. Such was her distraction when, taken off guard, she stumbled over a dead branch lying beneath the trodden snow.

"Mother!" Jessie exclaimed, rushing back to where Emma had fallen.

"It was only a stick," said Emma as Jessie helped her up.

"We can rest here for a while."

"Perhaps that would be good," trying to help as Jessie brushed snow from her coat, coming eye to eye with her

301

daughter as an involuntary shiver ran through her like the blade of a scythe.

Jessie called for Laureal, and hearing the anxiety in her mother's voice, Laureal rushed back with John on her heels.

"Grandma! Are you okay?"

"Yes dear," not fooling anyone but doing her best to feign a confident smile, "I'm only a little tired, that's all." And handing the rifle to John, "I'm sorry. I got snow in your gun."

Looking about, Jessie issued orders, "Laureal, build a fire. Build it right there in front of those two trees." Then turning to her son-in-law, "John, build a lean-to there," pointing to the same two trees, "build it so that the fire will radiate heat into it." Speaking next to her son, "Cody, gather firewood, lots of it." And finally looking to her cousin, "Mia and I will cut boughs and set up the tent."

"So much fuss for one old woman," Emma protested as Jessie took a caribou blanket and laid it on the back of the sled for her to sit on. The blanket's purpose was both simple and essential: prevent Emma from losing her precious body heat to frozen surfaces. And so it was that the change John spoke of came earlier than expected. Everyone refocused their energy and the family soon had a small but sturdy lean-to built. A blazing fire radiated heat into the natural structure where Emma lay resting on a bed of pine boughs covered in caribou hides.

Cody returned with another armload of firewood and seeing a ruffed grouse lying atop it, Jessie broke into a smile, "Where'd you get that?"

"It flushed as I was chopping limbs off a deadfall. I followed it and was able to get close enough for a shot." And setting the firewood down, he handed the bird to his mother, his tired eyes still yet the liveliest of the group, "It's a godsend Mom, just when we needed it, for Grandma."

"Yes it is Cody, and so are you."

The bird's precious meat, less than a pound altogether, was added to a handful of wild rice and herbs simmering in a pot beside the fire. Separately in a tiny pot, Jessie made broth of the bones, and because the bones of ruffed grouse taste bad for some inexplicable reason, she steeped the broth with pine needles to mask the unpleasant flavor. In a third pot, Jessie melted snow and steeped freshly picked leaves from a small evergreen plant abundant in those woods. Thus she made what had once been called Hudson Bay Tea.

Laureal returned from foraging with a bag containing soft strips of inner bark from birch and pine trees. Jessie gave a few of the raw strips to Emma to chew, as they were rich in vitamin C. The remaining strips were laid out on heated rocks to make roasted chips, to be pounded into powder as a substitute for bread flour.

"Laureal, where'd Cody go?"

"He went to help John."

"What are they doing?"

"Stripping bark to feed Ellie. John said they would go hunting for grouse and squirrels as soon as they were done." And lowering her voice so that the children would not hear, "He said that, if we are to live, it is important to keep Ellie alive."

Nodding in silent affirmation, Jessie turned to Emma, "Mother."

"Yes."

"Can you sit up?"

Emma opened her eyes, "Of course I can."

"Then sit up, please, and eat this. It will give you strength."

Sitting up and accepting the pot, Emma thanked Jessie before turning to Laureal, "Dear, would you please go and get John."

Yike and Nemo, tethered on the edge of camp, begged and wined so pathetically, Jessie had no choice but to order them to be quiet. For there was nothing to be done for them, and thus their cries served only to increase the family's distress.

Emma looked to Noah and Sophie, both huddled near the fire, both stoic, clearly frightened and, at the same time, knowing not to complain or cry. Grateful that they were still in good health, the Matriarch gestured with the steaming pot, "Would you kiddos like some stew?"

Noah had only begun to extend his hand when Sophie pushed it away, "No thank you, Emmy. We will eat soon enough."

"Aren't you hungry?" looking surprised.

Pavlov's dog had nothing on Noah except that Sophie sat closest to Emma, and therefore, he dared not beg on account of her glare.

Turning to Jessie, Emma attempted to hand the pot back, "I'll drink the broth, but I cannot eat while my family goes hungry."

"Mother," pushing the pot back, "you have caught a chill. You cannot travel, and that means none of us can. So stop arguing and eat before it gets cold." Then softening, "There will be enough for us all. We have rice and wheat flour in our stores, and we have all afternoon to find our dinner."

Jessie had spoken a half-truth and both women knew it. They had run dangerously low on wild rice and wheat flour. Worse yet, they understood that in that extreme environment, they could eat low-fat food like squirrel, grouse, and rice three times a day and still starve to death. They did not need to understand the science behind the calorie requirements of the human body to know the effects.

Meanwhile, John and Laureal traded places so that she could shave the outer bark from a birch tree that he and Cody had been working on. Cody could then follow her the same as he had followed John, shaving the inner bark.

"At least she's eating it," said Cody, speaking of the soft inner bark they had offered to Ellie.

John had tied Ellie there for fear she would wander far away in search of food. Presently, the giant ate handfuls of bark as well as nibbling twigs, tiredly digging for leaves, moss, lichens, anything she could reach.

"Did Emma say what she wanted?" asked John.

"No," shaking her head, watching as he ran his hand over Ellie's gaunt frame. Laureal had seen John heartsick before, like after one of their arguments. Now he was heartsick for Ellie. Her dire condition seemed to have crept up on them. A lot of things seemed to have crept up on them.

"We shouldn't feed her too much bark all at once," turning to Laureal, "it could make her sick."

"John."

"Yes."

"I'm so sorry."

"I'm sorry too," taking her shoulders in his hands. "I promise you, we will make it through this."

John started towards camp only to have Laureal ask after him, "John?"

"Yes," turning back.

"I just wondered, have you seen Weya today?"

"No. Have you?"

"No. And that makes three days."

"She may have gone her own way."

"Well," looking resigned, "perhaps it's for the best."

Back at camp, Emma asked John to sit by the fire. It was just about noon.

"Mom," Jessie interceded, "don't wear yourself out." And turning to John, "She needs to rest."

"I'll rest, dear…in a moment." And turning her eyes to the Seeker, "John, as you may recall from the charts we made, there's a stream that parallels our course to the south. And as I have said before, it is not a viable route even though it eventually leads to the lake."

Listening as Emma spoke, John already understood they were supposedly on the most direct route to the lake. He also understood that their mapmaking had not been a precise science by any means. Emma measured distance in time, whereas John measured distance in miles. Therefore, John had converted time to miles back when he drew his charts. Back then, to determine where to locate places on his charts, John would point due north, and Emma would then point in the direction of said place in relation to due north from their home. She would then estimate the travel time in hours required to reach said location. From her estimations, John converted time to miles to make his charts and, as he did, Emma reviewed them to determine if they resembled what she would expect to see if viewed from the eye of a high soaring eagle.

With a sip of her broth, the Matriarch continued, "With regards to that stream, on its approach to the lake, it flows into a bog. It does not disappear in the bog but winds through it. The bog is long, wide, and grassy. Large animals, particularly elk and moose know it as a place to dig grass in winter. When you reach it, you will look down on it from low wooded hills. From a hunter's perspective, you will be concealed with an excellent view. However, the wind will almost certainly be from the north, so you will need to cross to the wooded hills rising from the opposite side of the bog. Then you will have all the advantages. John, I feel certain we are near the lake, and because the stream parallels us, I am sure that if you were to strike out in that direction," lifting her hand to point south, "you would find the stream and bog in less than a day's travel. And with your rifle, you should be able to get us something large to eat. And also, in the process of doing so, you can verify our location in relation to the lake."

"I will go immediately."

"Eat this first," handing him the pot of grouse and rice, of which she had eaten a third. "It's not much but it will help sustain your strength. Take your tent, but do not travel more than a day from us. I hope to be better in the morning, at which time we can set out following your tracks. Therefore, choose your steps through the forest in a way that we may follow with Ellie and the sled. Once we join you in the bog, Ellie will have grass to eat and, hopefully, with the bounty of a successful hunt, we will regain our strength."

Emma set her empty cup on the ground and laid back. Then with eyes closed, "Jessie, would you please continue for me."

Covering her mother with caribou blankets, Jessie called a camp meeting—

"John is going hunting. We will follow in his tracks when Mother is able. Cody, for the rest of today you will hunt grouse, squirrel, whatever you can get without venturing too great a distance from camp. Laureal, you will set snares and look for nut caches. Mia, you and the twins will help me forage food for Ellie and gather firewood. We will stay around camp, and the dogs will stay with Mother."

John took a box from his packsaddle which, as we already know, contained chest-like boxes that doubled as backpacks. One particular box was always ready for emergencies, containing his tent and other essentials. Hoisting the box-pack on his back, John checked his compass before setting out. Laureal, having equipped herself with string for snares, went along to see John off on his errand.

"Please be careful," following close in a wood too crowded for walking side-by-side.

"I will. You too."

"Please turn back if it looks like the snow will cover your tracks."

Stopping, he turned to her, a smile in his tired eyes, "Don't you worry. Everything will be fine."

"I love you."

"I love you too," kissing her lips. "Take care of your grandmother."

"Will do."

Turning away, John spoke over his shoulder, "I'll bring you a steak."

Chapter 30

John soon stopped to remove layers of clothing, then continued on a southerly heading, keeping to a route the family could follow. Snow fell from almost every branch he touched, and while it wasn't wet snow, it seemed determined to tag along with him even as he did his best to avoid it.

Back at camp and approximately five stone throws into the wood, Laureal moved like a hungry cat, tired but aware, her eyes peeled for signs of red squirrels. Here and there, she stopped to make a snare, but mostly she looked for nut caches. She knew that red squirrels, unlike other squirrels, stashed all their nuts and seeds in one place called a midden. Hazelnuts and pine seeds; all excellent sources of healthy fats, protein, vitamins and minerals. Unfortunately, any cache she might find would be half empty, what with winter in its final months. Presently, a red squirrel dashed down a tree trunk and set to barking in protest. Laureal, digging its cache, stopped and drew her bow. No more had she taken aim, though, than the animal ran around the opposite side of the trunk. Hidden from sight, it continued to bark at her, perhaps saying something like, *"Hey, thief, I worked hard for those nuts, and if you take them, I'm as good as dead."*

On the opposite side of camp, perhaps as far as six stone throws into the forest, Cody hunted for squirrel, snowshoe hare, and grouse. The type of grouse he hunted roosted not on limbs but under the snow. And spotting one of their burrows, Cody took off his mitts, crept up carefully, and pounced while thrusting his hands down into the snow. He missed by a hair and the bird burst from the snow in a flurry. Cody made a dive but the grouse got away and the young hunter could only draw his bow and lay chase as it disappeared in the thick.

Just beyond the edge of camp, Jessie and Mia worked to harvest food from pine and birch trees. They stripped the coarse outer bark away, then peeled off the edible inner bark. The twins laid the bark in a temporary carrier, itself made from outer bark. The inner bark would soon be taken to camp and dried by the fire.

The women stopped feeding Ellie for fear that too much too quickly would make her sick. They treated the dogs in the same manner, giving them only a little to begin with. Yike and Nemo were not keen on the piney taste but slowly ate the bark out of starvation.

Returning to camp, Jessie checked on her mother and, seeing her sound asleep, turned her attention to drying out tree bark and maintaining the fire. Thick clouds of steam came from every breath as she used John's bucksaw to section a branch that, along with other dead branches, had been dragged in to make a pile of loose firewood on the edge of camp. Laureal appeared and, kneeling down, cleaned off a patch of packed snow in the cooking area where she poured out the contents of a small bag.

"It's not much, Mom."

"That's more than I expected at this time of year."

"Should we roast them?"

"Yes, we'll make bread cakes." And turning to the children, "Noah, Sophie…can you shell those nuts for me?"

"Be very careful not to waste any! And don't smash your fingers," their mother instructed, setting the kids up to work with mortar and pestle.

Cody showed up next, "I wish I'd gotten more," setting down two squirrels and one grouse.

"You did good, son. We'll make a fine supper of it."

"Mom—" painfully, as though everyone in the world knew it wasn't nearly enough to sustain five adults and two children living outdoors in the dead of winter.

"It will do, Cody. We'll have meat and fowl with rice. And flatbread with seeds and nuts baked in."

So the pot was filled with snow and put on to boil. Laureal and Cody skinned and dressed out the squirrels and grouse. Jessie was the chef, overseeing and putting everything together. Mia ground baked strips of pine bark into powder as a kind of flour extender to be mixed with wheat flour and warm water to knead and make breadcakes.

While they worked, the family members periodically stopped to warm their hands over the fire, their fingers aching in the cold. When at last supper was ready, Jessie turned to wake Emma—

"Mom."

"Yes," coming around slowly.

"How are you feeling?"

"Tired."

"Are you hungry?"

"A little."

"Can you sit up? We're ready to eat."

"After eating a supper which, under the circumstances, tasted good if not a little piney, the family huddled around their fire sipping hot tea.

"I pray John has found the bog," Emma murmured.

Cody lifted his eyes from his cup, "I hope he's carving tenderloins off a moose, and at this time tomorrow, we will be having a banquet."

Humble chuckles went around the fire, to which Mia added, "One thing's for sure...when we get out of this, I never want to eat tree bark again."

Tomorrow came and the family spent the morning gathering what food they could find. Emma remained in her lean-to before the fire. Jessie often stopped to check on her mother and, presently finding her resting quietly, turned to rummage through their food stores even though she knew there was next to nothing left.

"Jessie," meekly.

"Yes, Mother," coming to her side.

"Where is everyone?"

"Cody's hunting. Laureal's checking snares and looking for nut caches. Mia and the twins are gathering tree bark, firewood, and whatever else they can find. How are you feeling?"

"Well…I am very sorry to say, I do not think I will be able to travel today."

"There is no need for us to travel, Mom. John is certainly on his way back here. What do you want to bet he shows up this afternoon lugging a meat load."

"Let us hope so."

With a smile, Jessie returned to looking in food bags, hoping that perhaps she had missed something.

"What do we have?"

"A little rice and some wheat yet. We'll have more food when Cody and Laureal return. And Mia is certain to have some tender bark to eat. Oh, look! I found some breadroot!"

"Where?"

"In the fold of this bag."

"Jessie."

"What?"

"Come here for a moment, please."

Jessie seated herself on the edge of Emma's makeshift bed.

"I want you to know something," taking her daughter's hand. "It comforts me to know that when my time comes, our family will not perish because I have a daughter who is ready to take her place as Matriarch of the clan."

"Mom," responding as though it were a ridiculous notion, "your 'time' is a long way off."

"There are some things I wish I could do over…if only I could."

"We do the best we can," quoting one of her mother's own sayings.

"I tried to do what I thought best, but if I had it to do over again, I would…"

"Mom," cutting in, "don't be hard on yourself."

"Jessie," visibly distraught, "if only I had known the scar it would leave on your heart, I would have stood up for you."

Never had Jessie seen her mother so frail and, all at the same time, so deeply earnest. "Mom, there's no need to apologize." And stroking her hand, "Now I want you to know

311

something. I am certain that I could not have had a better mother. And you know what else? I'm not so sure that marrying Harley would have been a good thing. He was wilder than you know."

Jessie sighed as she looked back in time, "If Harley and I had married, life might not have worked out as well as it did, but things did work out well—wonderfully well. I have two wonderful children, a wonderful son-in-law, and soon, God willing, my first grandchild."

Jessie rose from the bed, "I'd better get back to work."

"Sit down, please...I'm not finished."

"Mom, everything is going to be fine," protesting even as she obeyed.

"When you are Matriarch, you will have to make some difficult decisions."

"I know, I've had a good teacher, and I'm thankful for it."

Emma clutched her daughter's hand, albeit without any real strength, "Jessie."

"What is it, Mother?"

"If John fails, you cannot forsake the rest of the family for the sake of saving me."

"Mom," visibly upset, "you're tired from fever, and you're thinking too much."

"Please, this is important! If I am to die here, I want to know that you will not let my passing change anything regarding the rebuilding of our family."

"Mom...please," fighting back tears.

"Every great tree begins as a tiny seed, and that seed is in your daughter. Now please, promise me that you will continue with our plan to rebuild."

"I promise, Mom," wiping at tears. "I promise."

Noontime came, and although no one had expected to see John before then, the afternoon was spent in anticipation of his arrival. He never came, and a meager supper passed with few words until each family member, huddling around the fire, sank into their own silent battle of hope and despair.

Then, as the light of day faded away, the figure of a man stepped out of the darkness, caked in ice and snow.

"John!" cried Laureal, quick to her feet.

Two days on the move without food and John scarcely had the strength to hold Laureal in his arms, a situation she quickly reversed, "Let me help you," taking his pack from his back and setting it beside the fire as a seat. Then, seating him on it, she took up the paddle comb and carefully knocked and brushed at the ice and snow that caked him.

Jessie poured John a cup of hot tea and all watched as he took a sip. The firelight shone into his hood, illuminating his grave expression. His eyes to the fire, he appeared too exhausted to speak.

"Did you not find the bog?" Emma asked lowly.

John only shook his head.

"How can that be?" asked Cody in disbelief.

"I went many miles," lifting his eyes to them, his countenance that of a defeated man, "I could find no stream, or lake, or end to these woods."

Noah's frightened little voice seemed almost birdlike, "What are we to do?"

"We have to go back the way we came," John replied.

"I concur," Jessie seconded, "we have no choice."

Painfully, John laid out a last-ditch plan, "I will go ahead of us. With the trail already cut, I should make the river in three days. Trout are plentiful there...we know that much. I'll load up a bag of them and head back this way. From your end, if Emma is up to it, you can slowly make your way back, traveling for half days, and foraging the other half."

Laureal, who'd been scrounging what food she could for John, looked to her mother in silent horror. John was in no shape to travel another mile. A picture of depletion, he would certainly perish if he attempted to reach the river. Nearly in tears but unable to afford the luxury of crying, she returned to the business at hand, gathering up what she could before coming to his side.

"Eat this, darling," handing him a small bowl of rice sprinkled with baked pine chips plus what few nuts and seeds remained.

"Eat slowly," she added, watching his every move.

"John," said Jessie.

"Yes," looking up from his bowl.

"Before we do anything, you need to rest for a day or two."

Returning his eyes to his bowl, John did not respond but as he ate in silence, everyone heard when Sophie turned to her mother and whispered, "Mommy, are we going to die?"

Chapter 31

Early the following morning while John was returning from the family's latrine, Jessie met him just paces outside their camp.

"John," speaking lowly.

"Yes."

"Emma and I have been talking, and, we've decided we cannot risk putting it off any longer. The time has come to do what we'd hoped not to do."

"The dogs?"

"Yes," shaking her head and pursing her lips tight. "Dear God, I hate to even think about it. Nemo has been such a faithful dog. But if we don't…well, we're not going to make it. And John, you cannot run for the river on nothing to eat. You would freeze to death."

In the gravity of the moment, she held his gaze. Then, glancing back towards camp, "We can keep the children in the tent. They don't have to know. We'll tell them that Nemo ran off in the night. Then you'll have something substantially more than a handful of rice to take with you. And we also will have something to sustain us."

"I'll do it." And grimly, he added, "I'll do it right now."

They hadn't taken three steps towards camp when John stopped and turned to Jessie, "I will get to the river and back, but, just in case…you have my horse. Do with her what you must to stay alive."

Once back in camp, John quietly took up Nemo's leash. Only Mia remained in the tent with the twins. Cody stoically split firewood with tears in his eyes. Laureal, also weeping quietly, filled a pot with snow and put it on the flames. Emma lay in her lean-to. Her lips pursed tight, she gave John a nod to silently say, *"It must be done."*

John turned to take Nemo into the woods, but no more had he begun than Yike set to whining and struggling against his leash like tomorrow would never come. Thus distracted, no one noticed Weya standing on the opposite edge of camp.

Suddenly seeing the wolf so near his wife and family, John dropped the leash and brought bow and arrow from his back all in one quick motion.

"Don't shoot her!" cried Laureal.

Nemo, having bounded over to Weya, jumped about like a pup before the wolf, wagging his tail, cringing in submission, and licking at her mouth. Weya then began to heave, her head down, her front paws placed apart. It seemed she would vomit. And sure enough she did—not once, but four times.

Cody cried out, "Look at all that meat!"

Like a wild man, John leaped over the campfire and kicked Nemo in the ribs, driving the starving dog off the pile before it could wolf down more than two bites. Nemo yipped but, suffering no serious injury, turned and dashed off to beg and dance around Weya who had moved several paces into the wood where, panting, she laid down like a sphinx to cool herself in the snow.

Laureal came alongside John, joined by Jessie and Cody altogether in astonishment, for steaming in the snow before them lay fifteen pounds of fresh undigested meat. Not just any meat but the meat that wolves instinctually prefer. The heart, liver, kidneys, and other organs were packed with essential fats, proteins, vitamins, and minerals. In a manner of speaking, just what the doctor ordered.

"This is from the hand of our Creator," Jessie uttered in awe. "In our moment of great need, he has answered our prayers, and, shown us his endless ways."

"Indeed he has," said John, starting into the wood with a light bulb going off in his head.

"Where are you going?" Laureal called after him.

"To follow her tracks," breaking into a trot, hollering over his shoulder, "She couldn't have come far with all that."

"John! You need to rest!" starting after him only to have Jessie grab her arm.

"He'll be alright, dear."

"Mom!"

"Stay here! Don't let Nemo near this pile!" And turning, Jessie went to fetch a pot.

Standing over the pile, Laureal was jolted from her thoughts when Weya suddenly set to growling and baring her teeth. As it turned out, the wolf was only telling Nemo to calm down and leave her be. Weya had only done what her parents had trained her to do; bring food home to the family. An adult timber wolf could consume over twenty-two pounds of meat at once, and a wolf of Weya's size could consume even more. She had only done what all good wolves do; she had carried the meat of a kill back to the den in her stomach and shared it there with her family members.

"This calls for a celebration," said Jessie, taking out the last of their breadroot which, along with some herbs, she added to the pot to make a savory stew like meat and potatoes with just the right spices.

Having followed Weya's tracks approximately two miles, John used the last of his strength to reach the crest of a gentle rise. From there the land fell away slowly to the east and, looking through gaps in the wood, he could see what appeared a snow-covered plain extending as far as the eye could see. Huffing clouds of steam and feeling lightheaded with legs heavy as lead, John could scarcely believe his eyes. For there it was, big as life, the Lake of the Swans.

Trudging wearily, John entered camp wearing a victorious smile.

"Did you find her kill?" Cody asked.

"I might have...had the lake not got in the way."

"What?"

"John," Laureal uttered in disbelief, "did you find the lake?"

"Not two miles that way, just over the crest of a low rise."

"I hunted squirrels along the base of that rise!" cried Cody.

"Had you walked to its top and looked east, you couldn't have missed it. And what's more, you would have seen a wide boggy flat along the shoreline. It looks to be an excellent hunting ground."

Looks of amazement went round the campfire, followed by joy and laughter.

"That lake is known for its trout!"

"And walleye too."

"John, there will be grass for Ellie."

"Yes, and when we've taken care of ourselves, I intend to do some shoveling so she can eat, just eat, without digging."

Emma sat up slowly and scooted forward, "Let us join hands and give thanks."

All bowed heads as Jessie led the prayer, after which the stew was doled out in wooden bowls and the family had plenty of good food for the first time in what seemed a long time.

Alive with hope and happiness, Laureal leaned into John, "What say you, darling? I say it's caribou. Mia thinks it elk?"

"Smelling his bowl, "Moose?"

"Oh, you diplomat!"

Laughs went round the fire.

Sitting up straight, John turned to look at the dogs. "Did Yike get a little?"

We gave him a few pounds, about as much as Nemo got. We don't want to feed them too much too fast anyway."

"I need to apologize to Nemo."

"John," asked Emma, "when you were on the rise, could you tell our location, I mean, with relation to the lake?"

"I cannot say for certain. But because the lake stretched away both to north and south, it would appear we overshot the south end and approached the west shore on a north-northeast diagonal. That would explain why I couldn't find the stream yesterday. Having overshot the southern half of the lake, we were farther from the stream than we thought."

The conversation continued until, at last setting his bowl down, John took a sip of hot tea and said, "That was some fine eating. Thank you, ladies."

"Would you like another helping, John?"

"In an hour or two, Jessie. Thank you."

A comfortable silence fell over the group, their present state like day and night when compared to an hour before. John and Laureal shared a smile. Lifted on a wave of hope, each with an arm around the other, the light in their young eyes told the tale. Love conquers all.

Finally, looking around the fire, John addressed their need for a plan, "How about we get a few hours of sleep, have an early lunch, and then Laureal, Cody, and I can go on a sortie to the lake. If our good fortune holds, the wind will not be severe. Ellie can eat grass while we forage. And hopefully, we'll return with a stringer of lake trout for supper, and perhaps some identifiable red meat."

Emma seconded John's suggestion, and soon thereafter all were fast asleep. A few hours later when they emerged from their tent, pleasant was their surprise. A mild breeze had come from the south. The cloud blanket had broken to reveal patches of blue sky. The sun never felt so good on their faces. And of course, Emma declared it a sign.

End of Book I